MW01488134

Advance Praise for *Seraphim*

"Apocalyptic in the truest sense of the word, Jon Michael Kelley's *Seraphim* is a stunning thriller with the very fate of the world at stake. Beautifully written, with prose as lush as it is chilling, Kelley is part poet, part prophet, but a true master of fear, through and through. This is top notch stuff of highest caliber!"

—Joe McKinney, Bram Stoker Award-winning author of *Flesh Eaters* and *Inheritance*

"*Seraphim* is a beautifully wrought tale of angels and demons that starts out strong and just gets better and better. A thoroughly enjoyable read. Jon Michael Kelley proves to be a mature, intelligent new voice in horror right out of the gate."

—Craig Saunders, author of *The Love of the Dead* and *A Stranger's Grave*

"Written with the finesse of a pro, *Seraphim* is one hell of a frightening horror novel. With bits of dark fantasy and humor mixed in, this one has it all! Hard to believe this is Jon Michael Kelley's first novel."

—David Bernstein, author of *Amongst the Dead* and *Tears of No Return*

Seraphim

Jon Michael Kelley

Seraphim

Jon Michael Kelley

Evil Jester Press

New York

For Ramona, my dearest and most lovely companion.
And guardian angel, to be sure.

Acknowledgements

The following people have my eternal gratitude, for without their encouragement this novel would still be smoldering in a wicker trunk. My mother and father, Joan and Charles Kelley, who, having raised me, know very well the guises evil can take, subtle and otherwise. Barbra Schilling, who graciously gave me the time to write it. Brandy Kelley, who supplied the inspiration while *in utero*. Charles Day for his tremendous ability at being the nicest guy you'd ever want to meet. And Peter Giglio, editor extraordinaire, true lapidarian of text—and also one hell of a nice guy. When he's not diluting my most purplish of prose, that is.

"Not for a moment dare we succumb to the illusion that an archtype can be finally explained and disposed of…the most we can do is dream the myth onwards and give it a modern dress."

– Dr. Carl Gustav Jung

Prologue

Eli Kagan was a maker of angels.

He appeared worshipful on bent knees, bowing over his creation. A deceiving pose, as Eli paid reverence to no one. Besides, the body that lay before him was only a caricature, a parody of faith. A cherubic pawn in a game he'd just recently been invited to play. Still, she was exquisite; stark and porcelain-fragile against these wild environs, a coastal region of the Pacific Northwest so untamed as to define primordial. But it was perfect in its seclusion, this chosen site. And even better for its loftiness.

An opportune place to test one's wings.

Some sixty yards ahead loomed a wood of Douglas fir, its jagged canopy now seared golden by the rising sun. Down below, within the olive drab, sashes of fog drifted along the ground, snagging upon the fern and verbena.

Eli smiled. Not so intangible after all.

He continued to watch the streamers anguish among the verdure. Floundering like the ghosts of drowned kittens reenacting their last, struggling moments of life.

Something moved just then, to his left, behind the tree line. The silhouette of a large dog, glaring at him, its eyes unnaturally aglow inside the murky perimeter.

Cautiously, Eli rose to his feet. The animal continued to stare, head hung low, ears pricked. If Eli didn't know any better, he'd swear it was a wolf. He picked up a stone and flung it at the voyeur. The rock fell way short, but the animal inferred its meaning and skulked back into the trees.

The thrown rock, or perhaps the dog itself, had disturbed a murder of sleeping crows, and, bursting from the wood, they protested the encroachment.

Beneath these sounds, his angel stirred, then finally opened her eyes.

Far out on the ocean, nature seethed. Storm clouds, darker than the fleeing night, heaved and roiled; entrails bulging from an eviscerated horizon. Behind them, nearly two-hundred feet below, waves lunged at the crag. Huddled along the rocks, cormorants braved the harsh surf with admirable indifference, their long, hooked bills aimed like trumpets at the approaching storm, ready to herald its arrival.

The air was sharp, honed by the misty updrafts shearing the rawboned cliffs.

His angel faced the sunrise. A dab of light had begun to creep along the upper fringe of her left wing, like a wary mouse edging along a baseboard. Soon, the sun swelled across both wings, bringing to them a luster that was almost...phantasmagorical.

Eli brought the Nikon to his face, aiming at the appendages that had been sewn deeply, securely, into the soft flesh of her back. Through the lens the feathers assumed a grainy texture, some of the larger, more loosely-fitted ones lifting on the gathering breeze.

Her eyes were the color of the water below, a frothy blue, the desperation within them equally savage. She was naked, except for the thin nylon rope that bound her wrists and ankles, tainting her otherwise virtuous image. But this was necessary, as was the duct tape that covered her mouth.

Angels screamed, Eli knew. Screamed loud.

She winced as the flash of the camera blinded her, her cries muffled behind the tape. Her head whipped to the right, then left, then right again, as if each blast of light were the backhand of a raging mother. The rope cinched and braided her flesh as she struggled, as did the heavy monofilament cross-stitched along her back. Eli wondered just how intense was her pain, but decided that it was endurable, and perhaps in these last moments nearly coveted, because it undoubtedly reminded her that she was still alive.

After all, children were loath to give up the ghost, ten-year-old girls being no exception.

He then reached into his knapsack and withdrew a jagged-edged piece of stained-glass.

*****

Summer was in full swing in Rock Bay, Massachusetts, all the shops and cafes along Chelsea Street open, their frontages dressed snugly for the tourist season. And it was especially brisk today, the bright midmorning sun and warm temperatures inveigling hordes of shoppers.

Rachel McNeil cupped the corners of her eyes, leaned forward, and peered through the window of Wayfarer's, an emporium full of choice antiques, most of them nautical. The window display was an old Faber trunk dressed up as a treasure chest, overflowing with spoofed regalia: strings of pearls, gold and silver bullion, gem-encrusted goblets...

She smiled, impressed. Some merchants had it down to a science. Rounding out the exhibit was an old US Navy diving helmet, tagged "Mark V, 1918." Its copper luster shone like new, and fresh strands of seaweed had been draped here and there for effect—just as had the very real human skull grinning at her from behind the helmet's hinged front-glass.

Gawd.

She stared back at the ghoulish diver. "Typical man," she mumbled. "Crimp his hose and he panics and dies."

Rachel was a native of Rock Bay, but this morning she felt more like a tourist on the last day of what had been, for the better part, a wondrously long and rewarding vacation. But now it was time to leave. Tomorrow, her husband's new job would steal them from this quaint seaside town, *her* home since birth, *theirs* for the past two. And had it not been for the recent and totally unexpected news of her pregnancy, then having to move to Los Angeles might have felt more like a new beginning and less like infanticide.

She was already afraid for the new life inside her. It was a prowling fear, circling her unborn like a lioness. And this fear was not, contrary to her husband's theory, borne of those Hansel-and-Gretel-like operas that every mother, expectant or otherwise, fantasizes from time to time. No, the anxiety that she'd been experiencing for the past two days, since having left the clinic with her wonderful but surprising news, was in no way, she firmly believed, the fallout from such musings. She had to admit that LA's infamous reputation had provoked in her all sorts of morbid scenarios, but this was something different. Something that continued to fester within her, still vague but persistent, as if it too were an embryo developing at its own torpid pace, content to let time determine its gender.

There was something else, too; lurking. A feeling of...what? Precognition? Was that the word?

She wished she could abort this dread, meet it with a coat hanger— then yank.

Her former psychiatrist, no doubt, would have identified this fear as a latent side-effect from the loss of her first and only child, four years earlier. *Guilt that's lain dormant,* she imagined him saying, *now suddenly awakened from its long hibernation by the news of your pregnancy.*

The Freudian fuck.

The guilt. It had nearly crippled her for good. It had taken everything she had and everyone she knew to help her survive the first two years following her daughter's death. Jessica had died of SIDS. And there was absolutely nothing she could have done to prevent it. But for so many months afterward she'd been convinced otherwise. If only she had shown more responsibility as a mother, her baby girl would still be alive. She should have seen it coming, should have laid her down differently in the crib that night, should have not wrapped her so tightly in that blanket, should have been there next to her, listening for her every breath.

The "Should Haves," she thought, *sequel to the popular "What Ifs," now playing at a theater near you!*

Oh dear lord, the guilt.

She nodded. Of course. That had to be the reason for her plaguing anxiety, the fear of losing this child as well.

Okay, so the Freudian fuck might have been right.

That explanation held for a few moments, then surrendered to doubt. No, no, there was something else, something...

Her reverie was broken when a figure emerged from the dusky interior, materializing on the other side of the glass like a ghost from the ethereal. The store's proprietor, a gaunt, plucky old man in crisp white Cracker Jacks, had obviously caught the faraway look in her eyes and mistook her for a pining tourist. He grinned as he curled an index finger, inviting her in.

Creepy. Rachel politely smiled, then moved on.

She paused in front of Confection Alley, a thriving little candy store owned and operated by one of her old high school classmates, Darlene Schwartzenburger, who was later rescued from that rambling moniker when Aaron Jakes, a successful entrepreneur from Salem, came along and swept her off her feet. But before Darlene Schwartzenburger-Jakes got her chocolate-covered mitts on the place, it had originally been, and for so many years, Clive's Clippers, as evidenced by the barber pole out front, still drilling away. Back in high school, Rachel had thought of Darlene as a real class-A bitch. Still did, actually. But that wasn't the reason why she'd never so much as sampled any of Darlene's famous fudge. Rather, it was the thought of biting down into one of those rich, creamy morsels and finding a relic hair from some fisherman's oily scalp meandering between the walnuts.

Here, the warm, ambrosial aroma of freshly pulled taffy was fighting for sidewalk space with frying onion and cilantro from an adjacent pub. These smells instantly triggered in her an exceptionally strong feeling of déjà vu. Yes, she had been here before, on this very sidewalk, in front of this very confectionery.

She turned wistfully toward the water, to savor what she had for so long taken for granted. To do what she'd intended: pay homage.

The bay glittered golden in the morning sun, as if the bullion of some far-flung and long-sunk armada had magically attained buoyancy and floated to its surface. Gulls bobbed and cawed above the wash of a departing lobster boat. Lovers strolled hand-in-hand along the boardwalk, and whale watchers waited eagerly in line for the next tour.

Deep in her chest, leaden memories slipped through the bottom of a frail pouch and fell slowly into a melancholy abyss.

It felt almost treasonous to have forgotten.

Yes, she was going to miss this town, this ocean; perhaps even more than she feared.

Lifting her face, she allowed the salty breeze to wash against her neck, her cheeks. She'd be leaving behind only a few acquaintances, no true friends, and a sales position at Michael's Department Store (a job she hadn't needed to keep after her marriage to Duncan McNeil, but had kept all the same). There would be no family begging her to stay. Her mother and father had long been deceased, courtesies of a drunk limousine driver in Vermont, and she had no brothers or sisters. The only living relative of any consequence was an aunt in Portland, Maine—and it had been, what, eighteen years since she'd last seen her? At her parent's funeral?

There were also two foster families, but she'd cut all ties with them long ago, estranged by the frequent lashings of a Baptist preacher, then later followed with her "deflowering" by a respected city councilman and his accomplice wife.

She had her share of ugly memories and had been more than infrequently haunted by them, mostly at night, back when her husband was "on the job." But ever since he'd begun keeping normal hours, most of them spent healing, those haunts had depreciated into the occasional— if not even playful—bump and rap.

And now her opportunity had come to uproot and see the world from a different angle. It would be a warped perspective, no doubt, given the view from LA, but she'd come—albeit grudgingly—to accept that destination. Her sense of destiny *had* been invigorated, she had to admit. As far back as she could remember, she'd felt fated. Not for fame, necessarily (although she wouldn't turn her nose up at the offer), but definitely something eventful.

Perhaps even pivotal.

But then, she figured everyone must have those kinds of delusions, at least to some extent. Without a sense of self-importance a person would languish in darkness and eventually succumb to the emptiness, to the meaninglessness of it all. She'd been there. Oh boy, had she ever. Fortunately for her, though, her knight in shining armor had finally arrived and would very soon be saving her from ever having to visit that murky kingdom again.

But...Los Angeles?

A year earlier, two bullets had nearly cost her husband his life. He'd been a homicide detective with the Boston Police Department. But now— thanks to those fortuitous bullets—they would both be leaving for LA tomorrow morning. His new job would be teaching Police Science to "a bunch of wanna-bes." And she was more than thankful for his career move. Cops' wives were destined to lay awake nights, waiting for the phone to ring, or that knock at the door in the small hours of the morning. But the vast majority of them could always expect a warm body to eventually come sauntering in, at least one free of serious injuries. Rachel, however, had been one of the few exceptions, having gotten that knock at the door, a uniformed officer behind it, fidgety beneath his grim errand.

But her husband had survived, and it did her heart well to know that he would never wear a badge again—knock on wood.

But...*Los Angeles*?

Growing up, she'd always dreamed of becoming an actress. But reality had chipped away at that boulder of a dream, as it eventually did the fancies of most girls, until, finally, there was nothing left but a hopeless pebble.

She smiled then, remembering that she never had to walk far before it'd shift around and dig into her heel, that pebble. She was quite often reminded of her unique attractiveness; was told that she had the good looks of a movie-star. Not beautiful, not gorgeous—but damned cute. And it wasn't just men who told her that, but women, too.

She brightened. *Why not,* she thought. *Hollywood, here I come!*

As she continued walking, the cobblestone sidewalk was eventually replaced by gray planking as she neared the boardwalk.

In front of the Swashbuckler, the most popular restaurant in town, a line had begun forming for their elaborate seafood brunch buffet. The sign hung above a medieval door and gangplank, with a smaller one below declaring, 'Arrr! The Finest Grub and Spirits This Side of Martha's Vineyard, Mates!' She'd eaten there many times. The food *was* fine, but not so as to be the envy of every chef between here and Cape Cod, she was sure.

She continued on, smiling as she passed the waiting patrons.

This end of the boardwalk was closest to the water, and the cool breeze made her nipples hard beneath the gossamer material of her summer dress. She blushed, feeling a bit ashamed for not having worn at least a camisole beneath something so sheer. There were more than a few men glancing, some lingering a little longer than manners would have allowed. She liked the attention, she had to admit, in a coquettish sort of way. Not only was she "damned cute," but was still shapely despite her years (a decrepit, cane-toting twenty-six), and the tragedies that are notorious for accelerating them.

Oh, yes, the tragedies...

Snap out of it, girl! she mentally slapped herself. *You're turning your stroll down memory lane into a roller coaster ride to hell! Stop feeling sorry for yourself and count your blessings, for Christ's sake!*

Yes, of course, she thought. *My blessings.*

"I'm going to have a *baby!*" she whispered excitedly, as if that news were still only minutes old.

God, she was feeling...*peculiar.*

More powerful than a whim, a sudden, inexplicable impulse made her back up, then take a left down another walkway—one she normally strayed from—that led to a haven of tourist shops.

She passed a smelly bait store, then a glass blower whose specialty was miniature masted ships, whales and hummingbirds, then another vendor selling beautiful sea shells, as well as other less attractive carcasses of marine and shore animals, then a clam shack, this one favored for its "Yards" of beer...

Next was one of those Old West photography studios where women got dressed up like saloon whores, and men as any one of your average sheep-herding, shit-kicking, tobacco-chewing, bandoleer-wearing cowboys. And every single person, she realized, had still managed to come out looking totally counterfeit; the lens wasn't fooled by the twenty-first century twinkle in their eyes.

A particular photograph stopped her. She peered in. A little girl, whom Rachel guessed to be nine or ten, was dressed up in a calico pinafore and bonnet, the woman next to her in suede chaps, spurs, gun belt and cowboy hat.

Rachel shook her head at the scowling woman, an outlaw with an attitude, her six-shooter stuffed sloppily into the waistline of her jeans. Her exaggerated stance implied that she was getting a kick out of the whole affair. The little girl, on the other hand, looked as if she were trying to salvage herself from what had been a particularly nasty flu.

Or the loss of a father? she wondered, surprised by the suddenness of the thought.

She bent forward, studying the woman's left hand, which was resting on her hip. There was no sign of a wedding ring. Rachel then stared at the little girl, regarding the faint smile that had started at one side of her pretty face; a smile that could have been famous for its vibrancy, she determined, had the malaise not been so inflexible.

Yes, that was it. The picture was not whole, not complete. A man was absent. A man who this little girl loved dearly. Not her real father, but someone as tantamount.

A man who had left them both very recently.

Rachel straightened, aware that she was not just pondering that possibility—she actually knew it to be true.

She leaned in even closer, her nose nearly touching the glass. Did she know this woman? This little girl? She didn't think so. No names threatened to bubble up from the well of her subconscious. No, in fact she was quite sure of it. But still, there was something hauntingly familiar about the little girl's *eyes*. And the longer she stared, the more she thought the child bore more than a passing resemblance to...well, to her *husband*.

Giggling, she threw a hand to her mouth. *Hormones,* she warned herself. *Yessirree, those obnoxious little bastards are already marching en masse out of your uterus and into your bloodstream. Soon they'll be digging trenches and rolling out the barbed wire like the freaking*

Gestapo. And when they're dug in reeeal deep, honey, your moods will swing faster than David Bowie, your taste buds will become psychotic and, of course, you'll start suspecting every child you see as an illegitimate product of your husband's virile past.

Christ, she'd almost forgotten the crazy things that happened during pregnancy. She was almost relieved—until she looked at the picture again. The little girl really *did* look like her husband. Or, more accordingly, like the pictures of him when he was around the same age.

She glanced around to the other photos displayed in the window, hoping that she wouldn't (but feeling like she might) recognize them as long lost relatives. There was a chubby man and even chubbier woman decorated like Napoleon and Josephine. An older couple sitting at a poker table, cards in one hand, shot of whiskey in the other. A young, shapely woman appearing loose and risqué in a snug corset, garters, and fishnet stockings. And at least a half-dozen more.

Strangers, every one of them. The familiar veneers of tourists, was all. Sightseers turning tricks.

But the little girl...

She looked back at the half-smiling child and was immediately overcome with panic; a feeling of dread so palpable that her knees began to shake and burn with the sudden glut of adrenaline.

A dry knot caught in her throat. A mother's fear gripped her.

The window display quickly boiled away, evaporating into another image not as crisp in its resolution; time was endeavoring to temper its contours, lull its implications. But time would fail this courtesy, she knew, as this particular travesty—no matter how many years might eventually separate then and now—would never consent to the shushing of its deafening edges. A white crib bathed in morning light now loomed before her. She peered timorously between the slats, upon the infant within. Jessica. Her baby girl. Motionless. Pale. Eyes half open, showing just the whites.

Rachel reached into the nightmare and shakily lifted her daughter from the crib. The child's arms and legs did not bend as they should. Her head did not loll, but lazed in a strained, macabre way.

Oh, oh...my...God...

What is happening to me?

She tried to shake away the memory, but it remained, steadfast with its accusations.

*****

Heart racing, hands trembling, Eli held the stained glass inches from her face, sunlight filtering through smoky hues. He concentrated the colors upon her wings, then slowly rotated the glass. The effect reminded him of the color wheel his mother used to put in front of the Christmas tree, one of those electric carrousels that swathed the whole display blue, then red, yellow, and green.

He fondly recalled the tin foil angels he'd made for her in Sunday school so many years ago, and remembered how they'd outshone all the other ornaments on the tree. They had been the simple winged kind, thin and flat, as if lopped from a cookie-cutter, their halos made of gold hobby wire. And every Christmas since—up to the one where she no longer gave a damn; had become senile—he'd given his mother a new assortment of his homespun angels. She would always crow, "They're even lovelier than last year's."

It was their wings that had made them special. He'd used real feathers with striking results, having meticulously arranged and layered them on the cardboard cutouts.

Eli stared into the girl's impossibly wide eyes, then anointed her forehead with the colors of the glass; a bizarre baptism as unholy as it was impromptu. But then, he'd always been impulsive.

When he was through, he kissed the piece of glass as if it were a rosary, returned it to his knapsack, then once again took the camera and brought it to his face.

*****

Rachel stared into the cauldron, watching that nightmarish morning of four years ago gurgle upward like some vile witch's brew...then spill over the edge and sweep her away.

She'd never told her husband about Jessica; was still too ashamed, she supposed.

An undertow, vile and impeaching, pulled her down. She couldn't breathe; was drowning.

There is no vaccine, Rachel, reminded the Freudian fuck. *I know you don't believe it now, but there will come a time when those cancerous feelings will seem in remission, when the pain in your heart will scar over. But the disease is insidious. It attacks scar tissue, opens up old wounds, thus allowing the guilt to flow freely again. Only with forgiveness can you suture them. But they will never heal completely. Accept that. And forgive yourself.*

"Oh, just shut up, you metaphor-infested quack!" she demanded aloud, startling herself back to the present.

A fat, freckled lady wearing black Spandex pants and a frond-woven sunhat slowed as she approached Rachel. The lady continued on, peering reprovingly down her nose.

Kiss my ass! Rachel thought. Then she felt something warm—a bead of sweat?—trickle down her leg. Oblivious to propriety, she reached under her dress and dabbed at her cotton panties, then her thigh.

Oh God, please don't let it be—

She brought her hand up and stared disbelievingly at the blood that now stained her fingertips.

Oh dear sweet God no, she silently pleaded. *Please, please, don't let me lose this one, too.*

Then something very strange and very wonderful happened: a presence reached inside and reassuringly touched what might have been the shoulder of her mind.

"Don't be afraid, Rachel," whispered a remarkable voice. "Your baby girl is fine."

*****

Her eyes were pleading with him, *imploring* him, but he just kept smiling behind the camera.

Defiantly then, she closed her eyes, squeezing out the relentless tears, determined to deprive the man the pleasure of ever seeing them open again. But a blast of pain flung them wide. Drawing in a sharp breath, she only provoked the agony.

The pain that had been earlier confined to her back was now pulsing through her entire body, sparing nothing. So thorough was this pain, the horror so transforming, that she literally believed she was melting.

Not the camera! her mind screamed. *No more camera!*

She turned her head away from the man and began to tenderly caress the soil with her cheek. Then, like some netted beast, she became suddenly rapacious. Grunting and growling, nostrils flaring, she scoured her face bloody as she gnawed ferociously at the dirt.

Then she saw the electronic flash wink across the ground.

For just the briefest moment she stopped thrashing, closed her eyes again. She heard another click, then a third. Only able to breathe through her nose, each respiration was carnally expelled. The loamy smell of earth tinctured her nostrils with its vitality, chilling her body and soul. She knew about the soil's alliance with death.

And then it struck her: *He's not going to bury me. He's going to—*

Her body began to wrench and jerk; some kind of seizure.

She was dying.

Woeful baying rose from the woods. Not just from one dog, but many.

Her spasms quickly subsided; now just shimmers of their former selves.

The man was staring into the shadow-rich timber where, amid the howls, orange dots of light now cavorted like windswept embers. She thought he looked scared, and that gave her some joy. After a few moments, he resumed his picture-taking.

Another flash struck her eyes. She blinked incessantly, but the blinding impression did not fade this time. Instead, the lingering dot of white brilliance kept getting larger and larger until it consumed her. She felt as if she'd been encased in a warm batch of Jell-O, not quite hardened to its full consistency.

The pain now began to quickly bleed out of her, the molten liquid flowing through her body, down into her legs, then finally out the taps that were once her ankles. There was a popping sound, then the sensation of being...*rounded*, a converging of all sides of thought and memory. This new sensation gave her the ridiculous yet convincing notion that she'd been turned into a bubble.

Then the most soothing voice she had ever heard spoke inside her head, a voice so tender and feminine. And somehow so very familiar. "Forgive your tormentor, for he is seduced."

"If Donut was here," she said, her words as clear to her ears as if she'd spoken them out loud, "this creep'd be going home in a body bag."

The voice had a pleasant, whispering laugh. "For just a little thing, you sound a lot like Charles Bronson. But don't worry, his time will come."

"Not soon enough!"

"Not soon enough," the voice agreed, "as you are only his second."

"He's going to kill more people?"

"Yes, more little girls. But if I said that you will pave the road for his eventual destruction, would that make you happy?"

"Sure, but I'll be dead, so how–"

"Come, Katherine," said the voice. "Let's leave the man to his work."

*****

Eli lifted his angel from the ground, then dangled her over the edge.

Far below them, the sounds of wind and ocean melded to be almost indistinguishable from one another. And in the reaching light, the rocky shore below looked like a gaping, frothing maw of black fangs.

In the distant wood, those glowing eyes flared; bobbing and streaking, ricocheting off the shadows, their yowls rising like suns, competing with the wind and surf.

"Fly," Eli shouted triumphantly, then released her.

And she did.

*****

Flying, flying...
Glitter and fireflies...

Fireflies sailing off of her, the release of each one a weighty burden gone, making her lighter, lighter...

Goodbye, Mommy...

Going were all the barbed and bitter pieces of pain and loss, the sweet petal smells of crayon marks, the multicolored sounds of silly laughter, plastic bracelets and Valentine candy, her friends and shiny bicycle spokes, carousel rides and Dairy Queen sundaes, dead skates washed upon the beach...

Going were the cameras and pictures and white feather wings.

All the good and bad men.

Memories glimpsed like vestiges of sunlight cast between the twirling blades of a windmill.

A pleasant wind rushing around her, through her. Eroding her.

Erasing.

All that was, all that had ever been, was molting off the orb, the bubble, falling away in a golden, sleeting rain; away into a vastness that was neither light nor dark, just unspeakably empty. She felt like a disintegrating comet plummeting through a strangely thick and infinite atmosphere, becoming even lighter now, lighter—

Someone beside her. Around her. Squeezing her?

Goodbye.

The bubble popped.

Now she was standing in warm, ankle-deep water.

The one beside her had no feet, no legs, but stood nonetheless. Just a faceless form. The one who had rescued her. Her protector.

"Where are we?" Katherine said.

"The Shallows. You've been here many times."

"I have?" She could not remember.

"Many, many times."

"Why?"

"Because you have."

"Smells salty, like the ocean."

"Tears."

"Tears?"

"Every one that has been shed, and all that will ever be."

Katherine reached down and wet her fingertips; drew them to her mouth.

"If you do, then you will *Know*," said her protector.

She didn't understand her sudden compulsion, but she had to *Know*. She brought her fingers to her lips and tasted the warm, briny water.

Instantly, she resumed her fall from the cliff. The wind grabbed her wings, pulling fiercely at the filament, ripping through her skin like talons. Horrible, searing pain. Her confusion was great. She had already forgotten.

Instinctively, she tried throwing out her arms, but her wrists were bound by rope. She screamed and screamed, but the tape across her mouth only permitted muffled barks.

Just a little girl. She began to cartwheel.

Delirious terror. One wing gone, whirling away from her like a dying feather kite. She could feel the icy sting of ocean spray, could taste the salt on her lips. An ocean of tears.

The other wing tearing loose now.

The hungry mouth below, yawning, cocking its jaws.

Closer, closer...

Please don't let it hurt, please don't let it–

She bounced upon a trampoline of light—a light of the most extraordinary brilliance and warmth. Her hands and feet were no longer bound, and as she rejoiced in her freedom the trampoline of light imploded, pulling her inward.

She was whisked into an inky, boundless chasm. All around her, as if sensing her arrival, the blackness began to peel away from itself in colossal, billowing sheets, revealing an even deeper blackness beyond. The absence of light did not interfere with awareness. She was observing everything with something much more perceptive than eyes, was *experiencing* with senses keener than she'd ever dreamed possible.

The sheets fell all around her, millions of them; an exfoliation of the blackest night. In noiseless procession they soared forth. At a great distance ahead, they converged, forming a planet-sized sphere, around which a golden atmosphere began to glow. As she drew closer, she saw that its surface was honeycombed, with each cavity splitting, dividing...

Despite her impression that she was being coerced, she had an underlying confidence that she could stop and turn back at any time. But she did not resist the obliging force—and quickly came to realize that to do so would leave her without subsistence, as it was this very force through which she was feeling-observing these incredible events; was an umbilicus tethering her to the Grandness, bringing her the Nourishment, feeding her the Incredibleness.

And upon that mentation, her *Knowing* fulfilled Itself. She was in the womb of God.

Nearly upon the surface of the sphere now, she saw one of the honeycombs begin to fill with what looked like molten silver. She instinctively curled into a fetal position—a bubble again—then willed herself into the opening. There was an actual sensation of splashing—

—then she was someone else.

There was a journey of lives revisited. The passing of each lifetime had felt incredibly long, and every one hopelessly unfulfilled. How many people had she been? She did not know. But the retention of all those lives—the cumulated cognizance, the plurality of awareness, the multiplicity of emotion—was unbearably fatiguing. She pleaded to be relieved of those souvenirs.

Now she was standing in the Shallows again, her amalgam of memories fading, fading...

But there still remained the *Knowing.*

"You see," her protector explained, "*your* tears are here, as well."

"Why did we come here?"

"So that you may *Know,* if you wish."

"But...I'll forget, won't I?"

"Perhaps."

"So, why keep bringing me back?"

"Because there will be a time when you will *not* forget, and that will be your salvation."

"When will that time be?"

"I am not the keeper of that key."

"Who is?"

"Your tears have already shown you."

A bubble again. Her *Knowing* burst from her into countless radiant shards of silver, tumbling away in all directions, end over jagged end. Away.

Disappearing...

But she wanted to keep the *Knowing.*

...disappearing...

Goodbye.

A warm, tight place now.

Something began to beat within the orb. Something wonderful.

"Where are we now?"

"The road I mentioned," said her protector. "The one you will pave."

The beating grew louder, absorbing the bubble and all transient memories left unshed. She peered within herself and saw the tiny pounding heart.

"Who will I be this time?" she said.

That whispering laugh again. "Hmmm, I wonder."

As she withdrew ever inward, she saw the second heart; as tiny as her own, and beating just as ferociously.

"Wait!" she called out. "There's somebody else in here!"

Her protector's voice was distant now, but no less playful. "Yes, there is."

...*disappearing...*

Goodbye.

*****

An internal, dizzying storm. Rachel swooned, the world tilting so precariously that she had to lean against the window to keep from falling. Nausea doubled her over. Sweat beaded across her brow. Bile singed the back of her throat, watering her eyes.

People slowed, staring in concern.

An employee from the studio peered around at her from inside the entrance. "You all right, ma'am?"

"Morning sickness," she told him, then managed a placating smile. "I'm fine. Really."

In the window, she saw the reflection of someone standing over her, an unusually tall, looming figure. But when she turned there was no one there. Then that strange and comforting touch again, as if someone were stroking her anxiety with warm, wispy fingers. The sensation was so profound, so *promising,* that any lingering dread of miscarrying her baby was quickly ushered from her thoughts.

The tempest passed. Then a brief but intense blinding flash of silver, followed by a strangely pleasant cramping sensation.

The tall figure again. In the window. Something spreading outward from behind its back, like...*wings.*

Magnificent, enormous wings, stretching triumphantly past the edges of the window, then beyond the peripheral vision of her mind. Folding inward now, enshrouding her, suffocating her with a palpable radiance that was indescribably serene.

Then it was over. All was normal again. Almost. The picture of the little girl remained. Behind the window. Staring back at her.

Those eyes!

And her sudden need to possess that photograph was so gripping, so consuming that she nearly wrenched the door from its hinges as she burst into the studio.

ELEVEN YEARS LATER

"If the religious projections of man correspond to a reality that is superhuman and supernatural, then it seems logical to look for traces of this reality in the projector himself."

– Peter L. Berger, *A Rumor of Angels*

Part One
Pictures

1.

Perched within the confines of a towering oak, it gazed down upon the playground, regarding each child predatorily. Immersed in a tangle of shadows, it had only stopped here to rest, to groom, but had inadvertently stumbled onto something. Something that roused in it a kind of primitive panic. An urgency to fight or flee.

And that *something* was infesting one of the rollicking bodies below.

Extending a leathery wing, it began to preen with swift precision. In seconds, the appendage was glistening, free of the dust and grime it had gathered in flight.

It tipped its head, pensive as it held the thin membrane taut against a dapple of sunlight, watching the blood pulse through the labyrinthine array of veins and capillaries. It was amused, but only briefly. It then turned and began cleaning the other wing, the children below never leaving its scrutiny for more than a second or two.

The scent wafted by again. It stretched out its neck and licked the air. It was a most unsettling odor; alarming in its individuality, in its *familiarness*, as it now believed it had once known such a stench. Snorting again, it shook its head wildly. Its inquisitiveness was paying the price for its tenacity; a bear willing to be stung many times to get the sweet honey within the hive.

It was growing more aroused, the hair bristling along its spine.

Then—as the face of the little girl came into full view—it *remembered*.

Like a seahorse, it moved in unison with the wind-stirred branches.

Just another limb, another bough swaying in a confusion of phantoms.

It would have to abandon its original errand and return to the place called Seattle. To alert the man who longed to fly.

The angel-maker.

2.

Before a barren patch of wall, Eli Kagan paced in circles. Some tight, some broad. Some not really circles at all, but more like the wobbly orbits of doomed satellites.

He was expecting the window to arrive any time now. Any moment.

Despite the relative coolness of his mother's basement, his undershirt was saturated, the wetness penetrating to the spine and armpits of his black clerical shirt.

But then, he was always a sweater.

Today's temperatures had dipped back down into the mid eighties, a welcome retreat from the preceding days' record heat.

Lips pursed bloodless, fingers interlocked behind his back, he recalled, as he went round and round, the story of Little Black Sambo. They shared some affinities, he and that tale, controversy not being the least of those. But the one foremost on his mind was: *If that fucking window doesn't show up in the next thirty seconds, I'm going to churn myself into butter!*

But those had been tigers running themselves into "ghi," he reminded himself, and that it was the boy with whom he had a lot in common. Just like Sambo, Eli had given his little Red Coat and little Blue Trousers and little Purple Shoes with Crimson Soles and Crimson Linings to the grandest Tiger in the Jungle.

But he still had his beautiful Green Umbrella to hide behind, known in other politically incorrect tales as the Catholic Priesthood.

Round and round and round he goes...

As do many aged and avid collectors of antiquities, Eli had become a deft authority on his obsession, that being archaic colored glass, ecclesiastical his forte. Although he often used the term himself, he knew that *stained glass* was a misnomer, as it is only *one* of the glasses so employed. Nevertheless, he was quite confident that this erroneous name would continue to be used for all time to inaccurately describe colored windows and their glass, simply because it had been so fixed in the public mind. Just as deeply and permanently as had become its naïve interpretations of Good and Evil.

However, Eli's windows—an inventory of six, so far—were not souvenirs filched from some medieval mosque or twelfth-century cathedral. They were rewards given to him by his mentor.

But more importantly, they were portals; sashes upon which the universe itself was hinged.

And through which he would soon have ingress.

"Come on, come on," he grumbled.

The empty space of wall before him was reserved for his seventh—and what was to be his last—window, its six predecessors spaced evenly and adjacently along the same gray cinder block, as if on display in some subterranean gallery renowned for its eclectic art. Each window had been tightly fastened to the masonry by what he could only describe as "magical means," as their framed edges appeared to have been *soldered* into the brick. And though each one only measured four-feet by six-feet, he was confident that they were pliant enough to allow Jupiter and its ever-growing number of moons to comfortably pass should they and this basement ever cross interstellar paths.

These were not windows in the availing sense, were not offering colorfully cloudy, misshapen perspectives of the Seattle afternoon. Rather, they were ornamented, framed pictorials, each one a hodgepodge of Roman, Byzantine, Gothic, and Renaissance persuasion and technique. Small, juxtaposed pieces of translucent glass artfully arranged into powerful images.

But while most praiseworthy colored glass portrayed biblical accounts—the kinds one would find in Le Mans, France, home of the famous *Ascension,* or Canterbury, England, where reside a magnificent series of twelfth-century windows representing the genealogy of Christ—Eli's windows might have been depicting choice passages from Dante's *Divine Comedy* or Milton's *Paradise Lost.* There were human figures cringing from gargoyle-like demons swooping down at them, others writhing and thrashing in pools of bright yellow fire, and still others impaled upon spires of eternal flame.

...and where he stops...

But that would not be his fate, he knew. No, his destiny was not profiled in the images before him, not blatantly and in such fabled conflagration, but rather in the peripheral regions not explored in the glass murals. Those areas where reality could be penciled in, then erased; brushed on, then whitewashed; scored, then filled, all at the artist's whim. And, all modesty aside, Eli considered himself a regular fucking Rembrandt. A prodigy.

Some twelve years had passed since he'd come into possession of the first window, each proceeding one having been acquired upon his simultaneous receipt of a ten-year-old girl.

Eli's love for glass tapestry was as old as his love for angel lore, ergo his assignments and rewards. His mentor had kindly integrated these passions into the playbook; had, in fact, built his stratagem around them. A compliment in and of itself.

...nobody knows.

The coach, however, had yet to make all the game's objectives known to him. Little bits and pieces learned over many years on the playing field, that was all. It was never even clear to him if his team was winning or losing.

But one thing was certain: he was still in the game.

Another safe bet was that the game balls—the angels and windows— were placebos for his cramped and near-sighted intellect; personifications to keep him focused, effigies to bolster his morale, moorings when he was blind-sided or took a knee to the groin. Supernaturally speaking, of course.

Throughout the years of looking beneath the surface for cryptic clues as to what his mentor might be up to, Eli often considered the possibility that there weren't any, that the powers that be were prone to simply act out impetuously sometimes, perhaps driven to whim by mere boredom. To set things in motion that fulfill nothing more than the need to keep their muscles from atrophying.

There was nothing furtive about a dog stretching itself on a rug after a long nap; no mystical bombshells about that. After all, eternity was forever. And that could get very old.

Eventually, though, he'd realized that the answers weren't likely going to be so anemic; that he just wasn't able to see beyond the facade. Some things were not for him to comprehend. Not yet. He was still an errand boy, a mere mortal, and knew there was plenty to forfeit should he lose that perspective.

He was so close now; the answers dangling this very moment from the talons of one of his mentor's more domesticated beasts.

Eli thought he couldn't wait to see the rest of *that* menagerie.

And if it turned out that the whole experience was nothing but a kind of hazing, a test of his will and devotion, perhaps something all inaugurates for the higher ranks had to endure, then he could live with that. For they had not been tribulations. He enjoyed the art of angel-making. Immensely so.

It sure as hell beat fasting for forty days and forty nights while playing stenographer to some burning bush. Eli didn't know what he was going to bring down from *this* mountain, but he was certain it wasn't going to be two stone tablets and a sunburn.

So far, he felt confident that he'd more than proved his loyalty, and would continue to do so no matter what shape or color or however allegorical the escapade.

But then, it was all allegory. Nothing but one contrived comparison to a systematized delusion after another, life and religion were. He'd reached that way of thinking long before his first day of catechism so many years ago. Then, he'd just referred to it less eloquently as "a crock of shit."

The scriptures couldn't fool him then, and—after three decades and counting as a Catholic priest—they most certainly couldn't fool him now.

On a scale of one to ten, Eli would have to set the marker at maybe two-point-five to indicate his belief in the *autonomous* existence of orthodoxy's God. Or any god, for that matter, all heavenly and not-so-heavenly creatures included. And given that same stipulation, he would have to place his own mentor at a six. *Maybe* seven. A generous placement indeed, for Eli didn't believe anything deserved an absolute ten, because nothing absolutely existed. Although he wasn't exactly a charter member of the "Reality Is a Self-Perpetuating Illusion" club, he'd snuck into enough meetings to finally come away persuaded. Hell, to rate anything an eight was charitable. Nine was downright altruistic. Ten and beyond were...well, the EEG tracings of a comatose Stephen Hawking.

He wasn't exactly sold on this ideology, or any other for that matter, but it continued to maintain a certain appeal; was alluring in a maverick sort of way, he supposed. And the obscured relationship he and Gamble maintained only added to the eccentricity. But this *folie a deux* sometimes caused him distress, as he would occasionally feel alienated from the rest of the world and would go searching for his sanity. Until he again realized that there was no such thing.

And throughout his years as an angel-maker, he'd become even more suspect that reality was just a land of mirrors. But *sometimes* the image staring back was something more than just the reflection of the one peering in. Staggeringly more.

Eli's mentor, case in point, was once himself the likeness of man's biggest fear (or so he claimed), but was now boasting a different visage, one smiling buoyantly back from that reflective surface, as he had finally removed himself from man's hip and was now his own free-floating person.

The mirror-makers, Eli thought, were likely in for some wild mimicry now. Eternal fire and brimstone would soon become passé, those reflections replaced by the faces of new and astounding horrors; tortures more chic and stylish, and more grisly than any man could ever dare imagine. His mentor had confided in him that much.

He snickered. Sometimes he just couldn't help but feel like a proud father.

A Jack of all Trades, Eli's mentor could now be found in the directory under his new name, Mr. Gamble. He'd once confided in Eli that the ones man had given him—Mephistopheles, Satan, Archenemy, and so on— were just a bit too conspicuous for his tastes, as he was his own plastic surgeon now, had reshaped his identity by nipping here and tucking there, and was truly a timid sort of fellow who could "certainly do without such sphincter-crimping introductions when entering a room."

Again, Eli wondered where truth began and reality ended, what was man's reflection and what wasn't, and what used to be but isn't anymore. It was *so* hard to even guess with his mentor. A veritable heap of integrity and guile, fact and fiction, Gamble was.

But at least his mentor showed up when paged. No one else had even returned his calls. Ever.

Heaven still might be a likelihood, Eli had to admit, but the mind of man—the *real* hell if there ever was one—was just a magical window away.

At least it would be for him.

Behind him, on a sheet-rocked wall, was a sweeping, shrine-like montage of black-and-white photographs; pictures of winged little girls. His angels. And the pain and terror shared by all were so extreme as to be the definitive expressions of looming death.

This he called the Wall of Faces.

Out of the nearly hundred pictures, there emerged six distinct girls.

Eli had arranged the snapshots into the shapes of two outspread wings. The right wing was complete, while the left lacked finality by a few dozen more photos, the ones he would soon take of his seventh and last angel. And the space between the two wings, the place where they would naturally join to a body, was a black chalk outline of his physical self, arms flat against his sides, traced by his own mother over a decade ago.

This seventh angel would provide him his own doorway to an infinite kingdom. And if he wanted, he could even pick out a crown and scepter on the way. This he'd been promised.

The anticipation finally overwhelming him, he stopped his pacing, unlocked his hands from behind his back, then pushed them against the sides of his head, noticing as he did the bloodless tips of his fingers, looking as if they'd been fitted with white thimbles. As he pushed them through his hair, into his scalp, he discovered that they were completely numb, as well.

He stepped up to the wall. "Why isn't it here yet!" he screamed at the empty space. Spittle flew with the words, arcing like a rainbow across the sixth window.

Mouth gaping, he stared at the indelicacy. He couldn't have been more mortified if he'd ejaculated on the Pope's Easter sermon.

Then, a distant commotion of wings. Coming from behind the same window. Getting close now. Closer. Eli peered into the mural, his despair now ebbing into stark dismay, confusion.

Finally, then, his last flicker of hope was doused.

The courier slammed into the back of the window, then continued to beat itself against the glass, desperate to come through.

Eli touched the mural and the courier materialized, pouring out from the window and its Romanesque traceries like dough through a sieve. It fell unmanageably to the floor, coalesced, then unfolded its wings; wings plenty large enough to conceal an adolescent girl.

But Eli already knew there was no girl, no angel; knew it the moment he heard the courier approaching from behind window number six, the same one from which it had been earlier dispatched. He knew then that sweet little girl number seven, for whatever reason, wasn't in the courier's custody.

Eli wavered unsteadily, and for a moment feared he just might faint.

The creature, agitated as hell, rose up on its haunches and began sniffing the air. It turned to Eli, regarded him with a suspicious glare, snorted, then leapt to the Wall of Faces, and began perusing the photographs.

Dumbstruck, Eli stood motionless, rapt in the courier's strange behavior.

Then, like some freakish hunting dog, the creature froze, its muzzle pointing directly at the felled bird. It began to hiss.

Eli moved alongside the courier, studying the face in the photograph. Although the creature had not singled out the largest picture of this particular angel, it had certainly chosen the most identifiable. Her face was almost square with the lens, and, in stark contrast with her other pictures, her suffering was absent. In this one she wore an expression of hopeless resignation, when he had captured the very moment the muscles in her face had finally tired of all the contorting, all the grimacing and clenching, and had slackened to the consistency of sun-warmed tar. Behind her eyes, it looked as if her soul were staring sorrowfully back at him—grievous not over *its* fate, but for his own.

Fuck you and your pity, he thought.

She'd definitely been his prettiest.

Many years had passed, but he'd not forgotten her name.

"Katherine Bently," he whispered. She'd been his second angel.

Now, why would the courier suddenly become obsessed with a photograph of a girl long dead? he wondered.

Then the most alarming thought struck him.

His right fist shot out violently, punching the creature across the side of its snout. "Just what the fuck are you trying to tell me?"

Cocking its head, the creature considered Eli with an expression that was nearly human; a look that said: *Do that again, chum, and I'll take it off at the elbow.* Then it began to slowly, demonstratively, flap its wings.

With avaricious eyes, Eli critiqued the display. Then: "She's *back*?"

The creature turned its muzzle back to the photograph and growled in the affirmative.

"Where?" Eli demanded.

Using the blood engendered by Eli's right hook, the creature leaned forward and, with a long, thin tongue, licked two crimson letters upon the face of the angel: *L A*

3.

"Hemorrhoids?" Duncan McNeil said, maintaining his composure. He removed his gray corduroy jacket, hung it on the brass coat tree standing beside the kitchen doorway, then loosened the knot in his tie.

Wednesday was his shortest day of the academic week, his last class usually extending no farther into the afternoon than one o'clock. Today's had ended mercifully at noon. He had seen to it. He liked teaching Criminal Justice, but it never failed to bring back memories, some good, some bad.

Today's had been bad, one of his Reliving days. And The Wounds were still throbbing.

The kitchen smelled strongly of sauerkraut, behind which his nose espied the presence of Kielbasa sausage. He shook his head. He hated that dish, but what infuriated him was that Juanita Santiago, the maid from hell, knew it, too, but kept on stuffing it into the oven anyway.

This, of course, was just one of her many and none-too-subtle ways of telling him that *she* was in charge.

Puta loco.

If it wasn't for the close relationship Juanita shared with his daughter Amy, he would have long ago Federal-Expressed the wench back to Tampico, Juarez, or whatever impoverished Mexican borough she was from.

He turned to his wife. "Hemorrhoids?" he said again, his poise quickly losing altitude.

"It's a job," Rachel said, absolving herself.

Duncan scratched his nose, as if that might stunt the grin forming below it. "Yeah, but...a *hemorrhoid* commercial?"

"Look, Dunc," she said defensively, "everyone's gotta start out somewhere."

Duncan lifted his shoulders. "Why not toilet paper, tampons, stuff for yeast infections? Hell, I can even see you pushing Midol. The afflicted housewife. God knows *that* would be a challenging role," he clucked. "But, geez, hon—*hemorrhoids*?" Then, in a pleading tone: "Tell me they're just going to dub in your voice, use only your hands to hold the—"

"Full frontal nudity," she declared.

He moaned. "Cable or Network?"

"Both. Networks don't make commercials anymore, unless they're plugging a show."

"Ointment or suppository?"

"Again, both."

He slumped against the refrigerator. "Holy inflatable seat donuts, Batman."

"Very funny," she said, drumming her long, manicured nails atop the dining room table. "I should have known this was coming."

Duncan finally sat down at the opposite end, facing her. Elbows on the table, he then bowed his head into his hands, feigning ruin. "What will the guys at the lodge say?" he whimpered. "The neighbors? Reverend Williams? *Mom?*"

A smile was slinking beneath her cool exterior. "*Reverend Williams?* Not in this lifetime."

He looked up at her, horror in his eyes. "You don't have to demonstrate its...*application!* Do you?"

She leaned forward. "Dammit, Dunc! Are you proud of me, or not?"

He straightened, the mischief in his voice waning. "Oh, of course I am, sweetheart." And he truly was, proud as punch, but this was just too grand an opportunity to let fully pass without some rib-poking.

He got up, walked over to her, put his arms around her shoulders. "Congratulations." He kissed the top of her head. "Just don't make an *ass* out of yourself."

She finally laughed. "My big break finally comes, and suddenly I'm feeling like Sally Struthers."

He started for the refrigerator. "Now *there's* an actress who could point you in the right direction, give you some up-front advice on the do's and don'ts of commercial making."

She lit a cigarette. "Pu-*leese.*" She blew a cloud of blue smoke in his direction. "Did I mention the hefty paycheck?"

He popped open a can of beer and said, "You mean you're doing it just for the money?"

"We're talking a hell of a start on Amy's college education," she said, ignoring his sarcasm. She pulled the contract from her purse, pointing to the figures that ran the full length of the right margin. "See?"

Perplexed, he said, "I thought we'd already pigeonholed enough for Amy's college tuition."

"Well, not graduate school, we haven't."

"My daughter, the doctor," he said, smiling proudly. "I can hear her now at the graduation ceremonies: 'And to my dear mother, who literally sold her ass so that I might one day—'"

"Enough with the butt jokes already," she warned, handing him the contract.

"Wow," he said. "Press hard for nine copies." He perused the legal jargon, nodding now and again, as if in agreement.

"Careful," she said, "the ink's still wet. And don't dribble any beer on it. I have to sign it and give it back to Stills first thing tomorrow."

"Speaking of Stills, I see here that your esteemed agent won't have to worry about *his* kids' college education, either."

"Yeah," she sighed. "Roughly thirty-percent, but that's standard. It's a fair arrangement."

His eyes bore down upon the paper. "Really? Let's see here: after Still's cut, there's the Screen Actors Guild, Uncle Sam—"

"Gawd, Duncan," she whined, "can't you for once just find the bright side to something?"

He gave her back the contract. "You're right. I'm being a poop—er, tease." He downed the rest of his beer, then belched wetly.

"Charming," she said.

"Okay, this is truly cause for celebration. Let's you, me, and Amy go out to dinner tonight. Any restaurant you want."

"But ... Juanita has din—"

"Let *her* eat it," he said, not hiding his revulsion. "By the way, where is the old hunchback?"

"Grocery store, then she'll swing by and pick Amy up from school." Rachel, her eleven years of residency in LA having made her overly cautious, did not allow Amy to take the bus when at all possible. "And, as her employer," she continued, "I don't think it's very sporting of you to name-call behind her back." She crushed out her cigarette. "I wish to hell you two would kiss and make up."

Duncan winced at the thought, then said, "Hey, isn't Amy getting her school picture taken today?"

"Fifth grade," Rachel said, her voice awed by the swift passage of time.

"Yeah," he fondly agreed. "Seems like it was just yesterday she was making presents in her diapers for Daddy."

"Oh? If they were *your* presents, then why did *I* always have the pleasure of opening them?"

"Woman's work," he said, waving it off, then quickly changed the subject. "Hey, your TV commercial reminds me of a joke."

"Oh, no," she moaned.

"There's these three missionaries in the jungle, see, and they get captured by this Amazon tribe of men. After taking them to their camp, the chief of the tribe says to the first missionary, 'The penalty for trespassing is either death or Bongo. Which do you chose?' 'Well,' the missionary says, 'I'll take Bongo. It can't possibly be as bad as death.' 'Bongo!' the chief shouts. The tribe cheers, and ten of these scary-looking natives line up behind the first missionary and start taking turns throwing him the ol' bologna pony." Duncan illustratively grabbed the air and pumped his hips. "After they've all finished, the first missionary says, 'Wow! That was pretty bad! But I guess it wasn't as bad as death.' Then it was the second missionary's turn. 'Death? Or Bongo?' the chief says to him. The second missionary says, 'Well, Bongo's pretty bad—but not as bad as death. I'll take Bongo.' The chief shouts, 'Bongo!' and the tribe cheers, but this time *twenty* natives take turns corn-holing him," he said, again pantomiming for her.

"Oh, please."

He continued. "When they were through, the second missionary goes, 'Oh, man! That was horrible! I should have chose death!' Then the chief looks at the third missionary, and says, 'Death? Or Bongo?' The third missionary says, 'No way am I taking Bongo. Give me death!' 'Death!' the chief shouts, '—*by Bongo!*'"

She just shook her head. "I saw that one coming a mile back."

"Oh, well," Duncan said, shrugging his shoulders. "They can't all be riots. Besides, it's in the lesson plan. See, I tell my students that joke on the very first day of every new semester, then explain to them that it's a paragon of futility. In other words, just when we think we've outwitted those who would screw us—whammo! We discover that we were screwed all along."

"Ya know what, Dunc?" Rachel calmly observed. "I used to think you were just cynical, pessimistic. But I'm beginning to see that you're far beyond that now. You've become totally misanthropic."

"Miss-and-what?"

"When did you become so, so...paranoid?"

Duncan shrugged. "When everyone started plotting against me. Anyway, I'm not letting any student of mine, badge-wearing or otherwise, loose on the streets still thinking he or she can make a difference."

Smiling, Rachel rose from her chair, threw her arms around his neck, and kissed him. "You're a desolate man, Duncan McNeil. But I love you anyway."

Duncan hugged her, softly kissed her ear, and whispered, "I love me, too."

She pushed away from him, and goosed his ribs. "I take it back. I don't even like you."

He laughed. "So, what'll it be for dinner? Korean? Mexican? LA-ian?"

"Curry," she said definitively.

"You're on the rag again, aren't you?" he said. "Seems lately that every time Aunt Flow comes to visit, your taste buds jet off to Calcutta." He shrugged then.

She shook her head. "Always the clown."

*****

But he was right, she had to admit. She'd not even realized it herself until just now—but yeah, those cravings had been nagging her for the last couple of months, yet had somehow managed to remain inconspicuous enough that she'd not connected them to her menstrual cycles. Of course, there were always those heightened desires for chocolates and their ilk, victuals that were strictly taboo as long as she remained an aspiring actress and part-time model. Sweet stuff. And maybe that was why she hadn't made the connection earlier. What she'd been craving lately was everything *but* sweet.

Still, there was nothing odd about women having cravings, she reminded herself. Like mood swings, they came with the territory. And Duncan, candid as blunt trauma, never failed to bring to her attention those certain times of the month when her disposition was approaching shrewish levels. But...to have recognized something as esoteric as her departure from sweets to curries—even before she had?

Well, she supposed not. That was the funny thing about her husband. Beneath his facetious, if not downright cynical, exterior there lurked keen intuition; a perception of people and situations that, at times, seemed to border clairvoyant. She'd long ago come to the conclusion that his years as a law officer had primed his awareness; that he'd acquired the "Blue Sense."

Sometimes, though, she wondered if it went deeper than that. Like now.

She sighed. Living with Duncan McNeil was like sharing a swamp with a herbivorous crocodile: you know it won't eat you, but it can still give you a start when it unexpectedly drifts by.

4.

"Tilt your head a little to the right, sweetheart," the photographer instructed. "There, right there. Hold it! Okay, now, smile big."

The girl tried to smile, but the effort was apparently too great. She nervously looked away.

The photographer bolted up from the viewfinder and sighed loudly. His patience, although always taxed when dealing with schoolchildren, was beginning to deteriorate this afternoon at a much faster rate than usual. He wondered if it was due to the heat combined with the lateness of the day. Since having begun at eight that morning, he'd soaked two handkerchiefs and gone through more than seventy-five fidgeting adolescents. Most had been eager, receptive, cooperative, but there were always those few...

At last count, there were five kids left in the hallway, their homeroom teacher slouched against the wall, looking in desperate need of a bar stool.

Frustrated, he pulled a hand down over his face. Maybe it was time to change careers, he thought. Sixteen years of portrait photography had not only caused deep, permanent creases on both sides of his mouth from demonstrating the correct smile, but had recently begun to strain his ego, as well. Lately, it seemed the only place people ever smiled was in front of his camera, and he behind it, both always fraudulently. And the clown-like tricks he'd been using over the years to extract those plastic simpers now seemed eager to surrender to less humorous kinds of coercion. Like brandishing an AK-47, for instance.

"Look, honey," he said tersely, "this isn't gonna hurt a bit."

He adjusted the two standing lights beside her and spread out a few wrinkles in the backdrop draped across the wall.

"What's your name, sweetheart?"

"Amy McNeil."

"How old are you, Amy?"

"Ten-and-a-half."

"Certainly you've had your picture taken before. Right?"

She nodded.

"Well then," he assured, "this is no different than when your grandma or mommy takes your picture with their little pocket brownies. Nothin' to it."

Yeah, right, pocket brownies, he thought. Christ, he was well into the 21st Century yet he continued to spout off comparisons as antiquated as his own equipment and techniques.

Seeing that she didn't have a clue as to what a brownie was, he said, "You know, digital cameras and such."

*****

Amy was reminded that she never liked having *those* kinds of pictures taken of herself either. Seeing her face in snapshots had always given her the creepy feeling that she was not really looking at herself, but at a twin sister who had been born—and continued to live and grow—in those glossy, rectangular patches of still life. A twin whose face always stared back at her with sad, *haunted* eyes. And she did not like seeing herself represented that way.

She was happy, always had been. At least she thought so.

Life had, so far, been good to her. She had a wonderful mom and dad, a nice big house, awesome clothes, had visited Disneyland and Knots Berry Farm and Sea World more times than she could count, always got straight A's (an achievement requiring little, if any, effort, and one that caused her occasional guilt), and a weekly allowance that confirmed her own suspicions that she was spoiled rotten. But she'd been careful never to flaunt her good fortune, and she attributed this bit of humility to an abundance of honest, well-intentioned friends. She was, in fact, instantly liked by nearly every person she met, adult and child alike. And to give thanks, she always knelt in prayer at bedtime—a nightly ritual encouraged by her best friend and family's live-in maid, Juanita Santiago.

Amy's parents weren't as outwardly religious, if they were religious at all, and they certainly didn't go around knocking on people's doors "pushing Christ like a vacuum cleaner," as her dad was fond of saying. They never attended church, much to Juanita's disapproval, but Amy felt that they all led a clean life. One without of any *major* sins, at least.

There was only one thing in the whole world that she hated (a word not often heard in her above-average vocabulary) and that was having her picture taken. She'd always felt the need to duck whenever a camera was pointed in her direction, to quickly glance away at the last second as if the shutter's intention was to capture more than just a moment in time. And more than a few of the snapshots taken of her (mostly the ones where she was three and older) were, from the neck up, blurred by this phobia.

To Amy, photographs were like silent lies. They quietly led the viewer away from the real truth with beguiling expressions; a concept, she imagined, that was certainly familiar to the sweating, rankled photographer before her.

She hated cameras, what they produced. And, strangely, always had. But today, that profound dislike was quickly turning into a kind of smothering fear, and she had no idea why. She wanted desperately to hop down from this wobbly stool and run. Run home. Already her heart was strumming in her ears. Her hands were trembling, and her knees felt cold and rubbery. She'd also begun to sweat and was aware of an awful odor coming from her armpits—a strong, skunk smell, much more powerful than the kind she sometimes noticed in gym class.

Frightened and ashamed, she pulled her arms tightly against her body.

"Let's try this one more time," said the photographer. "C'mon, how about a pretty smile."

Just as she was about to tell him that she wasn't feeling well, and that she would like to leave, he tripped the shutter.

The flash seared through her eyes and into her brain, exploding there like a balloon filled with silver helium. She blinked frantically, trying to reestablish her eyesight. She wobbled on the stool, then began to fall. But what should have only been a two-foot drop to the floor began to seem incredibly long. She could actually feel the wind rushing around her, powerfully so, as if she were falling from a skyscraper rather than a chair.

The roar of an ocean engulfed her ears. There was now an itching, tearing pain across her upper back, and she feared she'd somehow injured herself. Then the taste of saltwater filled her mouth and stung her nostrils, making tears form at the corners of her eyes.

Goodbye

She didn't remember hitting the floor, but could now feel the cold tile against her left cheek and arm.

The photographer rushed to her side. Gently taking her right arm, he said, "Easy sweetie, easy."

Her vision hazily restored, Amy reached for the stool to steady herself, but missed. Her right hand landed on the lower edge of the photographer's backdrop, a watercolor miasma of grays, whites, violets, and blues. Then, as if some supernatural sponge, her hand began to absorb the colors from the canvas. Surging just beneath the skin, those tinctures spiraled around her wrist, then into the rest of her exposed arm, giving the limb the appearance of having been hideously bruised.

She found the stool with her other hand, pulled herself up to her feet.

The photographer stumbled backward, tripping over one of his umbrella reflectors. He fell hard on his butt, then shuffled backward on palms and heels until he wedged himself into a corner, not once taking his eyes from the cyclonic attack.

Amy stared at her predicament with attentive wonder, unsure if her eyes were playing tricks, or if her hand was actually sucking up the cloudy colors. She was experiencing no pain, just a droning in her arm; a tingling, as if its circulation had been crimped.

Very afraid now, she tried to jerk her hand away, but found that she could not. Instead, her efforts seemed to have the opposite effect, her hand plunging deeper into the canvass. She didn't feel like she was being forcefully *pulled* in; rather, it felt more like she was *sinking*. There was no doubt in her mind that the rest of her body would soon follow.

Crying now, she tugged again and again, harder and harder. Turning her wide, wet eyes to the photographer, she pleaded, "Make it stop. P-please make it stop."

The man's jaw moved up and down, up and down, but nothing audible fell out.

Everything below her elbow was now gone.

Within seconds the backdrop was drained of color.

Nearly hysterical now, Amy planted her right foot against the wall, then yanked with all her might. To her surprise, her hand slid free. Off-balance, arms flailing, she pirouetted away like a drunken ballerina. Her left arm struck the photographer's tripod, sending it and his camera crashing to the floor, while nearly sending herself there as she tripped over one of his splayed legs. The man recoiled in fear. He pulled his knees tight against his chest and warned her to stay away.

Catching her balance, Amy held out her hand. This was not an obligatory gesture to help the man up, but to inspect the colors swirling tempestuously within her arm. Then, quickly, the pigment of her pale, freckled skin returned as the colors submerged, taking with them the pin-prick sensations that had grown to an electrical buzz.

She glanced back at the wall and noticed that her hand had not filched all the colors from the backdrop. There were still a few smudges left. And as her vision returned to near-normalcy, she believed that those smudges were actually words.

Wiping her eyes, she inched closer until she could read them. Yes, they were words; easy words. She had no difficulty reading the sentence they formed. It was *deciphering* the sentence where she found she was having trouble.

HE KNOWS WHERE YOU'VE FLOWN

Then another flash blinded her.

The room went topsy-turvy, and she spiraled into a bottomless sea of silver.

5.

As Rachel and Duncan stepped through the emergency room entrance of the hospital, they were greeted by Amy's school principal/English teacher, John Kincaid, who had called them with the news of her accident. They'd met Kincaid before, mostly at award ceremonies honoring students who'd made the Principle's Honor Roll. Not much taller than a schoolboy himself, Kincaid looked even mousier next to Duncan's six-three, bear frame. The principal's thinning white hair and weary stoop made him look twenty years older than he probably was, which, Duncan guessed, was somewhere in the mid-forties.

"Not to worry, not to worry," Kincaid said with practiced, soothing urgency, sounding as he did over the phone. "She's just fine. Took a tumble off a chair is all." A broad smile widened his face. "I assure you both that her admittance here is purely cautionary."

As they passed the admitting desk, Duncan noticed two paramedics working listlessly over documents, talking quietly to one another; whispering. They both looked up as Kincaid ushered him and Rachel by, their eyes following them down the gleaming corridor. By their grim, round-eyed expressions, Duncan supposed that they'd just brought in the lurid remains of a homicide victim, or something equally gruesome.

They checked in at the security desk, a mandatory procedure.

The guard, a retired cop (Duncan could spot them a mile away), ran his finger down the computer screen. "Amy McNeil, you said? Admitted within the last hour or so?"

"That's right," Duncan said, launching sarcastically into cop rhetoric: "Adolescent Caucasian female, ten years old, approximately four-and-a-half feet tall, reddish-blond hair, greenish blue eyes, usually has in her possession at least one item with a Barbie logo."

The guard looked up, not amused. "She's not showing up on my—"

"The child from Jefferson Elementary," Kincaid reminded, stepping out from behind Duncan. "I arrived shortly after the ambulance. I'm her principal." He pointed to the visitor badge affixed to the lapel of his modish jacket. "Surely you remember *me*."

"'Course I do," said the guard, swiveling the monitor around. He pointed to the screen. "But the girl *you're* referring to was registered as Katherine Bently, not Amy McNeil."

Duncan and Rachel exchanged bewildered glances.

Kincaid sighed. "A mistake, sir, just as I authenticated initially. And one which you obviously failed to correct in the interim. Now please, these are her parents—"

"Alright, alright, I believe you," insisted the guard, smiling now. After retrieving the necessary information, he issued Duncan and Rachel visitor badges.

"Bay four," said the guard. "It'll be the second door on your right."

"'Bay' four?" Duncan said, insulted for his daughter. "What, is she getting her tires rotated?"

The guard shrugged, brandishing another impish grin at Kincaid as he walked by, as if the man were a drag queen instead of a self-respecting principal.

They paused in the doorway. Amy lay on a bed, appearing to be asleep. A male nurse was standing over her, adjusting a saline drip that had been inserted into her right hand.

The nurse saw them in the doorway and motioned for them to enter.

"I'll leave you folks alone," Kincaid said. "If someone should need to speak with me, I'll be in the waiting area." Then he disappeared down the hallway.

"You must be Katherine's parents," the nurse said with an appeasing smile. "She's going to be fine. Probably just had the wind knocked out of her."

Rolling her eyes, Rachel said, "Her name is Amy." She reached into her purse and removed a pen. "Here," she said to the nurse, "you might want to scribble that down somewhere."

Taking in the scene, Duncan was beginning to wonder if Amy's situation might be a little more serious than they'd been led to believe.

He followed Rachel to the bed, then bent down and kissed Amy's cheek. "Hey, baby cakes," he whispered in her ear.

Rachel, worry sagging from her face, softly placed a hand upon her daughter's forehead.

The nurse was reading the admission form. "Well, there's obviously some mistake. She's been registered as Katherine Bently." Hunching his shoulders, he looked up at them. "Name ring a bell?"

Disgusted, Rachel shook her head.

Although the name wasn't arousing any carillons in Duncan's belfry, he had to admit that it *was* giving the rope a slight tug.

"Being her parents and all," Duncan said, "we're almost positive her name is Amy McNeil."

The nurse studied the admission form some more, then the papers beneath. "Well, what obviously happened is the people at admissions copied the information straight off the medic's report. The ambulance driver just got his names mixed-up," he said, as if that kind of cute little blunder happened all the time. He made some notations on the forms, referenced the new name, then handed the clipboard to Duncan. "Go ahead and look over the paperwork and feel free to make any other corrections. Once you're through, just go ahead and give it to the doc. And don't forget to go by the front desk and give those folks the right info. They'll want to know what insurance to bill, as well." He stepped out of the "bay" and began pulling the curtain closed. "Constance Strickland is the ER doc on duty. She's already checked Amy out. I'll see if I can track her down for you."

"Thank you," Rachel said.

"Yes, do that," Duncan urged.

The nurse drew the curtain closed, leaving them to their privacy.

Duncan shuffled through the papers, wanting to confirm for himself what the nurse had just told them.

Rachel leaned over and cooed into Amy's ear. "Mommy's here, baby. Everything's all right now."

Amy stirred restlessly but remained asleep.

"They've got everything wrong," Duncan said, comparing documents. He was seething now. "Fucking incompetents. None of this is right. Christ! This is someone else's information! The phone number's all wrong, the address—" He stared at the address.

Rachel glanced back at Duncan with a look that said she was growing a little perturbed with his seemingly misguided concern.

"I wonder why she's sleeping so hard," she said. "Did they give her something, you think?"

"Hawthorne Avenue, Rock Bay," Duncan said, more to himself.

"Uh-huh," Rachel said, obviously not listening. She was craning over Amy, looking like she wanted desperately to grab her shoulders and shake her out of her stupor.

"Rock Bay," he repeated, louder. "Little coastal town in Massachusetts. Your home town, my dear. You know, the one we were *married* in."

She turned, giving him her full attention. "What?"

He showed her the papers. "Katherine Bently, 1402 Hawthorne Avenue, Rock Bay, Mass." And as he spoke those words, heard his own voice say them, an ambiguous memory glittered in the deep darkness of his mind, like a lone firefly trying to illuminate a vast, starless night. It was so brief, so transitory that he barely noticed it before it was gone.

"Small world," Rachel said.

Duncan, however, wasn't ready to believe the world was *that* dinky.

*****

Doctor Constance Strickland was a tall woman, lanky, and had a face that Duncan instantly labeled a "Two-Hundred Yarder," an old cop expression for homely women: not nauseatingly ugly, but definitely a few football fields away from ever gracing *Vogue*.

She entered ebulliently, so much so that Duncan wondered if she was writing her own prescriptions for amphetamines.

The doctor introduced herself, extending a hand to Duncan, then Rachel. "I understand that there's been a mix-up with your daughter's name?" She regarded them with subdued suspicion, as if they might be impostors.

"The paramedics apparently got her confused with another patient, or something like that," Duncan said, bewilderment having tempered his anger.

Doctor Strickland took the clipboard from Duncan's hand. "Strange," she said. "I saw her when she first came in, and she clearly told me her name was Kathy Bently."

Duncan lifted his eyes to the ceiling.

"Oh, you know," Rachel offered suddenly, "I don't know if this means anything, but Amy had an imaginary playmate by the name of Kathy for...well, a good while."

Strickland didn't seem concerned. "About how old was she when you stopped hearing about this playmate?"

Rachel looked at Duncan. "Oh, say four? Maybe five?"

Duncan had forgotten all about "Kathy" until just now. He thought a moment, needing to catch up with Rachel. He finally nodded. "Yeah, four or five."

"Well," Strickland said, "it may be coincidental, it may not. But I'll make note of it."

"Why is she sleeping so hard?" Rachel said. "I can't seem to rouse her."

"We've given her a sedative," Strickland explained. "She was quite upset when she came in, and from there became uncontrollable. Please understand—we needed to calm her down for her own safety."

The concern on Rachel's face surrendered to fear.

"What the hell happened to her?" Duncan quietly demanded. "Did she hit her head, suffer a concussion?"

"She was apparently having her picture taken at school and, according to her principal, just slipped off of her chair and fell to the floor," Strickland said. "And as far as suffering some kind of head injury, I'm not convinced. There's no signs of trauma or swelling, anything like that." She sighed. "But in light of her apparent *identity crisis*, I'd like to go ahead and schedule her for a CAT scan, just to be sure. I would also like to keep her here overnight, for observation."

"Yes, of course," Rachel said.

"If she doesn't have a head injury," Duncan persisted, "then would you please tell us why she would suddenly assume someone else's identity?"

Doctor Strickland removed the patient's blank medical history form from the clipboard, then craned over it with a pen, seeming to ignore Duncan's question. "Has your daughter ever suffered from seizures?"

"You mean like epilepsy?" Rachel said.

"No," Duncan said. "Never."

"Has she ever sustained a severe head injury?"

"No," he repeated, feeling his chest tighten with each question.

"Any history of diabetes in either family? Psychiatric disorders?"

They shook their heads.

Doctor Strickland asked more questions, the final one eliciting a murderous gaze from Duncan.

"Drugs?" he hissed. "You're barking up the wrong tree!"

Strickland remained composed. "I realize she's only in elementary school, but I have to ask. Sadly, it's not uncommon anymore to see children her age abusing drugs."

Rachel took Duncan's hand, and this calmed him.

"Test her for drugs, then," he said. "I'll guarantee that you won't find her peeing anything stronger than Kool-Aid."

The doctor smiled sympathetically, shook her head. "Mr. McNeil, I'm pretty sure drugs aren't to blame. Although she didn't display all the classic symptoms, I'm inclined to believe that your daughter suffered some sort of seizure, most likely provoked by an outside stimulus."

"Such as...?" Duncan said.

"The strobe flash of a camera," Strickland said, as if that should have been highly obvious.

6.

Duncan left Rachel with Amy and hurried his way back to the ER waiting area, hoping that Amy's principal had not yet left the hospital.

With each step he felt more like a neglectful parent. Contrary to Rachel's ambivalent ogling back in the "bay," he was concerned for Amy; passionately so. But he just couldn't ignore his gut instinct, and right now it was telling him that something wasn't right; that perhaps something had been missed. This perception wasn't entirely palpable, just a scent in a mild breeze. But if it was already raising his hackles at this early stage then he would give it his full, undivided attention.

Katherine Bently, he thought. *Damned if that doesn't have a peculiar ring.*

He was reminded that he'd not had such potent intuitions, at least in any constabulary sense, since his days on the force. Back then, his inklings and hunches had always proven themselves dead-on, and more than one among his peers had, at one time or other, cast their suspicion that his charmed nose was more precognitive than instinctive. Perhaps even divine. Duncan had just thought himself streetwise, and a good judge of character; still did. Whatever the reasons, he'd quickly garnered a reputation worthy of any blue-ribbon bloodhound.

And any dust that may have settled on those olfactory glands since had just been blown away. *Clean* away.

Duncan found Kincaid sitting in a small waiting area gazing up at a television screen and eating pumpkin seeds, shells and all. He appeared engrossed with some Japanese chef, who was passionately demonstrating the fine art of shucking shrimp and the English language.

Eight chairs were arranged in an L-pattern in the small room. A giant, balding black man was rocking slowly back and forth in his seat. He held a blood-soaked bandage over his right shoulder, chanting "Cecil Mendez, that cocksucker," as if practicing his court testimony. In the corner opposite Kincaid sat an elderly couple, weeping quietly as they held one another.

"Kincaid?" Duncan said, standing over the man. "We need to talk."

Kincaid looked up and smiled. "Of course, of course." He jubilantly patted the cushion next to him. "I was just about to come check. How is Amy feeling?"

Duncan remained standing. "We're not really sure. Listen, I want the name, address, and phone number of the photographer who took my daughter's picture. I'm assuming it was a man."

"That's correct," Kincaid said, his eyes narrowing ever so slightly, his smile dimming at the edges, forming an expression that said he knew where this was heading: straight to court. "But Mr. McNeil, I can assure you that the person in question is beyond reproach. Why, he's been photographing our kids for years, the old-fashioned way, and we've never had a—"

"I'm not accusing him of any wrongdoing. I just want to talk to him." Duncan shrugged. "Call me silly, but being a parent and all, I guess I'm just a bit concerned."

Discomfited, Kincaid thought for a moment, then said, "I'm not comfortable at this time to reveal that information. Please understand my position. If I give you the man's address and phone number, then, as an acting representative of the school, I might be inviting a lawsuit should something...unpleasant come of it."

"...that *cocksucker*," the black man continued to chant, getting louder.

Duncan finally sat down next to Kincaid, and, speaking very softly, said, "Please understand *my* position. This isn't an issue of confidentiality. The photographer hasn't been charged with a crime. I simply want to find out everything I can concerning the accident that *my* daughter suffered at *your* school this afternoon. However, if I *do* find sufficient evidence to suggest that this Kodak provocateur acted inappropriately, negligently or criminally, and that you or someone else at the school had knowledge of indiscreet acts committed by him prior to his contractual employment with Jefferson Elementary, then your days of haunting lunch rooms and wiping snotty noses will be over. Now, I can get the info from you, or I can acquire it independently. If I'm forced to do the latter, however, I'll be rather upset. And seeing how I don't really like you anyway, I might vent my frustrations in a manner that might only be described as something ... *unpleasant*." Duncan stood. "It's your call."

Head craned, Kincaid turned his eyes back to the shrimp-happy chef, who was now either greatly alarmed over the blazing skillet in his hand or just excited to be flambéing the scampi. Hard to tell.

Kneading his package of pumpkin seeds like a manic child with Play-Dough, Kincaid said, "Are you threatening me, sir?"

Duncan smiled. "In every sense of the word."

Finally, reluctantly, Kincaid reached into the inner sanctum of his jacket and withdrew a pen and a business card, upon which he shakily wrote a name.

Wise move, Duncan thought. Still, he felt a bit saddened that he wasn't going to be forced, after all, to drag this gnomish principal/English teacher to the roof and dangle him like a participle over its edge.

"Here," Kincaid said, handing Duncan the card. "The man's name is on the back. If you'll contact my secretary, Ms. Annison, and explain to her the situation, I'm confident she'll be most helpful in finding you his address and phone." He glanced at his wristwatch. "She's normally there until five, so you have plenty—"

"Thank you," Duncan said, already through the door. Then he abruptly stopped, turned. "Any idea why my daughter would think her name is Katherine Bently?"

Kincaid thought for a moment. "No. *Should* I?"

"You don't have a student by that name?"

Kincaid brought his trembling hands together and rested his chin on his fingers. "No, I'm afraid the closest thing we have is a Denise Benton."

"Thanks," Duncan said. "Oh, for what it's worth, I really do appreciate you sticking around like this. Amy will be glad to know that you did."

"Not at all," Kincaid replied, his eyes indicating otherwise.

7.

COMPUTERIZED AXIAL TOMOGRAPHY (CAT) was stenciled in big white letters across the double doors. In the waiting area, Juanita Santiago paced like a caged cat, treading up and down the full length of the waiting room, her rubber thongs smacking wetly against the buffed tile.

Rachel sat in a burgundy chair, studying her upturned hands. She was so engrossed with her subjects that she might have been a palmist rendering her own reading, searching specifically for that one line or juncture that might reveal the medical reason for her daughter's admittance.

"Pardon me for saying, Mrs. McNeil," Juanita said, "but why does Señor Duncan not stay to comfort his very own child in her time of need? Is he not a concerned father?"

Juanita, having tried picking Amy up from school as arranged, had rushed to the hospital after learning of the accident from Amy's homeroom teacher.

A rosary was clutched tightly in her right hand.

"He had an important errand to run," Rachel said, still preoccupied with her palms. "Besides, Amy's going to be fine. There's no reason we should all be here acting like expectant fathers."

"Well, at least there is dinner for him in the oven," Juanita sighed, secretly hoping a large piece of Kielbasa sausage would lodge in his uncaring wind pipe just long enough to see him flopping like a mackerel on the kitchen Linoleum.

"Juanita?" Rachel said, holding out her palms. "Do my hands look funny to you?"

Juanita clutched Rachel's hands and stared at the lines and bifurcations like a lost motorist. Finally, she shook her head. "They are not funny. You have beautiful hands, Mrs. McNeil. Smooth like a baby's bottom."

"Exactly," Rachel said, a bit troubled. "It's as if...all of my lines are fading away."

"It is those creams and lotions you use," Juanita said. "A couple of more years and you will be a teenage girl again." The she added, "Unless you put them back in a hot, soapy sink of dishes."

Rachel looked up reprovingly. "That's not going to happen."

Then, almost direly, Juanita said, "Señor Duncan, he fire me soon, you see."

"Over my cold, dead body," Rachel promised. Then she leaned close and whispered, "My God, I screwed up making macaroni and cheese last Thursday night when you were at bingo!"

"*Si*," Juanita gloated. "And you burned the pan, too. It's no good now."

Perpetually strutting in arrogance more befitting a Queen than a maid, Juanita Santiago had never experienced the burden of having too many friends. In fact, she practiced the art of intimidation daily. But once past the initial urge to run like hell, one could begin to perceive a powerful wisdom beneath her effrontery, potent enough to vindicate her, to forgive her brazen disposition. Most people, however, never took the few extra minutes to detect this.

Duncan was one of those people, the impatient kind. And in the nearly nine years Juanita had spent in his house—the thousands of hours spent feeding him and his family, taking care of his daughter, washing his dirty drawers and cleaning up his messes—he'd never once taken those few extra minutes to get to know her.

Although, she had to admit, *her* first impression of Señor Duncan was not exactly fleeting. He was a man with secrets. Crippling secrets. From the moment their eyes first met, she'd more than just intuited this: she literally beheld it like she would a monsoon-driven rain nettling her cheeks. She'd kept those mistrusts stored in the cellar of her soul; locked up and preserved like award-winning jams.

Her mission in life was to safeguard his daughter whom she had vowed to protect more than thirty-five years earlier, at the tender age of sixteen. Of course, she'd never informed the McNeils of this. She was a lot of things, but *loco* wasn't one of them.

Those many years ago, in the tiny town of Chinipas, Mexico, the Virgin herself had appeared from the fourth pinewood pew in Our Lady of Guadalupe, a disintegrating church in the center of what was her equally decaying birthplace. The Radiant Mother had bestowed upon her a revelation of such earthly cataclysm that had she not already been on her knees, it would have surely driven her there.

In this apocalyptic vision, broken glass oceans issued forth the legions of hell. Multitudes of winged demons swarmed out from the gigantic cracks and fissures that craggily traversed to all horizons. And beneath these aerial armies lay a child, so terribly alone on that vast expanse of glass; the only casualty in the War of wars. But this potent metaphor was not lost on Juanita, for she understood that this seemingly lone victim, in truth, epitomized all mankind.

Weeping, curled like a fetus at the base of the altar, she then received her instructions from the Blessed Mother.

Her appointed mission was not messianic, was not to warn the backsliding masses to repent, that Armageddon was fast upon them. It was a more narrowly focused one, to look after a little girl named Amy, to keep her out of harm's way. Be her sentinel.

The Marian apparition then changed into the image of that chosen girl, one aged ten or twelve, with a sweet, beautifully innocent face. The theory behind this designed manifestation, Juanita felt, was so that she would recognize the girl when finally confronted with her. This had shaken her considerably and continued to for a great long time, as she had not wanted her memory entrusted to what was obviously going to be a custodial responsibility of biblical proportions.

From then on, up until the glorious day when she and Amy finally found one another, Juanita had delighted in daily self-flagellation. Merciless throughout all those years, she'd whipped herself with popular morality tales, aided to deeper depths with the honed, stalwart blades of religious parables, then deeper still by the enduring, perennially whet sabers of scriptural parallels until, finally, her psychological state of mind had become so horrendously avulsed, her soul so variegated with the scars and welts of self-pity that the Devil himself might have convalesced her wounds with a salve to rival Heaven's own had he to endure even one more second of her insufferable mewling.

The most recurring Bible story, she recalled, had been that of the Pharaoh's daughter, when she'd found Moses on the river, floating in an arc of bulrushes. Juanita (her appointed mission having felt for so long punitive by comparison) had always been quick to remind herself, though, that there was a very sound and legitimate reason why *her* appointed package couldn't have been sent to her as effortlessly. That reason being her own sinful nature. Oh, sure, the Pharaoh's daughter had been full of sin, too. But that was a time long before the birth of Christ, and it just went to figure that God overlooked a lot more back then.

It wasn't until many years later when her searching was ended; when her employment agency called and asked if she'd like to be interviewed for a housekeeping position. That one phone call and she'd been relieved from the relentless task of searching for that child's face wherever she went. Oh, how she'd searched so diligently, so devotedly, all those years.

One simple phone call, but hardly routine. Received at seven a.m. on the seventh day of the seventh month.

Later that same evening, she'd interviewed with the McNeil family. During introductions, she'd learned that the child's name was, indeed, Amy. Upon that affirmation, she began showering the poor thing with gushing affection. It had taken all she had to keep from kneeling before the bundled form and weeping.

It wasn't long into the informal interview when she sensed Señor Duncan's fear of her, and it was likewise during this time that her distrust of him was born. She'd since learned that Rachel had the "final say" in the matter, and had hired her despite Duncan's protests. She'd also since learned that when Rachel McNeil had the "final say," God Himself couldn't have carved the pronouncement any deeper in stone.

But now she didn't know what to think of Señor McNeil; hadn't for a good year or so. He was a mysterious and certainly troubled man. Of this she was sure. But evil? Evil enough to do his own daughter harm? She now doubted it. Something had begun many months back to persuade her otherwise. Nothing tangible, nothing that he'd said or done, only a nagging feeling that maybe she'd been spending far too much time and energy suspecting her employer. The deep, troubling secrets she intuited from the man, she had to finally admit, were probably not worthy of her longstanding suspicions.

No, it was now arguable that Señor Duncan was not Satan incognito. He was just an asshole with issues.

She continued to pace, driven by fear. Earlier that morning, something had occurred within her, a sense of heightened alert, as if someone had climbed to the crow's nest of her mind, waving frantically to the rest of her being, her soul, signaling the approach of doom on the horizon.

Polishing her rosary, she mumbled, *"Va haber un desmadre."*

Yes, all hell was going to break loose, she was sure. And soon.

*****

Juanita continued to pace.

Rachel, no longer intrigued with her hands, was leafing through a two-year-old edition of *People* magazine when a young man in a blue and white uniform walked up to her. He was one of the paramedics she'd seen earlier in the ER. He was still wearing a troubled face.

"Excuse me," he said, "but are you the mother of the little girl we transported from Jefferson Elementary?"

"Yes," Rachel said, "I am."

"May I talk with you?" He glanced nervously around. "Privately?"

"Keep the chair warm for me, Juanita," she said, grabbing her purse.

The paramedic placed a gentle hand on Rachel's elbow and led her, somewhat urgently, into an elevator.

Descending from the seventh floor, neither spoke. By the time they'd reached the lobby, Rachel was surprised the medic hadn't chewed his lower lip bloody.

The air was still hot despite the sun's position, which teetered like a steel orange on the Pacific Ocean. It was the last week of September, and was promising to be the start of one of the hottest and muggiest autumns this city had ever seen. But LA wasn't the only place suffering third degree burns. Nearly the whole country was in the midst of a tenacious heat wave.

He pulled a pack of Camels from his shirt pocket. Offering a cigarette to Rachel, he said, "Nasty habit, huh?"

"What's this all about?" she said, accepting. Dave Schilling was stenciled on his name tag.

"I'm not crazy," he whispered. "And my partner won't back me up. He refuses to talk about it."

"Okay," Rachel said "Talk about what?"

Dave lit her cigarette. "Ya know, I've seen some bizarre things in this city," he continued in a low voice. "A car wreck so bad there were intestines splattered across a billboard thirty yards from impact. A hobo whose face was eaten off by two Chihuahuas as he lay passed out in an alley. A crazy old woman who choked to death on her pet hamster." He stared at the noisy interstate that ran adjacent to the hospital. He took a drag off his cigarette, inhaled deeply. "Shit," he laughed nervously, "and we were able to save the hamster."

She glanced sidelong at the medic. "Excuse me, but isn't that just an urban legend?"

"No," he said, "you're confusing that with Richard Gere getting caught with a gerbil up his ass. *That's* an urban legend." He stared at her, nonplused. "Isn't it?" Then he shrugged his shoulders and clucked. "Oh hell, lady, in this city, if it's not one orifice, it's another."

"Name's Rachel," she said patiently. "And what do these experiences have to do with my daughter?"

He turned a pair of mystified eyes to her. "What I saw and heard today was totally unlike anything I've ever experienced." He flicked his half-finished cigarette to the ground, crushed it beneath his shoe. "At one point while your daughter was inside the ambulance, she began...seizing. Nothing full blown, like a grand mal, just some minor shaking. Anyway, as I was holding her down, trying to listen to her heart and lung sounds, she grabbed hold of my stethoscope. The second she did, I heard the strangest voice. It was like I'd tapped into a kind of, of telepathic conversation between your daughter and..."

"And...?" Rachel nudged.

"And God," he finally said. "I mean, the voice was so *out there* that it couldn't have been...*human*."

"And what did *He* say?" Rachel said. There was a genuineness, a sincerity about him that kept her from rushing back inside to find a pair of burly guys in white coats.

"It wasn't a *He*—it was a *She*."

Chalk up another one for women's lib, she thought. "Alright, what was *She* saying?"

"'He knows where you've flown.'"

"Excuse me?"

"That's what the voice kept saying, over and over. 'He knows where you've flown.'"

"*Who* knows where *who's* flown?"

Dave shrugged. "I was kind of hoping that you'd know, or at least have a hunch. You see, the reason I'm telling you this is because I interpreted it as a kind of warning. It didn't necessarily sound like one, but I *felt* it was a warning." He stared at his shoes. "Man, my ass is history if you talk to anybody about this."

"My lips are sealed," she promised. "You said it was a conversation. What was my daughter saying?"

"'It hurts, it hurts.' And she kept clawing at her back, too," he said, demonstrating the awkward scratching, "as if something was really irritating it. Burning it, maybe."

"That's it?" Rachel said, as if that wasn't enough.

"No," he said, shakily lighting another cigarette. "Now comes the weird part."

Rachel's jaw actually dropped. "The *weird* part?"

"Just as we pulled up to the hospital, Kathy jumped—"

"Amy," she corrected. "Her name is Amy."

"Really?" David said, confused. "Her teacher said her name was Amy, too, but as we were getting her into the ambulance, your daughter told us quite lucidly—well, she insisted!—that her name was Kath—"

"I know, I know," Rachel nodded pressingly, "but continue."

"Well, she—Amy—jumped up from the pram just as we pulled to a stop in front of the ER. She placed both hands on one of the two rear windows of the ambulance and...and a picture appeared, a *moving* picture, as if the glass had somehow turned into a..." Slumping against the wall, he exhaled loudly. "You're not buying any of this, are you?"

"I'm trying," Rachel said. "What did you see in the window?"

"There was a man sitting in a chair. It was like I was looking right into his living room. He was busy with his hands. At first I thought he was crocheting, or something like that, but then he stood up, and in his hands was a set of wings. Like a prop, you know? Angel wings someone might make for a Christmas play? But they looked real enough. Too real. And they were big. Maybe from a swan? Anyway, the scene disappeared as we pulled her away from the doors. I only saw half his face."

"Angel wings?"

"I know it sounds crazy, ma'am, but, on my mother's grave I swear to you—"

"I believe you," she said, surprising herself. Something about it made sense to her, though she hadn't the vaguest idea why.

Or had she? Something swept through her just then, like a breath passing through her soul.

Now oblivious to everything around her, she searched desperately for that bit of salience, as resistive to the pull of recall as a bat is to daylight. *Dammit!* It was important; vitally so, she was sure. She had to remember. *Had to.* It had something to do with wings...

Angel wings.

"Are you okay, ma'am?" Dave said.

She had entered that vault where such memories lay stored and catalogued; was pulling desperately at the file drawers like an heir to a billion-dollar estate, searching for the lone key that would allow her entry into unimaginable wealth.

Then, as the last sliver of sun winked off the horizon, the memory dawned in her mind.

8.

A shellacked portrait of Jesus Christ—that popular rendering where he's clean shaven and appears to be posing meekly for his senior high school yearbook, circa 1978—hung crooked over the kitchen sink.

Josephine Kagan removed the Stouffer's entree from the microwave, peeled back the plastic cover, then placed it on the floor.

She'd lost her faith years ago.

"Alright, Jacob, eat up," she barked with a grouchy fondness only the elderly can master. Jacob was a monkey-bat, a term she'd christened for the animals that had started prowling her house years ago, ever since Eli's first window appeared on her basement wall.

Perhaps her son was right: she'd not lost her faith, but had simply misplaced it, given her failing memory. Not that he gave a shit.

Jacob primped felinely as his dinner cooled, backlit against the two glass patio doors of the adjoining dining room. There, the curtains were partially drawn, revealing the warped planks of the cedar deck outside. A white plastic table and chairs sat in the middle, each piece home to a puddle of stagnant water replete with leaves, birdshit, and hatching mosquitoes. Against the railing stood a rusting gas grill, the upper right half lost behind the overhanging branches of a willow tree. The entire backyard lay beneath a willow canopy, allowing in only sparse dapples of sunlight.

She was remiss. But then, she was invalid. In body and soul.

If she could hasten her dementia, she surely would. She'd been treading crazy waters for so long that her mind was exhausted, shriveled like a prune.

She was ready to go home.

Throughout the years, she'd seen the monkey-bats come and go. But out of the hundreds that had passed through, there were a few strays that always came sniffing back around. For these particular gypsies, she maintained a certain affinity.

All the others could go straight back to hell.

They were smart, too. Human smart, she was sure.

"Well, what are you waiting for?" she said. "It's Yankee Pot Roast, your favorite."

Jacob leaned over and whiffed. Satisfied, he began eating.

Oh, who was she fooling. She'd already sank and drowned in those waters; had already died and brought the craziness with her. Maybe her son was right, that everything was just one big man-made illusion. That heaven and hell were only real when the synapses were firing *en masse*, were only legitimate when the "majority mind" believed them to be, and simply evaporated for those leaving the congregate; those who finally die and disconnect. While the brain was alive, went her son's theory, God wavered like a mirage. Upon death, He just faded away.

As did everything else, she supposed, only to open up another existence to a "majority mind" even crazier than the last.

Or perhaps just a single mind was necessary to create this new dimension she was in.

She knocked her cane twice on the kitchen floor.

Crazy, crippled, and dead. Still trying to play the game, but the old rules no longer applied.

Stuck between floors.

Some years back, she'd approached Eli about getting her favorite monkey-bats collars and little round nametags. Eli had nearly come unglued, reminding her that the couriers weren't poodles, or Persians she could take to show. No emotional attachments allowed; that was the law. He'd told her how painful rabies vaccines would be if she was lucky, and how costly it would be to reattach a limb if she wasn't.

But she'd never been so much as nipped by the buggers, although, she had to admit, her cane had a few playful gouges.

What did Eli know anyway? He was crazier than she was.

A fallen priest.

A killer of little girls.

She thumped her cane twice more, smiling. She especially liked helping him with the little girls.

9.

With the sauerkraut and Kielbasa resting in a garbage can outside, the kitchen was almost free of that repugnant odor. Duncan stuffed his head inside the large paper bag and inhaled. The warm aroma of mandarin beef, cashew shrimp, and sweet and sour pork aroused his senses. He was famished.

On his way home from the hospital he'd stopped at the China Palace and loaded up on Mandarin takeout. He'd tried calling the photographer at home, but no one answered, not even electronically. So he figured he'd have a bite to eat, then try again.

He took the three steaming boxes from the bag, left the fortune cookie behind (because that was nonsense), grabbed a fork from the utensil drawer, and descended to the room he'd consecrated years ago as his "sanctuary."

Books of all kinds were stacked pell-mell in high, wobbly pillars. Given these textual stalagmites, many a visitor had paused to wonder aloud why its denizen hadn't gone to the extra expense of putting in bookshelves.

The south wall was cluttered with various awards, honorary plaques, teaching certificates, college diplomas, the Police Medal of Valor, assorted newspaper clippings, and other derivations of nostalgia that one would expect to find on an educated ex-cop's wall.

And still in the same cheerless, wood frame as when it was given to him by his father, just before his death sixteen years earlier, was a picture of Gregory McNeil, his uncle. Not a handsome man by any standards, but he'd been a damn funny one. Irish to the bone and ornery as hell, he'd become quite the success story in the family. After serving ten distinguished years with the New York City Police Department, he went on and made his fortune in beer. But it wasn't a bar he'd opened. It was a brewery. Then a distributorship. Upon his death—just two weeks after Duncan and Rachel had moved to Los Angeles with hardly a pot to piss in or a window to throw it out of—Duncan and his sister Anna became wealthy. They'd not inherited Uncle Greg's entire estate, which was consequential, but just two little old trust funds, each worth about one point two million dollars.

Duncan shook his head. It wasn't nearly the fortune now he'd thought it was a decade ago. And since that time, although he and Rachel had plenty to show for it, the numbers had gone down considerably. Not so much that anyone in his household was ever going to go hungry, but still...

Man, did it fly.

Although he and Uncle Greg weren't the closest of relatives, he kept the picture on his desk out of respect. And as a reminder that he was the luckiest man alive.

And probably the most troubled.

He shook his head again.

"Guilty," he meekly confessed to his uncle's portrait. Uncle Greg just stared back with piquant eyes and a wily grin. No shame there, no regrets, just a love for life. A persevering man, Duncan thought, who'd been far wealthier in spirit than pocket book.

Duncan envied him.

He was partway into his dinner when the phone rang. He grabbed the cordless on his desk. It was Rachel.

"Hello?"

"Oh, uh...I was expecting the answering machine," she said, winded. "I thought you were going to go see that photographer—"

"He's not home," he said. "Are you in labor?"

"I, I just ran to the phone is all."

"Have another cigarette," he chided. "Oh hell, have two."

"Yeah, yeah."

"What did the tomographies show?"

"They haven't told me yet," she said hurriedly. "Listen, Dunc, I need you to do me a favor. In the chest at the foot of the bed—or wait, maybe it's in the cellar in one of the crates that are stacked by the wine racks— Christ, it's been so long! Anyway, I need you to find a manila envelope. I believe it's marked 'Scraps' or 'Memories,' something like that. Actually, you'll find quite a few that are marked that way, but they should all be together. There's an eight-by-ten picture of a little girl and her mother; you know, one of those Old West-type pictures where you get dressed up like Jesse James?"

"Sure, I know what you mean, but—"

"Listen, Dunc, it's very important that you find that picture. I'm not exactly sure *why* yet, but I need to see it again, okay?"

"Yeah, okay, but...hello?"

She'd hung up.

"Woman's crazier than a peach orchard boar," he mumbled, then wondered from what backwoods Georgia feed-and-grain he'd picked up that expression. To his urban thinking, it didn't make a bit of sense.

But then, he reminded himself, neither did women. Rural or otherwise.

The urgency in Rachel's voice lingered, prompting him to waste no time. He pushed himself away from the desk, stood, pointed at the containers of Chinese food, as if they were three begging Pekinese, and said, "Stay."

10.

Eli sat in the confessional. His thick, black hair was drenched in sweat, and in the muted light there was a burnished, glistening quality about his face, as if it were running with honey rather than perspiration. He always tried keeping the temperature inside St. Patrick's hovering between sixty-eight and seventy-two degrees, and had been managing very well of late despite the unseasonably warm temps. But within the confessional it felt as if a conduit to hell lay directly beneath.

Eli didn't like being scared. And Mr. Gamble frightened him to no end. *Like a kidney stone with a parachute.* That would be the brand of comparison Gamble would make. But Eli found no humor in the situation. So, he sat, waiting; waiting like a scared, naughty boy for his father to come home and deliver his punishment.

During their first meeting, Eli had asked Gamble how he'd come to be. "Once planted in man's corrupt soul," Gamble had explained, "one grain of God will grow an eternity of demons. I am the first of those to have achieved cognizance, and if I don't eradicate obscurity then I'll most certainly not be the last. You see, Father, for me to aspire to, and remain, king, I have to abolish all the countless degrees of resemblance and dissimilarity between right and wrong, acceptance and rejection, between what is faulty and what has allegedly been repaired. I must accomplish upon creation the singleness of *me*. Otherwise, the soil will forever produce challengers, foes and compatriots alike. And I, my dear padre, don't intend to have weeds growing in my garden." Pure, unadulterated Gamble-*ese*. What an asshole.

Oh, and he was so near the end now. Throughout all the planning, all the productive and inspiring meetings with Mr. Gamble, all the tedious hours of making the wings and applying them just so, all the photographs he'd taken and developed himself, there had never been a blunder.

And now this.

Like Marley's ghost, Katherine Bently was back to haunt the Scrooge in him.

Well, I've got news for that little bitch! he thought. *If she thinks a visit from the Ghost of Dead Girls Past will scare me into reconsidering, then she's in for a rude awakening!*

Finally, casual footfalls echoed in the empty church. They were Gamble's. Over the years, from within this very confessional, Eli had come to recognize his mentor's perfunctory stroll just as well as he could other people's voices.

As they grew nearer, he shuffled nervously in the cramped space.

Gamble entered the adjacent closet, his door opening and closing with a resounding *clack*. They were now just inches apart, but their faces remained hidden from one another, just as they always had throughout their years of secret trysts.

"Bless me, Father, for I have sinned," Gamble said, following the shrift with a wispy cackle.

Eli cleared his throat, but said nothing; wishing only that Gamble would get some new material.

"I understand that you were quite a fright at mass this evening," said Gamble. "Nervous as a whore in church, if you'll pardon the expression."

As it was no doubt intended, the irony of his mentor's last statement angered Eli. "I've had better services," he said.

"Spilled more wine than a palsied waiter," Gamble said, suddenly humorless.

Eli could smell his mentor's rancid breath seeping through the fabric screen. This evening it was more acrid than usual, which meant only one thing: he was pissed.

"You might say I was a bit preoccupied," Eli chuckled, attempting some levity.

There was a long, suffocating pause, and Eli had to stifle a whimper. Although he considered the silver cross presently dangling down his surplice as nothing but cheap costume jewelry, the urge to suddenly take hold of it was a strong one, as he expected a vampire of considerable rank to come crashing through the paneling at any moment and feed ferociously on his neck.

Breaking his silence, Gamble said, "We have a major problem. It appears that one of your angels—your second—has returned."

"Yes, I...I know. I've been extremely upset since learning of it this afternoon."

"Upset?" Gamble said. "No, no, *I'm* the one who's upset, Father. On the other hand, I'm surprised that *you* haven't found something to insert rectally so as to stifle what should be a gushing case of terror-induced incontinence."

"I did exactly as I—"

"This 'catch and release' policy of yours might be vigorously applauded by the Colorado Division of Wildlife, but it hardly sits well with me."

There was a dry, audible click as Eli swallowed. "How could I have anticipated...how could I have predicted such a thing? I, I..."

Gamble said, "You don't believe in God, do you, padre?"

Eli literally lurched in his seat, his groveling brought to a crashing stop as it collided with Gamble's question. "Are...are you saying that there actually exists a *real* God? You even said yourself that—"

"All I said was that if Abraham's God *did* exist, He was most likely walking around in a much more comfortable cut of pant leg than the ironed, hip-hugging, butt-cheek-lifting denim you Catholic boys always have Him wearing. What you inferred from that is your own business, padre. But I never once said there was no *real* God." He gasped. "Why, I would never even insinuate such a thing."

Feeling like a sweaty slab of marble waiting to be inscribed, Eli whispered, "I don't know what to believe anymore. It's all so..." He didn't finish.

"But you do believe in *me*, don'tcha, Tonto? Oh, I know, I know, the antipode doesn't meet with you like I do. But I just have two words to say on that: Rumor Mill. I mean, can you imagine the ensuing gossip if someone were to learn that you and God were chit-chatting in this confessional on a regular basis? Christ Almighty, Father, rivers would run backwards, the moon would shit cheese balls, and the Bakers would be back on Cable in no time!"

Eli detested Gamble's brand of raillery. "So, I'm supposed to believe that this...meddler is...God?"

"Well, somebody's fucking with the gears of our machine. Who knows, maybe Katherine Bently *is* that proverbial wrench, lodged by the hand of the Almighty Himself! Amen! Then again, maybe not. I don't know. What I *do* know is that you didn't *hear* it coming. Why? Because you haven't been *listening*. You didn't *see* it coming. Why? Because you haven't been *looking*. Quite frankly, Father, Helen Keller had keener senses."

Eli said nothing, could barely breathe. He hated this ambiguous shit; Gamble's vague, circuitous approach to everything. His sophomoric insults.

Gamble sighed. "If your devotion to this whole matter is in a state of collapse, then perhaps we should start making arrangements for your dismissal."

"No, no, please," Eli choked. "That won't be necessary. My allegiance is as strong as ever."

"I sincerely hope so, because if it isn't then you will have not only dishonored yourself, but you will have pissed me mightily off. And I assure you, Father, that the latter will pain you far more than the former."

Suppressing his urge to scream, Eli bit hard into his clenched fist, nearly drawing blood.

"Now, pay very close attention," Gamble said. "After you've recaptured the second angel, there's something I want you to do for me. I've left a package for you in the pulpit. Handling instructions have been included. If all goes well, then we won't have to worry about this sort of thing happening again."

"If only I knew what this...*resurrection* meant?" Eli said.

"How many angels can dance on the head of a pin, Father?"

Why, the same number of them it takes to screw in a light bulb, Eli thought to say, but dared not. He reflected for a moment, then took a deep breath. "As you know, I'm more a theologian than a philosopher, but your question, of course, is an aged and rhetorical one; a metaphor to demonstrate the unimaginable, the incalculable—"

"Oh, shut up, Father," Gamble groaned. "The answer I was looking for is: none. Because angels have much better things to do with their time than frolic on sewing utensils. Or, as I've just demonstrated, to try and explain calculus to a tadpole. So, just concern yourself with finding Katherine Bently, and let me ponder the whys and how-comes."

"Yes, of course."

"One more little detail," Gamble said. "It's come to my attention that you assumed some rather harsh liberties with one of the couriers."

"Li-liberties?" Eli said, having no idea to what Gamble was referring.

"You lashed out angrily, Father."

"Oh, yes—*that*," Eli stammered, now remembering how he'd struck the creature's face. "I was angry, flustered, confused—"

"If you ever touch one of my beasties again—ever so much as raise your voice to them one octave higher than the genial norm—I will unleash upon your soul the wickedest of carnivores. Are we clear on this matter?"

"My sincerest apologies," Eli said, his voice almost a whisper. "It will never happen again."

"See that it doesn't," Gamble said. "And while we're on the subject of beastie mistreatment, I'll remind you that your mother wields her cane like a cattle prod. If she does not cease and desist, then I will advance her state of osteoporosis so far that you'll have to *pour* her into bed."

"I understand."

Before allowing himself to cry, Eli waited until he could no longer hear Gamble's heavy, rhythmic breathing, smell his foul breath. There was no opening and closing of the door, no footsteps receding down the aisle while he whistled a catchy tune.

Mr. Gamble exited in his customary manner: without a sound.

11.

Duncan found Rachel's photograph. On the back, stenciled in gold brush script:

FRANKY AND JOHNNIE'S OLDE TYME PHOTOGRAPHY

321 Porpoise Avenue, Rock Bay, Massachusetts

Hand-written in red ink below that was a date, and what Duncan assumed was an invoice or purchase number. If the date was factual, then the picture was just over twelve years old.

It was a trick; had to be. And a very nasty one at that.

In the damp, fuzzy-gray fluorescence of the basement, now littered with schmaltzy memorabilia, Duncan was sure that the little girl staring back from the picture was Amy. His very own daughter. No doubt about it.

But what convinced him that *she couldn't be* was the woman next to her, an apparition herself. A beautiful wraith spooking up the past from the dark, dusty corners of his heart. Legions of black tiny wings were rushing forward, flocking, converging in the twilight. Becoming memories.

A hot blush erupted on his cheeks.

The woman in the photo was dressed like a cowgirl, sporting an old six-shooter and a villainous expression. In reality, however, she had been someone entirely different; someone who preferred only *Karan, Lagerfeld, Oscar de la Renta*, never *Levi's* or *Wrangler*. Someone who he'd secretly loved in the shadow of his own new marriage.

A lover for whom he had literally taken two bullets.

Her name was Patricia. Patty, when they'd been close.

"Oh shit, oh shit," he whispered. "Patricia, what are you doing here?"

As he brought the picture closer to his face, a thin, silver line of light rolled across its matte surface. Radar sweeping his past.

"Wait a minute," he said, slowing himself down. "Patricia had a daughter—" Dropping the picture, Duncan mashed his face into his hands. The name and address on the hospital admission form flashed across his mind. That star-like twinkling of recollection he'd had earlier at the hospital was now going nova.

"Shit! Shit! Shit!" he barked, his right palm slapping his forehead. "Kathy! Patricia and *Katherine Bently!*"

He picked up the photo and stared again at the facsimile of his daughter. Grainy memories began sluicing through his mind; a drenching, hodgepodge, cut-and-paste reel of an evanescent life, one to which he'd been unwillingly regressed: *the tip of Cape Cod, Provincetown, scoops of ice cream in waffle cones, Katherine wearing a Red Sox baseball cap, Patricia laughing in his ear, digging clams, Katherine throwing a Frisbee, a restaurant patio, lime wedges and bottles of Corona, laughter, soft kisses passionate kisses whispered promises shame love remorse the taste of salt Katherine running after him shouting, Daddy! Daddy! Daddy!*

Closing his eyes, a circus of memories continued unremittingly, tossed one after another like the pins of a vaudevillian juggler.

His memories of what Katherine Bently looked like could not be right. He tried to convince himself that the image of Amy was simply interfering with his recollection, was superimposing itself where Katherine's own face should have been. Guilt, the culprit.

But if the picture and date were authentic...

Impossible.

Their affair had been brief, having lasted four months or so. Patricia had then just lost her husband, and Katherine a step-father, to a criminal and his gun. Although they'd lived in Rock Bay, Patricia's husband worked out of downtown Boston. His body had been discovered in a parking lot two blocks from his office, dead from a single gunshot to the head. Since it was an obvious homicide, Duncan and his partner had been assigned the case. And it was during the investigation when he'd come to know Patricia, and her daughter Katherine. Like a knight in shining armor, he'd come to their rescue; had trotted haughtily up on his steed and swept them out of their mourning. It was the stuff of gallant comic strips—up to, and including, the moment he traded in his Prince Valiant costume for that of Robin Hood.

When he'd risked everything for them. Even his life.

After *The Wounds*, he never saw them again.

Until now.

God, he now remembered how much he had loved that little girl, perhaps even more so than her own mother. So, what had happened to his memories of them? Oh, they were there, but most had become like virga, wispy and vague, evaporating long before they ever reached full recollection.

Once upon a time, the constant reminders like his scars, and the "ghost pains" (at least according to his doctor) that radiated from those areas, the relevant newspaper clippings and Police Medal of Valor hanging on the wall of his study—all had invoked a daily retinue of sights and sounds and smells from that epoch. But for a long while now, he just realized, maybe even years, those catalysts had been triggering nothing but the same redundant images, tame as they were fleeting.

Selective memory? he asked himself. Survivor's Guilt? Possibly. Were these kinds of episodes of reality going astray inevitable for victims of trauma? Again, possibly. He'd been told by some of the best shrinks in the business that he could expect some kind of stress-induced psychosis (most likely transitory, at least initially). Given that, then this very experience could be such a manifestation.

But not today, he thought. No, he firmly believed that he was still in every way, shape and form in full possession of his faculties. The only rational explanation here, he finally decided, was that he was sane and that it was the rest of the world suddenly having a psychotic break.

This dispossession of memory had occurred so surreptitiously and over such a long stretch of time that it hadn't even dawned on him until just now that he'd been forgetting anything at all. But now it was all coming back—and so vividly that he could feel the sun setting behind him, could taste the mustard from Katherine's kraut dog, could smell the shampoo in Patricia's hair, could hear their laughter, see his purple windbreaker rippling in the wind.

I am not losing my mind.

These didn't feel like memories of old. They were still damp with saltwater.

Christ!

Overwhelmed, he opened his eyes. Both faces stared back at him, their expressions having changed, questions now loitering in their eyes; questions that asked why he'd left so soon, why so suddenly, and why when they needed him the most?

Why did Rachel want to see this photograph *now*? he wondered. Better yet, who did she get it from? Franky and Johnnie's studio, or Patricia herself? Had she kept it as a souvenir after learning of his affair, to finally bring it out after all this time to blackmail him? He doubted it. Rachel, like any proud woman, he was sure, would have yanked off his cock and cleaned him out in court years ago.

Besides, there was still the little girl, Katherine, who didn't just resemble Amy, but could be her identical twin—assuming that the photograph was genuine, of course. That was the peculiar part, the one that segregated the entire matter from mere chance, coincidence, and placed it into an entirely different category. Something like fate or destiny—abstractions that his analytic side wasn't comfortable with—was at work here. Perhaps something even more arcane.

But...that was just pure nonsense.

He shook his head, disgusted with himself. "There's a logical explanation," he groaned, dragging a hand over his soaked red hair. "Has to be."

The world to which Rachel had earlier alluded as being very small, given the countless occurrences of so-called coincidence, was beginning to feel to Duncan like a very cramped closet; a closet now shared with the ghost of a daughter who couldn't be, and the ghost of a woman who should never have been at all.

12.

Sitting in the front pew of St. Patrick's Church, hands folded and resting comfortably in his lap, Eli stared up at the pulpit with private trepidation. He was afraid of what Gamble had left behind. *What could it be?*

There was just no telling.

Up until now, the only things Gamble had ever left him were six bags of feathers. "Plucked from man's own personas of grace, as diminutive as they are fragile," he'd once told Eli. More cryptic bullshit. At least that's as far as it got with him back then, back when his innocence was blinding. But he believed he'd since deciphered its meaning, that Gamble had literally scalped the feathers from the wings of angels. Those created by the collective mind, of course: Gamble's very own mother. And Gamble often crowed about how he'd killed them all, those angels.

Eli grinned. It was fratricide, if one got right down to it.

The interior of the church echoed with the deafening stillness of a mausoleum. Even the sounds of his own breathing drifted upward and were quickly lost, perhaps to seek out and inflate the inert lungs of the angels cast upon the domed ceiling; to give them a dimensional quality that the painter's brush could have never achieved.

He recalled with fondness his adolescent years when he had fallen in love with angels. Though no longer that naive little boy, the captivation was still there, but a more grounded one, the years having washed over that puerile enchantment, smoothing out its rough edges and boyish imaginings the way a river does a stone.

On their first meeting, Gamble had enlightened Eli, had confided in him—albeit equivocally—things that were contrary to popular Christian beliefs, things antithetic to Holy Scripture. In fact, Gamble had advised him to find a flatulent hippopotamus, take the "Good Book" firmly in hand, and shove it up the hippo's ass, as that was all it was *good* for.

More truth could be found at a liars' convention, Gamble had said.

Eli, however, had become no more disillusioned than he already was. He'd long suspected as much.

But now Gamble had insinuated—contrary to Eli's long-standing belief—that there might be a God after all. The real God of infamy. And that *He* might even be responsible for Katherine Bently's return.

Shaking his head, chuckling to himself, Eli supposed he shouldn't be so surprised. Gamble, after all, was just being Gamble—the enigmatic asshole.

He found himself once again coveting the winged and haloed figures above, each one a representation of the nine orders of God's angels. In descending order: the mighty six-winged Seraphim, nearest to God; then the Cherubim, Dominions, Thrones, Principalities, Powers, Virtues, Archangels, and Angels. This was the choir ranking according to St. Ambrose, the fourth-century bishop of Milan, and the first great Latin doctor of the Church. A few centuries later, pseudo-Dionysius had switched the orders around some and divided them into three groups, expounding upon individual duties.

Eli, however, had decided to go with St. Ambrose's arrangement, given the man's heritage.

Taking his interpretations of this *man-made* order to their colorful limits, Eli had nonetheless created a virtual masterpiece, as if Michelangelo himself had possessed every brush stroke, for their brilliant gowns and adorned wings flowed with an archaic fluidity reminiscent of the Renaissance artist.

It had taken him nearly three years to paint them, the first two months alone spent erecting the scaffolding. Funded primarily by the diocese, this stupendous effort was not only followed by a broadening congregation and heftier collection plates (at least for awhile, anyway), but had satisfied the bishop, among others, to no end.

This artistic achievement had come on the heels of a truly inspiring visit to St. Michael's Church, some eight years earlier. *The* St. Michael's in New York City, famous for its seven magnificent stained-glass windows. Created by Louis Comfort Tiffany, each long window portrayed an Archangel (Michael, Gabriel and Raphael being the most notable) and placed them into illustrious, angel-filled scenarios. When all were lit at the uppermost levels by daylight, it appeared that the Light of God shone down upon them. The lower portion of the central window had been Eli's favorite, depicting the Archangel Michael freeing the Court of Heaven from the disobedient angels who'd raised their wills to their Creator.

And just as Michelangelo was now long-extinct, so were the heavenly beliefs that Eli once entertained as a child, that when people died they became angels and were issued their golden haloes and white, gossamer wings at the Pearly Gates by old St. Peter himself—if, of course, they were fortunate enough to have gone that northerly direction.

But the figures on the ceiling still enkindled absolute awe. It was, and would always be, their *loftiness* that invited him.

Eli knew of another brotherhood of lofty being, a fraternity where a mortal man *could* ascend in status and rank. Then into a pair of wings, if he so desired. And Eli so desired. And so what if it was for nothing but vain, aesthetic reasons. All his life he'd longed for his own wings. They were symbols of power and strength and seniority, but most of all they were tokens of flight. And he truly wished to fly; to achieve an altitude that would finally let him look down upon all that existed and gloat in his supremacy. To be where destiny wanted him. Needed him.

And he was so close now. Just one more angel.

Two, he reminded himself. *There's the matter of the Bently girl in Los Angeles.*

The City of Angels.

"Touché", he whispered, glancing craftily at the Holy Virgin centered in the reliquary above the altar.

Eli rose and walked over to the pulpit; looked inside. Gamble had left him an ordinary, rectangular cardboard box, one large enough to comfortably fit a pair of running shoes. A harsh, loamy smell wandered from the package.

He leaned in and listened. Its contents made faint, squishy sounds.

"Oh shit," he mumbled; a phrase, he often argued, that should have been the *real* shortest verse in the Bible. "Jesus wept?" Huh-uh. He *cussed* that night, baby. Like a sailor.

A limerick, written on a plain 3x5 index card in Gamble's traditional old-world flair, was taped to the box:

> *There once was an angel named Katherine*
> *Ten years old and full of Saccharine*
> *She flew the wrong way*
> *On a dark, stormy day*
> *So get the bitch before she starts a'yackin'!*

Inured to such verse, Eli just shook his head.

He removed the lid. Inside was a mass of what appeared to be earthworms in a shovel-full of black, wet soil, writhing and squirming as if electrically charged. On top of the dirt rested another limerick:

> *This is a box of night crawlers*
> *They do nothing but squirm for hours*

But if placed in the ground
Where flesh, blood and bone abound
Then they'll demonstrate their nasty powers!

This time Eli let out a giggle, a shifty little titter reminiscent of a bully who, from nearby shadows, has just witnessed the finale of a vicious and well-orchestrated prank.

Deciphering years of this kind of acrostic, nonsensical instruction, Eli knew instantly what he was supposed to do.

And he couldn't wait.

13.

Back in his study, sitting frumpily behind his desk, Duncan finally shifted his eyes from the photo to his half-eaten dinner. The smells had begun to make him nauseous, and those red Chinese dragons undulating around each box weren't helping matters. Unheedingly, he pushed an arm out and, as if they were a trio of reluctant lemmings, swiped the containers over the edge and into the wicker wastebasket below.

Rachel had called again, this time giving him the CAT scan results. The tomographies, she'd said, had been examined by three resident specialists, and all had passed Amy's head with a clean bill of health. She'd gone on to say that Doctor Strickland was now under the firm belief that Amy had suffered a seizure, and that it was a transitory episode and would most likely not happen again.

Worst case scenario? The attacks would continue to occur, but infrequently.

He'd felt ashamed for not sounding more excited by her good news, having still been numbed by the photograph. He had lied to her when asked if he'd found the picture, not wanting to discuss the matter over the phone. He'd listened intently, but there had been no tell-tale inflections in her voice, no hint that she was on to him. Just wonderful relief that Amy was going to be all right.

She'd told him that she was going to stay a little while longer, that it wasn't necessary to come get her, that she would hitch a ride home with Juanita.

And for him to please, *please* continue searching for the photograph.

Once again the name and address on the hospital admission form floated to the surface of his mind, drifting there like slicks of crude oil, threatening the nearby pristine shores of reason.

Katherine Bently, 1402 Hawthorne Avenue, Rock Bay, Massachusetts.

Why in God's name had Amy told the medics and ER staff that her name was Katherine Bently? The very name of the daughter of a mistress for whom he had once risked everything? And why had Amy given them that particular address in Rock Bay? Though he was no longer sure that he could fully trust his memory, that address sounded, well...more than familiar.

And now a picture of Patricia lay before him, as young and pretty as he remembered her, with Kathy Bently, her daughter, staring back at him with his own daughter's face.

Coincidence? A fluke?

Sure, he thought, and if you put enough monkeys and typewriters together you'd eventually have some of Shakespeare's finest pushing up the slush pile.

Maybe Amy had heard the name Katherine Bently elsewhere, he desperately reasoned; had overheard Rachel while in some fit of rage over learning of his affair, mention it, and from her mother's tone had somehow inferred its disastrous meaning on a subconscious level, only to be recalled in a state of delirium like the one she'd experienced today.

But the address, too? No, that was stretching some already thin speculation. It was preposterous, really. Besides, it still wouldn't explain Amy and Katherine's uncanny resemblance.

Or would it? What if the picture was a forgery? What if Rachel had hired an expert to inlay a photo of Amy next to Patricia's...? Oh, hell, who was he kidding? He shook his head. Rachel would not have gone to all that trouble and expense, not when a simple "Get out you no-good rotten son of a bitch!" would have sufficed. And when he got right down to it, she would have to be a certifiable lunatic to even attempt such a thing. Though occasionally showing promise, like signing contracts to do hemorrhoid commercials, he was sure she was nothing of the sort.

He continued to use the sheer art of deduction, trying to shape and form all potentialities like dough into neat, palatable cookies. And so far none of them tasted logical. Not remotely so.

Though he didn't want to listen, his old cop instinct—that intuition that he would have normally embraced with every ounce of his trust—was telling him that something beyond his comprehension was at work here; something so far beyond rational explanation that to try and figure it out with just these few puzzle pieces would be an exercise in futility.

Any answers—*reasonable* answers—would have to remain forthcoming until Rachel got home.

He picked up the phone and tried the photographer again.

Nadda. Probably moonlighting at Foto Mart.

14.

Amy McNeil was startled awake by the sound of thunder. It wasn't the blast that did it so much as it was the rattling window before her. She was on her knees, her thin hospital gown feeling like nothing but an oversized paper towel around her body.

Droplets of rain, as big as quarters, pelted the glass with wind-driven force, melting away the city lights over and over.

Lightning impulsively stung the night.

She glanced around, confused. No one else was in the room with her, as best as she could see. The lighting was dim, coming from a pair of Yosemite Sam night lights glaring at each other from across opposite ends of the room, poised in gunslinger fashion.

Strange machine-shapes occupied the shadows.

The silhouettes of other Looney-Tune characters danced on the wallpaper. There was Elmer Fudd chasing that "wascally wabbit," Bugs Bunny. There was Daffy Duck, Porky Pig, all her favorites. There were red and green dots of light above the bed next to her; her bed, she presumed. There was another bed, as well; one with a curtain pulled all the way around, like a shower.

The smell of alcohol was faint, but unmistakable.

I'm in a hospital, she concluded with little effort.

She'd been having a dream, could recall it vividly. The strange thing was, in the dream her name was Kathy.

In a bewildered gesture, she raised her hands to her face, wanting to inspect them, to make sure that they were free of injury. On her right forearm was some kind of splint (to keep her lower arm immobile, she suspected. But why?), and she noticed a plastic tube, secured with transparent tape, jutting from the back of her hand. Further inspection found two small round tags with silver nipples stuck to her chest, then two more on her lower abdomen.

With puzzled scrutiny, she examined her legs, then poked subtly at her stomach, her chest. She methodically ran a hand through her hair, then tugged a few strands as if to make sure they were securely embedded.

Relief slowly washed over her after realizing that she was, as she suspected, all right. At least as far as her eyes and fingers could tell. She *felt* okay. Almost. There was a slight tingling, burning sensation on her upper back, as if someone had just sprayed Bactine on her sunburn.

But she didn't have a sunburn. And as she considered this, the feeling on her back dwindled away.

Initially in her dream she'd been standing on the edge of a very high cliff, looking out over a violent ocean where waves crashed thunderously against black, volcanic-like rock. A feeling that someone was standing behind her had caused her to turn around. Finding no one, she'd turned back to the ocean. Instantly, it had changed. The water had flattened, had turned glassy, and mirrored the blue sky above and its gauzy streams of clouds without a single, rippling blemish. It was as if God had suddenly inhaled. And that calm had set upon her a feeling like no other she had ever known. A wonderful, magnificent peace had settled within her heart, her soul, warming her internally.

Now, while recalling it, it felt as if she'd been standing there and staring out over that blue expanse for hundreds of years.

And then, deep within the water, she had watched a shape slowly rise; a dot at first, gradually growing bigger and bigger, as if a great whale was on its way to the surface for a breath of air. Then a breeze had begun to stir, which quickly turned into a mighty wind that whipped her sandy-blonde hair across her forehead and eyes. Then a roar, like hundreds of trains speeding toward her, engulfed her ears.

The water below, however, had remained crystalline, undisturbed.

Then, as she glanced upward to find the source of the thunderous noise, she'd realized that the shape in the water below could not have been a whale but was actually the reflection of something coming down from the sky. Something staggeringly huge. Something charging headlong on the power of gigantic, multiple, luminous wings.

Then someone had called out a name: "Katherine?"

The voice kept calling the name, over and over; frantic, like a mother searching for her lost child. In the dream she had truly believed that Kathy was her name, had responded to it without hesitation, just as if it were the name given to her at birth.

Just as she would have reacted now if someone were to call out "Amy?"

"I'm here," she had replied. "I'm here, I'm here." But she and the voice never found one another. The storm outside had roused her awake before they could meet.

At no time in the dream had she been scared. Not the slightest bit.

But she was scared now.

What happened to me? she wondered. *Why am I in front of this window?*

The last thing she remembered before waking in this room was sitting in front of a man who was going to take her picture. Where was her mother? Her Daddy? Juanita?

She began to rise to her feet, being extra quiet just in case someone was in the other bed. She didn't think there was because she couldn't hear any breathing or moaning, but just in case...

She placed a hand on the window sill to steady herself, then put her other hand on the glass. And the moment she did, a blinding flash of light erupted from the window, so immediate and intense that the pane of glass might have been a cloud shedding a bolt of lightning.

Then the dream resumed.

15.

Rachel stared at the photograph while pensively twirling a finger through her wet hair. She and Juanita had gotten drenched in the short distance between the driveway and the front door, having been unable to go through the garage because the opener in Juanita's car was on the fritz.

As she studied the picture, Duncan thought her poise was laudable.

Of the two windows in the room, the one closest to them faced west, confronting the storm. Lightning flickered habitually across the glass, as if the window sat in the periphery of a welder's arc.

Thunder reverberated throughout the house, reminding Duncan of the earthquake they'd all sat through just a few days earlier. A minor one, five-point-two on the ol' Richter scale.

Now, deep in his heart, he could feel the rumblings of another; this one powerful enough to split continents.

"She's a dead-ringer," she finally said. "I mean ...wow."

Duncan leaned forward in his chair. "When and where did you get that picture?"

"Well," Rachel said, "I've been putting dates and events together since remembering the photograph earlier today, and I believe..."

"Yes?"

She straightened in her chair. "Do you recall when we first found out we were pregnant?"

Although quite sure only one of them had been with embryo, Duncan nodded.

"Right before we left Rock Bay, to come here?"

"Yes, yes, I remember," he insisted.

"Well, I was in town one day and ran across this picture. Actually, it was right before we left for LA. Anyway, this picture kind of grabbed me from the start. I felt...compelled. I mean, I had to have it. The guy behind the counter thought I was crazy. He didn't want to sell it to me at first, but I put on the waterworks, probably said something like they were long lost relatives, and he finally gave in."

"What *compelled* you?" Duncan said, then wondered if he might have sounded a bit too suspicious.

"I...I don't know. I do remember that I almost fainted at one point." She looked up at him, bemused. "And that I saw an angel."

"I'm sorry, did you say an *angel*?"

"Funny, huh?" she said, looking down at the picture again. "God, she really does look like Amy."

"That *is* Amy. Has to be," Duncan said, still not really believing it but wanting to solicit a reaction from Rachel.

She considered him carefully. "That's not possible, Dunc. I bought this—"

"Over eleven years ago," he finished for her. "But *why*? What on earth would force you to buy this photograph? And why have you kept it hidden from me all these years?" His tone was sharp now; accusatorial. "Are you keeping something from me, Rachel?" The question crashed in his chest, hurling sharp, icy debris into his heart. He was now convinced that Rachel was just as mystified by the picture, at least by the image of Amy, and that if anyone was keeping secrets, it was him.

What a miserable hypocrite, he thought.

"I wasn't intentionally keeping it from you," she snapped, meeting his hostility. "I simply tucked it away because later I felt foolish for buying it. I did run across it five or six years ago while going through some old stuff, but it didn't leave any particular impression because Amy was still too young, I suppose, for the resemblance to strike me. I boxed it up with a bunch of other odds and ends and once again forgot about it."

"Okay," Duncan said, tempering his voice. "If it means nothing to you—if it was simply a compulsive, spur-of-the-moment thing way back when—then why didn't you just throw it out when you came across it again those five or six years ago?"

This time, she considered him suspiciously. "Why the third degree, Dunc?"

He leaned back in his chair. "I just—I just want to know why this picture is so important to you," he entreated, "and why you just happened to remember it today."

With some diffidence, Rachel related the conversation she'd had earlier with the paramedic.

Nervously, Duncan laughed. "What a load of horseshit."

"He was telling the truth," she insisted.

Before Duncan could rebut, Juanita crept through the doorway carrying cream, sugar, and three cups of steaming coffee on a circular tray. It was obvious to Duncan that she'd not even toweled herself dry, given the shiny black octopus squatting on her head.

The china clinked dangerously together as she abruptly paused. "Excuse, Mrs. McNeil, but should I come back—"

"No, Juanita," Rachel said. "Please, come in."

Juanita set the tray down on the edge of Duncan's desk and began putting the customary amounts of sugar and cream into Rachel's coffee. Duncan preferred his black, though he was sure that if rat poison were an available condiment, Juanita would have added enough lumps to guarantee convulsions, then coma, after the second sip.

"This picture," Juanita said. "It is the cause of your argument?"

Rachel held the picture up for Juanita to see.

"It is Amy," Juanita said confidently, "but I do not recognize the woman next to her."

"Neither do I," Rachel said. "And that's *not* Amy."

Juanita stared down at Rachel as if she'd just confessed to having opened the city's first free abortion clinic. "Pardon me, Mrs. McNeil, but I know my Amy, and that girl is her."

"If I didn't know where it came from, and how old it is," Rachel said, "then I would have to agree with you."

"This picture is not new?" Juanita said, exasperation in her eyes.

"Rachel found it before Amy was ever born," Duncan said. "Back in Massachusetts."

Juanita crossed herself, mumbled a short prayer. "God help us, she has a doppelganger."

"Apparently," Rachel agreed.

Duncan knew what a doppelganger was, but was surprised as hell to hear such a word come from Juanita's mouth. In fact, it even seemed a bit too exotic for Rachel's vocabulary.

"*Did have* a double," he reminded them. "Their likenesses would have to be contemporaneous to qualify that noun. Besides, you both watch too much daytime TV."

"Alright, Professor McNeil, then you explain the uncanny resemblance," Rachel said. "In fact, why don't you just neatly square the whole thing away for us right now."

Duncan sighed. "I can't. At least not..."

"At least not *what*?" Rachel said, her eyes narrowing.

As the land masses of his life began to buckle and grind, he averted his eyes.

"Spit it out, Dunc," Rachel insisted. "You're not the only one around here who can read people like a book, you know."

He still couldn't look at her, but could feel her eyes drilling into the top of his skull as he stared into his lap.

Did he dare tell her?

"Fess up," she urged. There was already a shaky quality in her voice, as if she were prodding a hesitant doctor to reveal the results of her mammogram. "Now!"

He finally looked up at Juanita. "Would you excuse us?"

Juanita glanced expectantly at Rachel, as if she might invalidate Duncan's order. She didn't, though, and a few moments later Rachel and Duncan were alone.

"Well?"

"You're not going to like me very much," Duncan promised.

Sighing, Rachel nodded her understanding. "Alright, who's the woman?"

16.

Amy was back, standing on the edge of the cliff, but was now observing rather than experiencing the same dream she'd had earlier. And this time from a different perspective. She was watching it unfold in the window directly before her, as if the pane of glass had turned into a kind of television screen, one capable of three-dimensional imagery.

She did not have the wide panoramic view of the cliffs that she'd had previously, but was now standing on their very edge, if she was to trust her eyes. She felt that if she were to step forward, up and over the window sill, she would surely fall the hundreds of feet down to the tranquil ocean below.

She could still hear the rain outside pecking against the glass, but could no longer see it. Unlike her emotional state in the previous dream, she was frightened.

Shakily leaning forward, she peered down, and was instantly overcome with that woozy, wavering feeling that she got when riding in elevators.

As hard as she tried, she could not remove her hand from the window. It was the weirdest feeling. Her sense of touch told her this was a solid object; smooth glass. But her eyes and stomach were telling her something entirely different.

Her name was Amy McNeil, not Katherine, and she was sure this was not a dream.

Then, just as before, the multi-winged image appeared, reflected on the mirror-like surface of the water below. Small at first, it quickly grew in size as it descended from the sky.

She looked up, and again the sounds of many approaching trains filled the air, rapidly becoming a deafening blare.

The immense shape plummeted directly in front of her, and for more than a second blocked out her view entirely. A blinding flash of light and hot gust of wind rushed instantly through the window, the concussive force literally blowing her off her feet. Had her right hand not been so bizarrely anchored to the glass, she believed she would have been thrown clear across the room.

At once her lips became chapped, her mouth and eyes sucked of moisture. Her hair whipped crazily about her face.

She cried out.

Then a thunderous, crashing noise erupted from the water below. She looked down. The multi-winged creature had plunged into the water—which wasn't water anymore, but glass. A volcanic eruption of glittering fragments, like the silvery pieces of a mirror, sprayed into the air.

Seconds later, a conglomeration of remnants sailed past her, heaven-bound. She saw that each one was an individual segment of either body or wing, exquisitely detailed, capturing every aspect and minuscule feature of scale and feather as if cast from the most delicate of molds. She even saw, in some of the closer ones, portions of her own astonished reflection.

The soaring fragments did not dive back to earth, as she'd expected. Instead, the pieces kept soaring upward, twinkled like stars for a moment, then vanished altogether.

Glancing back down at the ocean, she saw that there was now a gigantic, craggy hole where the impact had occurred. And she instantly knew with all of her soul that within the infinite blackness beneath...there waited monsters.

Monsters preparing for a feast of man.

Then the vision became a rain-splattered window again, so suddenly that it jarred her backward. No longer stuck to the glass, she fell butt-first to the hard floor.

Dazed, she glanced around the shadowy room. Very near her, something twinkled on the floor.

In the hallway outside, there was a scramble of soft footsteps. Careful not to cut herself, she snatched the piece of glass, then hurried to the open bed.

The door opened just as she slipped beneath the covers.

Two nurses scrambled in.

"What's goin' on in here?" one of the nurses said, looking around the room, appearing surprised that it wasn't in shambles. "And just how, mind you tellin' me, did you disconnect yourself from your IV and cardiac monitor without Houston gettin' wind of the problem?"

Amy pulled the sheets up to her chin, swallowing hard. "I don't know. Guess I was just having a nightmare."

"Nightmare?" said the other nurse. "Mercy! It sounded like King Kong was throwing a tantrum in here!"

17.

As Deacon Samuel Flannery walked down the central aisle of St. Patrick's Church, ready to call it a day, he paid his usual reverence to the nine swirling angels gracing its domed ceiling. He paused, then slowly began turning in a tight circle as he gazed upward, entwined with the angels' spiraling, heavenly ascension. Then he stopped, his thick, black eyebrows dipping prominently between his puzzled eyes.

Father Kagan emerged from the sacristy. No longer draped in the silky vestments he'd worn at mass, he was now down to his black Rabat, black slacks, and clerical shirt with its white Roman collar.

He was whistling.

Samuel turned as Eli approached him. "Ah, Father Kagan. You seem to be feeling much better," he said, referring to Eli's earlier, weary state at mass.

"Yes, much so, thank you," Eli said. "Admiring my work, I see."

"God has truly gifted you, Father," Samuel agreed. "An inspirational masterpiece. By far the most adored this side of Pompey. But, I must say, I'm a bit stumped."

"Oh?" Eli said. "And why is that?"

"Well," Flannery said, again gazing upward, "you see the largest angel there? The, um…"

"Seraph," Eli said, not bothering to look up.

"Seraph, yes. Well, I've studied your exquisite mural many times, Father, have indulged in its holy meaning, but I must say…I don't recall that particular angel wielding a *sword*."

This time Eli looked up.

In the seraph's right hand was, indeed, a great sword, poised as if ready to deliver a lashing blow.

After an uncomfortable moment, Eli smiled. "Your faculties are failing you, Samuel. The sword has always been there. And a nice touch, if you ask me."

Samuel leered at Eli. "Are you sure, Father?"

"I painted it, didn't I?"

"Of course, of course, but I…"

"Perhaps you partook of too much wine at sacrament this evening?" Eli winked, chuckling.

"Never," Samuel vowed with a wave of his hand.

Eli slapped him on the back, laughed. "Go get a good night's rest. It's good for the soul. And the *eyes*."

Samuel sighed, reluctant to give in. "Maybe you're right. I'm not a young man anymore, Father."

"Neither of us are," Eli agreed.

"By the way," Samuel said, "how old are you, if you don't mind me asking?"

"Not at all," Eli smiled. "I'm fifty-two, and feel better than I ever have," he said, punctuating the declaration with two hard slaps to his flat stomach.

"Yes, yes, you're a fit man, Father, and hide your age well," Samuel agreed. "But—and also something I've apparently overlooked—the gray at your temples," he observed. "It seems to me that just this previous Sunday your hair was free of such maturity."

Eli said nothing. Though maintaining his smile, his scrutiny seemed reproachful to Samuel.

Nervously, Samuel chuckled. "Perhaps you're right, Father. My faculties are not as loyal as they used to be."

Eli's smile widened. "A good night's rest," he assured.

"Thank you, Father," Samuel said, glancing one more time at the angels above. He slowly shook his head, then started for the front doors. "Oh, one more thing, Father. The Broncos are coming to town Monday night," he offered, "and I just happen to have two tickets. They're not the best seats, mind you—you might say we'd be way up there rooting with God—but if you're as big a Seahawks fan as I am—"

"That's thoughtful of you, Samuel," Eli said, "but I've plans for that evening."

"If you change your mind—"

"I'll let you know."

Flannery walked through the doors and into the mist-enshrouded Seattle night. "Goodnight, Father."

*****

"Yes, yes, goodnight, Samuel," Eli said, then under his breath: "You nosey cocksucker."

Eli stared up at the seraph, regarding its facial changes with a hatred and loathing so intense that he thought he might explode. The seraph now wore a kind of deprecating yet challenging expression, as if its eyes were inviting him to dance—him, the ugliest girl at the ball!—and were not willing to take no for an answer.

He shook a fist at the soaring image, furious at its newfound arrogance. "You don't scare me!" he shouted. "I'm nearly finished, and when the last one flies, we'll meet on mutual ground. Then we'll see whose sword is mightier!"

Raging in his bolstered belief in the Almighty, he was looking far beyond the seraph now and defying God Himself. "When the last one flies!" he roared.

"When the last one flies!"

18.

The photograph lay in her lap; a crushing, immovable stone.

Rachel gazed through the window, watching a storm not nearly as tempestuous as the one gathering within her. Thunder rumbled through her heart, gales howled around the eaves of her mind, lightning coiled in her fingertips. If she could muster the fury, she'd have this house and its resident adulterer well on their way to the Land of Oz. There, her husband could get a heart, a brain, and some courage. The rotten bastard.

And while he was waiting, she thought coldly, he could retain himself an attorney. The line was guaranteed to be full of them.

Staring down at the photograph—way down now, beyond the baffling coincidences and into a new opening savagely rent by Duncan's admitted infidelity—she considered the darkness awaiting her at its threshold. To venture in, she would need light. But she wasn't sure just yet if she could handle Duncan igniting those torches.

The fact that it happened over a decade ago might have softened the blow for someone else, but it did nothing for her.

"So, you called it off while you were in the hospital?" she finally said, her voice low, reticent.

Duncan, face in his hands, said, "I called off a lot of things after I got shot. Sprawled out like that for three weeks...I had a lot of time to...consider my options."

"Saw the errors of your ways, huh?"

"I'm not that man, anymore, Rachel. Haven't been for over ten years."

She turned away from the window; faced him. Nearly a whisper, she said, "If you were any kind of a man, you wouldn't have waited all this time to tell me."

Duncan nodded.

Rachel sighed. "And you're sure her daughter's name was Katherine?"

"Positive."

"She would be, what, twenty, twenty-one-years old by now?"

"Yeah, somewhere around there."

Rachel stared at the picture, focusing on the little girl. "You'd have had one hell of a time denying paternity," she said. "Did it ever come up?"

Something occurred then at the corners of his mouth; something that might have passed unnoticed by an untrained eye. But Rachel instantly and unmistakably recognized it for what it was: fond reminiscence.

She could have killed him right then and there.

"Earlier," he said, "when all the memories came flooding back, I remembered how we joked about it one night at Giacomo's. The resemblance, I mean. We sort of just...laughed it away as a funny coincidence."

"Oh, it's a real hoot," she agreed. "And if I remember correctly, isn't Giacomo's the same goddamn restaurant where you proposed to me?"

Nostalgia eased itself from his face, then tipped-toed out the room just as mortification came rushing in. "Oh...oh, shit."

"Christ, Duncan," she said, more surprised than disgusted, "that's just plain tacky."

"I'm not that man anymore," he restated, his voice fast approaching desperation. "I swear, it was the only time I was unfaithful to you."

"Uh-huh. And what else have you remembered that you might want to tell me?"

"Donut," he said.

"Excuse me?"

"Katherine used to call me 'Donut,'" he explained. "A play on my name. You know, 'Dunkin Donut.'"

"Oh? Well, isn't that sweet," she said, her voice slurred with melodic sarcasm. "And does Dunky Donut remember being called by any other nicky-names? Perhaps while he was in the middle of humping Kathy's Mommy?"

"Dammit, Rachel!" he yelled. "Aren't you going to throw something at me? Spit in my face and call me a filthy rotten pig?" He pulled open the top desk drawer, grabbed a letter opener that could have passed for a decent steak knife, offered it to her, and said, "Here! Stab me in the heart! Cut off my wang and throw it out the car window! Slit my throat! Hell, *do something!* But don't just sit there and gloat like some self-righteous bitch!"

She remained stoic, undaunted, as if he'd told her that unleaded had just gone up two cents a gallon.

He stood up so forcefully that his chair went spinning across the floor. "It happened a long, long time ago, Rachel! So kill me, forgive me— something! But do it now, because I would like to try to get to the deeper meaning of the whole crazy fucking thing!"

She turned back to the window and folded her arms, as if to ponder between the two choices.

"Well?"

"Death," she finally said, "by Bongo!" Then she started laughing; then crying; then laughing again.

Duncan walked over and embraced her, held her tight. She did not resist, but neither did she respond.

"It happened a lifetime ago," he whispered in her ear. "And right now I desperately need you to forgive me. *We* need to forgive me if we're to sort out this...bizarre mess."

"Oh, I'll work with you on this," she said irrefutably. "But forgive you? I don't know, Duncan. I just don't know."

Then she finally asked him: "Did you love her?"

He waited, then sighed: "I think I might have."

Rachel shook her head. "Goddamn you."

19.

After having reattached Amy's leads and saline IV, fluffed her pillows, inspected her and the room for damage, poured her a glass of water, all the while admonishing her for creating all that racket (though she'd fervently denied causing the noise, having blamed it on the storm outside), both nurses finally left, scratching their heads.

Lightning blanched the cartoon characters on the wall, eerily animating them in a millisecond of silver-white light. She flinched at the sudden toll of thunder, sounding as if it had been vented in the very next room.

Amy held the piece of glass up to her face, and saw only her distorted reflection. The item fit awkwardly into the palm of her hand, portions of its uneven circumference extending farther outward than others. It looked like a blotch of resinous silver that had been thickly and arbitrarily applied to a bird's wing, then carefully peeled away after hardening, except that the large, replicated feathers were *raised*, not *indented*.

She curled her fingers around what she could and discovered that it had a pliable quality. She could actually bend it, though she was very careful not to exert too much pressure. She did not want to break her newfound toy, one that sang to her insides.

The music was like warm water, and finally lulled her to sleep.

She did not dream this time of cliffs and glass oceans and shiny winged behemoths in the sky. Instead, she dreamed again of a place called Rock Bay. There was a man who looked just like her daddy, but he wasn't her daddy in the dream. There was a woman, too, a woman she called Mommy; a pretty woman, but a different kind of pretty than her waking mom, Rachel McNeil, possessed.

She ran through the tide, chasing after the man, erroneously shouting "Daddy! Daddy! Daddy!" There was another name she called him, too, when she was being silly: "Donut."

It was the same recurring dream; the same dream that left her feeling empty when she woke from it; left her feeling...abandoned.

Suddenly then, a kind of merging occurred. *She* was now the ten-year-old girl named Katherine Bently, now deceased, whose step-father was also dead, whose real father—dead or otherwise—remained anonymous, and whose mother still ached for her, still lived and breathed in a cloud of grief and despair. And the only thing sustaining her mother's empty life was the hope that she would one day meet face-to-face the person responsible for abducting her daughter, and with her closely gnawed fingernails have the great pleasure of stripping him to the bone with an eternity of slow, agonizing strokes.

That she actually knew these things to be true, or was simply inserting probabilities where such facts were missing, she did not know.

Strange. She was experiencing both roles simultaneously—then suddenly realized she always had. It was weird, as if Amy and Katherine were Siamese twins, nocturnally tethered; intangibly fused by a *shared mind*. It was confusing, and yet it wasn't.

In some fantastical way, Amy McNeil and Katherine Bently were one, yet separate.

All this came to her so swiftly and fluidly that it felt as if a great void had been filled within her soul.

Upon this sudden realization an incredible peace and acceptance swallowed her, then swept her away in dream-speed from Rock Bay's serene beaches and landed her upon the distant, craggy, beautifully turbulent shores of the Pacific Northwest.

A place where she—Katherine—had been cast upon the wind with improvised wings, and told to fly. And where she—Amy—had caught her soul, saving her from experiencing a cruel *death*.

Even in its mature form, she now recognized the voice of Katherine's protector those many years ago as her own. It had been, in fact, both Amy and Katherine's voice.

Confusing. Yet, on another level so perfectly, so harmoniously imagined.

20.

The wipers were chopping Elton John's "Nakita" into little communist pieces.

Duncan thought he could sympathize, what with his manhood having just barely escaped a demonstration of his wife's cutlery skills. He'd discovered that, just like murder, there was no statute of limitations for adultery.

Except for the porch light, the photographer's one-level home was dark. Duncan eased the BMW to the edge of the road and parked. There were no concrete curbs or elevated sidewalks in this residential area, only shiny black asphalt merging into loose gravel shoulders skirted by long, neglected rows of lilac bushes, bisected every fifty feet or so by a cracked and oil-stained driveway.

He hadn't tried calling the photographer again before leaving the house. He'd needed to get out, take a drive, sort his thoughts. So, he figured he'd just drop by on his way to nowhere and see if Mitch Dillard was home and, if so, up to talking shop with a Mick ex-cop.

And if the shutterbug wasn't home, or was but wasn't in the mood to have a man-to-man, then Duncan would just have to let himself in.

Just like the good ol' days.

God, he was pissed at himself.

Ice granules had all but replaced the rain, sizzling like bacon atop the BMW's roof. The lightning, having grown bored with golf courses and chimneys, seemed content for now to merely skitter across the belly of the storm, stitching seams in the nimbus with dazzling neon thread. Thunder prowled the sky, growling. All roared out, for now.

Eerily, it felt to him that the storm wasn't abating, but bowing obsequiously beneath the passing of a larger, more abhorrent one.

In fact, it seemed like the whole night was cowering.

The neighborhood was old, its trees massive, looming like thunderheads over the roofs of the peeling cracker boxes. The rain here, Duncan guessed, was going to have to fall a lot longer and a lot harder if its intentions were to wash away the sooty film of broken dreams.

As he pulled on a black pair of Isotoner gloves, Duncan understood that this wasn't the worst part of town, but it was bad enough. Then again, crazy lived everywhere.

Luck of the Irish, don't fail me now.

He exited the vehicle and dashed umbrella-less across the narrow street, making the porch in a dozen strides. He rang the bell, then gave the door three hard raps for good measure.

A voice cried out immediately: "Hey, in here! Help me, I'm trapped!"

Duncan froze, listened. The plea sounded like it came from right inside the house; yet...there was an airy, buoyant quality to the voice, an acoustical dichotomy, as if it had originated from a nearby amphitheater rather than from these insulated confines.

The voice *echoed.*

Duncan imagined the cries of a lost, desperate hiker, then snorted in disgust. He was growing perturbed with his recent cockeyed interpretations of things.

"Hey, if you're Duncan McNeil, then I've got a message for you!" hollered the voice.

"Duncan McNeil?" Duncan mumbled, as if that name sounded familiar. Did someone know he was coming? Of course not. Hell, he wasn't even sure *he* was coming until...*wait a minute!* Amy's principal knew, and must have given the photographer the heads-up that her sue-happy father would likely be calling.

Duncan gritted his teeth.

Incensed, he tried the door, hopeful that he would have to bust it down with either of his shoulders (a feat, it now occurred to him, that he'd not once had to exercise while acting as a cop).

Sadly, the knob turned; the door opened effortlessly.

Duncan reached one arm in and felt around for a switch. He found the plate and flipped up the lever, instantly transforming the darkness into a tiny living room decorated in 20th-century sloven. The light was coming through the tasseled shade of a floor lamp, one so old and listing so badly that he was surprised it didn't have an attending nurse.

An odor that reminded him of Vic's Vapor Rub hung in the room.

"Don't leave, don't leave!" implored the voice. "Is that you, McNeil?"

Duncan did not look around the room, but kept very still, as if by turning his head he might miss the culprit dash from behind the curtains and hide, say, behind the back of the sofa.

Games. Someone was playing games.

In the center of a round rattan coffee table rose one of the largest hookah pipes he thought he'd ever seen. And he'd seen plenty.

Eight hoses sprouted from near the base; a medusa, of sorts.

He leaned over the prodigal pipe, and inhaled.

Hashish, of course. That explained the smell.

Memories started flooding back. He shook his head, as if he'd conjured a cloud of gnats, then stepped silently toward the kitchen.

The living room and kitchen merged where dingy carpet had collided disastrously with wood flooring. Champagne-colored ringlets and curls corkscrewed their way up from the long, quarter-inch trench, ensnaring floor splinters and cigarette butts and Captain Crunch and God knew what else.

Compared to the living room, however, the kitchen was surprisingly tidy.

"Hey, over here!" cried the man. "Please tell me you're that kid's father."

This time, Duncan got a bearing on the voice. He stepped cautiously to the south wall where hung an Ansel Adams poster. Modestly framed, this black-and-white photo depicted a placid lake surrounded by aspen and pine and snow-capped mountains. The caption below offered "Mirror Lake and Mount Watkins, Yosemite National Park, California".

It was vintage Ansel Adams; the vista so serene, so inviting that it made a guy just want to crawl into the picture with his fishing pole and drown a few worms. And as hard as Duncan was trying not to believe it, it appeared to him that someone had done just that, minus tackle.

On the narrow patch of shore located in the bottom left corner of the print, also in black-and-white, was a gaunt man in striped pajamas. Barefoot, he was pacing along the bank, hugging himself. He appeared to be in his late forties, bald, and was sporting a gray goatee. His pate glinted dully beneath the overcast sky.

Duncan fought a curious urge to yell. "Are you Mitch Dillard?" he said, feeling truly stupid.

Startled, the man pivoted shakily. Not quite facing Duncan, he gazed skyward and spoke like an oracle addressing the Messiah: "Are you Duncan McNeil?"

"I asked you first."

"Look," the man began, disconcerted, "I can't see you, but I can hear you." He rubbed his hands briskly together. "All I can see are mountains and trees and picnic tables. So unless you're Ricky Ranger, Duncan McNeil, or Smokey the fucking Bear, get the hell out of my house!"

"You didn't answer my question," Duncan reminded, searching the ceiling and walls for hidden projectors, laser lights, Alan Fundt's successor—anything that would expose the prank, or at least allude to one, and quell the strange panic blooming in his gut.

The man squinted. "What question was that?"

"Are you Mitch Dillard, the photographer?"

He laughed. "I used to be, but now I'm Mitch Dillard, flashback schizophrenic." He hugged himself tighter. "Let me tell you, it's colder than a well digger's ass in Wyoming out here!"

"California," Duncan corrected. "Yosemite National Park."

"I know where the hell I am!" Mitch crowed. "It's my poster!"

"And it appears to be springtime," Duncan said, making idle conversation while poking around an oval oak table teeming with wadded Twinkies packages and 35mm film canisters. Cigarette burns were so plentiful on the table and surrounding carpet that they often crisscrossed one another, looking to Duncan like a herd of black, fuzzy caterpillars had migrated to this very spot and died. "I can almost smell the blooms from here," he said. "I'm guessing it's 65, maybe 75 degrees in there."

"Celsius or Fahrenheit?" Mitch cried, pulling exaggeratedly at the waist of his pajama bottoms. "So I have a low threshold to the cold! I yell *bonzi!* every time there's a *nip* in the air! Big deal!" He was literally jumping up and down. *"Haven't you noticed the rather peculiar situation I'm in?"*

"I've noticed," Duncan said. "So, how...did you get in there?"

Mitch began rubbing his hands along his thighs. "Couple three hours ago, this guy pays me a visit, says his name's Gamble, and that he wanted me to give someone a message. Basically, I told him where he could stick his message, that I'd had enough loopy shit for one day, and was most certainly not in any mood to play mailman opposite some fruitcake."

"And he said...?"

"He said, 'My friend, you don't know the first thing about crazy,' then recited a lame limerick—and presto! I'm in this glossy freezing my nads off!"

"What did he look like?"

Mitch blew into his cupped hands. "You won't believe me."

"Like I'm believing any of this."

"David Copperfield," he confessed.

"The book, or the magician?" Duncan felt it was a legitimate question, given the scenario.

"The hocus-pocus guy, smart ass," he said. "Black suit, boyish good looks, the whole nine yards. But he didn't fool me. I've seen better Cher impersonators, and I told him so."

"Magic, huh?" Duncan said. "Well, that might explain a lot. How much hash did you smoke before this Gamble guy arrived?"

Mitch laughed. "How much did *you?*"

He thought for a moment. "Good point."

"I'll damn sure guarantee you that this ain't the kind of Rocky

Mountain High John Denver had in mind."

Well, that was debatable, Duncan thought. Besides, Mitch was in the Sierra Nevada range, not the Rocky Mountains. But this wasn't the time to nitpick.

He lifted the picture off its hook and examined it from front to back. While doing so, it vaguely occurred to him that he might be pitching the poster's animate resident about like a bug in a jar.

Of course, that was a ridiculous notion.

There was nothing on the wall except a ghostly rectangle of brighter paint, indicating only that the print had been there for some time.

Duncan returned it to the wall and regarded Mitch—still upright and appearing no worse off than before—with remorse; not sad for the man, but woeful that he himself might be spending the next six months or so as a guest of the state, where he would interpret inkblots, debate with his fellow convalescents the ethical ramifications of electroshock therapy, and match wits with an unscrupulous nursing staff. And, in the meantime, hopefully befriend any humongous oafs who could bench-press any of the facility's marble commodes and bust his ass out, preferably before his prescribed lobotomy.

"Fuck," Duncan groaned. "This is not happening."

Mitch held up a finger. "Hey, it could be worse. Instead of Ansel Adams, I could be up to my ass in H.R. Giger."

Duncan poked the glass with an index finger, and was relieved when he felt solid resistance. But could he reach into the scene if the glass wasn't there? he wondered. He wanted very badly to remove his glove, convinced that it was not allowing for the tactility necessary to experience this remarkable brand of bizarreness. He kept both gloves on, though, reminded that—even without his fingerprints—the District Attorney could probably make a convincing case that he had the motive and opportunity should the photographer's corpse later be found floating in the reflective waters of Mirror Lake.

"He's the guy who designed the creatures in the old *Alien* movies," Mitch said.

Duncan was massaging his temples with vigor. "What?"

"H.R. Giger. He's the one—"

"Yeah, yeah, I know who he is."

"Hey," Mitch hollered, "this is just as hard on me, you know."

Duncan closed his eyes, inhaled deeply.

"What happened at the school today?" he finally said. "With my daughter?"

"Ah hah, I knew it!" Mitch yelled, clapping. "You *are* McNeil!"

"The one and only," he said. "Now, what about my daughter?"

"She...she didn't tell you?"

"Yes, she did," Duncan lied. "But I want to hear your version of events."

Mitch began pacing again, gesturing dramatically as he spilled the story.

"Let me get this straight," Duncan said. "Amy's hand *sucked* the colors from your canvas?"

"Like cat hair up a Kirby." Mitch shrugged his shoulders. "Given the fact you're talking to a guy in a chintzy poster, is that so unbelievable?"

Duncan supposed not. "And the note that was left—this 'Special Bulletin'—said, 'He knows where you've flown'?" Upon that, he vaguely recalled something Rachel had told him earlier. Didn't she say that the ambulance driver experienced something very similar? At the hospital?

"That's what it said," Mitch affirmed.

"Where *who's* flown? And who the hell is 'He'?"

"Mr. McNeil, your daughter didn't answer any of my questions, which should come as no surprise seeing how I was too busy wetting my pants to ask her any."

Duncan concentrated. There was something else the medic had told Rachel. Something about moving images on glass? Christ, he couldn't remember.

He cursed himself, wishing now he'd been more attentive.

Headlights spun across the living room curtains. Across the street, car doors opened, releasing a drunken chorus of profanities and giddy laughter. The voices entered a neighboring house, then all was quiet.

"McNeil?" Mitch yelled. "You still with me?"

Duncan continued to stare at the curtains. "Yeah. I'm just trying to figure a way to get you out of there."

Mitch whooped. "I'm glad you brought that up. See, this guy Gamble said he expected you to show up sooner or later, and that he'd let me out once you did. But that I'd have to read you a message first. So, if you don't mind..."

Very curious now, Duncan turned to Mitch. "Okay, let's hear it."

Mitch delightedly removed a folded piece of plain notebook paper from his pajama pants' pocket, cleared his throat, then began reading: "'There once was a detective named McNeil, A suitcase full of money he did steal, Amid the moral strife, He saved a child's life, And gained a dead one in the deal.' He signed it, 'Sincerely, Mr. Gamble'."

Jack London's short story "To Build a Fire" came to Duncan's mind as his body temperature suddenly plummeted to forty below zero, with the tundra around his heart made even more frigid by the wind chill. For a long moment he could barely breathe, and seriously considered burning the poster and the photographer within it before he lost consciousness. But he was already so numb that a match would have been useless in his fingers.

"Don't you rabbit on me yet, McNeil!" shouted the photographer.

"There's more, a P.S. at the bottom. You ready?"

"Go ahead," Duncan said, wondering if his chest would ever thaw.

"'P.S. Given her recent cravings, tell your wife there's a wonderful little restaurant over by Hollenbeck Park. Middle Eastern. I strongly recommend she start out with the *Fatoosh*. It's excellent. Then, to whet her appetite for lamb, she should go for the *Koozy*. Best in town. For dessert, there's nothing better than their *Basbousa*. I know, I know, she's watching that cute little figure. But guess what? So am I! Mmmm-mm! Tell her to put it on my tab.'"

After what might have been either several seconds or several hours, the picture and photographer wavered back into view. Duncan, just barely recalling that last part, said, "What was that about my wife and Koozy in Hollenbeck Park?"

"Want me to read it again?"

Duncan shook his head. "No, no, forget it. I think I get the intention."

"Their couscous is good too," Mitch offered. "If you're into that shit."

Duncan glanced around, not knowing whether to expect a genie to pop out of Mitch's hookah, the walls to ooze blood, or his wife to deliver him a swift elbow, order him to roll over, then curse his obnoxious snoring before falling herself back to sleep.

Finally, Duncan turned to the photographer. "Well, I'm still here, and you're still in there."

Mitch was already slugging himself in the sides. "Damn it! Maybe I didn't read it right!"

"No," Duncan assured, "you did just fine."

Just then, Duncan saw a distortion on the surface of the lake, just off the opposite shore. The photographer must have heard what Duncan saw, for he turned and stared.

There it was again. Something huge rolled just beneath the lake's glassy surface.

"What the fuck is that?" Duncan said. "A sturgeon?"

"Way my day's been going," Mitch groused, "it's probably the Incredible Mr. Limpett."

Don Knotts dressed up like a carp? Duncan leaned in, fascinated. *Why not?*

Then his eyes grew wide as he stepped back from the poster. "Mitch, get away from the lake," he ordered. "Now! Run!"

"Run? And go where?" Mitch implored. "I'm in bare feet. I can barely walk!"

"Just...Christ, just start heading toward Mount Watkins!" Duncan said, beginning to panic.

The thing in the lake was surfacing. But the lake was no longer water. It had turned into glass. With a quick upward thrust, the monster broke through in an explosion of twinkling shards and nuggets.

Duncan felt the room vibrate.

Mitch stood transfixed, gaping at the mutant as it oozed up from the hole and onto the fractured surface.

The creature looked like a giant slug, and was mostly transparent; its internal organs less so, but see-through all the same. As it moved toward Mitch, it did so raucously and with the blunt determination of an earthmover, scouring the surface and pulverizing the chunks of glass strewn in its path.

Its optical tentacles telescoped out and fixed upon the photographer. It was nearly upon him now.

"Get out of its way!" Duncan squealed, his voice pinched with fear.

Mitch began stomping the ground again. "We had a deal, Gamble!" he screamed at the sky. Then he turned in Duncan's direction: "I think he's coming for your daughter, McNeil! I think it's Gamble who knows where Amy's flown—"

The gastropod seized Mitch by the head, and quickly imbibed him. Duncan watched the man's progression through the slug's diaphanous body, from esophagus to stomach. During the violent ingestion, Mitch's pajama top had been pulled from him and was now floating in the creature's jellied throat.

To foil a tactless urge to laugh, Duncan slapped a hand to his mouth.

There once was a Detective named McNeil...

Everything in the picture, even the slug, remained black and white – except for the blood now rising like steam off the photographer's entire body, effusing a wispy crimson aura.

But Mitch was not dead. Duncan could see the facial contortions, the torpid movements of his limbs, as if he were pushing out against a million rubber bands. Craggy holes were already blossoming outward in his pajama bottoms, exposing muscle and bone. Then the tissue on his chest began to flare. Within moments, his sternum began peeking through, then the connecting ribs...

The photographer's screams were strangled, but ever-present.

A gust of wind stirred a distant copse of pine, the sound traveling across the lake like a fizzling pop bottle rocket.

In a cumulus of blood, Mitch's right leg slid away from the hip, buoying grotesquely in the loose gel.

He was being digested.

...A suitcase full of money he did steal...

Duncan bolted for the front door, his right hand still covering his mouth. He was no longer stifling a laugh, but was now fighting back the urge to vomit.

...Amid the moral strife, He saved a child's life...

...And gained a dead one in the deal.

Duncan stumbled off the porch and onto the photographer's dirt lawn. Nausea had already paled and slackened his face, and was now working on his stature.

The rain had stopped, and a breeze cooled his sweaty cheeks and forehead.

Doubled-over, Duncan dropped to his knees.

"A salt shaker," he mumbled, laughing amid tears. "If only I could've gotten a salt shaker."

Then he leaned forward and reintroduced to Los Angeles some of its finest mandarin cuisine.

"May the universe in some strange way be 'brought into being' by the participation of those who participate?"

—John Wheeler, physicist

Part Two
Windows

1.

A fetid stink crowded the basement; had blossomed overnight, it seemed.

Beneath each of the six stained glass windows rested a large plastic dog dish. And from these the stench of rotting meat had once again risen to levels that would, according to his crass mother, "knock a vulture off a shit wagon!"

Eli would have to get her down here to clean up. She would once again rant and rave about his compulsion to feed the "monkey-bats," reminding him that they obviously didn't like Mighty Dog or chicken livers or Nine Lives, and why couldn't he just get that through his depraved skull, blah, blah, blah.

He teasingly tapped the glass murals as he walked by them, inciting their blurry occupants into wild Pavlovian responses.

Except for those of the developing room, and a lengthwise section in the middle for his Wall of Faces, all the basement walls remained unfinished. Two bare, hundred-watt bulbs hung from either end of the ceiling, casting dark, distorted twins of every stud left exposed by the absence of sheet rock, lending each undeveloped chamber the look and feel of a cold, drab penal cell.

Moodier still were the shadows ogling from those confines; the ghosts of inmates past, recidivists even after death, and still the rubbernecking bunch they were before the warden pulled their numbers.

Head bowed, eyes closed, Eli knelt before the sixth window in the procession. His lips moved silently, hurriedly, appealing to the window's inhabitant to once again seek out the last angel, to fetch and bring her back to this very sanctum.

This same errand had been attempted yesterday, but was foiled when the courier inadvertently stumbled upon the Bently girl in Los Angeles, alive and no worse for wear according to rumor. He would dispatch another courier for her today, as well, and shuddered to think of the consequences should the runty, trouble-making bitch slip by him *this* time.

Katherine Bently aside, Eli never knew who he was getting until she arrived, and only that the girl would be ten years old and fatherless. And in this day and age, that left a lot to choose from. But whether the child was picked at random or was pre-selected, he did not know. His hunch, though, had always been that each one was singled out for possessing special qualities; qualities Mr. Gamble himself must have looked highly upon, as it was he who made the shopping list.

Besides, he imagined that the couriers did a fine job leaving the FBI and local authorities with nothing but the Jersey Devil to investigate. And any witnesses—no matter how compromised the authorities might come to consider them—were dealt with personally by Gamble.

Some of his fondest moments, Gamble had once told Eli, were the times when he questioned the witnesses himself. "I tell ya," he'd bragged, "I can shake down a snitch like you wouldn't believe."

Eli could only imagine Gamble's methods of interrogation.

Then again, maybe he couldn't. And that was probably for the best.

Although Eli had been kept in the dark all these years about what Gamble was truly up to, he couldn't help but wonder on occasion what his good mentor hoped to harvest from seven dead girls. But the restless nights when he pondered such mysteries had grown rarer with time, and he was more content now than ever to remain in the closet. For the most part, he was satisfied to be left alone to build and cherish his window collection, and perfect the incomparable craft of angel-making.

Most important of all, though, was the gratuity he'd earned for his unflagging devotion to Mr. Gamble and his cryptic cause. That being, he'd been given full artistic control over his imminent rebirth. He could be whoever or whatever he wanted when the time came—given the thumbs-up, of course, from his mentor.

That's what Eli was hoping *his* side of the crop would yield.

He desperately wanted his own wings, had ever since he could remember, and thus had set out creating the Wall of Faces. He figured even the most reserved connoisseurs of contemporary art would admit to seeing the obvious corollaries between a black-and-white montage of dead, winged little girls and a mad priest's obsession to fly.

If they could see starving Ethiopian children in a can of Campbell's Tomato Soup, he thought, then they could see anything. And if the critics *were* to ever come back nay-saying, then he'd just kindly direct them to the dome of St. Patrick's Church.

Let Andy Warhol top that!

Satisfied that his wishes had been made clear, he opened his eyes and slowly rose before the window. He then touched the glass with one finger, dispatching the entity from its multicolored, puzzle-pieced medium and into a similar world where edges come together almost as dramatically; where borders and margins are sharply pronounced, separating color and demography. Into a world where scenery is now more often segregated by manmade lines and boundaries than allowed to naturally blend.

Man's need for structure was evident in everything he touched, Eli knew. Especially his faith.

Unleashed, the apparition swiftly grew distant behind the glass, fluttering like a leaf down a well.

Eli then walked the length of the basement wall and hesitated before the second window in the series; the second one he'd obtained. "The Dawning," he'd named it long ago; appropriately so, for the bottom of the window portrayed a black sun rising beyond a horizon blazing with orange-red flames. Farther up in the mural, near its center, those tongues of fire eerily metamorphosed into vaulting demonic figures, the higher and more complete ones bending and arching downward like divers off of springboards, cannon-balling and belly-flopping back down into the flames that had given birth to them.

But the image he adored most was near the top, the likeness of a little girl-angel falling headfirst from a golden sky, her feather wings tearing apart in her swift descent, her white gown rippling like a mast in a squall. Her face was terror-stricken; mouth agape, eyes wide. And there were many hands reaching down from the sky, trying to catch her, to snatch her up before being consumed by the fires below.

Until yesterday afternoon, it had never occurred to him that they might prove successful.

Perhaps those hands have managed some kind of desperate clutch after all, he thought.

"Kathy, Kathy, Kathy," he whispered, shaking his head. "Someone has clipped your wings. But who?"

He stared at "The Dawning," then into it, focusing on its inhabitant, whose wings fluttered then, as if in eager anticipation of his impending instructions.

"And you, my old and ornery friend," he commanded, "will once again bring back to me the little bitch called Katherine!"

He touched the glass: "To the City of Angels!"

2.

Duncan sat at his desk, staring at a Chagall lithograph on the opposite wall. He'd not slept a wink since having returned from the photographer's place, but already it had begun to feel like a dream; that point where reality elbows its way in as the eyes flutter open, and a sigh raises the drawbridge, leaving any monsters in fast pursuit to the discretion of the mote's black, bottomless waters.

Duncan's eyes were open, but he hadn't yet exhaled; was still holding that breath, wanting to sift a little longer through the macabre flotsam.

Although the likelihood was good that someone had stopped payment on his reality check, it had by no means reached a foregone conclusion. In fact, he was feeling quite lucid, despite some cheap tequila that now had his brain shimmering like a patch of sun-baked asphalt.

Not too long ago, Rachel had finally come out and accused him of being an alcoholic. Insulted, he'd quickly countered that he was a drunk, not an alcoholic. Alcoholics, he explained, went to meetings.

In his right hand was a cordless phone, one he'd been caressing, fondling, petting for the last four hours or so. In a few minutes he would have to call the college and talk with Matt Doyle, Dean of Criminal Justice, and advise him that he would not be in today, as he was sick. Although *psychotic* might be the better clinical term, he had no desire to leave his good friend and boss with mental pictures of him naked and apish on his roof, throwing feces at passing cars. And Matt Doyle was just the sort of guy to drudge up those very images, being an ex-cop himself.

His idle cuddling of the phone was not manifest anticipation of that call, but rather for another he would very soon have to make.

The morning sun was just now snooping through the vertical blinds, revealing upon each burgundy slat Juanita's streaked endeavors with a damp sponge.

Lazy as well as loco, he thought.

"You look like something the cat dragged in," Rachel observed from behind a mask of facial cream the color of jade. She was in a knee-length blue silk robe with big white orchids. Little balls of cotton were pinned between her painted toes.

Duncan thought she looked like a geisha with a sheep-kicking fetish.

"You didn't come to bed," she said. "Been down here all night?"

He nodded, a bit bewildered. Last he checked, "down here" was the Dog House. And after having confessed his love affair with Patricia Bently, he was damned surprised that he wasn't staring down at a Motel Six continental breakfast.

"It's a bit early for that, don't you think?" she said, pointing to the shot glass and bottle of tequila on his desk.

"Early?" he said. "In dog years, it's practically dinnertime."

"Uh-huh," she said, looking at him curiously. "How did it go with that Mike Dillard guy?"

"*Mitch* Dillard," he said, more suspicious than surprised. "And what makes you think I saw him?"

She smiled. "I just know."

Well, Super Sleuth she was not. After all, it had been his very intention to do just that. He was still a little jumpy, he supposed. No. A lot jumpy, and the last thing he needed to be right now was paranoid. But he was definitely not going to relive those events with Rachel; not now. He didn't need his wife placating him with phony smiles and goo-goo talk while she phoned the state hospital.

"The guy was okay", he said, staring again at Chagall's stone-signed litho. "He had nothing to do with what happened to Amy." He clucked, then added sourly, "Whatever *that* might have been." Then, more chipper: "Got a joke for ya. Two nuns are bicycling through town, as they often do. One says, 'Hey, I've never come this way before.' And the other nun says, 'Yeah, it's the cobblestones.'"

"Uh-huh," she grunted, obviously too afraid to laugh lest she fragment the moo goo gai pan on her face. "So, what was it like playing detective again?"

"The flood of sweet sentiment was more than I could bear."

"Great," she said. "So, what's with the Chagall?"

"The what?" Duncan said, baffled.

She pointed: "The Chagall. You've been staring at it. Is it crooked or something?"

Duncan ignored her question. "I have to call her, Rachel."

Rachel grew silent, then disappeared back into the bathroom.

What am I going to tell Patricia? How am I going to tell her? Duncan had been asking himself those questions all morning and, so far, had not heard back with any sane suggestions.

All serious psychosis aside, he was now convinced that something had been set into motion. But he was still short an abstract, so what could he possibly say to Patricia—or anyone else, for that matter—without coming off as a total loon? *Hi, Patricia! Just thought I'd call and let you know what a hell of an impression you left, seeing how my ten-year-old daughter not only looks exactly like yours did at the same age, but actually believes herself to be your daughter! So, how've ya been?*

Hell, if he approached it like that, he thought, then he might as well include the news that all Ansel Adams pictures were about to be recalled by the Department of Agriculture, having been deemed a threat to all crops, gardens, and old hippie photographers.

Pesky slugs.

He poured another shot.

No, the only way to get Patricia's undivided attention would be to plop Amy right on her doorstep.

Still, he had to call her, to prime the situation. Regardless of her reaction, Duncan could say that she had at least been warned. And if for nothing else, he blandly thought, meeting Katherine would prepare him for what Amy would look like in eleven years.

Rachel reappeared with a toothbrush in her mouth. "I'm not real keen on this, Dunc. Besides, isn't it just a tad early to be calling on ex-lovers?"

"It's mid-morning on the East coast," he reminded her.

"Well, I see you thought of everything," she said, shoulders sagging, as if he'd personally created the time zones just to facilitate the phone call.

He glowered at her. "Look, Miss Saigon, I think we both know it's necessary."

Giving her toothbrush a breather, she folded her arms across her chest. "Alright, but let *me* talk to the slut."

He rolled his bloodshot eyes. "Jesus, Rachel, that horse is deceased already."

"Oh, hell" she said, brushing again, "they probably don't even live there anymore."

Duncan just stared at the phone.

Astonished, Rachel yanked the toothbrush again from her mouth. "You've already tracked her down, haven't you, detective!"

"Please, it's not like I hired Sherlock Holmes at great expense," he said. "Information didn't have a listing for a Patricia Bently in Rock Bay, but it did have one for her mother, Joan Pendleton. She still lives at the same address as when I'd met her, the very one Amy gave the paramedics. Patricia had only taken me there a few times, so I suppose that's why it didn't jump right out at me at the hospital."

Her eyes lit up. "She took you home to meet Mom? How charming."

Without making a face, Duncan swallowed the remark. "Anyway, back then, Mrs. Pendleton wasn't doing so hot," he said. "Arthritis, I think. And as I recall it, Patricia was planning to move in and take care of her. Maybe that's why Amy gave that address, because it's where Patricia and Katherine are living now." His hands came off his lap and spread out, as if to catch a low-thrown basketball. "Of course, I'm just speculating."

"Of course you are," she said. "I mean, what reasons would I have to doubt that you would be anything but totally on the up-and-up with me."

"Damn it, Rachel, I never lied to you," he said. "I just...didn't tell you."

"Spoken like a true man," she proclaimed. "With those kinds of scruples, you're a shoe-in for Commander-in-Chief."

Duncan shook his head, ashamed of himself. "Jesus, you're right. I'm sorry."

She emancipated a long sigh, their paranormal situation obviously winning over her feminine principles. "Okay, call her. But I want to be here when you do."

"I have an even better idea," he said. "When I make the call, why don't you just pick up in the other room, then you can eavesdrop to your heart's content."

This proposal writhed inside Duncan, not so unlike the bag of worms Patricia would open if she felt in the mood to reminisce. Just the wrong word, the wrong phrase and Patricia could have him on his knees begging for mercy in a variety of civil and criminal poses. He quailed. Rachel now knew of his affair with Patricia Bently, but she didn't know the whole story. Not the half of it.

"Eavesdrop," Rachel grinned mischievously. "*Now* you're thinking like a woman."

"This concerns both of us, Rachel," he reminded her, "because it concerns Amy."

"I agree," she said, walking toward the door. "Try her now."

Duncan nodded, then dialed the number.

Rachel picked up on the other extension.

"One ringy-dingy," he said, overcome with a childish urge to heckle her. "Two ringy-dingies—"

"Grow up," Rachel said.

Please don't be there, he thought. But his bull's-eye intuition told him she would be.

"Hello?" answered a lady's voice.

Duncan paused, then: "Uh, Patricia? Patricia Bently?"

Incertitude hung in the pause. Then: "This is she."

"Hi, Patricia, this is...is Duncan McNeil," he confessed, the words clicking on the parched roof of his mouth.

For a moment, Duncan was sure he had only a conch pressed to his ear.

"Patricia?" he prompted.

"My God, you're the last person I thought I'd ever hear from," she finally, somberly, replied.

"Yeah," Duncan said. "It's been awhile. Geez, almost—"

"Twelve years," she said. "Last time I saw you, you were leaving the hospital in a wheelchair."

"I'll never forget how the sun felt on my face," he said. "But...I don't recall you ever being at the hospital."

"Your wife and police buddies were around, so Katherine and I just sort of watched you from a distance."

He winced. "Wow. I mean, I had no idea..."

"The prefix on my caller ID indicates that you're phoning from California. Is that right?"

"Yes, LA."

"Uh-huh," she said suspiciously. "My question is, why would *you* be calling from anywhere at all?"

"Well, it's about my daughter," he began. "Funny story. You see, she's in the hospital and, oddly enough, she told the hospital staff that she lives at the same address that...well, you're currently at."

"I don't remember you having a daughter—"

"I didn't...not, not when I, you—"

"She's how old then?"

"She's ten."

"Ten", she said timidly, as if haunted by that number.

There was a tremendously long pause, and Duncan was almost sure she'd hung up.

Finally, Patricia cleared her throat. "What's your daughter's name?"

"Amy."

She bounced the name back to him. Then: "Assuming that this isn't a joke—and I'm not—that would be quite the coincidence, don't you think, for your daughter to give my address as her place of residence?"

"Well, there's more," Duncan said. "At one point, Amy also believed that her...that her name was Katherine Bently."

"This *is* a joke, you sick bastard!" Patricia snarled.

"Whoa, calm down, calm down," Duncan softly urged. "Why would you think that?"

"You know why!"

"No, I swear, I..."

Patricia was bawling now. "Katherine's been missing for eleven years!"

Duncan nearly fell out of his chair. *Missing for eleven years?*

"Oh, Jesus," he said. "Patricia, I'm so sorry—"

"Screw you, McNeil! No matter how indebted I am to you, it will never be enough for me to tolerate this...this kind of bullshit!"

Duncan stood up. "Patricia, don't hang up! Please, there's something else—"

"This isn't a joke, Mrs. Bently," Rachel interjected. "I promise you."

"Who the hell are you?" Patricia demanded, sniffling.

"I'm Rachel, Duncan's wife."

She cackled. "Oh, I see. The family that tricks together sticks together."

"Listen," Duncan said, "I...we have a picture of you and Katherine, all dressed up in western get-up. It was found in Rock Bay—"

"So?"

"So," Duncan said, "Katherine is approximately ten years old in the photo, and she's the spitting image of Amy, could be her identical twin."

Having controlled her emotions somewhat, Patricia said to Duncan, "I remember that picture. It's on the fireplace mantel. I'm heading over to it right now, as a matter of fact. But if I remember correctly, it was taken *after* you disappeared from our lives. So how and where did you get it?"

Duncan waited for Rachel to respond.

"Well..." he started.

"The Olde Tyme Photography Studio in Rock Bay," Rachel finally said. "I saw it on display in the window. I didn't know about you or Katherine then, but for some reason I had to have it."

"You know," Patricia said, "I think you should both be ashamed of yourselves. Especially you, *hero!* Now, if you'll excuse me, I have to make a phone call to the telephone company and request that my number be changed immediately. Goodbye."

"No, wait!" Duncan yelled, "Please don't hang—ahhh, shit!"

"Let her go, Dunc," Rachel said, then disconnected.

Duncan flopped back down into his chair. *Oh my God. Katherine Bently went missing over a decade ago.*

Elbows on the desk, Duncan rested his face in his hands. He was still bothered about not having immediately recognized the name Katherine Bently when he first heard it come from the guard, then the nurse, at the hospital. He supposed he could forgive himself that. He wasn't a pup anymore. But to have still remained clueless after discovering its relationship to Rock Bay as he read the admissions form—that should have set off all sorts of red flags and obnoxious buzzers.

The *essence* of that turbulent time had not been forgotten; yet, somehow, in a censoring sort of way, the players had been.

But now everything was so clear. The images he'd captured just yesterday were still fresh, drying on the walls of his mind. And today the ones he continued to pull from the emulsion tray radiated with a sheen that was almost supernatural. Those memories were coming back to him with such speed and startling clarity that the present seemed vague and distant in comparison.

He wasn't so much bothered that the distance between forgotten and remembered had closed on him so quickly—as any number of stimuli can provoke lost memories, he knew—but rather by the uncanny detail the memories continued to bring. Queerly, he felt suddenly on the verge of living two different lives simultaneously, as if those memories of Patricia and Katherine Bently had snapped their demarcating tethers of time and were now floating back into the here and now of his consciousness.

In either reality or delusion, though, he was quite sure that Rachel wasn't going to like sharing him again.

Rachel entered with a towel in her hair, the goop gone from her face. "Are you thinking what I'm thinking? I mean, Christ, over eleven years—"

"Look, I know where you're heading, but I think we can dismiss reincarnation as the culprit here. Besides, missing doesn't mean dead."

"Is that what the cop in you believes?"

Duncan shook his head. "No, the optimist."

Rachel laughed. "My dear man, you don't have an optimistic bone in your body."

"Okay," he grudgingly agreed, "my pragmatic side, then."

Scooting one of the director's chairs to the front of his desk, she sat down. "Look, Duncan, Katherine's obviously dead. We're dealing with something here that may very well defy rational explanation. I know that's hard for you to accept. It's hard for me, too, but I'm afraid we're going to have to start approaching this from a very different perspective."

He poured himself another shot. "I already have."

"Oh? And what might that be?" she said, then saw the answer in his eyes. "Oh no, you want to take Amy to Rock Bay, don't you?"

"Yes."

"To see your old flame."

"Yes again."

She was bristling now. "And what's that going to prove?"

"I'm not sure."

She threw up her arms. "Well, it wouldn't be a total loss. I mean, you could still get your dick wet!"

Although his judicious side strongly advised against it, he laughed at her. "Could you stop it for just five minutes? Could you? Just long enough to hear me out?"

Smoldering, Rachel folder her arms. "Alright. I'm listening."

"I don't know what will happen if I take Amy to see Patricia. But I know it has to be done, that's all."

"Why?"

"Because," Duncan said, "I don't think Amy's safe here anymore." *Maybe none of us are*, he almost added. But even if he decided to tell her everything else, every sordid detail about his visit with the photographer, he wasn't about to include Gamble's restaurant recommendation. It was just too damn silly, if not downright terrifying in its implications.

Suddenly concerned, Rachel said, "Why do you think that?"

"Something the photographer told me last night. A man by the name of Gamble may have an interest in Amy."

"Whoa!" Rachel said, pushing out her palms. "Wait a minute! You're telling me that the same guy who took Amy's school pictures knows another guy who has an 'interest' in our daughter? What *kind* of interest, Duncan?"

"I don't know."

"Is he a talent scout from Sesame Street? A pedophile? What?"

"I said, I don't know."

Rachel leaned forward, grabbing the edge of his desk with both hands. "I want the police notified immediately. I want this photographer guy questioned—"

"He's dead."

Rachel eased back into her chair, eyes narrowing in suspicion. "Really?" she said, stretching out the word like it was taffy.

Duncan simply smiled. "I didn't kill him, if that's what you're thinking."

Rachel smiled back. "You're not telling me everything."

"No, I'm not," he confessed. "But if you'll go with us, I'll catch you up on events. We'll get Amy, then hop the first flight available."

"I can't. In case you forgot, I have a commercial to shoot tomorrow morning. But you just go right on ahead keeping secrets, Captain Donut! Juanita and I will take very good care of Amy."

"I'm taking Amy with me."

"Oh no you're not."

"Don't fight me on this, Rachel."

She bolted up from her chair. "Tooth and nail!" she promised, then stomped away, leaving cotton balls in her wake. "P.S." she added. "Go fuck yourself!"

Funny, he thought. *That's just what that guy Gamble had said in his postscript, more or less.*

3.

Patricia Bently raised her hands toward the sylvan mantle above the fireplace, stopped suddenly, then lowered them. She rubbed her fingers against both her pant legs, wiping away the natural oils that had built up since her shower three hours earlier, not wanting to smudge the glass or the beautiful pewter frame. Or worse, have it slip from her grasp and fall to the brick hearth below.

She raised her hands once more and again hesitated at the edge of the mantle, a plank of knotty pine sanded to a silken grade.

She just couldn't bring herself to touch the photo, afraid that if she did her daughter's image would disappear, leaving her alone in the picture.

But that was stupid. No, it was downright silly. She'd never had this problem before.

"McNeil, you crazy bastard," she mumbled to herself. "What do you think you're doing?"

"Patty dear, who was that on the phone?" Joan Pendleton said as she ambled into the room, dusting rag in one hand, a fresh replacement of doilies in the other.

Nonchalantly, Patricia said, "Oh, that was just Tooney." Before the rows of pictures, she pretended to be reminiscing, keeping her puffy eyes away from her mother's scrutiny. If she told her mother who had really phoned, more importantly *why* (not that she believed any of his bullshit for a second), she'd have Patricia on the first plane to Los Angeles, ready to commit the crime of *this* century, complete with her own homemade ladder and a medium to contact Bruno Richard Hauptmann just in case she should lose her nerve.

"Jim Tooney from the bowling alley?" her mother said.

"No, Ma," she said, rolling her eyes, "Jim Tooney from Jed's Bait and Tackle. Christ, how many Tooneys do you know in this rathole?"

After giving it serious thought, she said, "Well, just the one, I suppose. What did he want?"

"League jackets are in." That was a truth, but not a recent one.

Poised with rag over an imitation Tiffany lamp shade, Joan said, "Well, I was hardly eavesdropping, but the conversation sounded pretty spirited for just a jacket, dear—"

"Look, Mother, not that it's any of your business, but he...he just keeps asking me to go out with him, and I finally had to let him down hard, is all." Another fib. God, she hated stretching them out like this. And, although her mother may have been failing in many respects, her bullshit detector pinged away just fine much of the time.

"I see," Joan said. "But really, dear, you *do* need to get out more."

"As you remind me all the time."

Patricia stared at the photo. Then, finally, she turned to her mother: "Ma, you still think...Katherine's alive?" She knew the answer, of course, and hated herself for asking. But, at least for the moment, she needed to share her mother's perennial delusion.

Joan didn't even look up. "Of course she is, dear," she said. "You just mark my words. One day, Kathy's going to show up on our doorstep and the mystery will be over."

Over? Patricia wondered, turning back to her daughter's face. *Or just beginning?*

4.

Juanita Santiago stood in the pediatrics' waiting area, trying to summon enough courage to embrace the candy machine and shake it hard enough to free a Heath Bar from its clutches. The traitorous machine had eaten her last bit of change, and she was hungry.

She pointed at the candy bar. "You are mine. I pay for you fair and square."

Juanita had spent the night at the hospital, in Amy's room. She'd gotten there late, but the staff had no problem with her staying. In fact, some of the nurses even brought in a special chair for her, one that reclined.

While Señor Duncan and Mrs. McNeil had argued over some old and interesting picture, she'd returned to the hospital. Her need to be with Amy had grown dire. Something was coming. She didn't yet know what that *something* was, but it sure wasn't going to be Julio Iglesias. And that was really too bad as far as Juanita was concerned.

When she arrived last night, she'd been told at the nurses' station that something loud and strange had occurred in Amy's room just prior to her arrival. The nurses had been vague, and even laughed about it, but Juanita was sure it was no laughing matter, and chastised herself severely for not having gotten there sooner.

She'd been neglectful of her responsibility to Amy, had not been on her toes, and vowed it would never happen again.

Having decided that a bear hug would be more than her short, flabby arms could handle, she looked both ways, kissed the rosary in her right hand, then punched the plexiglass.

It rattled pretty good, smarted even better, but nothing fell.

She glanced down the hallway where Amy was in her bed, staring down at a bowl of oatmeal, toast and jelly, two sausage links, a cup of apple sauce, a cup of hot chocolate, orange juice, cranberry juice, and a small banana. What a spread.

Kissing her beads, she *kicked* the machine.

Overestimating her strength, she stumbled backward, falling on her rear.

Heavily cushioned, she got up uninjured, dusted herself off, then peered into the machine's repository. She hadn't gotten her Heath, but did succeed in dislodging a packet of plain M&M's, a roll of breath mints, and some angry stares and finger-shaking from a few nurses down the hall.

She looked at their respective prices, and discovered that the combined cost of both items exceeded that of the Heath bar.

To hell with it, she thought, then withdrew her pilfered snacks. It was stealing, no doubt about it. But hunger was a cruel temptress. Besides, she'd been saying her rosaries all morning. A few more weren't going to hurt.

A doctor approached. A very tall, handsome man, he wore green scrubs and a warm smile. He stopped in front of the candy machine. A beautiful silver necklace hung around his neck. "I understand you stayed with the Bently girl last night," he said. His voice was captivating.

"Oh, no, señor," Juanita said, speaking cautiously. "I stay with Amy McNeil."

He deposited two quarters in the machine. "Tomorrow, you must go with the McNeils and Katherine to Rock Bay."

"Katherine?" Juanita said, mystified. "Rock Bay?"

The doctor entered the code, and the item fell almost silently into the tray below. "Very soon, the little girl you stayed with last night will no longer be the entirety of Amy McNeil, but will resume to be mostly Katherine Bently."

Her hands trembling, Juanita whispered, "But, señor, where then is my Amy?"

"Here and there."

"Are you sent here from God?"

"Not...exactly."

Fearing the worst, Juanita brought her rosary to her bosom and took a cautious step backward. "The Devil?"

Humored, the doctor reached into the machine, removed his selection, and said, "I'm not here on *his* behalf, either."

Each time the doctor spoke, Juanita was waylaid by a variety of smells, and experienced protracted though very subtle moments of déjà vu. They weren't singular aromas, but powerful ensembles, as if someone with an eyedropper were selectively dripping water on the dehydrated patches of her life and thereby reconstituting the essence of each chosen moment. The visual clarity that followed was no less extraordinary.

The experiences, however, were sorely bittersweet, and her eyes were misting with melancholy.

Juanita stared at the doctor. "How do I know you are not just crazy talking?"

"Here," he said, "I'll trade you." He handed her the candy bar, then took her items. He opened the M&M's as he began walking away, plopping them one at a time into his mouth.

The package in her hand felt too thin, as if nothing existed within the wrappers.

"You must not let anything happen to Katherine," the doctor said without looking back. "The day is nearly upon us. At all costs, we must protect the Shallows." He raised a finger and added, "And don't forget: What's the most important meal of the day?"

Juanita stared down at her candy bar. "Blessed Mother of Christ, give me strength," she whispered.

Carefully removing the wrapper, she found a communion wafer, loose within the foil.

The instant she placed the unleavened bread on her tongue, nausea blossomed in her stomach. Fearing that she'd been poisoned, she turned to vomit—then a strange thing occurred: she instantly found herself being chaperoned across a vast pulsing landscape. One that might be heaven, she thought.

This chaperone, a dark, pillow-like thing, sped ahead of her, then morphed into a portal that she fell through—with no sense of up and down—into a chasm where an incredible presence seemed to sweep her away. A warm, tender wind. She: like a dandelion seed riding a gentle chinook.

With profound gratitude, a voice said, "Time has fallen about your face like a leather veil, yet the raiments of servitude still wear well about you. I am thankful. The road journeyed has led you back to me. But there remains a length to go, so know now that if you pass on my right the fields are thin and bane, pass on my left and the river runs but a fiery wind. Continue onward and you will be blessed with the Father's own mighty hand." A warm, blustery pause, then: "Do you wish to linger a moment and receive?"

Tears poured from Juanita's eyes, and she knew this gentle voice could only belong to the Holy Mother.

Shuddering, trying to muster all her strength, Juanita replied, "*Si*."

The Holy Mother asked again, with emphasis: "Do you wish to *linger* a moment?"

"*Si, si*, yes!"

"Then receive."

Although she hadn't remembered closing them, Juanita opened her eyes—and was back in the hospital. For a brief moment, the sensation that she was still floating remained, and she nearly fell head-first into the window of the vending machine.

Hands against the Plexiglass, she steadied herself as her equilibrium returned.

Like an inmate with a guilty conscience, she then patted herself all over, feeling for contraband. She really wasn't expecting to find any, but when crossing a border separating two different worlds, it was best to check oneself for all kinds of hitchhikers. These were tips she'd learned long ago from her many encounters with the Border Patrol and other customs officials, and was thankful that they'd come in handy once again, at least as cautious gestures.

Just what had she received? And what was this place the doctor had called *the Shallows?*

Well, she felt all right. No, better than all right. She felt...*in charge.* More so than usual.

Looking down, she saw the candy wrapper at her feet and was suddenly ashamed. She was tidy, not a pig. Not like Señor Duncan, tossing his dirty Fruit of the Looms here and there.

As she bent down for the wrapper, she noticed a reflection in the Plexiglass of someone behind her. It was an old man in a wheelchair. Gray and gaunt, he was nearly lost inside a red and black flannel robe. And his fuzzy slippers, each one planted squarely against a waffled footrest, reminded her of snow shoes. There was a pile of quarters in his lap, maybe five dollars worth, and he was staring up at her, his concern soured with impatience.

She was too afraid to ask how long he'd been waiting.

"You one of them narcolepsy people," he said, "just shut off whenever and wherever the damn thing strikes ya? Or are ya just plain catatonic, hon?"

Juanita put a hand to her mouth. "Oh, please forgive. I did not know you were there!"

Anxious, as if about to cross a busy highway in his electric two-wheeler, he looked both ways, then said, "Apology accepted. Now move aside, señorita. If they catch me this time, they'll move the goddamn snacks again, and I'll never find 'em."

5.

As Duncan and Rachel entered the room, Juanita immediately jumped from her chair and assumed a rigid stance beside Amy's bed.

Duncan countered with a brisk salute. "At ease."

The moment she saw them, Amy immediately sensed the silence surrounding her parents. Both were pretending that nothing was wrong, of course, all for her benefit. But she could tell they'd been fighting. Something they did a lot more of these days. Judging by their faces—the wider the smile, the hairier the fight—it must have been one heck of a knock-down-drag-out, she decided.

Beneath the sheets, Amy rubbed the glass fragment between her right forefinger and thumb like a worry stone. Having to stay overnight in a hospital was probably her own fault, something she could have prevented if she weren't so young, so...childish. And not knowing why she was here only deepened her guilt. She could recall the previous day's events just fine, up until the time she was about to have her picture taken. Then she'd wakened in this room, in front of that window, all the in-between points seemingly erased.

Other than the dreams...

To hold on to those brief but distinct memories, afraid that they might somehow go away, too, she tightly squeezed the object.

Duncan bent over and kissed her forehead. "Ready to get out of here, pumpkin?"

She smelled Old Spice, her favorite. And booze. "Sure. But it's been okay here," she said, hoping to placate her father. He'd been worried sick, she was sure, as he didn't usually start drinking until dinnertime.

"Amy?" Rachel said, as if she wasn't quite sure. "How are you feeling, sweetheart?"

"Great," she said.

Duncan took some bills out of his wallet, then handed them to Juanita. "Here. Chapel's open. First floor. The vendor out front has some quake-damaged dashboard Madonnas from Argentina, fifty-percent off. Knock yourself out."

Peeved, Rachel glanced sidelong at Duncan, then said to Juanita, "You look starved. Go on down to the cafeteria, hon. We'll catch up shortly."

"Thank you, Mrs. McNeil," Juanita said, then mumbled something in Spanish as she pushed by Duncan. She waddled out the door, toward the elevators.

"Why do you and Juanita hate each other, Daddy?"

Jumping in, Rachel explained, "They don't hate each other, sweetheart. Your father's still bitter because I wouldn't let him hire that cute little *thang* from Memphis."

In a passable British accent, Duncan countered, "The young professional to whom your mother is referring was more than skilled for the job. It was her long legs, full lips, and firm bosom that disqualified her. As for Juanita, well—"

"They just sense in each other things that make them both...uncomfortable," Rachel said.

Amy stared across at her toes as she wriggled them beneath the thin white sheets. "Like when I *sense* that you and Daddy have been fighting, even though you try to hide it?"

Rachel glanced at Duncan, abashed. "Yeah, something like that."

"Is it that obvious?" Duncan said.

Amy nodded.

Rachel cleared her throat. "Well, I won, if that makes any difference."

Leaning in, just inches from her ear now, Duncan said to Amy, "Smart girl. Very perceptive. Care to divulge any of your current feelings about Wall Street? Interactive Television? How many fathoms the Andria Gail is under?"

Amy giggled.

"Or maybe you're just plain psychic," he offered suspiciously, "like that Uri fellow we all saw on TV the other night."

He took the fork from her breakfast tray, then slowly swung it back and forth in front of her face like a hypnotist's pocket watch. "Now concentrate," he said slowly, deliberately drawing out the words. "I want you to bend this with your *miiiiiiind*."

She giggled even louder.

"I know you can *doooooo* it. Just pretend that your brain is a garbage *dispooooosal*."

Amy sank into her pillow, laughing uproariously.

"Go on, girl!" he prodded.

"I can't," Amy said, tittering as if her ribs were being goosed. She sensed the gaps closing, felt her guilt subsiding, and knew she was just moments away from walking out of this small, sanitary room and back into LA's hot autumn sunshine.

Rachel scooted a chair to the edge of the bed and sat. "How would you like to take a vacation, princess?"

Duncan's eyebrows shot upward, but he remained silent.

"A vacation?" Amy said, delighted. The glass in her hand began to tingle and burn slightly.

"Yes, with your father," she said, turning to Duncan's waylaid expression. "To Massachusetts."

"Lobster Country," her father said, pronouncing it *lobstah*, reminding her of the way her mom sometimes sounded.

"Rock Bay, to be exact," Rachel said. "My hometown."

On these last words, as if on cue, the glass in Amy's hand began to lose its solidity, becoming loose between her fingers like warm, runny dough. It tickled.

"Why are we going there?" Amy said, then recognized that something inside her knew, but was keeping it secret.

"To see an old friend of your father's," her mother said with a strained smile. "Someone you're going to like very much. And who's going to like you as well, I'm sure." She winked.

Amy was suddenly concerned. "But what about school?"

"You're in fourth grade, sweetheart, not Harvard Medical," her mother reminded.

"Oh, okay then," she said, satisfied. "But why can't you come?"

"I've got a commercial to shoot tomorrow. It's Mommy's big break, kiddo, and she can't miss it."

Duncan grinned. "Yeah, your mom's gonna—"

"Don't start," Rachel warned.

Entwining like rose vine, the warm, resinous glass spread urgently up and around her wrist and lower arm, tightening. Then she could feel it begin to seep parasitically into her pores, then her bloodstream. This did not alarm her, though; was not painful, or even uncomfortable. Oddly, it felt as natural as breathing air.

She lay back down. She did not cry out to her parents, for the nursing staff, did not hurl her arm out from beneath the covers, shouting "Look!" This was something personal, something no one else would understand. She'd realized this the moment her fingers rescued the fragment from the cold hospital floor.

Rachel leaned in. "Amy?"

Amy stared unblinkingly ahead. A wonderful sensation was surging through her body now, one that made her feel feather-heavy. Her surroundings wavered into clearer focus, and the fringes of her peripheral vision began to stretch toward the front of her, as if the walls, the ceiling, were nothing but Hollywood *trompe l'oeil* being rolled away from her soap-operatic sound stage.

Everything continued traveling forward until she felt drawn into the center of the room and could see everything without turning her head. It was as if her eyes, her pupils, had elongated, had wrapped around the sides of her head and converged on the backside. Her vision had been distended to a full three-hundred-and-sixty degrees.

The reality seized her then that she was not seeing with her eyes, but was experiencing a truly magical form of cognizance. And she was confident that it would extend infinitely in any or all directions, given the notion.

As she lay there, she re-experienced an unfathomable passing of time. Starting out as a protozoan in the warm virgin oceans of Earth, she saw this one-celled animal through every transmutation, branching out with each descendant, and its descendant's descendants, aware of every thought, every minuscule twinkling of consciousness, every glint and pulsation of energy leading up to its species' present awareness. The cycle would repeat, each time a different organism, a different evolutionary process. Then onward to different worlds. Finally, after countless eternities, she'd come to know everything there was to know about *everything*. She didn't understand the workings of the universe and all within it—she'd become the universe. Or perhaps something even grander.

"Amy?" Rachel prodded. "Honey, are you all right?"

Amy winked back in, her binocular vision restored. Something colossal recoiled out of her at such velocity that she was certain nothing had been there at all.

Then a portion of that something returned. And nested. Something incredible.

"Y'okay, kiddo?" Duncan said.

Realizing only a few seconds had passed instead of consecutive millennia, Amy glanced around the room, wanting to inspect her surroundings a bit more closely before committing herself to an answer.

"I feel fine," she said finally. "Can we have McDonald's for lunch?"

6.

Doctor Constance Strickland entered the room in a graceful flurry. So many patients, so little time. "How are we feeling this morning?" she asked the chart in her hand.

This bit of insouciance provoked Duncan. "Well, *I'm* feeling just ducky, thanks," he offered, "despite a little indigestion I picked up this morning from a tequila worm. And my beautiful daughter here appears to be spry as a March hare." He turned to Rachel. "And if you'll overlook the scowl on my wife's face, you'll probably find that she's just as happy and healthy as a pig in a turd patch."

Amy giggled.

Rachel elbowed Duncan in the ribs. He grunted.

Strickland looked up from her chart, countering with a sense of humor that surprised Duncan. "Considering your abundant use of animal analogies," she observed, "one might be inclined to believe that you were raised on a farm—if one overlooks all the other obvious signs, that is."

"Hey, not bad," Duncan said.

"You'll have to excuse my husband," Rachel said. "He has a particular dislike for hospitals."

Strickland smiled at Duncan. "Bad childhood memories? Let me guess: Tonsillectomy? Appendectomy?"

"Gunshotectomy," Duncan said.

"Oh?" Strickland said warily. "War wound?"

Duncan shifted uncomfortably. "You could say that."

"Show her your scars, Daddy," Amy said.

Strickland waved a hand. "Keep your clothes on, I'm not a scar monger." She looked at Amy and added, "But I'm sure they're *quite* awful."

Amy nodded slowly.

"Duncan was shot in the line of duty," Rachel said, then glanced at Duncan as if she might have said too much.

Strickland said, "You're a police officer?"

"Was," Duncan said stiffly, wanting to end the conversation. "It was a long time ago in a galaxy far, far away."

"He's a hero," Amy vouched, now sitting in the middle of her bed, raring to plunge right into the subject. "He saved some lives and got a medal for it."

Duncan gazed at Amy with eyes that said, *secrets should never be revealed*, then raised a finger to his lips.

Amy said, "They still hurt him, too, especially at night. The scars, I mean. Sometimes I can hear him crying—"

"Amy," Duncan sighed.

"She's just concerned, Duncan," Rachel said. "Maybe it's not just psychosomatic, like you say. Maybe now's a good time to—"

"To what?" Duncan said. "Air my dirty laundry?"

Rachel exhaled loudly, dropping her shoulders so low that Duncan was sure they would disengage from their sockets. She said, "My God, Duncan, what is so horrible about being a hero? I can understand a healthy display of modesty, but you become downright defensive whenever the subject comes up. It's as if—"

"Just drop it!" he snapped.

Strickland jumped in. "I can see that this is a very touchy subject, so before we leave the matter entirely, let me just say that I can refer a doctor who specializes in post-traumatic disorders, if you like."

Duncan guffawed. "Been there, done that."

Strickland raised both hands in defense. "Okay, okay, I'll take that as a no and consider the matter closed. Now, let me take one last look at your daughter before I sign her walking papers."

"Stubborn, stubborn man," Rachel said.

"Look, it was a long time ago—"

"I know, I know, in a galaxy far, far away."

But not far enough, Duncan knew. His own personal time-traveling rocket ship had taken him back thousands of times. And each and every one of those times he was forced to make one of two decisions through the narrow sights of a Smith and Wesson, and each and every one of those times he'd chosen the same one. He'd more than entertained the idea that it was the infant in the deranged woman's arms who finally swayed him into making that decision, that tiny little bundle who could not have understood its mother's heroin addiction any more than it could have the true reason why he and his partner were there that tragic night.

Taking two bullets to save the child's life would have certainly been a noble reason for his decision, one that would at least justify the medal hanging on his wall.

But the sad and lonely truth that forced him to lower his gun that night, he'd eventually admitted to himself, was death. He'd wanted to die, to make final atonement for sins committed against his brethren officers, against all that was supposed to be decent, against himself.

But he hadn't died. Close, but no cigar.

Deep down, and sometimes not so deeply, death still tempted him; called out to him in the quiet night, perched like a sylph on black, memory-worn rock, urging him, taunting him, singing to him as he lay there, listening.

And he was convinced that the only thing that had so far kept him from dancing to that temptress' song was the adoration staring up at him from his daughter's eyes.

Rachel nudged him from his trance.

"...photosensitive epilepsy," Strickland was saying, "is normally caused by light passing through regularly spaced objects, like trees or light poles along a roadway, as seen from a moving automobile. Stationary patterns of striped lines. Even the flickering of a television set or computer monitor. In Japan some years back, for example, the same thing happened to over six hundred children. All of them simultaneously suffered seizures while watching a popular animated TV show. Cycling colors were blamed."

"In Amy's case, a strobe flash," Rachel said.

"Exactly," said Strickland.

"Is that your diagnosis?" Duncan said.

"Everything else checks normal." she said. "But if she experiences any other attacks, mild or otherwise, then bring her in immediately. But really, I'm not the least bit worried. Your daughter here is about as hearty as they come." She offered a confident smile. "I'm sure this was a just a one-time thing."

Yesterday, Duncan would have accepted the "Photosensitive Epilepsy" diagnosis without question. His faith in doctors had yet to be aggrieved by the same suspicions of malfeasance that had long ago ruined his trust in nearly every other occupation.

Of course, had those doctors twelve years ago not performed a medical miracle by saving his sorry ass...

But now, after last night's escapades at the photographer's house, it had become wickedly obvious that Western medicine was going to fail his daughter, though not through any fault of its own. What Amy really needed, he feared, was a voodoo priest to shake a headless chicken over her body and mumble purging incantations, as it might be the only way to rid her of that possessive spirit called Katherine.

He sensed that Rachel wasn't buying the seizure explanation either and, like himself, was just being patient and polite.

"I'm not sick anymore?" Amy said.

"Nope," Strickland said. "And if you stay away from stampeding elephants and fatty foods, then I think you'll be just fine." She scribbled her name on the release form. "You're free to go, sweetie."

Juanita, who'd been standing in the doorway for God knew how long, rushed over with a bagel and cream cheese in one hand and a brown shopping bag in the other.

"Here," Juanita said, handing Amy the bag and keeping the bagel for herself. "I wash these for you last night. Socks, your favorite jeans and shirt." She leaned in, and whispered discreetly, "Your panties are hiding in-between."

Amy was smiling, but not at Juanita. She was beaming at the doctor. "That's a beautiful necklace," she said.

The doctor smiled back, then pulled the chain up from her blouse, revealing a round, silver emblem. "Thank you. It was a gift from a *friend*."

Right before Duncan's eyes, Amy had relayed some kind of understanding to the doctor. And he was equally sure the doctor had assented with a relative expression.

Whatever just happened between them, he thought, definitely went beyond any kind of doctor-patient relationship. It was too deep, too personal. Was more like...camaraderie. But the more he thought about it, even that seemed too soft a description.

He chewed on it some more, searching.

Then it finally came to him: Allegiance.

Then, coming from somewhere inside the sane quadrant of his mind, a strangled voice said, *Don't you think the world has enough conspiracies without you adding to the pot?*

He didn't answer the voice, just regarded the blood pressure machine mounted on the wall, wondering if there was any similar instrument available for the healthy monitoring of one's sanity.

7.

As they neared the nurses' station, Duncan led Rachel aside.

"Why the sudden change of heart?" he said.

She crumpled a piece of Juicy Fruit into her mouth. "During the drive here, I reminded myself that it's not you who's crazy. It's the situation. Your dick, on the other hand, could use some therapy. Anyway, given the circumstances, a trip to Rock Bay to see whatsername does feel like the next logical step. Therefore, I would only be pampering my own womanly sensitivities if I didn't let Amy go with you to Massachusetts."

"I'm...flattered. I guess."

She reached up and jabbed a finger into his chest: "Yeah? Well before you go and officially open up your own fan club, take note, buster. I'm still hugely pissed off about you and whatsername. I don't care if it happened twelve years ago or twelve minutes ago, you're just damned lucky I haven't called my lawyer."

"*Our* lawyer."

Sneering, she poked him again, harder.

Wincing from the pain, he said, "Now all I have to do is convince you to go with us. And don't try and tell me the commercial shoot is still holding you back."

Rachel sighed. "Look, you don't know how tempted I am. It's just that I...I don't think it would be a good idea, Dunc. I mean..."

"It's not like you to avoid a cat fight," he said. "Besides, Patricia's not your enemy, Rachel. This isn't about me and her."

She threw her head back and laughed, then reached into her purse and pulled out a twenty. "Here, go buy yourself a collie and a cane."

Duncan wasn't surprised. When trying to make a point, Rachel often engaged the theatrical. It was an occupational hazard.

He took the money. "I don't follow."

She rolled her eyes. "Would you please come off your guilt trip. Even a blind man would see all the so-called *coincidences* piling up. I mean, I can barely walk, the synchronicity's so deep. Aren't you getting it yet? You and Patricia *are* linked somehow, someway. And I have to tell you, it's scaring the living shit out of me."

As far as he was concerned, the only connection he and Patricia shared was their past love affair. And, of course, the events leading up to, and including, the night he was shot. He'd only told Rachel half the story, the affair part. But what Patricia's role in the incident, or the affair itself, could possibly have to do with doppelgangers, a dead photographer, a giant slug, and a limerick writer by the name of Gamble—

Hold on a second. From the moment he heard it, he'd been shamefully aware that the author of that jingle was referring to the night he was shot. The limerick didn't mention Patricia, or even allude to her, but it did talk about a child. Two, as a matter of fact.

He saved a child's life...And gained a dead one in the deal.

Just what did that mean?

True, the infant was unharmed that night, but it wasn't so much that he *saved* the child's life as it was his refusal to shoot and accidentally take it. But still...

And gained a dead one...

Patricia's daughter had been missing for more than a decade, and was more than likely dead. So, did that mean Amy really *was* the reincarnation of Katherine Bently?

Suddenly, Gamble's limerick was making a lot more sense, not that it was all that cryptic to begin with. He'd just been needing to give it some thought. Hell, maybe Rachel was on to something after all.

The twin issue was the kicker, of course. The uncanny resemblance Amy and Katherine shared, at least at their respective ages of ten, would have been remarkable enough had it occurred randomly. And the strong possibility that it *hadn't* was indication—if he wanted to accept it—of some kind of discriminative motive; one reaching beyond his and Patricia's scandalous history, yet still linked with it in a way he couldn't begin to fathom.

Okay, so maybe there *was* a link. Now that Rachel knew of the affair, he supposed he was just trying to keep the matter subdued; placate her (and maybe himself) by maintaining as much emotional distance as possible between Patricia and Katherine. But those kinds of sheltering maneuvers, he had to grudgingly admit, would only estrange him and everyone else further from the truth, from what was really happening.

It was time to stop avoiding the past, as toxic as some of it was.

He thought it odd that Rachel hadn't already accused him of being Katherine's real father, that he'd known Patricia far longer than he was admitting. But then, maybe she'd come to the same conclusion he had: what would be the odds of fathering two identical girls, eleven years apart, from two totally different women? If he had, in fact, impregnated Patricia so many years ago, he could have probably forced himself into accepting such a fluke. But he hadn't met Patricia Bently until a year into his marriage with Rachel. And that was a fact.

In the years before he and Rachel met, he'd been promiscuous as a cop. But there hadn't been so many women that he'd lost count, and when he did the math he'd only been with one woman during the time Patricia could have conceivably gotten pregnant with Katherine.

But...reincarnation? C'mon, a person could dislocate something, reaching that far.

A memory struck him then. His late partner, a real UFO buff, had once said to him: "If aliens landed on the White House lawn, millions of people would still not be convinced that extraterrestrial life exists. Why?

Simply because those people don't want to believe, they don't want their cozy little lives threatened. And you, my friend, are one of those inflexible chickenshits who'd switch from CNN's live coverage of such an event to *The Dukes of Hazard* simply to avoid the trauma."

Okay, so he was pigheaded.

Rachel walked up to him, holding out a can of soda. "Here, be a Pepper," she said.

Christ, he hadn't even realized she'd left him.

He took the can, popped the top. "I'll try and be more open-minded," he promised.

"Please do."

Amy and Juanita were waiting at the nurses' station. Juanita—Amy in one hand, a duffel bag in the other—looked like she was going to war.

"Let's get lunch," he said to Rachel.

She held out her hand. "Not so fast."

"What?"

"Give me back my twenty."

He reached into his trousers and brought out the folded bill. "I thought I was supposed to buy a gimp outfit with this?"

She snatched the bill from his fingers. "*You* don't need a costume. And from now on, you're mine. You'll be staying in *my* house, eating *my* food, driving *my* car, taking *my* daughter to New England, kicking around *my* maid." She took his hand. "Think of it as a surrogate divorce."

They began walking.

"Whatever happened to that sweet, innocent little lady I married back East?"

"She grew up."

"She got rowdy."

Rachel looked up into his eyes. "I have a feeling I'm going to have to."

"Maybe. Besides, you're right to be angry with me. I've had an ass-whipping coming."

"Long overdue," she agreed.

8.

It realized itself. It knew what it was, and what it wasn't.

It was what it wasn't. It wasn't what it was.

But it took great pleasure in its current form; liked the feel of the air, the snow upon its wings.

Oh, the pleasures I have known!

What it *was* was anything man wished it to be, chiseled from his own hard interpretations of evil. Literal personifications of any current and widely accepted illusions of malevolence. It could duplicate itself, masquerade as many, with each conjured form acting independently from the whole.

It was one of any number of spokes subservient to a new and evolving hub.

But it was no illusion. Man breathed life into it, sustaining it with his own belief in its existence.

It drew its life from man, and breathed life back into him.

It could hibernate without man. It had in the maelstrom before him. Man, though, could not exist without it. Man would perish without it, just as surely as he would without other forms of sustenance, spiritual and otherwise.

It was man. And it was not.

It could not remember *not being*. It had lived before man in nebulous, static form, but had nevertheless been conscious of itself. Only then had it known its true guise. Since, man had given it many, just as he is inclined to give physical, polar forms to those he calls Good; to give semblance to Jehovah, Christ, Buddha, God, and a host of others.

Man's preoccupation with putting faces on things best left faceless.

Despite whatever forms man imagined it to be, though, its essence remained unchanged.

It wasn't what it was. And it was what it wasn't.

But very soon it would become something different, was going to metamorphose into a revelation, a truer, more mature image of itself. Was going to alter forever man's naive interpretations of Evil. And, in consequence, it knew that man's exegeses of Good would have to also change. Of this it was sure.

For it was both Good and Evil.

And it was not.

A *"monkey-bat" indeed!*

Investing itself within the white weather, it circled above the small Iowa town, waiting for the little girl.

The last one.

The seventh angel.

9.

It was close to noon when they exited the hospital.

Amy shielded her eyes from the brightness, as if she'd just been rescued from an ogre's dungeon rather than the stark fluorescence of an infirmary. It was hot, the temperatures already well into the eighties. Large puddles of rainwater from last night's storm mottled the alleyway's east graveled shoulder, their edges slowly receding, still in shadow. Once the sun passed from behind the eclipsing structure, however, they would implode in quick fashion.

"Piggyback!" Amy instructed.

Duncan stopped, squatted. "Last train to McDonalds, have your tickets ready!"

Clearly distressed over the idea, Juanita nevertheless dropped her bag of items and hefted Amy onto Duncan's shoulders.

Amy threw her arms around her dad's neck, then spurred his sides. "Giddyup!"

Grabbing her ankles, Duncan slowly rose. "I'm a train, not a horse," he reminded her.

"I beg to differ," Rachel said to Amy. "Your father bears many equestrian likenesses. One in particular comes to mind."

"*Si,*" Juanita heartily agreed.

Duncan ignored them. Out of the three women in his household, he could handle Rachel and Juanita thinking him a horse's ass. But not Amy.

"Tickets, please," he hollered in true porter fashion.

Amy promptly kissed the top of his head.

"Paid in full!" he announced, smiling proudly.

As it had so many times in the past, especially the last twenty-some-odd hours, it struck him that if he were to lose Amy to illness, accident or goblin, he was confident that his remaining days would be few, tortured by an emptiness more agonizing than any medieval paring of the Cat's Paw, braiding on the Wheel, or skewering by the Iron Maiden.

His heart went out to Patricia Bently. No instrument of torment then or now could ever inflict the ferocious pain as the one that steals children. And he was in awe of those parents who still managed to persevere despite such inconceivable suffering.

Surely they were mad.

Mussing his hair, Amy said, "Can't you go any faster?"

"No faster," Juanita pleaded.

Abandoning the train idea, Duncan whinnied, and began to trot. "Go easy on your old man, he's lame."

A dark shadow rippled across the alleyway. Rachel and Juanita immediately tipped their heads skyward.

"Was that a hanging glider?" Juanita said, squinting.

"*Hang* glider," Rachel said. "And not likely. Not here in the city."

The long, narrow alleyway was flanked by two multistoried buildings that comprised the entire hospital. Bonaventure-esque in style, the two structures loomed on either side like sleek glacial walls. A moat of gray-blue sky bowed between the structures, where it was then captured and imparted downward to each building's hundreds of reflective windows.

Another shadow (or perhaps the same one) rolled across the pavement, this time from the opposite direction.

Cupping her eyes, Rachel said, "That's strange. I don't see a damn thing."

Duncan, too, was tightly pivoting now, gazing upward. As he searched between the two buildings, sunlight burst across the windows' chromed edges, flashing like paparazzi at a celebrity gala.

"Vultures," he offered. "It wouldn't be the first time Juanita was mistaken for dead. I mean, have you seen the house lately?"

"Ignore him, Juanita," Rachel advised. "God knows I try to."

"It's here," Amy said excitedly.

"What's here?" Rachel said, still squinting skyward.

"My ride!" Then her voice turned glum: "But we've got a visitor, too."

Wide-eyed, Juanita looked up at the girl. "What is this *visitor*?"

The tag of a dark specter began to pull across the sky, unzipping the dirty blue veil. And spilling from the seam came something resembling a dark shroud, billowing out like the cloak of a famed horseman fast afoot, whose head was no more apparent now than it had been during his moonlit haunts.

No, not a cloak, Duncan now realized, but large, black wings.

There was a perceptible *tink*, as if a pebble had been tossed against their glass reality.

Then, as the wings fully unfolded, Duncan could make out the suggestion of a body, a head. Then a long, thrashing tail.

Within seconds, advanced twilight had settled upon Los Angeles. The sky was now the pitted, undulating rind of a moldy orange. An almost palpable hush swept through like an enchanted wind, and the temperature dropped a good thirty degrees.

The creature circled as it descended from the unearthly awning, finally alighting next to a steel Dumpster some twenty feet away. It folded its wings and squatted, regarding them with a vile grimace. Duncan thought it looked like something straight off the lofty precipices of Quasimodo's immortal belfry. But more slim and sharp, like a hood ornament. One leading the charge on Satan's Seville.

Duncan turned to warn Rachel and Juanita—but they were no longer there. And for a strange instant he wondered if they had ever been there at all. He called out to them, but his voice sounded vacuous, seeming to travel no farther from his face than the length of a cigar.

Except for the exotic sky, and the insane addition of the creature before them, the world had not noticeably changed. However, Duncan felt that they'd been relocated, that he and Amy and this section of LA had somehow been scooped up and transported to another world and were now the main attraction for some curious race of aliens. An episode of the old *Outer Limits* came to mind.

"Not again." He closed his eyes. "Somebody please pinch me."

"You're not dreaming, Dad," Amy said. "But you're not too far from there."

Duncan was struck by the sudden acumen bridling his daughter's voice. She still sounded like a ten-year-old girl—but now there was an additional identity behind that pubescence, as if some guru had hopped aboard and grabbed the reins of her innocence.

He opened his eyes. The creature was still there, now rubbing itself lithely against a corner of the Dumpster, grinning like a wolf. He thought there was something profane about the way it moved; suggestive of something...lecherous.

And its teeth, as black and deep as his shame.

"Okay," he said, heart thrumming in his chest. "Any idea what kind of animal that is?"

"Don't worry. It wants Kathy, not us."

"Katherine *Bently?*"

Cat-quick, the creature leapt, voicing an eerie cry, and took flight. It flew down the alleyway, rising to maybe a hundred feet, turned, then dove at them. Just as it was aiming its sharp talons at Amy's shoulders, something unseen swatted it to the ground as if it were an insect.

The creature struck the asphalt hard, tumbling along like a napkin in a gale. It finally rolled to a stop and lay there for a moment, lifeless. Then it tottered to its feet and hastily made its way back to the Dumpster, apparently wanting something large and heavy to put between itself and the next invisible punch. Bloody scuffs of road rash were visible, as was a long tear in its left wing.

Lifting a leg, the creature regarded them with contempt as it peed, more blood than urine, onto the receptacle. It stayed there, at the edge of the trash bin, licking its wounds.

"Coward," Amy accused.

Duncan knelt, allowing Amy to slide from his shoulders.

Now face-to-face with her, he said, "Any idea what's protecting us?"

"A *friend.*"

Duncan was reminded of the way Doctor Strickland had similarly accentuated the word *friend* when she'd earlier explained to Amy the origin of her silver necklace.

He remained on his knees. "Well. That's, um, some kind of friend."

She sniggered. "Now you know why nobody picks on me at recess."

"You've got your old man's sense of humor," he said reprovingly. Then, glancing back at the creature, he said, "So, where's Katherine Bently?"

"She's right here," she said, poking at her chest. Something flittered across her eyes then, and the same voice as his daughter's—the same yet cusped with a new, genuine delight—spoke from her lips: "Hi, Donut!"

More amused than shocked, Duncan just stared at her, as if that bombshell had only ejected party confetti instead of the intended shrapnel.

"You just can't see the forest for the trees. But don't worry, the answers will come soon enough."

"But...I want the answers *now*."

Sighing, she said, "Dad, you don't even know the questions yet."

"Alright. Alright," he said, mustering his wits. "Just a clue then. *Please?*"

For once, her face was fretful. "Something's happened. Something that maybe even God didn't anticipate."

"What, God made a boo-boo?"

"It's really hard to know. But in a nutshell, there's an additional reality now, and we have to erase it." She shrugged. "If we can't, then we're screwed."

Duncan let the expletive slide. "Define *we*."

"Well, it's going to kind of depend on me, but it's going to depend on you, too."

"On me?"

"And Mom, Juanita, and Kathy. There will be some other people, too. You're going to make a journey."

"*Our* Juanita?"

Amy smiled. "She's okay, you'll see."

"A journey, huh. To where?"

She whispered in his ear: "A place where angels are born, among others."

"Sounds messy."

"Only when you have to deliver one."

Wincing, he said, "Is that on the agenda?"

"Yep."

Although Amy didn't seem at all apprehensive about the creature's presence, Duncan had been maintaining a vigilant watch. Still by the Dumpster, the creature continued its tongue bath. For now, it appeared content to remain there.

Nodding toward the creature, he said, "So, what's Fido's beef with Katherine?"

She looked at the creature, a taunting grin broadening across her face. "You always want most what you can never have." Then, turning back to Duncan: "He's just pissed off is all."

Soft but firm, he grabbed her shoulders. "Tell me what's going on, young lady, or I'll rinse your mouth out with soap."

She laughed at the threat. "What once was thought extinct is about to make a grand comeback."

"Oh," he said, rolling his eyes. "*Now* I understand."

"Just know there's a seraph loose."

"A *seraph*? As in an angel kind of seraph?"

"Uh-huh. The seraphs were the wardens of eternity. But they've been wiped out...all except one."

Feigning less shock than he was legitimately suffering, he said, "The Wardens of Eternity? Wiped out? Wait! Let me guess: The Devil?"

Almost ashamedly, she said, "Yes. And no."

"You're starting to sound like your mother," he warned her.

She just glared at him.

He held up his hands, surrendering. "Okay, okay. So, where's this sole-surviving angel?"

"Seraph," she affirmed, as if it preferred that luminary title. "And that's going to be part of your journey, to find out."

"What, the Vatican wasn't available? C'mon, kiddo, I can't even find my car keys half the time!"

"Just ask yourself—where would a seraph hide?"

He glared at her.

She smiled warmly. "Dad, I know you want to understand, but you can't. Not yet. I know you're very scared, but all you have to do is go with the flow. And trust your *instincts*." She took his hand, squeezed it. "*Just go with the flow.*"

With urgency, he said, "Have I gone totally insane?"

"Just a little." She winked.

"I mean...you sound...odd, sweetheart. Besides Katherine, who else is in there with you?"

"Kathy's not *in* me, Dad. Just think of me as all grown up."

"Grown up? Last I checked Ken and Barbie were still groping each other on the veranda."

"They were not!" she said, mortified.

Staring deeply into her eyes then, he said, "My little girl's still in there, isn't she?"

A new voice now; older, feminine. And strangely familiar: "Your daughter's still very much here," the voice assured. "But she also has another family, and they desperately need her right now."

Suddenly, Duncan felt a crippling emptiness in his chest, as if he and Amy were exchanging last goodbyes.

He stood, brushing pebbles from his knees. "Alright. Where does this journey begin?"

Amy's voice again: "Where do you think it should begin?"

"Okay, Rock Bay," he said. "Then what?"

"Follow the Yellow Brick Road."

He shook his finger at her. "Don't think I won't bend you over my knee!"

An endearing smile. "Don't ever lose your sense of humor, Dad. God might not forgive you if you did." Then, as if fondly recalling something, she said, "You know, God is really very funny, loves to laugh. It's the only sound He makes that's even close to human."

"But He's not laughing now, is that it?"

She turned from him, her face solemn. In a mixture of voices, she said, "We don't know *what* He's doing."

The assertion was now inescapable. He listened for the groans of any eavesdropping nihilists, then groaned himself. "So, this is all biblically related.

"It is what it is."

"Now you're starting to sound like Moses."

Her eyes turned discerning. "You're not so unlike Moses. History will remember you both as emancipators."

"What if I mess up?"

She shrugged. "Then this sitcom will never see the light of syndication."

"Clown," he said. "Do I get a staff? Something that'll turn the rivers to blood? Summon plagues?"

"I can get you another 'Get Out of Jail Free' card," she offered.

Another...? Unbelieving, Duncan whispered, "You know about why I got shot?"

"I had some friends who were there."

"But...that's not possible."

"Dad, you won't believe what's possible."

Ashamed, he turned his eyes away. "I'm not the hero everyone thinks I am."

"If you go in with bad intentions, that doesn't mean you can't come out a hero."

"Translate."

"That fateful night isn't through with you."

"You got that right," he said. "It'll never be through with me."

"I think what you mean is that you'll never be through with *it*."

He nodded. "Smart girl."

"Just remember what George Bernard Shaw said. 'If you cannot get rid of the family skeleton you might as well make it dance.'"

"What if me and Mr. Bones don't wish go to the ball?"

"Then you won't," she said, her puppy eyes blooming. "But you'll dance for me, won't you, Daddy?"

He put his face in his hands. "Oh boy, I have a feeling we're all in big trouble if mankind is counting on me and the maid."

"Don't forget about Mom and the others," she reminded. "And me."

Duncan shook his head. "I don't think your mother will be going. She's kinda mad at me, kiddo."

"She'll come around. You'll see."

"I won't hold my breath. Besides, I'm no Deliverer."

"Your tears will show you who you are."

"My *tears*—" He wanted to reach out and strangle her. "Could you possibly be any more obscure?"

"Just get everyone to Rock Bay, Dad."

"But...*Juanita?*"

"Juanita doesn't need you telling her who she is," Amy scolded. "She has her own idea."

"So how come I don't get the benefit of knowing who *I* am?"

"Very soon, you will once again hold on the tip of your tongue all that is, all that was, and all that ever will be. And you will *Know*."

"Know *what?*"

"Who you are, silly."

Duncan felt as if he were descending in a faulty bathysphere, the pressure building to crushing proportions. His brain wasn't buying any of it, but his soul trembled in the assuredness that it was all real and true.

His brain still firmly in control, he said, "You *do* know that I don't believe in God, right?"

"I know. But it won't hurt God's feelings." Then a frown emerged, one much too serious for a child. "Unfortunately, He's not quite as wrathful as legend has Him."

The creature was growling now, spreading its wings, appearing like it might attempt another blitz.

"Time to go," she said.

"Is this the part where I wake up?"

"No" she said, almost plaintively. "But very soon, you will."

In a blink, it was over. The temperature steadily rose, and the commotion of the city, it seemed, had rebounded to an even more oppressive din than before.

He was back, standing once again with Amy on his shoulders. Rachel and Juanita were still gazing skyward, apparently not having missed them.

Then, upon the mirrored buildings, the silhouettes of two immense hands plunged downward, as if meaning to pluck both structures from their foundations.

Amy hugged Duncan's neck and whispered in his ear. "Goodbye, Dad. Be very careful. Take good care of Kathy. And no matter how it all finally turns out, I'll always and forever know you were a hero." She kissed the top of his head. "Oh, and be nice to the dead man."

Duncan squeezed Amy's hands. "What dead man?"

"Señor Duncan!" Juanita gasped.

"Oh, my God," Rachel cried. "Look!"

He followed Rachel's finger to the reflective window before them. Both Juanita and Rachel were looking at Amy, then the window, then Amy again.

Duncan could feel her weight on his shoulders, could feel her hands in his hands, but something was missing from the burnished portrait before them.

They stood there, their own astonished reflections staring back. All but Amy's.

10.

"Put me down, Donut," she laughed, poking the back of his head.

He watched her image in the window. For a long second, it seemed, her reflection had not been there.

"Did you just call Señor Duncan 'Donut'?" Juanita said.

"Dunkin' Donut," she affirmed.

"My God, Duncan," Rachel said, "Did you see that—or not see that—in the window?"

"Quite frankly, I think I've seen and heard quite enough."

Rachel stared at him. "Are you all right?"

"I'm not sure," he said. "Can messiah's have bad days?"

"Excuse me?"

"Never mind."

Juanita helped the child down from Duncan's shoulders.

"You're Juanita San Diego," said the girl.

"San*tiago*," she corrected. "And you are Katherine Bently?"

"Yes, ma'am," she said. "But you can call me Kathy."

"Not again," Rachel moaned. She knelt in front of the child and, sternly, said, "I am your mother, this is your dad and Juanita, and you're Amy McNeil."

Shaking her head, she said, "Amy's not here anymore, Mrs. McNeil. She went to get her sword."

Forced to take a step backward, Juanita gasped as she wildly signed the cross, appearing more like a nose-picking epileptic than she did a devout Catholic. Duncan actually felt for her.

Rachel, now almost nose to nose with the girl, said, "I'm sorry, hon, she went to get her what?"

"It's a long story," she sighed.

Rachel glanced back at the hospital doors, as if trying to decide whether Amy would go peacefully, or if orderlies would be needed.

Juanita placed a shaky hand on Rachel's shoulder. "Mrs. McNeil, I know it is hard to believe, but she, I think, *is* Katherine Bently."

Rachel stared accusingly at Duncan. "You're being awfully quiet."

"Cat's got my tongue," he said. The tequila worm he'd had for breakfast, he feared, had cocooned in his stomach and was about to hatch into a species of Lepidoptera not indigenous to the jungles of Mexico, but rather the kind found in old Japanese movies.

"Okay, what's your mommy's name, sweetheart?" Rachel said.

"Patty."

"Patricia Bently?"

"Yes ma'am."

"Your daddy's name?"

"My step dad's dead."

Rachel frowned. "I'm so sorry. What was his name?"

"Charlie Bently."

"I see. He was your step-father?"

Kathy nodded. "He adopted me."

"And your real father's name?"

She looked up at Duncan. "I don't know."

"Do you know who Duncan is?"

Mindfully, she smiled. "He used to be friends with my mom."

"Uh-huh. And Juanita here?"

"Sure. She's here to watch over Amy and me."

Rachel stood up, grabbed Duncan's arm and escorted him to a private area some thirty feet away.

She took a deep breath, then exhaled slowly. "My God, I had no idea her delusion was this...involved. Doctor Strickland said to bring her back immediately if she—"

"Whoa," Duncan said. "I thought you were the one who needed the least convincing. Now you believe it's just seizures, or that she's delusional?"

"That's Amy, our daughter!" she snapped. "She is not Kathy Bently, Bridey Murphy, Peter Proud, or anyone else!"

"Who are you trying to convince?"

She looked stunned. "You don't actually believe her, do you?"

"I'm afraid I do."

"You...you do?"

"Absolutely."

"Oh bullshit."

"By the way," Duncan said, "Juanita's going with me and...uh...Kathy to Rock Bay. She's part of this."

"Part of what?"

"Whatever this is."

Suddenly dazed, she said, "Oh, alright then..."

"You have to come with us, hon."

Tears welling in her eyes, Rachel hugged herself. "Our baby's not really gone, is she?"

Duncan watched a man in an adjacent portico erect a ladder and begin the tedious chore of changing light bulbs.

"She's gone, but not for good," he said. "Looks like Kathy's going to help us from here." He glanced back at the girl. "Seems she and Amy are linked in some way."

Emphatic, Rachel said, "What happened back there? Huh? Are we the only ones who saw it?" She was blubbering now, searching her purse for a tissue. "Why aren't there people screaming, babies being thrown out of windows, car horns blaring, sirens in symphony?" She blew her nose. *"Just what in God's name happened to the sky?"*

He pulled her to his chest. "Face it, reality's gone on the rag." Then he stepped back from their embrace and held her arms. "Tomorrow the journey begins."

She began dabbing her eyes. "First class or coach."

Duncan smiled at her. "Now there's the woman I know and love."

Choosing her words carefully, she said, "Back there I...I turned and, for a split second, could've sworn you and Amy were...gone."

"We were." With some reserve, Duncan gave Rachel the abridged version of what had happened.

After he finished, Rachel waited for the punch line. It didn't come.

"You have *got* to be shitting me."

"Wish I was," Duncan said. Then he gazed into her eyes. "Have I ever told you how attractive you are when your mascara's running?"

"Oh, Duncan," she balked, "are you getting mushy on me?"

"Just an observation."

"Good. Because it gives me the heebie-jeebies whenever you start breaking out the flattery."

"Have I really been that neglectful?"

"You could use a refresher course."

"Sign me up. Can I practice with anyone I want?"

"As long as you put her back in the closet when you're done."

"I thought you had a fear of dark, tight places."

She snorted. "God knows your dick certainly doesn't."

"Ouch. Cease fire."

She was looking beyond him now, into the past. "I wonder how much Rock Bay has changed in all these years."

"Don't know," Duncan said, peering himself beyond its dunes, at the collapsing tide. "But it'll never outgrow its ghosts."

"Ghosts?"

"Well, my ghosts."

Very concerned now, Rachel said, "Nice ghosts or mean ghosts?"

"I think Dan Akroyd should answer that."

"Are you in trouble, Duncan?"

He said nothing.

"Damn it, Dunc! If I have to dust off the Ouija Board and drill the bastards myself, I will."

"Those ghosts aren't talking. There's something called the 'Code of Honor.'"

"Oh, I see. Something to do with you and your police pals?"

He just shrugged.

"Alright. Fine. Don't tell me. But I have a sneaking suspicion that I'm gonna find out soon enough."

"So do I, darlin'. So do I."

He took her hand, and they began walking.

Rachel snuggled close. "Have you thought about the possible trauma Patricia Bently might suffer when she see's that her daughter hasn't aged since the day she disappeared?"

"Tell you the truth, I've been more concerned about my own mental health," he said. "But yeah, it's crossed my mind."

"Just know one thing, buddy," she warned him. "If that little romance gets rekindled, I'll do to you things Lorena Bobbitt never dreamed of."

"Not even one little kiss?"

"Don't fuck with me on this," she said. "I mean it."

"I'm glad you're coming with us."

"Me too. I think. But there's one condition."

Duncan sighed. "There always is."

She motioned for him to bend down so she could whisper in his ear. On her tip-toes, she said, "I want to know why Patricia is *indebted* to you."

He'd been waiting for that one. "Those ghosts aren't talking, remember?"

She was shocked. "So Patricia Bently *is* involved."

"Sort of. I think so. I'm not really sure."

She grabbed his shirt. "You'd better tell me what in Christ's name is going on!"

"Enough. I don't have it figured out yet, but when I do, you'll be the first to know."

Reluctantly, she released him. "I told you this revolved around you and her," she smugly reminded. "Didn't I?"

"I suppose." Then, anxious to change the subject, he said, "So, what about your commercial tomorrow?"

"I'll call Stills tonight, tell him I have a family emergency to tend to back East. Maybe they can postpone the shoot a couple days." She shrugged. "If not, then something else will come along."

"Okay. But this time why not put on some rubber gloves, tie a scarf over your head, and go for something really challenging, like floor wax or toilet bowl cleaner? Really, Rachel, once you've been seen doing hemorrhoid commercials, you're instantly stereotyped. Your career will never get out of the medicine cabinet."

"How come I always feel like I'm in a Billy Crystal movie when I'm with you?"

He laughed.

They collected Juanita and Kathy and proceeded to the car.

11.

Melanie Sands tucked her black flute case beneath her arm, looked both ways, then stepped from the curb.

Newton, Iowa: "...Home of the Maytag washing machine—and won't *that* be something to tell the grandkids," her mother would lambaste when in one of her hateful states, when she was gunning for men, putting holes in everything that got in her way, towns included.

Large snowflakes floated dreamily down from a slate-gray ceiling; one that, from this distance at least, looked to be no more than rooftop-high. For a moment, Melanie stood transfixed, positing that the snowflakes had to be responsible for dropping the clouds. Because of their scissor-cut edges, she reasoned, they snagged like thistles onto the gray gossamer, dragging it slowly down.

It was a theory worth committing to, she decided with a token nod.

There was not so much as a whisper of a breeze, and within this absence of wind there hung an unnatural calm; a stillness so profound that, strangely, colors appeared more resplendent to her than ever.

Not so far behind her, Tinder Elementary School was evaporating, the old, red brick facade fading, fading...

Finally, it disappeared altogether.

Now, if it would only stay that way, she thought.

Already the snow was up to her knees, and she was just willing to bet that it wasn't going to let up anytime soon. Well, she was hoping, really.

She could hear soft creaks and groans coming from a queue of ancient maple trees to her right, and it took her a moment to realize that these sounds were the whimpering of branches weighted down from the wet snow; the maples' rust- and saffron-tinted leaves acting as nets, coerced into treason by an impetuous winter.

Soon, she thought, the ground would be littered with broken limbs. But this was only vague conjecture. She did not have an abundance of autumns and early snows behind her to accurately deduce such carnage. She was only ten and couldn't have cared less anyway. Thoughts of building snowmen and ice skating and drinking hot cider with cinnamon currently preoccupied her, with an occasional—and most often nasty—opinion about Suzie Stapleton, her arch enemy and sometime-friend.

She kicked up globs of snow as she continued along Fourth Street.

Across the slushy road, a school bus lumbered by, some of her classmates waving through the fogged windows. She could not hear their voices and could barely see their bouncing faces behind the rows of rectangular cataracts. But she did not find herself craving their comfort.

To show them all (especially Suzie Stapleton, if she was looking) that she was just as pleased as peas to be walking home, she stuck out her tongue and in no time collected a dozen wet, billowy flakes. Then she quickly rolled it back in, afraid that her peers might misconstrue her intentions and think she was jealous.

The yellow bus turned down Madison Avenue, its rear-end belching a plume of exhaust as the driver shifted down. She finally waved back as it disappeared behind a complex of red-shingled town homes.

She once more stuck out her tongue, whetting a fatuous appetite endemic only to children.

Luckily, Melanie's mother (who had, upon gazing out their kitchen window that morning, declared the sky a "London Special") had prepared her for the forecasted, and most certainly premature, incursion of winter. Melanie had been equipped with a down parka, wool muffler and gloves, and green galoshes, the latter still in her backpack. Her parka had a fleece-lined hood, but for now she chose not to bring it over her head, her ears, as she enjoyed the dreamy, tingly feel of the snow in her hair.

It was only a quarter-mile or so from Tinder Elementary to her house on Rampart Avenue, but she wished now that it were ten. She was relishing the white weather; liked the way it squelched under her shoes.

She waved to Mr. Altman. "Old Limp Wrist," her mother called him, whatever that meant.

He'd already shoveled the snow from his walkway and was clearing a path to his front door, his shiny Aluminum shovel rasping across the cement. This struck her as odd, considering it was still snowing. Why didn't he just wait until it stopped?

Adults were weird, she concluded.

Mr. Altman looked up from his chores, then glanced at his wristwatch. "My goodness, Ms. Sands! Is school out already?"

Nodding enthusiastically, she said, "They let us out early cuz'a'the snow." Mr. Altman always addressed her as "Ms. Sands", and she liked the way that sounded. It had a noble quality about it; was distinct from the childish, sing-song preamble that most adults often used when greeting her: "Hiya, Mel! How's phonics treatin' ya?" (Mr. Hampton from the Kwik Way), or, "Well, if it ain't that sweet little angel, Melanie Sands!" (Mrs. Rusch, her next-door neighbor), or, "Stop the presses and darn yer dresses, it's that gal from the fifth grade!" (Mr. Tessier, one of her mother's old school teachers, from the library).

But when Mr. Altman spoke to her, he always made her feel *grown-up*.

Expertly manicured evergreen shrubs lined the man's curving walkway on the outside, while a tall, white trellis of checkerboard design flanked the other, crawling with the spindly remains of woodbine and clematis. A few green leaves, overlooked by a scavenging autumn, still clung to the skeletons like bits of flesh; morsels left for winter's sharper, more ravenous beak.

His house was a remodeled, turn-of-the-century, expansive four-story structure adorned with dormer windows and charming gingerbread ornamentation. Melanie called it a mansion. Her mother, on the other hand, liked to refer to it as "Faggot Central," whatever that meant. Melanie thought it might have something to do with decorating, for she'd overheard her mother mention to Mrs. Huntington at the grocery store— and on more than one occasion—that she should have ol' Limp Wrist over to refurbish her house; that he could do a much better job than she at picking out drapes and matching wallpaper. And oh my the wonders he could do with her flower garden. Then they'd *laugh*.

Yes, Melanie concluded once again, adults could be very strange.

A short and rotund man, and very bald, Mr. Altman continued to plow laboriously, his vaporous breath pulsing out of his mouth like smoke from an old locomotive. And as she drew closer, she could see steam rising off of his shiny pate.

She snickered, then blurted out, "Your head's smoking!"

Taking a breather, he swiped sweat from his brow. "Looks like winter's sneaked up behind us." He shook his head. "And just when you thought the Almanac couldn't be wrong."

The sniffles having set in, Melanie ran a coat sleeve across her nose. "Mom says it's a 'London Special.'"

Mr. Altman looked at the sky as if to verify this. "Well, more like an Anchorage Special, but I know where she's coming from."

Melanie laughed, sure that what he said was supposed to be funny.

She paused and glanced down Fourth Street, barely able to see her house through the falling snow.

There would be no one home to greet her, of course; wouldn't be for another three hours. She was an only child, and what her mother affectionately called a "latch-key kid." Her mother had also told her that she could thank the ever-increasing cost of child care and an absent, no-good derelict father for her predicament. But she didn't mind those few hours alone. She looked forward to them, in fact. And as for her father, well...He really hadn't hung around long enough for her to have profound feelings for him. And if the truth be known, she probably wouldn't be able to identify him if he were the only suspect standing in a police line-up; a likely scenario that, according to her mother, would probably be her last and only hope of ever seeing him again. That, or a "postmortem visit to the morgue," whatever that meant.

Her mom had told her that the reason they didn't have any pictures of her dad was because he was "camera shy." Melanie just figured that her mom had tossed them after the divorce. Or worse.

Setting her flute case aside, she plopped backward into a hillock of snow, courtesy of Mr. Altman's shovel and, as if practicing the back stroke, began to sweep her arms back and forth. She then jumped up, brushed the snow from the back of her head, and regarded the snow angel she'd made. It wasn't bad, but not quite up to her standards.

She shrugged, reminding herself that she had most of fall and a whole winter ahead to perfect the art.

From the column of maple trees beside her, something growled; a low, predacious sound, very much like a lion would make.

She turned, startled. In the tree closest to her, a few hand-sized clumps of snow began falling from the uppermost limbs, immediately inciting a fusillade of mini avalanches that quickly swept the girth of the tree, finally leaving it naked among its snow-draped peers.

She saw that Mr. Altman had heard the sounds, too, for he had stopped his shoveling and was looking up at the tree.

Something was there within the maple's tangled interior. Something *alive*. An animal of some kind. Growling at her.

It clung to a branch like an old world chameleon.

Then she saw its eyes; eyes that spawned in her feelings of complete and utter fear. Those orbs of glowing light seized her, and instantly she knew that she was not staring into the eyes of an animal but into the infinite depths of despair.

Ravenous despair.

The animal exploded into a shuddering, squealing, menacing mass of energy. Something that looked like a pair of wings unfolded partway from behind its back, and then a long barbed tail whipped out from behind it, the end twitching slowly back and forth in predatory, cat-like musing; an eerie contrast to the violent paroxysms shaking the rest of its body. Its dog-like muzzle flaunted four ranks of gnarled, pointed teeth, as shiny-black as polished obsidian. And she was convinced that if it were to eat her, her shredded pieces would not slide down into its belly but would take an unnatural excursion into the bottomless depths of its eyes. And ultimately be reassembled then agonizingly digested there for all time.

She begged her legs to move, but they stubbornly remained planted in the snow.

"Run, Ms. Sands, run!" Mr. Altman yelled, but his voice sounded small and tinny to her ears, as if it were coming from a cheap pocket radio buried nearby in the snow. The creature's mesmerizing gaze not only stole her breath away, but had numbed her senses, had filched every ounce of fuel from her muscles.

Mr. Altman trampled toward her, plumes of snow bursting at his feet, his gelatinous belly bouncing up and down.

Melanie opened her mouth to scream, but only visible breath escaped.

Raising the shovel above his head, Mr. Altman cried, "For the love of God, girl, *run!*"

In a chorus of snapping limbs and hideous guttural sounds, the creature leaped from the interior of the tree, wings aggrandized.

12.

As Eli walked into the church, Deacon Samuel Flannery was in the central section of pews, gazing skyward with a magazine in his hands.

"What are you doing, Samuel?" But Eli already knew.

"Ah, Father Kagan," he said drearily. "It appears that you were quite wrong about the sword. You see, the pictures in the Standard don't show the sword to be there."

Upon its unveiling, Eli's masterpiece had quickly become so beloved by not only the Catholic community but the general public at large that *The Catholic Standard* actually gave it five whole pages in its following edition, one devoted entirely to "Hallowed Architecture and Art."

"See?" Samuel said, pointing at the magazine's pictures. "No sword."

Eli did not have to look at any pictures. He was the artist, for Christ's sake, and had every minute detail committed to memory. He was certain that he could point out things not even the good deacon had yet to notice, especially the little eccentricities that had shown up on the mural within the last twenty-four hours. Facial expressions, mostly. All the angels' lips had begun to ever so slightly dip into frowns. And their eyes...Their eyes were narrowing.

Thus far, only Samuel had approached him about the sword.

"Who else have you told about this?" Eli inquired.

"No one, Father," he assured him. "I just came from the church library where I found this issue, and—"

Thrusting out a hand, Eli said, "Give me the Standard."

"Father?"

"The magazine, you asshole! Give it to me!"

Hesitantly, Samuel handed Eli the Standard. "Are you angry about something, Father?"

Eli rolled the magazine up tight, then stepped face-to-face with Samuel. "Listen up good, Friar Fuck! If you turn this church into another Fatima, not only will I make sure that you catch a real nasty case of stigmata, but I'll have a dose of hemophilia thrown in for no extra charge!"

Eyes round as saucers, Samuel swallowed hard.

"In a few more days—maybe even sooner—I'll be getting my wings," Eli continued, "and I don't need some nosey subordinate tripping me up!"

Samuel was visibly trembling now. "Something's about to happen, isn't it?" He pointed to the ceiling. "Something about the sword—"

"*I'm* what's about to happen! Very soon, dear Samuel, I'll have a bird's-eye view as reality gets turned on its nose."

"You're not well," Samuel whispered. "So help me God, you're not."

"Sammy boy," Eli snarled, "you have no idea."

13.

As she and Duncan picked at their fries, Kathy and Juanita stuffed their faces with burgers.

Rachel sighed. "Okay, Juanita. Look, I'm not a very religious person, so I'll ask you."

"Yes, Mrs. McNeil?"

"What the hell's going on?"

"I do not know, Mrs. McNeil."

"Then who does?"

"God."

"Well, I don't have His cell number. Anyone else?"

Juanita patted Rachel's hand and said, "You just have to ask, and He will tell you."

"Oh, well, if that's all, then let me make a list." Employing the melodramatic, Rachel reached into her purse and pulled out her day runner and a pen. Poised for dictation, she turned to Duncan. "Do you have any questions you'd like to ask the Almighty?"

Duncan cleared his throat. "Well, I *would* like to know if the Raiders are gonna go all the way this season."

Kathy giggled as she picked onion bits from a cheeseburger.

Juanita slammed her Coke down hard. "No wonder God does not give you answers! He is too upset!"

"God doesn't get upset," Kathy said. "And it could be His undoing."

Duncan cocked an ear. "Say again?"

"She does not know what she is saying," Juanita huffed.

"I know one thing," Kathy said. "There are some angels who're very pissed off right now."

Juanita gasped. "You know no such thing!"

Kathy slurped her drink and shrugged. "Stick around."

"Nasty angels are no big secret," Duncan said to Kathy. "So what makes these guys so special?"

"Because Amy said so," she declared around a mouthful of fries. "She said since God wasn't up to kicking butt, then she knew some angels who were."

Leaning over, now eye-to-eye with Kathy, Juanita said, "Somebody needs to kick *your* butt, young lady." She straightened, then added, "All the way down the street."

Amused, Rachel said, "So Amy's buds with God, huh?"

"Oh yeah," she said. "She's told me all kinds of things about God and stuff. And hardly any of it's like what they teach in Sunday school." She glanced hesitantly at Juanita. "Not even close."

"Amy's a regular in heaven?" Duncan said. "Like Norm on *Cheers*?"

"Sure," Kathy said. "We all are. It's just that we forget all about it each time we leave because just a piece of its memory would slice us to bits."

"One more time?" Rachel said.

Kathy sighed. "Okay. Amy said that heaven is made of something like glass, and to remember even the tiniest piece could nick the skin of our reality and deflate it like a balloon. Or something like that."

Rachel leaned forward. "Then how come Amy gets to remember without getting sliced up?"

"Because she *Knows*."

"Knows what?"

Kathy smiled. "Who she is"

"Heaven is not made of glass, young lady," Juanita said with all the charm and certainty of a truly propagandized fanatic. "It is beautiful and clean, like the Earth once was."

"That's absolutely right," Duncan confirmed. "You listen to your pal Juanita. Heaven is a tropical, fully-clothed, alcohol-free resort where you lounge all day by a pool that nobody pees in, where Don Ho impersonators take turns singing Hawaiian love songs in straw gazebos, and Jehovah's Witnesses wait on you hand and foot." He winked at Juanita, taunting her. "Hey, it's all in the brochure I picked up last week. You know, at Our Sisters of Mercy Me?"

Giggling, Kathy cupped a hand over her mouth.

Juanita's stared contemptuously into Duncan's eyes.

Rachel elbowed him. "Knock it off. You're becoming obnoxious."

"You're still a wiseacre, Donut," Kathy declared.

Duncan leaned back stiffly in his chair and said, "That's what your mom nicknamed me. 'Wiseacre.'"

"My mom used to say that your clowning around was just your armor," Kathy said. "What did she mean by that?"

For once, Duncan was positively pensive. "I think she meant that some people just handle the stresses of life differently than others. Some, like Rachel here, cry a lot to relieve the tension, while other people drink—"

"Like Duncan here," Rachel interjected.

"—or take drugs, act all macho when they're really not. And then there's people like me who try and cope with life by laughing it away—"

"*Drinking* it away," Rachel calmly insisted.

"—when all we're really doing is avoiding our true feelings and insecurities. Mine's a front, a bluff, but just one of the more outwardly gentler ones."

"Gentler?" Rachel said. "Not your jokes."

"*Si*," Juanita agreed.

With a wicked smile, Duncan said, "But don't think I'm gonna change now just because the cat's out of the bag."

Rachel leaned forward and whispered to Kathy, "At least 'Wiseacre' is cleaner than the one I normally use."

"Me too," Juanita added.

"I'm confused," Rachel said, "When, exactly, did you and Amy have time to sit and chat about all of this?"

"In our dreams," she said. "It's the only time we see each other."

Slackening a bit, Duncan said, "Tell us some of Amy's hangouts. When she's not hanging with you, I mean."

Kathy thought for a moment. "Well, she likes to talk a lot about a place called the Shallows."

As if the word were a preprogrammed trigger to release her from a hypnotic trance, Juanita turned to Kathy, and said direly, "*What is this place you said, the Shallows?*"

Kathy, having been nearly pushed off her seat by Juanita's verve, said, "It's where eternity is." She straightened in her chair. "Geez."

"'I am Alpha and Omega, the beginning and the ending, saith the Lord'," Duncan said, his Catholic birthright showing through. "Revelations. Chapter one, verse six."

"Verse eight," Juanita corrected.

Duncan leered at her. "I've got a twenty in Rachel's purse that says it's verse six."

"I do not bet," Juanita said. "You do not pay me enough to."

"Then what do you call your Thursday night bingo parties?"

"Tithing."

Rachel, bewildered, said, "Wait a minute. For eternity, there is no beginning or ending." She looked at Duncan. "Is there?"

He was rubbing his eyes. "I think that was my point."

"Amy says that eternity is like a dog chasing its tail," Kathy said, "and that our souls will go on forever because they'll never catch up to themselves."

Elbows on the table, Rachel rested her chin in her hands. With a regaled sparkle in her eyes, she said, "Do you understand everything Amy tells you?"

"Mostly," she said. "Amy also said that the Shallows is everyone's home eventually."

Juanita patted Kathy on the shoulder. "It's true. Once you die, you have everlasting life," she assured her. "That is God's promise."

"As either a harpist or cord of kindling," Duncan agreed.

Kathy shook her head. "It's not like that at all."

"Then what is it like?" Rachel said, now showing serious interest.

"Amy says heaven's like a pizza. It's round, and you can have whatever you want put on it."

"Round meaning eternal?" Rachel said.

"I guess so."

Duncan said, "What did she say hell was?"

"Anchovies."

"Oh."

Rachel said, "What else has Amy told you?"

"That there is only love and fear, stuff like that. Oh, and that her dad, Mr. McNeil, used to be a Seminole."

Proudly pushing out his chest, Duncan said to Rachel, "Told you I was a half-breed."

"Oh, please," Rachel said. "You're a lot of things, carrot top, but Indian ain't one of 'em."

Looking very confused, Kathy said, "A Seminole is an Indian?"

"Native American," Duncan corrected.

"Oh," Kathy said. "But...I don't think that's what Amy meant. I think she meant someone else used to guard the Shallows."

Rachel was left spinning in the dust again. "What *are* you talking about?"

Duncan, however, suddenly looked like a patron who was deciding if the piece of BigMac in his throat was wedged sufficiently enough to start panicking.

With something resembling concern, Juanita said, "Señor Duncan, are you all right?"

"Fine," he finally said, looking at Kathy. "Hon, are you sure it was 'Seminole?'" He glanced back at the cashiers, the lines of patrons, as if an eavesdropper might be in their midst. Turning back to Kathy, he said, "Could Amy have said 'sentinel?'"

"Sure, I guess."

"What about 'criminal?'" Juanita offered. "It's a good possibility, and a better rhyme."

His alarm had receded now to a witless mien. Oblivious to Juanita's jibes, he continued to stare intently at the girl, as if the answers to life were hidden in a series of anagrams scrawled across her forehead.

The seraphs were the wardens of eternity, Amy had told him.

"Wardens," he murmured, his rapt gaze having surrendered to a tenant of bohemian ancestry, as premonitions now oozed down the backs of his eyes like the driveled curses of a toothless gypsy.

Sentinels.

"You're scaring her, Duncan," Rachel said. She waved a hand in front of his face. "Hey, knock it off."

Duncan continued to stare at Kathy. "Did Amy say anything about what's happening now? Something about to happen? A war, maybe?"

Concentrating, Kathy said, "A long time ago, the mind of man found a wandering piece of God, trapped it, and has been building on it ever since. Now, a nation has risen from there to defeat the keepers of the Shallows." She gave a big nod and smiled winningly, obviously quite pleased with herself.

"Whoa," Duncan said. "You just left skid marks from here all the way to Nazareth."

Rachel leaned in. "In other words, you lost us, hon."

"I didn't get it at first, either," Kathy admitted. "So, Amy said that there's another place now, another hell, a fake hell, and it's fighting the real heaven for the Shallows."

Duncan said, "This other place, this 'fake' hell, came from the wandering piece of God Amy talked about?"

"Uh-huh. So did the fake heaven, but she said the fake hell pretty much got rid of it."

"So," Rachel said, "is there a fake devil in this fake hell? And a fake god in the fake heaven?"

"Sure," Kathy said. "Who else would there be?"

Being the deft authority on such matters, Juanita said, quoting the First Commandment, "'Thou shalt have none other gods before me'. There is only one God, one heaven—and you will go to only one hell for believing anything else."

Duncan glowered at Juanita. "Then we're all in *beeg* trouble. Really, do you think the alleged God in all His infinite compassion would punish an innocent little girl for her beliefs? Sentence her to eternal damnation?"

"*Si*," she whispered. "In the blink of an eye."

In a voice not her own, Kathy said, "Imagine the true Heaven as a place of magnificent light, and Hell as whatever light that does not pass through you. You see, the true Hell is just a place to hang your shadows. But the impostor hell is all you've envisioned, and more. It believes it can achieve celibate harmony, and does not care about the fragile balance."

Wide-eyed, Kathy took a sip through her straw, as if to wash down the possessing spirit, then said in her normal but shaky voice, "That freaks me out when they do that."

"They?" Rachel said, now leering distrustfully at the girl.

"Uh-huh. They say things in a neater way than I do."

Rachel nodded. "I've noticed."

"They use bigger words, too," Kathy added.

"I'll say."

Juanita just sat there; staring, silent and disturbed.

"Hang our shadows?" Duncan said somberly. "You mean, the real hell's nothing but a coat rack?"

As Kathy sniggered at the thought, Juanita made the sign of the cross, yet another self-inoculation against that lurking virus called blasphemy.

Rachel said, "Where's God during all of this? The real God, I mean?"

The sober, taken-aback expression was almost comical on her ten-year-old face. "Amy didn't say."

"Well," Rachel chortled, "smoke 'em if you got 'em, right? Because if the fake hell triumphs, it won't matter how clean a life or however many we've led, we're still going to burn when we die?" She looked at Kathy. "Is that it, basically?"

Kathy shook her head. "If the fake hell wins," she said, "it won't wait for us to die."

14.

George Altman hid behind the door as if he'd just stepped from the shower and was embarrassed by his two hundred and forty pounds of dripping nakedness. To his left, a flute case lay propped in a corner, orphaned. He'd rescued it from the snow bank where Ms. Sand's boot prints ended abruptly. Tufts of snow still clung to its edges, from where rivulets of water sashayed routes of least resistance across the black, corrugated leather, finally pooling on his swank, imported stone tiles.

He momentarily regarded it as if it were an incriminating piece of evidence, the smoking gun that would link him to a crime he did not commit.

With only one wary eye visible, he spoke tremulously through the narrow crack. "Whatever you're selling, I'm not interested."

The man in the tailored suit raised a detective's badge to Altman's lone eye. "I'm not selling encyclopedias or Jehovah this afternoon," he said, somewhat wearily. "I'm here to get a statement from you regarding the disappearance of a neighbor girl."

George Altman's eyes grew wider. He hadn't yet called the authorities, was still too frightened. Hell, the incident had only happened fifteen, maybe twenty minutes earlier, and he was still worried about the state of his sanity, frantically trying to make some rational sense of it all.

Thumb over his shoulder, the detective offered, "Ms. Higgins across the street thought she saw something suspicious and called it in."

"Oh," was all George could muster. He watched the snow descend thickly and lazily around the man, but was confused as to why none of those flakes seemed to fall *upon* him; his head, his shoulders. He continued to stare.

The detective shifted his weight from one leg to the other and sighed. "Are you going to invite me in, or am I going to have to get a flu shot?"

George slowly opened the door and waved the detective in. Just before he shut the door, he glanced up and down the slushy street. Except for a few familiar cars belonging to his neighbors, there were no other vehicles in sight.

Oh shit, George thought miserably. *Shit, shit, shit.*

They walked through a richly furnished foyer, the detective curiously leading, as if it were his house and George the visitor, then into an expansive living room of cleanliness and order.

"Dainty," the detective said, glancing around.

George, his voice back but at a squeakier pitch, said, "I beg your pardon?" He felt a bucketful of adrenaline dump into his chest, but didn't have the vaguest idea why.

Or maybe he did.

"Your furnishings," the detective said. "They're dainty. You know, 'Fussy.' Christ, this place doesn't have a woman's touch—it's got her fucking *hand prints* all over it!" He turned to George, and winked. "You must have one heck of a darling wife."

"No wife," George said, firmly believing he was being paid an insult.

A crafty, one-sided grin cracked the detective's face. "Oh, you're one of *those*," he said, the pinky on his right hand jutting out as if he were sipping tea at a London bath house.

"Yes, I'm gay, if that's what you mean," said George. But George had the instant impression that this detective already knew that; that this detective knew quite a lot of things. "Are you normally this rude to every witness before you take their statement, Detective...?"

"Gamble," he said. "And, yes, I normally am." He glanced around the room again, put a finger to his lips, as if to ponder upon the stupendous decorating effort, and said, "Tell me, fat boy, was all this your doing, or did you request the expertise of some of your persnickety, limp-wristed butt-buddies?"

George just gaped.

"Oh, come now," Gamble urged. "Surely you don't expect me to believe that a cum-drunk queen like yourself did all this? All by your lonesome? Really?"

The adrenaline rushing through George's veins was turning cold and sluggish. Now he truly felt naked, exposed, vulnerable, just like he did when he found himself in one of his notorious dreams where he was walking around his favorite department store, or down the locker-lined hallways of his old high school, only to look down at himself and discover that he was naked. But the worst part about those dreams, he'd always complained, was that poor L'il Willy was never any bigger than he was in reality. Seemed even more shriveled than normal, in fact. But his big fat gut would prevail realistically.

It wasn't fair.

Like a full meal deal from Burger King, dreams were often super-sized. Timid little woodland creatures suddenly became carnivorous giants nipping at your heels. A simple elm tree could grow to be the gigantic Kraken of myth, its branches turned into grasping tentacles, its leaves transformed into suction cups big enough to pluck the smoke stacks off a Norwegian cruise ship.

Yes, it seemed that, in dreams, extra large was the order of the day. The order for everything, that was, except his own genitalia. For George, it was one of life's spiteful peculiarities.

Gamble waited, still frozen in expectation of an answer, that thin half-grin pulling up his cheek like a crooked blind.

No, this tactless man was not a police detective, George was now convinced. But who, exactly, was he?

Deciding that he did not want to entertain the possibilities, he pointed to the door. "I want you to leave right now. Right this very instant!" His lower lip trembled, and a slight lisp had crept into his voice, a mannerism induced not by his 'fussy' side, but by a dry mouth. "If you don't, then I swear I'll notify the *real* police."

"Be my guest," Gamble chuckled. "But first things first. Tell them that you witnessed a hideous winged beastie snatch poor little Melanie Sands from your front yard, and that you bludgeoned said beastie with your snow shovel—that you have the dents to prove it, by God!—but despite your heroics it managed to fly off with her anyway, but not before it squatted over that cute little snow angel she'd made and left a big stinking calling card. Tell them that. And then, after they take your fat-ass measurements for a straightjacket, you go ahead and tell them about little ol' me."

At that moment, George Altman knew that he was going to die. Very soon. He was going to pay the ultimate price for meddling in something that had not concerned him. He'd been in the wrong place at the wrong time, but was now certain that he'd sealed his fate by swinging that snow shovel—not once, but thrice—at the creature that kidnapped the poor child.

Gamble continued to smile his droll, one-sided smile, then offered up a limerick. "There once was a fairy named George. By the look of his belly he did gorge. Although fond of the same sex, it was food he loved best. And one day ate himself to the core."

George raised an eyebrow. *Ate himself to the core? What does that mean? Christ, it barely even rhymes.*

Something pattered across the oak floor, rat-heavy, just to his right. George turned, stared curiously, then began to laugh the way a man laughs when he's just discovered that sanity is a very loose thing, tethered to one's being the way a carnival balloon is loosely knotted around a child's finger, apt to just suddenly unsnarl, then quietly drift away.

And be lost forever.

Hunkered down like a sprinter awaiting the gun, just beside a polished leg of the coffee table, a naked little fat man winked up at George, then joined him in laughter.

Over by the couch, another spliced in with rolling mirth.

George laughed even louder.

Then a third, over by the reproduction High Boy, holding his bouncing belly like old St. Nick as he howled.

The chorus was quickly joined by dozens more, but George Altman was beyond caring now, was too busy trying to keep his eyes shut as his own laughter (or was he crying?) continued to shake him; was too busy wondering if L'il Willy was ever going to stop playing turtle and poke his head out and finally reveal to all those lookie loos in the mall, in the hallways of his alma mater, that he was really the famed Kraken of myth.

Then George realized that the laughter had stopped, and he was now the only one in the room making a sound. He stifled himself, then mustered up enough courage to open one eye. There were now dozens upon dozens of fat, naked little Georges staring at him from atop the dining room table, from lamp shades, bookshelves, the arms of chairs, curtain rods, the rims of clay planters...They were everywhere, in every nook and corner, their tiny L'il Willies hidden beneath their overhanging bellies.

Their merriment had been replaced with black, beady eyes, voracious in their intensity.

George finally looked at Gamble, who was now in possession of Melanie Sand's flute case.

"How about a little dinner music?" Gamble said as he unfastened the silver clasps. "Any requests?"

George couldn't speak.

"No? Well, I have one. It's called, 'Don't Hurt The Beasties.' I think you'll like it."

The melody was that of "Don't Eat The Daisies," the song made famous by Doris Day in the film by the same name. But the music was quickly crushed beneath the charging of wee little feet.

Then another tune erupted, unmelodic and very high-pitched, as hundreds of ravenous, Lilliputian mouths devoured George Altman.

To the core.

15.

They arrived home, wearing their moods like monogrammed sweaters. Juanita was poking and lurking around like a third world bodyguard, Rachel was so infectiously wired that Duncan's extremities began to tingle when he stood too close to her, and Katherine Bently was just plain chipper. She watched HBO and ate Juanita's peanut butter cookies.

As for himself, Duncan felt overwhelmed. Goofy-tired.

Weary-eyed, he sat behind his desk, harking back to that infamous day when two bullets dashed through his torso.

It was a funny thing, but not once did anyone from Internal Affairs come slithering around; not when he was in the hospital, and not after his release. Those fellas never gave him so much as a dirty look. And all he could ever remember getting from his cronies were a lot of atta-boys and backslapping. He'd received get-well cards from practically every cop within a hundred-mile radius, and dozens more from police departments around the country. There was even one from Israel.

And having lost his partner on top of it, sympathy had been in abundant supply. Hell, he'd been downright pampered. In fact, on the day of his release, a mariachi band, hired by some of his buddies, played "Hail to the Chief" just outside the doors as they wheeled him out.

Everyone thought he was a hero. He'd almost believed it was true.

But he was sure his partner, Tyler Everton, would disagree. If he were alive.

The day of Tyler's funeral was the most sobering of Duncan's life. Though he had still been in intensive care and couldn't attend, he couldn't shake the sense that he was a murderer. That feeling had less to do with the funeral and more to do with his decision to stick to Lieutenant Mo White's somewhat fictionalized version of events.

"No sense in the department losing two good cops" had been Mo's justification.

Jesus, he was so gigantically screwed up then.

Then? Oh yeah, right, he thought. *Now I'm the epicenter of sanity.*

The poster child for Prozac.

And a murderer!

If he could do it again, he knew exactly what he would change.

Everything.

Tyler Everton was a good cop. Good meaning beguiled. Tyler had operated under the inveigled impression that people were basically good and well-intentioned. Duncan, on the other hand, had joined the force knowing full well that human beings were very flawed animals. And it wasn't until he had a few years under his Safari Land basket-weave belt that he understood just how miserably fucked they really were.

Police officers were by no means the exception. On the contrary...

Theirs had not been the partnership upon which cop movies were made, but he and Tyler had nonetheless developed a relationship as trusting as any he had ever had, despite some rather poignant differences of opinion.

You watch my back, I'll watch yours: an aphorism Duncan had written on the front of his locker when he was a rookie. It was a reminder to himself, not his fellow officers, that no matter how insignificant or trivial or inconsequential the job, or life, might seem, he would never surrender a colleague's safety.

He'd known that the cop fraternity was riddled with nothing but cynical, alienated, disenchanted people, sworn to protect and to serve, and to uphold the law through the bloodshot eyes of hypocrisy. When he'd joined the force, his intentions were not to save the world, or even his little corner of it, but to hopefully experience the thrill and excitement that law enforcement promised. Unfortunately, even that illusion was eventually shattered, especially when he was in uniform and cruising the districts. To steal a phrase his captain was fond of: "It's weeks and weeks of boredom punctuated by seconds of sheer terror."

That just about summed it up. And, despite the presumed odds, a large percentage of police officers retired from the force without ever having drawn their weapons. Of course, there were always those very few who could never seem to keep them holstered.

Society was briskly going to hell down a dark vertical shaft, but not so much greased by violence as it was apathy, regardless of what TV and its glut of real-cops-in-action programming would have one think. Those shows didn't often privy the viewing audience to malnourished toddlers living in their own excrement because their mother was too busy whoring to support her drug habit, or the middle-class, upstanding parents who swapped prurient photographs of their six-year-old son with other pedophiles over the Internet.

No, that shit was depressing. People wanted to see fists and cuffs. Hear squealing tires and bleeped-out dialogue. But to the disappointment of all, the vast majority of calls were easy on the knuckles. And the treads.

Hard as hell on the soul.

The list was endless. At least it was for a cop. Because that's what cops did. They lived in decadence day in and day out.

Shit magnets.

They lived reality.

The badge didn't differentiate the good people from the bad, he knew. The "Thin Blue Line" that allegedly separated order from anarchy was just an urban legend. Cops didn't prevent chaos...they controlled it.

It was all just a game; a game where the winners went home in one piece (at least physically), and the losers were left staring down at the shattered remains of what they had for so long thought was truth.

What was truth?

Rachel, after finishing a Joseph Wambaugh novel—they were both avid fans—once said, "There's no way cops are really like that."

Duncan had smiled back. "You're right, babe...they're worse."

Cops. What a funny, pathetic, enduring, decadent, heroic breed they were.

Duncan thought that Baxter Slate, a character from Joseph Wambaugh's *The Choir Boys*, summed it perfectly: *"The very best, most optimistic hope we can cling to is that we're tick birds who ride the rhino's back and eat the parasites out of the flesh and keep the beast from disease and hope we're not parasites too. In the end we suspect it's all vanity and delusion. Parasites, all of us."*

And the night he was shot, Duncan realized just what kind of parasite he'd become. Or worse, what kind of parasite he'd always been. Ironically, while lying there, bleeding to death, it had finally gelled with him that any contrasts existing between the good guys and bad were, truly, only the dense bricks upon which wallflowers grew.

That night, as Lieutenant Mo White was plugging Duncan's wounds with his fingers, he'd assured him that he would personally take care of everything, that they'd all come out heroes, smelling like roses.

Oh, he'd acquired a smell all right, but it wasn't anything like a bouquet of Betty Boops.

As it turned out, Mo himself was a parasite; one of the biggest and most respected bugs to ever create an itch on Boston's crotch.

Duncan had taken his second bullet for Mo; probably had, in fact, saved Mo's life.

And the favor was returned in spades.

Mo White: The baddest, blackest cop on the force. Everybody loved Mo. Everybody.

Duncan had suffered a collapsed lung, and lost nearly four pints of blood and a kidney. Why he hadn't ended up in the morgue was the most asked question by his attending surgeons. They called it a miracle.

Privately, Duncan called it a travesty. He should have died.

Deserved to die.

Like Mo, Duncan had also been well received by his peers and superiors. He'd made a lot of friends in high places over the years, although he never considered it politicking. Not then. It wasn't until later when he realized just what he'd been doing, and how clandestinely he'd been doing it.

Ergo his decision to remain a detective rather than advance in rank, which he could have done effortlessly.

Actus non facit reum nisi mens sit rea: it is Latin, meaning, "an act does not make a person guilty unless the mind is guilty." *Mens rea*: Mental culpability. Duncan had not believed himself culpable of trying to gain favors. But after careful review, that had been exactly his intent. And the funniest thing of all, he eventually learned, was that he was not just doing the priming, but that it was he who was also being groomed. Not for anything in particular, just the back-burner variety.

Don't call us, we'll call you.

Just look the other way.

And he had. Hell, he'd turned his head so many times he developed a cough.

Law-enforcement was definitely a close-knit family, and ratting on a fellow officer was the civilian equivalent of screwing your best friend's wife, sending him the pictures, and charging the hotel room to his VISA. It was not tolerated, and met with its own brand of justice.

And because of his loyal adherence to this policy, Duncan had been cared for by his family.

It was all of this and more that eventually led him to radically renounce conventional justice, and to create his own, the crusade reaching its zenith the moment he'd decided to help Patricia Bently in her desperate moment of need. The death of Charles Bently, her husband, had left her in financial ruin, and he'd found a remedy for that.

For so many years, guilt stalked him like a determined beast. Somewhere along the way, though, he'd stopped running, and the monster gained on him.

And now, according to his daughter (and whoever else was in there with her), he was somehow going to help save mankind like some bearded relic from the Old Testament.

Not the rain forests. Not the whales.

The fucking world!

Check, please!

16.

Summoned by the call of banging glass, Eli made it down the stairs just as the courier came though.

"Impatient bastard," he grumbled.

The creature hopped down from the window, grinned its black, double saw-blade dentition at him, then jerked its wings back from its body like some dwarf exhibitionist, as if to say, *Take a look at this puppy!*

Eli scowled. Its *puppy* wasn't anything to be showing off, but there was even less of Katherine Bently. And that was even more perverted. Blushingly so.

"Son. Of. A. Bitch!" he barked. "Now what?"

On a scoured leg, the creature hobbled to the remnants of what had once been a child's mattress, now beached upon the basement's concrete shores, wads of ticking clustering around the carcass like tide foam.

Given its overall tousled appearance, and the blood trail from the window to the mattress, it was more than obvious that the courier had been involved in some kind of fracas.

It squatted on the cotton remains and began preening. This the couriers did constantly, injuries or not, and at a level that made cats look lazy and squalid in comparison. Eli wondered if it had anything to do with their befouled origins; a stink they kept trying to lick away.

If they'd devote as much time and effort to finding the Bently girl, he thought, *I'd have nine of her by now.*

Glaring at the courier, Eli folded his arms across his chest and said,

"My, my, did we fall off our tricycle?"

The creature kept on grooming, but Eli could tell it didn't much like the innuendo. If it could have effectively raised a middle finger, he was certain it would have thrust one out, wiggling it a few times for emphasis.

"So now what?" Eli said. "Do I send you out again, or replace you with something a bit more competent, say...a blind titmouse?"

The courier hissed at him.

Eli hissed right back. "Kiss my ass! If you don't bring me Katherine Bently before tomorrow morning, I'll have your ass on a skewer." Then something struck him. "Or, is finding her the *easy* part?"

He studied the creature some more, then said, "She's the one who did this to you, isn't she? Got your ass kicked by a little girl."

The courier sheepishly looked away.

"Pussy."

Then more banging erupted. From behind one of the other windows.

Eli turned, and for a moment stood confused. There was something not quite right with the wall, or perhaps the basement itself.

And then it struck him as nothing else ever had.

The seventh window! It's here!

He blinked a few times, stared some more, then—very slowly—turned back to the courier.

In a guarded whisper, he said, "Am I hallucinating, or do you see that, too?"

The creature, engrossed with the ceiling as it worked a large knot up and down its slender throat, ignored Eli altogether. Then it hacked up a hairball.

Too shocked to be disgusted, Eli took a deep breath as he turned back around.

The seventh window was still there, another courier behind it, banging again; louder this time. Although he'd been expecting it, deliriously so, he hadn't realized until just now how emotionally unprepared he was for its arrival.

He finally exhaled, purging his lungs and lingering doubt, surveying the seventh window rather than just ogling it. It appeared to share the same dimensions as the other six—No, Eli thought, that wasn't exactly true. There was one dimension where it digressed from all the others: Depth. And it's design of colored glasses was wonderfully grandiose: the image of a man—it was him—stepping into a black, rectangular portal, his right lower leg disappearing into the abyss. And he was especially taken with the way the artist delineated the victory—*the triumph!*—in his smile.

Actually, it reminded him a little too much of Elton John's "Goodbye Yellow Brick Road" album cover where the bespectacled entertainer was stepping into a picture and onto the road Dorothy and Toto allegedly traveled.

But most of all he was enraptured with those enormous feathered wings, jutting majestically from his back. Elton's glittered pumps paled in comparison, he thought wryly.

He couldn't move. It felt as if some kind of refrigerant had been injected into his neck, as the circulation there had grown cold, the iciness now exuding down his spine, tickling every follicle, erecting every hair as it coursed beneath the dermis.

He supposed he'd expected this one to arrive differently than the others; with some fanfare, maybe...noise makers, balloons, streamers, champagne on ice.

The courier continued to rap behind the glass, obviously eager to be rid of the weight of the little girl.

The seventh angel.

Tears welled in Eli's eyes, and the next eight steps were the longest and most memorable he had ever taken.

17.

Melanie Sands opened her eyes. She was naked, stretched out on her left side. The cement beneath her was numbing in its coldness. Her shoulders ached, and she was incredibly thirsty.

As she pushed herself to her knees, she saw that she'd peed the floor. There was blood, too—

Something behind her retched like a cat.

She turned and, at the sight of the creature, instantly remembered her abduction from Mr. Altman's front yard. The animal, apparently having roused itself awake by its own vulgar noises, regarded her with a part-startled, part-groggy expression.

Then it licked itself *down there.*

Gross.

It was obviously a boy creature because it had a pee-pee just like Jake, her beagle.

Then, just as Jake would have probably done, the creature leaned forward and sniffed the wet spot on the cement, then proceeded to her crotch.

"Shoo," she said, her tone only a glimmer of what she'd intended.

The creature tipped its head, considered her for what seemed like forever, then looked down at its privates. And stared. Immodestly, perversely, carnally...

Just. Stared.

But what horrified Melanie was its smile, a thin, calculating, curling-at-the-edges Grinch-grin.

As she backed away, expecting the attack to come at any moment, the creature slowly lifted its head. Still grinning, it followed her with lustful eyes as she scooted along the cement floor.

She eventually backed herself against a joist, cleaving her bare back with its splintered edges. White sparkles of pain danced before her as her heels kept scuffing a retreat. She had no intentions of ever stopping, of ever taking her eyes off the monster. But as her heart settled with the slow realization that she was going to be left alone, at least for now, she relaxed a bit and began inspecting her surroundings more closely, always keeping the creature well within her peripheral range of vision.

The room was about the same size as her bedroom back home, except this one didn't have any walls, just boards. And through these wood beams she could see the simple floor plan of the basement. Most of it, anyway. To her right was an adjoining room, unfinished as well, and in it was another animal, same kind as the one with her, squatting on a torn-up old mattress. She thought it looked hurt, had maybe been in a fight with a big dog or something. Surprisingly, she found herself feeling a bit sorry for it.

In front of her was another room, this one much larger. And way across on the opposite wall she could see what looked like church windows. She counted three, and got the impression there were more, but her view was blocked by the half-finished section of wall that ran lengthwise down the center of the basement. And on the far end wall, near the windows, she could see an open doorway accessing a wooden flight of stairs.

Stark and shadowy, the overall layout was largely incomplete. There did appear to be an enclosed room this side of, and closest to, the stairs. Maybe half the size of the room she was in. She thought she could see a thread of red light running along its upper edge where the facing wall and ceiling weren't quite flush.

She then looked down at herself and began inspecting her shoulders, arms, chest...She had puncture wounds everywhere. One hole in her left chest was still bleeding badly. *They should be hurting like the dickens*, she thought. But they weren't; just kinda throbbed.

She stared accusingly at her captor's sharp talons, then glanced at the other creature in the next room, not feeling a bit sorry for it anymore.

Then she heard footsteps. Someone coming down the stairs.

Reflexively, she straightened against the joist, then began pushing against it, struggling again, hoping and praying she could burst through and fall back down the dream hole that was surely hovering above her nice, warm bed back home.

"My, my," the man said as he entered the room. "Up from our nap?"

She pulled her knees to her chin. She'd seen those kinds of clothes before, the kind the man was wearing. He was a minister or something. But that didn't make her feel any better. Maybe even worse.

There was a camera in his right hand.

The man stepped aside, then motioned for the creature to leave.

It snorted its disapproval, then hobbled indignantly through the doorway. It made its way over to one of the church windows, then—magically—jumped inside. And was gone.

She froze as the man knelt before her.

He stroked her hair. "The ones before you were exceptionally pretty. But I just might have to concede that you're the prettiest of them all." He leaned over and kissed the top of her head. "I guess they saved the best for last."

She buried her face between her knees.

"Legs down, chin up," he ordered. "I want all of that beautiful face."

Knowing that her mind wouldn't dare move them on its own, she pushed her knees down with her hands.

"What's your name?" he said brusquely.

She didn't answer.

"Vee haf vays of maykink you talk."

"Melanie," she whimpered.

"Melanie ... *what?*"

"Sands."

He brought the camera to his face. "Well, Melanie Sands, I'm in something of a hurry, as I have to get back to the church. So, if you'll just bear with me..."

The flashes were blinding.

She raised her arms to shield her eyes. Voice hitching, she said, "May I have my clothes back?"

"No can do," he said. "But not to worry. I've got something that's going to fit you *just right.*"

He began circling her, taking picture after picture after picture. Oddly, the electronic whirring noise made by the camera's auto advance seemed to intensify her thirst.

"Sir, can I please have a glass of water?"

"Very thirsty, are you?"

"Real bad thirsty," she said, trying so very hard not to cry.

He sat the camera gingerly on the floor. "How about some lemonade instead?"

Melanie nodded, her chin quivering.

"Alright then," the man said as he began to unzip his pants. "One glass of lemonade coming right up."

"Eli!" shouted a voice from the stairs, that of an old woman. She raised her cane and aimed it at the man like a rifle. "I'll get her some water from the tap, so zip it up!"

He quickly obeyed the woman. "Haven't I warned you about sneaking around, Mother?"

"The world ain't yours yet," she said. "Until then, this is my house. If you don't like it, then go back to your cot at St. Patrick's."

Chuckling, he said, "Alright, get her some water then. And while you're at it, bring me down a beer, will you?"

18.

As if he'd just emerged from an office filled with whining faxes and whirring printers, the sounds of his camera still haunted his ears. And his crotch. Those sounds were, without fail, the only things in this world that could give him an erection—whether he wanted one or not.

After having captured two rolls of black and white images of Melanie Sands, Eli hurried back to the church. The little girl remained in the custody of his deranged mother, who he instructed to begin preparations for the wings. He'd also dispatched two couriers: one to contact Gamble, as he urgently needed to speak with him, and another to search out and recapture the Bently girl.

Now he sat in the confessional, which was feeling exceptionally close today. Christ, it was hot. Five more minutes and he thought he just might smother to death.

Then footsteps.

Finally, the adjacent door opened and closed.

"You rang?" said Gamble.

Eli inhaled deeply. "I believe that Samuel Flannery is going to pursue his findings."

"You're referring to the sword imbroglio, I presume?"

"Yes."

"You have to admit, Father, it's damned clever. Oh sure, it's amateurish, puerility at its most basic, yet still manages to deliver its message with discerning *savoir-faire*. Don't you agree?"

"Um, yes, of course."

Eli waited uncomfortably for Gamble to speak. Nearly a minute passed before he finally did.

"Very well," Gamble said cheerily. "I'll make sure that Flannery doesn't become the town crier."

"I wouldn't mind doing it myself."

"Nonsense! You have other things requiring your full and immediate attention. And let me just say how proud I am of you. Although congratulations aren't quite in order just yet, you now have your seventh angel and window, padre! You're almost there! You're sliding into home base! Wow! I imagine that you're extremely excited, yes?"

Eli managed a smile. "Excited is not quite the word I would use."

Gamble let go with a charitable laugh. "Just don't wet yourself prematurely, Father. Keep painting by the numbers and we'll all come out well."

"Melanie flies tomorrow."

"Does she? Very well, then. But don't forget about Katherine."

"Oh, I haven't," he promised through clenched teeth. "I have another courier looking for her this very moment. That little cow's going to rue the day she was born."

Gamble pressed his face against the screen. "I think you meant to say *days*."

"*Days*, yes, of course," Eli said, rolling his eyes at Gamble's affinity for the arcane. "Also, there's one thing I've been...been meaning to ask you." His hands were trembling in his lap.

"Yes?"

"It's about Katherine Bently. You see, I can understand how...how she might have easily remained secluded from *me* these past years. But I was curious as to how she got past...*you*."

The burgeoning silence began to liquefy and was soon a cold, drizzling dread saturating his skin, leaching the air from his lungs, numbing his soul like Novocain. Eli could not enlist so much as a wheeze to verify that Gamble had not already turned him into a bloating corpse. Or worse.

Gamble cleared his throat. "That's a valid question, Father. In fact, I'm surprised you didn't approach me about this earlier. Well, I imagine you were somewhat fainthearted to confront me with such a quiz. Am I right?"

"Y-yes."

"Well, the truth of the matter is, I *did* know of Katherine's whereabouts. Naturally, when she didn't show up after her nasty fall, I went looking for her. I eventually found her, but in a place, shall we say, that was not graciously accessible to me. So, I just left her alone, knowing that she'd rear her ugly head eventually."

"So, may I be...absolved from any negligence regarding the little bitch?"

"Exculpated, vindicated, exonerated—why, Father, consider yourself pardoned."

"Thank you," Eli said, near tears.

"You're welcome. But if you don't catch and keep her this time, I'll personally handpick the bacteria necessary to ensure that the excruciating ingestion of your flesh not only endure eternity, but also its successors."

"Of course," Eli whispered.

19.

After his meeting with Gamble, Eli hurried back to his mother's house.

He stood once again before the seventh window, enraptured.

Knowing that he shouldn't, but unable to resist the urge any longer, he pushed his hand through the window. Instantly, he was passing through stratums of time, his fingers resonating across the layers as if he were strumming the cords of a vast celestial harp. Pushing onward, his groping fingers began to feel planets revolving around alien suns, galaxies teeming with life, infant universes growing on the frontiers of creation, suckling from the pulsing lifeblood of that which is eternal.

The mobiles of gods.

The tactility he was experiencing was not suggestive in any way. He was actually feeling these things on so literate a scale as to be acutely unimaginable; touching not with the fingers of his hand, but with the phalanges of something so powerful, so omnipotent, that the light of creation would be snuffed with one little pinch should the decision be made to do so.

Oh, how superbly grand!

He smiled triumphantly. He would be ruler of these realms once Gamble released him.

He withdrew his arm, which he'd submerged up to his elbow, and studied it. Although it looked no different, it felt bewitched with a sensation of denseness and hollowness at the same time; here and not here.

Grand, yet humble.

Within seconds, however, the arm felt like its old self.

Eli was intoxicated.

The fruition of his many years of hard work was about to be fully realized.

20.

As Rachel and Duncan left the room, having just tucked her in, Kathy said, "Thanks for letting Juanita come with us." She sat up suddenly in bed. "I mean, you did tell her she's coming, right?"

"Of course we did," Rachel said.

Duncan scowled. "I had to give her my window seat. She started blubbering about having never flown before, wants to 'see *thee* world from a *beeg* height,' so..."

"See," Kathy said. "Amy didn't believe me when I told her that you really *liked* Juanita."

"That's a vicious rumor," he balked.

She flopped back down, laughing. "You can't fool me, Donut. I know you like her."

"Okay," he said, "she's all right. Sometimes." He put his hand on the light switch. "Now go to sleep. Our flight leaves very early."

"When we take off it'll still be dark," Rachel said. Then, just as she always did with Amy every night, she blew Kathy a kiss from the doorway. "Sweet dreams."

Hurriedly, Kathy said, "Rock Bay isn't the end of the world."

"Of course it's not," Duncan said. "I believe that title belongs to New Jersey."

Rachel stared at her curiously. "Why would you say that?"

"Just because," she said. "See ya in the morning."

Then the light went out.

"The angel of death has been abroad throughout the land; you may almost hear the beating of his wings."

–John Bright

Part Three
Reunion

1.

The sun was a good thirty minutes away, and already the airport was bustling.

In the line for United, the woman standing in front of Chris Kaddison was a bit shorter than him, but much broader about the shoulders. Her carrot-red hair was cropped military-style, and the back of her bare neck offered a galaxy of freckles, with a few eraser-size moles added for celestial dimension. But it was the silkscreen on her back—two grinning, leather-clad skeletons straddling a Harley Davidson motorcycle—that was adjuring him to betray his better judgment.

The man next to her, a tall, thickset ape with a shaved head and Fu Manchu mustache (and pierced in places even Chris hadn't considered), carried his own proverb: *If you can read this*, proclaimed the back of his shirt, *then the bitch fell off*.

Chris could no longer contain himself. "Biker cunt!"

From the adjacent lines of travelers, an erudite brunette (with the biggest pearl necklace he'd ever seen) went slack-jawed, gaping at him in disbelief; a dark-skinned man, who Chris guessed was of Muslim descent, was studying him with the black, abhorring eyes of Allah. And to his immediate left a rather refined gent in a gray tweed jacket was nodding in agreement.

The redhead glanced casually around, as if the accusation had surely been directed at someone else.

"Biker cunt!" he charged again. A nervous tick had begun to somersault across the left side of his face. As if to quell a threatening burp, he pressed the top half of his one-way ticket to his pursed lips. *Damn!* His mouth was going to get him into trouble once again.

This time, the redhead turned slowly around. Her front looked every bit as masculine as her back insinuated. Chris even thought she might have a bright future as a short lumberjack.

The Ape had turned around as well, and was regarding Chris dolefully; sorrowful, perhaps, that he was going to have to squash this little bug.

Standing a few persons ahead of the redheaded biker was an older woman who looked and dressed like a Rockwell schoolmarm. She was ogling him, her huge bosom swelling around her crocheted carry-on as if it were the eyes and ears of a child, protecting it from the wickedness that abounded in this world.

Staring directly now into her eyes, Chris quickly countered himself. "Like, I'm really sorry, lady. It's just that I—*cunt!*—have a condition."

Her eyes narrowed. "A condition, huh?" she said in a voice that was more feminine than Chris had anticipated. "How would you like me to cut—"

"Kick-stand mama!" Chris barked.

"—your balls off and shove them down your throat?"

"That might be an undertakin'," said a tall, urban cowboy, his chivalry as garish as his belt buckle, "considerin' the fact that this asshole's obviously got a pair the size of bowlin' balls between his legs."

"Split-tail on wheels!" Chris accused.

"Potty-mouths," Schoolmarm accused, indignant. "The both of you!"

The urban cowboy laughed. "Don't go gettin' your cotton undies all bunched up, grandma. I believe what this pissant needs is for me to stomp his ass into a mud hole."

The Ape stepped in. "I'll take care of this," he said wearily. "You can have sloppy seconds."

Although a few passing travelers had paused to observe the quarrel, most continued on without giving a second glance. Those waiting in line, however, were forced to endure the situation, some with scathing resentment, still others with ribald amusement, but most with indifference. After all, Chris thought, this was LAX, where fracases like this were as much a part of the scenery as those Rama-Rama-Ding-Ding guys and their Hare Krishna bibles—although he hadn't really seen any of those people hanging around this morning. It had been quite some years since he'd been in LAX, or any airport for that matter, and he wondered if they'd been kicked out for good, or if they'd just opened up their own website like everybody else.

The quiver on his face was growing spastic.

A pretty flight attendant, blonde, clad in a tight, navy skirt and vest, towing a miniature dolly stacked with luggage, hesitated as she went by. "Everything all right here?" she said with a practiced smile.

"It's about to be," promised the Ape.

"Chrome blower!" Chris said, backing away from the promising beginnings of a lynch mob. God, how he hated lynch mobs. He'd been the focus of many throughout his years as an intrepid loudmouth.

*****

Kathy tugged Duncan's pant leg. "What's a chrome-blower?"

"A poor choice of words," Duncan said, watching the commotion with keen interest.

"Are they going to beat him up?"

"More like *throttle* him, I think," Duncan said, but Kathy missed the joke.

"Stay out of this, Duncan," Rachel warned. "You're not the law anymore."

But Duncan was already on his way.

"Damn it, Duncan!" Rachel shouted after him.

The young man—still in laudable control considering the mess he was in—gestured with his hands pleadingly, but his mouth kept betraying him.

Duncan pushed his way in. "Ever heard of Tourette's Syndrome?"

The afflicted man nodded.

"No," said the Ape, "but I've heard of people getting hurt when they don't mind their own business. So step aside, asshole."

"Of course!" said the pretty flight attendant. "Oh my God, of course!"

"Spontaneous, uncontrollable outbursts," Duncan explained. "This young man suffers from a medical affliction, not a moral one."

"You tellin' me this asshole's got a prescription to spout off at the mouth whenever and whatever he wants?" said the garish cowboy, stepping toward Duncan.

Duncan met the advance: "I don't remember him calling you a shitkicker. Get my drift?"

The cowboy stood his ground for a moment, reconsidered, then dropped back a few paces. Throwing up his arms, he said, "Hey, I was just tryin' to help."

"You wanna help," said the redheaded biker, "then fuck off already."

Emasculated, the cowboy cowered into the crowd.

"John Wayne!" Chris called after him.

Although the Ape stood his ground, his steely if not somewhat groggy eyes conveyed a look of surrender, as if he could smell a badge, retired or not. "Can't you put a muzzle on him?"

"Afraid not," Duncan said. "He's not my dog."

"Isn't there a pill you can take for that?" said the redheaded biker.

Chris nodded. "Yeah, there is. Quite a few, actually. But I don't—*bitch!*—take any medication because it screws with my telepathic abilities."

She looked stunned. "Only in LA!" she exclaimed, shaking her head. She grabbed her apish partner, both huffing and elbowing and excusing themselves back into line.

"Thanks, dude," Chris said to Duncan. "But, like, how did you know I have Tourette's?"

Duncan smiled. "Let's just say that I made the same mistake once."

He looked Duncan up and down. "Cost someone the use of their lip, I'll bet."

"And two days' suspension for me," Duncan admitted. "You seem fine now."

Chris offered a devilish grin. "I was fine three minutes ago. Sometimes a guy just has to make his point."

"And what point would that be?" Duncan said. "That you're a bigot?"

"Hey, dude, most of it was legitimate," he assured, not the least bit insulted.

Chuckling, Duncan said, "So, you're heading to Boston, too?"

"Yeah," Chris said. "Business trip."

"Ahh."

"Hey, like, thanks for helping me out." He extended a hand. "Name's Chris."

"Duncan," he said, taking Chris's hand. "And don't mention it."

Chris's face pulled back in sudden shock. "McNeil? *You're* Duncan McNeil?"

Duncan tightened his grip. "Yes. I am."

"Wow!" Chris said. "This is too *bonzoid!*"

"Translate."

"Like, you're why I'm going to Massachusetts. Flyspeck called Rock Bay. I'm supposed to meet you at some chick's place—*owh, owh...*" Grimacing, twisting back and forth, Chris said, "Dude, my hand!"

Duncan released him. "The name of this chick?"

"Patricia...something," Chris said as he dug into his blue jeans pocket. He withdrew a crumpled piece of yellow notebook paper. "I wrote it down. Yeah. Here it is. Patricia Bently. Her address is—"

"I know her address," Duncan said. Upon the wrinkled piece of paper, below Patricia's name and residential information, he observed the names Kathy, Amy, Wife Rachel, Juanita, and his own.

"There's just one 'L' in McNeil," Duncan said. "It was the *only* habit my ancestors dropped when they came over."

"Sorry," Chris said. "Like, I just write down what the voices tell me."

What the voices tell him?

"Voices?" Duncan said, his legs beginning to buckle.

"Peter, Paul, and Mary," Chris said. "The voices in my refrigerator." He shrugged. "Well, this week's crew, anyway."

Up until this point, Duncan supposed he was in denial, was still holding on to the hope that it was all just a nightmare aggravated by a severe stroke. He would like to believe that at this very moment some nurse in an ICU ward was making his comatose ass comfy while preparing to give him his low fat, low sodium breakfast intravenously.

"Excuse me a moment," Duncan mumbled. Dizzy, he backed into a row of chairs and plopped himself down. "These voices: Peter, Paul, and Mary. You don't mean the, um...the people who sang, 'Monday, Monday,' do you?"

"No, dude," Chris said, sounding slightly annoyed. "You're thinking of the Mamas and the Papas. And they aren't the ones mentioned in the *Bible*, so don't take that exit either. I mean, c'mon, don't make this any weirder than it has to be."

Although his face was now hovering above his knees, Duncan was coming around. "Oh, wait, yeah, they were the ones who did, 'Leaving On a Jet Plane.'" He slowly lifted his head, regarded his surroundings with a bit of wonderment, and said, "Doesn't that strike you as being a rather odd coincidence?"

"Naw, it's too vague. I mean, if it was 'Leaving on a Jet Plane to Rock Bay to Kick Ass,' then that might get my attention. Or, for instance, they also did 'Puff the Magic Dragon,' and if they'd asked me to meet you in the Hotel Honah Lee, and you'd just made reservations with a desk clerk by the name of Jackie Paper who sold sealing wax on the side, then I might be swayed. But, hey, don't get me wrong, synchronicity's par for the course."

Duncan was sorry he asked. "So, you're clairvoyant, huh?"

"Among other things," he stated proudly.

"I see," Duncan said, shakily rising from the chair. "Then I assume you're foreseeing a safe flight for us this morning?"

"Oh, for sure." Then, appearing slightly worried, he said, "But, like, I can't see beyond tomorrow. It's all blank after that. It just keeps going deeper and deeper until it eventually turns itself inside out. Then it repeats."

"What repeats?"

"The nothingness."

Duncan was starting to feel like he did when Juanita took her native tongue to speeds and levels beyond his comprehension. Satirizing the gallant cowboy, he offered, "Maybe you just got a catch in yer get-along."

"Ain't nuttin wrong with my get-along, pardner," Chris rebutted. "I jest 'spect it's cuz I've been lopin' my mule too much."

"Well, there's yer answer," Duncan said. "Ya done finally went and gone blind."

Chris pointed. "Is that yer missus over yonder, lookin' madder'n a tick on roadkill?"

Duncan nodded. "I reckon it is."

He grabbed Chris's carry-on, shouldered it, and started walking. "Where you from?"

"San Diego," Chris said. "I just hope it's there after tomorrow."

Interested, Duncan looked down at the young man. "Why wouldn't it be?"

"Dude, you really don't know what's going on, do you?"

2.

As he drove away from the Texaco, leaving Gloucester proper, Duncan set the cruise control to five miles over the posted limit and started wondering again why he'd suddenly developed a fear of flying.

He'd flown in aircraft all of his life, from rotor- to fixed-wing, and not once had he ever given it a second thought. Until today. Thankfully, he was already on the ground when the phobia struck. Just as they entered Salem...Witch country. Probably just an errant spell, he'd reasoned, floating around like a cold virus. Maybe it was nothing. Maybe it was something. Hell, he just couldn't figure it out.

But he was confident that it had nothing to do with either crisis he'd faced earlier while at 32,000 feet.

The first calamity was encountered about forty-five minutes after takeoff from LAX. A rather homely stewardess had explained to everyone in coach that the Harrison Ford movie that was scheduled would not be shown after all, as they were experiencing technical difficulties. Somehow, Duncan had managed to hide his grief. Rachel, on the other hand, wouldn't have looked more shocked if an oxygen mask had dropped in front of her face. And the meager jeers that followed only confirmed what the passenger manifest already knew: the plane was practically empty.

And Duncan still thought that damned odd.

Approximately one hour later, the second catastrophe occurred. For no apparent reason, Kathy suddenly reached across Juanita, who was sitting in the window seat, and turned the little capsule-shaped porthole into an RCA color television set, prompting Duncan to blow Corona out his nose, and Juanita to mime the entire King James version of the Old Testament.

The picture appeared for maybe forty-five seconds, if that, and winked out when Kathy finally freed her hand from the porthole. The scene was unimaginative, to say the least, appearing to have been a drab, everyday living room straight out of the mid-sixties.

Juanita had quickly covered the window with her pillow, but the severe lack of passengers turned the intrepid move into a pointless one.

And then there was Chris. Chris was sitting in the seat directly in front of Duncan, asleep when the incident began. Just before Kathy disconnected from the window, Duncan told Juanita to move the goddamn pillow, nudged Chris awake, then directed him to the image.

Chris glanced at the window, then back at Duncan, smirked, and said, "Wake me when she turns the cockpit into a Taco Bell."

Rachel, sitting in the aisle seat, dozing herself, had missed most of it, but had caught enough to ask the ugly stewardess for two vodkas, neat please, twists of lemon in both, hold the rocks.

When Duncan asked Kathy how she did it, she sheepishly replied, "That was an oops. You guys weren't supposed to see that yet. Sometimes my hand sticks, and, well..."

When Rachel asked her if what happened in the ambulance was an "oops," Kathy tried to pin the blame on Amy. That didn't go down well with Rachel, and, eventually, Kathy recanted, admitting she had a problem, that she couldn't help herself sometimes, that she liked the feeling it gave her. Duncan asked her if she knew of a twelve-step program available for her addiction, but she didn't know what he was talking about, thus doing to levity what icy wings had done for DC-10s.

They connected in St. Louis, and the flight from there to Boston was uneventful.

Yes, Duncan was quite certain that the answer to his sudden phobia lurked elsewhere.

Throughout the trip, Juanita had assumed the role of Kathy's shadow, even to the point of not only taking her to the bathroom but insisting that she go with her into the stall. That's where Kathy drew the line.

Chris's succotash-surfer slang was a bit much sometimes, as was his glib attitude, but both were tolerable, as were his facial tics and the other impetuous body motions that seized him without warning.

Massachusetts was in the grip of a heat wave that had lately been singeing both seaboards and most of the south. Only the upper central states appeared to have the opposite problem. Heavy snows were forecasted for a second straight day in the lower Great Lakes regions, and Des Moines, Iowa was already under twelve inches of the stuff.

Wild.

On the radio, Mike "Mad Dog" Malhooney, the DJ for KMRX out of Boston, stated rather flippantly that the unseasonably hot weather was a wake-up call from God. Mad Dog suggested that his listeners not consult with their local clergy but rather the mercury in their front porch thermometers for spiritual guidance.

"Are these the End Times?" Mad Dog spookily asked, then cut to commercial.

Well, it was hot, no doubt about it. But FEMA wasn't passing out flame-retardant knickers just yet. Mad Dog was just being facetious, but his point was well taken.

Duncan was grateful that they weren't traveling through the Deep South. Airwaves through the Bible-Belt were no doubt hotter than the current heat wave.

He turned left on Hawthorne Avenue and began reading the numbers on the houses. They were only two blocks away.

Rachel had been exceptionally quiet during most of the drive, taking in the scenery much the same way an emphysema patient takes in oxygen. She'd asked him to drive slowly through each town. In Ipswich, she made him stop at Madge's Bakery ("It's still here!" she'd blubbered), where she bought everyone a pastry and an espresso for herself and Juanita.

She was home.

Kathy appeared to be developing a bond with Chris, one that was more father-daughter than brother-sister.

Juanita didn't look happy about Chris's presence, although, in Duncan's estimation, she was doing a damn fine job of keeping her feelings to herself. Duncan liked Chris, but he understood Juanita's apprehension. He was feeling it, too.

3.

In front of the house, Duncan eased the rented Thunderbird to a stop.

It was a big place—maybe 3,500 square feet, not including the basement. The paint looked old, a piss yellow. The chain-link fence was new, and the hulking, twisted cottonwood out front was so massive that twelve years' growth would have gone unnoticed.

"Well," Rachel sighed, "are we going to just sit here, or are we going to get this over with?"

"Get it *over* with?" Chris laughed. "Sweet Cakes, this party's just starting!"

"I've asked you once," Rachel snarled, "and I'll ask you again—Don't call me 'Sweet Cakes.'"

Chris pushed out his hands. "Yikes, chill, sorry."

"Let's go," Duncan said, killing the ignition. He unlatched his safety belt, opened the door. His palms were sweating, hands shaking.

In the lead and grinning madly, Chris opened the gate—and instantly stopped. He kneeled down on the scorched lawn, bent over and pressed his right ear onto the brown blades of grass.

Duncan stood over Chris. "Just what the hell are you doing?"

"Maybe the dead are talking to him," Rachel posited.

Chris held a finger to his lips.

Juanita looked around nervously, then whispered, "He is crazy, Señor Duncan. He is going to bring us much trouble."

Just as Duncan was reaching down to grab him by his shirt collar,

Chris said, "There's something down there."

"Moles?" Duncan said, feigning true concern.

Chris stood up. "I'm serious. The worms are all worked up."

"Oh, brother," Rachel moaned, rolling her eyes.

Juanita couldn't believe it. "You tried to talk with the worms?"

"I can talk to any animal," Chris said, appearing offended that he was not preceded by his reputation. "I have something like a universal translator."

"Is that what they're calling it now?" Rachel said, then grabbed Duncan's arm. "Let's just go."

Chris pointed to the ground. "I'm telling you, dude, there's something down there, and it ain't the Avon Lady."

Appearing spooked, Kathy carefully tip-toed off the grass and back onto the cement walkway.

Duncan bristled. "You, Dr. Doolittle, will behave, or I will personally upgrade your connection to the spirit world."

Chris saluted. "Aye, aye, captain."

They walked toward the porch while Chris straggled behind like a moping teenager.

Duncan rang the bell.

An elderly woman answered, and Duncan instantly recognized her as Patricia's mother.

"May I help you?" She smiled.

Sheepishly, Duncan smiled back. "Mrs. Pendleton."

She shuffled closer to the screen, where a breeze caught and parted her silver bangs. "You're damned familiar," she said in a friendly way. "Have we met?"

"Yes ma'am. Long time ago."

She did not seem to hear him, her gaze now focused on Kathy. Duncan could see the color evaporating from her face.

Joan Pendleton opened the screened door, lowered herself unsteadily to her knees, and gaped in astonishment at the little girl.

"Hi, Grammy." Kathy smiled, holding her arms out for a hug.

Joan, eyes filling with tears, held out her own arms, and they embraced.

"I missed you," Kathy whispered. She brushed the tears from her grammy's face. "Is Mommy here?"

"I'm here," Patricia said from behind the screen. She was staring at Kathy, but not the way someone would who suspects a hateful prank. Instead, in her eyes was inured acceptance, as if the child before her was the same wandering ghost who passed through her walls daily, never quite solid enough to take away the insanity of their *own* embraces.

"Mommy!" Kathy cried, rushing to the screen.

Patricia stayed behind the door, holding it shut.

Duncan thought she looked remarkably well, considering her losses. Apparently no longer a prisoner to high fashion, she wore a simple white blouse, blue jeans with a hole in the left knee, and a tan pair of flip-flops. Her raven hair was off her shoulders, and her thick lips still affected that lachrymose pout that he'd once found so irresistibly kissable.

She looked damned good in rural, he had to admit, and guessed that Rachel was thinking the same thing, but with far less admiration.

An old, fat dachshund waddled up to Patricia's feet and, upon seeing Kathy, emphatically began whining and pawing at the screen, its tail a blur.

"Pillsbury!" Kathy cheered.

Patricia opened the door just enough to let the dog through.

There was a reunion of yelping and licking and elated giggles.

Joan was still on her knees. "I don't feel so well," she moaned, wavering dangerously.

Rachel and Duncan immediately helped the woman to her feet.

"She needs to lie down," Duncan said to Patricia.

Patricia did not open the door; just stood there fidgeting with the bracelet on her wrist. "Who the hell are you people?" she said curiously.

Duncan realized that, just as her mother, Patricia was reeling from the ambush.

"Patricia," he instructed, "we need to bring your mother in and get her knees elevated."

"Donut's right," Kathy said. "Please, Mom?"

Patricia hesitated, then guardedly pushed open the door.

They put Joan on the couch and slipped two throw pillows beneath her feet.

Duncan turned to Patricia and saw that she and Kathy were staring at one another from opposite ends of the room.

Apprehension owned Patricia's features.

Kathy continued to wear her patient, understanding smile.

"Patricia?" Duncan said. "Meet Katherine Bently."

Sounding amused, if not a little condescending, Patricia said to Kathy, "You're not my daughter."

Kathy said nothing; just kept smiling.

Patricia took a step forward. "Did you hear me?"

Kathy nodded that she did.

Laughing now, Patricia said, "I mean, that's the most ridiculous thing I've ever heard. It's crazy. There is no way on God's green Earth that you could be my daughter. I mean, sure, there's a resemblance, but she...she would have been a lot older than you now, and...and I'll bet that, oh hell, I'll bet that you don't even remember...wait, *that you don't even know my middle name.*"

Kathy smiled even wider.

Hands on her hips, Patricia said, "Well? Speak up. See, you couldn't be my daughter because my daughter has my middle name, too."

Patricia turned to the group. "See? Case solved. She can't be my daughter—"

Kathy mumbled something.

"—as if there was ever a doubt."

Kathy stepped forward until she was ten feet from Patricia. Raising her voice, she said, "I know what your middle name is."

Very confident now, Patricia said, "I don't believe you do."

Kathy stepped even closer, now just two feet away. Holding out her hand, she said, "Bet?"

Shocked, as if she couldn't believe the gall, Patricia turned back to the group for support; to her mother, to Chris, then Duncan, Juanita, even Rachel. She had a wide-eyed look of consternation, as if she'd just returned from the proctologist and was afraid that the gritty aftertaste in the back of her mouth really was Latex.

Getting no support from the group, she turned back to Kathy. "Alright, what's the bet?"

"If I guess your middle name, then you have to forgive yourself."

"For what?"

"You know."

"Oh, fine, whatever," she said. "Now, if I win, then you and your traveling companions have to get the hell out of this house and never come back."

"Deal," Kathy said.

"Wait!" Patricia said. "And you have to spell it right, too."

"Deal," she said again, and they shook hands.

For a long moment, Kathy and Patricia just stared at each other.

"Well, little miss," Patricia said finally, "let's have it."

Head low, she said ashamedly, "I lied. I can't spell your middle name."

Triumphant, Patricia turned to Duncan. "Bingo! Now, I want you and your dysfunctional family out of my house—pronto!"

"Patty!" gasped Joan. "They brought our Kathy back! How can you—"

"Oh, horseshit, mother! If you believe that then you're as sick as they are!" She flipped her eyes back to Duncan. "Now get out!"

Now at Patricia's side, Kathy said, "Excuse me, please."

"What?" Patricia snarled. "What? *What?*"

With a smile as meek and vestal as a newborn fawn, and a voice just as downy, Kathy said, "The reason I can't spell your middle name is because you don't have one, Mommy. Just like me."

Patricia flashed a hint of surprise, then began to slowly shake her head. "Duncan told you that I have no middle name, just like he told you the name of the dog."

"Pillsbury?" said Joan, now trying desperately to sit up. "Patty, we didn't get Pillsbury until after"—she glanced uncomfortably at Rachel—"until after you and...Mr. McNeil stopped, well, you know what I mean."

"Thanks Mother," she sighed. "But tell me, how can you remember something like that when you can't even remember your granddaughter's birthday?"

"I do so know my granddaughter's birthday," she countered indignantly. "If you remember, I'm the one who baked her cake this year, the one with poppy seed frosting and—"

"And how many candles did we light, Mom? How many candles were on that cake?"

As Joan stared at her daughter, a smile barely broke the surface of her face, then disappeared, then a tiny ripple again, like a wily trout plucking mayflies. But just as her smile remained elusive, a sort of comical frustration grew more and more evident within her eyes.

Duncan thought it looked an awful lot like denial. Maybe shock. Probably both.

"How many, Mother?" Patricia demanded.

Joan was now wringing her hands with such conviction that she might have been demonstrating to a bunch of upstart surgeons the proper way to scrub. Then that elusive smile broke through. She clasped her hands together in front of her chest and said, "Who would like some nice iced tea?"

Chris, sitting in the living room in front of a blank television, raised his hand. "Got any non-decaf herbal?"

Joan hobbled over to Chris and took him by the elbow. "You just follow me straight into the pantry, and I'll show you the menu."

As they both entered the kitchen, Patricia's mother hummed Nat King Cole's "Unforgettable."

"Proud of yourselves?" Patricia said, plopping herself down at the dining room table. Directly across from her sat Juanita, as still and quiet as a trained Doberman, appearing every bit as harmless.

"Patricia?" Duncan said. "I'm really sorry we came unannounced, but it was the only way—"

"Only way to what? Drive me and my mother to the funny farm?"

Rachel stepped forward. "We knew this was going to be a shock. It's a shock to us, believe me. But once you see that she's—"

"Where did you find her?" Patricia said, pointing at Kathy. "And isn't this creepy enough without her staring at me like that? Just stands there and stares. Jesus, she reminds me of those kids in *Village of the Damned*."

"She's just being polite," Duncan said. "Now listen, the natural course for you or anyone is to start in Denial, then Anger, etcetera, etcetera, until you eventually come to Acceptance. Now, because we're kind of strapped for time, we need you to skip from Denial to Acceptance, and leave the cream filling alone."

Patricia clucked. "You haven't changed a bit."

"Just give her a chance," Duncan said.

"This isn't all about Kathy," Rachel said, "or someone who you think just looks like Kathy. This is about something infinitely bigger."

"We are on a mission from God," Juanita boasted.

Patricia buried her face in her hands. "Oh, shit. It's Revival Ministries Hour." Then she looked at Duncan. "What is this, some kind of cult? Wait, don't tell me! You want me to chuck all of my belongings, rent a room at the Ramada, make myself a nice strychnine sandwich, then wait for either Hale Bopp to come back around, or those little gray guys to take me home, right?"

"Listen," Duncan urged, "we're not here to push the Watch Tower, or tell you why Jesus Christ died for your sins. We're here because our daughters want us here." He gave Juanita a scolding glance. "We don't know or pretend to know why we're in Rock Bay. We only know that we have to be here. The answers will be coming soon enough."

"We really need you, Mommy," Kathy said.

Patricia turned in her chair and stared at the girl. "I am not your mommy. So, from now on you'll address me as Mrs. Bently. Understood?"

"Yes, ma'am."

Rachel stepped behind Kathy and put a hand on her head. "I gave birth to this child. I nursed her. I bathed her. I read her *Cinderella* and *The Pokey Little Puppy* and *Jack and the Beanstalk* and a million others. I sent her off to school and was a lot more frightened that first day, I can tell you, than she was. I helped her with her homework. I took her to ice skating and ballet lessons. I took her to the park and let her feed the geese. And I watched her grow into this fine young lady." Then she stepped away from Kathy, renouncing her. "But I am not her mother. You are."

Rachel sat back down.

"I help raise her, too," Juanita said. "Amy, I mean."

"That's right," Rachel said. "Juanita's been with Amy from almost the very start."

Patricia was shaking her head, looking like she didn't know whether to laugh or start pulling out fistfuls of hair. *"But that's just not possible."*

"Of course it isn't," said Duncan. "But that's the way it is."

"Look," Rachel said, "we don't expect you to just take our word for it. So do whatever you think is necessary to either prove or disprove to yourself this little girl's identity. But please hurry because Duncan's right, we don't have a lot of time."

Duncan began to rise. "Look, we'd planned to take a motel in—"

"No!" Joan blurted, eavesdropping from the kitchen doorway. "Absolutely not! I'll have no such thing! You are our guests and will be treated as such. Right, Patty?"

Patricia rose from the table, disgusted. "Fine, Mom, whatever," she said. "Make yourselves right at home." Then she sneered at Duncan. "Anybody wants me, I'll be upstairs scooping out my 'cream filling.'"

Juanita said, "Okay to bring in some luggage, Mrs. Bently?"

"Knock yourself out, Maria."

"Excuse, but my name is Juanita."

"My mistake."

Patricia stormed by just as Chris was leaving the kitchen.

"Twinkie?" he offered.

"Shove it."

4.

Patricia slammed her bedroom door hard enough to evict an expensive cloisonné vase and two ivory figurines from their pinewood retreat on the south wall. Directly below, on her grandmother's French coffer, the red, lily-like flowers of a beautiful amaryllis plant failed to cushion their falls.

"Fuck!"

This. Is. Insane.

How could that bastard McNeil after almost twelve years show up on her front doorstep with his cutesy wife, a fat Guatemalan lady, a lowlife hood, and some little girl who thinks she's Katherine Bently incarnate?

The very nerve of him!

The little girl downstairs was not her daughter. Not her at all. And to even entertain such possibilities, she reminded herself, could quickly find a person finger painting old pill charts with a bunch of groping, weenie-wagging perverts.

She began pacing back and forth.

They brainwashed her, the little girl. That's what happened. Picked her up somewhere in a mall, a shoe store maybe, that playground inside McDonald's...They kidnaped her, Duncan and his gang, his cult, just because she looks a little—okay, a lot—like Katherine used to look. Then they forced her to learn all about Rock Bay and Pillsbury and everyone's middle names. And they were so successful that now the little girl really believes it herself, that she's my daughter. They're here to extort me, threaten to take Katherine away if I don't cough up the money.

The money Duncan never got. Not a penny.

She reached under her bed and brought out two photo albums, then sat them on the forest green comforter. As she reached to open one, her hand hesitated above the leather binding. It hung there for a moment, quivering, then she called it back.

Well, Duncan isn't going to get away with it. He's had twelve years to claim his share of the loot, and if he feels it necessary to go to these extreme measures...these crazy measures to...these crazy, insane, absurd, outlandish means—

"—that are even more unbelievable than having Katherine back!" she blurted, then buried her face in her hands.

"Oh my God, I'm losing it," she bawled. "I've lost my baby girl, I've lost my self respect, and now I've lost my mind." She yanked back a corner of the comforter and pulled it across her face.

Still hitching, she rolled onto her side and stared at the busted heirlooms on the wood floor. Well, at least now she had an excuse to shitcan the ivory pieces. Her father had passed them on to her, but she'd always felt guilty for having them, knowing that some majestic elephant had been slaughtered just so someone could fill their curio cabinet. Or her bedroom.

Nope, in the ground they would go. She'd give them a proper burial. Dad would understand.

As for the cloisonné vase, well...Good riddance to bad rubbish. She never liked that aunt anyway.

The intercom on her night stand transformed her normally emollient mother into a loud, nasally waitress from the Bronx. "Patty, honey?"

Patricia ignored her. Years ago, when her mother's arthritis had gotten so bad that she couldn't climb the stairs for days at a time, she had an intercom system installed throughout the entire house. This was one of those many moments when she wished she hadn't.

Her voice trembling with excitement, Joan said, "I know you're upset, darling, but I think you should come down and listen to what these people have to say. It's incredible!"

She wriggled up to the headboard and let her face sink into a pillow.

"Patty? Are you in there? Are you in the toilet, honey? Okay, I'll just try there. Bye."

Patricia lay there, engrossed with the smell of fabric softener. She brushed her cheek across the linen, caressing it, nuzzling it like a man's chest. That smell was so...*something*; so...

She sat up suddenly and held the pillow at arms' length. She wanted desperately to pitch it across the room, yet was unwilling to let it go.

"Leave me alone!" she spat at the pillow, then shook it as if it were a possessed child. "Just leave me the fuck alone! You're just a pillow, you're nothing!" Now she was punching it. "They all have it! Not just mine!"

Rocking on her knees, she pulled the pillow to her chest, folding and squashing and mashing it with an anger she hadn't known in years.

"They all have it!" she admonished the ceiling, and whatever gods might have been eavesdropping from the rafters. Her tears came so hard it was difficult to see. "Every last one of them! Right down to their Barbie socks and matching underwear! So why are you reminding me now? *Why?*"

She mashed her face into the pillow and kicked her feet. "They all have it! All of them!"

Then she threw the pillow across the room, shouting after it, "They all have it! All little girls have that smell!"

5.

Patricia descended the stairs with two photo albums, although she was sure one would suffice.

Everyone was gathered at the dining room table. Her mother must have had Duncan put in the leaves, as it had grown considerably longer since her last visit. A large coffee maker was brewing on the server, beside which were stacked enough Styrofoam cups to see the local AA meetings through to Christmas. Packets of sugar and creamer filled a small wicker boat, and the napkins and plastic spoons had been artfully arranged. A pitcher of iced tea and another of lemonade were off to the side, both sweating on the white linen. The scene reminded Patricia of the days back at the VFW where she, her mother, and several volunteers had met every morning before going out and pasting practically all of New England with Katherine's fliers.

She'd first lost Charles, her husband, then Katherine in the space of sixteen months. While preparing for his funeral, she'd gone ahead and bought two additional plots, hers on one side of Charles, Katherine on the other. Then two years ago, when she'd finally given up hope of ever seeing her daughter again, she had the headstones placed for Katherine and herself.

Although more profound in some aspects, it was only one day in countless many when she'd truly felt dead.

The air conditioner blasted, and three large floor fans, situated throughout the large dining room, whirred, their combined efforts barely touching the heat.

The little girl who looked like her daughter sat next to the Guatemalan lady, eating cookies from a round silver tray. Duncan and Rachel sat together on the opposite side of Katherine and appeared to be having a sobering conversation with her mother. The junkie, parolee, whatever the hell he was, sat at the head of the table, rockin' to some heavy tunes piped in through his Walkman CD player.

She sat down between the girl and the wired weirdo.

Removing only one of his earphones, Chris leaned over and quietly said, "Someone was looking for you in the john."

"How thoughtful of you to say."

"I mean, all of a sudden this unworldly voice was filling the can," he continued. "Scared the living you-know-what outta me. It was like a damned good thing I was already parked, or I might've had to chuck the briefs."

"I'll alert the press."

"It's just that I'm not used to getting hit like that. It just kept saying, 'Patty? Patty dear? Are you in there, honey?' Normally, I'm in the kitchen when I hear the voices. Audibly, I mean, not just inside my head. Like, I hear voices in my head all the time, but the ones that come from my refrigerator are special." He replanted the earphone, leaned back, and closed his eyes. "It's wild. I mean, how many times do you have to have a philosophical discussion with your vegetable crisper before you start feeling really stupid?"

"Thanks for sharing," she said. But he clearly didn't hear her.

Joan spoke up with maternal urgency. "Patricia, the McNeils have some interesting tales to tell about why they're here, so I think it would behoove you to listen."

"Before I listen to anything," Patricia said, "I have something that I would like 'Katherine' to see." She tapped her finger on the photo album as she went around the table, meeting everyone's eyes. "Time to play Truth or Dare."

Glaring now, Joan said, "I really don't see why that's necessary—"

"That's because you're temporarily insane, Mother."

"It's okay, Grammy," assured the girl. "Mommy—I mean Mrs. Bently—just wants to show me some pictures."

Patricia said, "Care to make any bets this time?"

The girl just shook her head, smiling all the same.

"No?" Patricia opened the album to a random page. She pointed to a color photograph showing two intense men in camouflage overalls. A dead doe lay at their feet. Off to the side, almost out of the picture, was another man looking on. He was older than the other two.

"Name everyone in this picture," Patricia instructed.

She pointed to each as she called off their names: "Uncle Kelly, Uncle Richard, Bambi, and, um, Mr. Carlson from the a...the post office. Oh, and everybody called Mr. Carlson 'Skipper' because he used to have a lot of boats, or something." She looked up at Patricia. "Next."

As if she'd just sat on a kitten, Joan jumped up from her chair and cried, "Oh my God!"

Exceedingly calm, Patricia flipped the page. "Who's the lady in the bottom picture?"

Crinkling her nose, the girl said, "That's Toni, the babysitter. She was always mean to me. I don't remember her last name...but I think it was like a nut."

"Akhorn," Patricia said, then closed the album; gently, delicately, as if she were a minister closing her *Bible* on the last words of an unusually poignant sermon.

Chris, tugging the rings on his right ear the way Carol Burnett used to, said, "Way to smoke 'em, dude!"

Duncan said, "Patricia, I know it's the hardest damned thing in the world to believe, but you have to stay calm. Don't go flipping out. There's nothing wrong with you." He turned to Joan. "Either one of you."

"We know what you're going through," Rachel said. "You have your Katherine back, but now it's our little girl who's gone."

"The one who was in the hospital?" Patricia said. "Amy, right?"

"Yes," Rachel said. "She suffered some kind of...seizure."

Although their eyes locked, Rachel's soul looked away after a moment, and Patricia saw in the vacancy a desperation so sharp, so relentlessly keen, as to be an unstoppable force. Patricia knew of another woman who'd been driven by such despair, but she hadn't led the charge in years. Hope, like her rapiers, had dulled and rusted.

Patricia tipped her head toward the girl. "But—this is her, right? This is Amy?"

Duncan raised his eyebrows. "Not anymore."

"She *was* Amy," Rachel said. "Now she's *your* daughter."

Patricia held up a finger. "Um, let me see if I'm getting this: your daughter Amy, who is only ten years old, winds up in the hospital, believing her name to be Katherine Bently, my daughter from Rock Bay, Massachusetts. The very same Katherine Bently who disappeared from the boardwalk over eleven years ago. And, as it just so happens, Amy looks exactly like my Katherine looked when she was ten years old. And not only does she walk the walk, but she talks a good talk, too," she said, patting the photo album. "And to top it all off, the biological parents of this little girl, out of the billions available, just happen to be our own Rachel and Duncan McNeil, the latter with whom I once shared more than just a motel room." She cleared her throat. "How am I doing so far?"

"So far, so good," said Duncan.

"What is this about motel rooms?" Juanita said.

The girl snickered.

Patricia slowly shook her head. *"I...just...can't...accept it."* She turned to the girl. "I'm sorry, but you are not my daughter."

"Excuse me, but I think we can all appreciate just how unbelievable this all is," Joan said, appearing as if she didn't really appreciate the unbelievable at all. "But just remember, Patty, that God works in mysterious ways."

Patricia slammed her fist on the table. "God has never worked a day in His life, mother," she reminded. "He's a loafer, a lazybones."

Juanita crossed herself as a shocked Joan clutched the big gold cross dangling above her cleavage. Patricia had not seen her mother wear that necklace since she'd thrown it at the television when *America's Most Wanted* ran the last discouraging update on Katherine's disappearance, six years ago.

"Oh, *puh-leese*, Mother," Patricia moaned. "One little ghost and already you're pushing your way past the ushers. Before too long, you'll be singing again in the front row of the choir—if you can make the steps, that is." She was standing now. "But that shouldn't be a problem because God works in mysterious ways, right, Mom? He'll not only cure your arthritis, but as a bonus for hopping back on the minstrel wagon, He'll make it so you'll sound just like Etta James—"

"Okay, okay, okay," Duncan said. "Patricia, sit down. Please."

Patricia lowered her head, suddenly ashamed. "Oh...Mom, I'm so sorry."

"It's all right, Patty dear," her mother said. "I love you."

"I love you, too, Mom. Honest."

As Patricia gathered herself, Duncan used the moment to confiscate Chris's Walkman, and to finally make introductions.

Patricia looked at Juanita. "I'm sorry, but you're here because...?"

"I make sure that nothing happens to the girl."

"Why? Is something supposed to happen to her?"

"*Si*," she said with heavy certainty.

Patricia turned to the girl. "And how do you feel about that?"

Smiling, she said, "Juanita worries too much, but I guess I feel safer having her around."

Now to Chris: "And you have ESP?"

"That acronym encompasses all paranormal abilities and should, like, never be used to designate individual talents," Chris lectured. Then he grinned. "But in my case, it pretty much sums it up."

Patricia nodded, indulging him. "In other words, you're a sort of supernatural jack of all trades?"

"And master of none," Juanita grumpily added.

Chris glared at Juanita, poking his chest. "Hey, man, I just go where they tell me."

"Do they ever tell you to go to hell?" Juanita said into her coffee.

"Juanita!" Rachel gasped, appearing both shocked and amused.

Juanita bit into a lemon cookie and shrugged.

Patricia half-smiled as she looked around the table. "This is just the tip of something, isn't it? I can see it in everyone's eyes. You're not telling us everything."

"We're just as lost as you are," Duncan assured.

"Juanita," she said, "tell me what happens from here?"

"I do not know, Mrs. Bently."

"What about you?" she said to Chris. "What are your psychic antennae picking up?"

"I know this: At sunrise tomorrow, your nice little town will go down in history as the place where it all began to end."

"You mean like end of the world kind've stuff?"

"It will be like nothing you've ever imagined," he assured.

Patricia was trying not to laugh. "In that case, I guess I'd better get some laundry on. I don't want to gallop off with the Horsemen of the Apocalypse wearing a dirty bustle."

"Think I'm full of it?" Chris said, soft but sinister. There was now a faint tick beneath his left eye. "Think I'm some idiot dealing Tarot Cards here?"

"Easy, Chris," Duncan cautioned.

"Think I burn incense and gaze into crystal balls?" he continued with rising malevolence. "Then get a load of this. You haven't been laid in over four years. You and your bowling buddies just got new jackets but they misspelled your name on the front. Pretty boy Marco at the Phillips 66 just robbed you of over three hundred bucks last week when he did absolutely nothing to your Accord except change the air filter. Your best friend in high school was K-Karen Koch who died three days ago in that Amtrak c-crash that killed f-forty-one people. She says hello and not t-to worry anymore about—about that diamond ring you stole f-from her mother's j-j-jewelry box. And—and—" Chris fell from his chair, convulsing.

Patricia remained seated, staring at the spot he'd just left vacant.

Duncan and Rachel reached him immediately. The spasms were primarily occurring on his left side. His eyes rolled to the whites, and his hands, rigid and bent at the wrists, jerked and twitched above his chest. He looked like a praying mantis on crank.

Rachel, on her knees, stared down into his face. Panicked, she said, "Is he trying to swallow his tongue? I think he's swallowing his tongue."

"He can't swallow his tongue," Duncan said. "We just have to wait it out. That's all we can do. Just keep him from hurting himself until it passes."

"Is he high on drugs?" Juanita said, now standing at Chris's right shoulder. With her rosary dangling from both hands, she appeared ready and more than willing to give last rites.

"No, it's just his...disease," Rachel said.

Chris, still quivering and jerking, rolled his eyes back down, then winked at Duncan.

After the initial shock, Duncan grabbed a handful of shirt and pulled Chris to his face. "Just what the *fuck* is your major malfunction?"

"You asshole!" Patricia shouted, now back with the living.

Rachel, eyes closed, appeared to be searching for the manual that provided a list of all the retaliatory measures utilized by decent, God-fearing people who've been duped by lowlife punks with ESP. Finally, she opened her eyes, got up, and kicked Chris's leg. Then she kicked him twice more before silently striding back to the table, fists clenched.

Chris was laughing hysterically now. He kept trying to say something but couldn't find a wide enough spot to get the words through.

"I ought to kick your ass right here in front of God and everybody," Duncan said, appearing to be an eyelash away from doing just that. "I mean, so far up between your shoulders that you'll have to pull your shirt off to take a shit."

Chris howled even louder.

The girl kneeled next to Chris's red, twisting face. "You have a mean streak in you." She grinned, then whispered, "I like that. A lot."

Joan, raising her voice over the commotion, said to Patricia, "Darling, did you really steal a diamond ring from Mrs. Koch's jewelry box?"

"Jesus, Mother," Patricia said. "Not now!"

"You are sick!" Juanita said, bending over Chris, quivering with anger. Eyes black and portentous, she shook her fists. "Sick! Sick! We do not have time for this bullshit!" Then, like some raving exorcist, she slammed her rosary into his stomach. But the look on Chris's face indicated that she had struck him with something considerably larger. A dump truck, perhaps.

He lay frozen in an odd posture, as if he'd been attempting to get to his hands and knees, but had slipped a disc halfway through the roll.

Just as the rosary had struck Chris, evicting all demons and giving the rest of his motley tenants something to think about, a powerful noise burst from the stairway; a shattering, crackling, glass-like sound.

6.

Duncan was already up and moving toward the stairs, as was Pillsbury, hackles up on both.

"Pillsy, you get back over here," Patricia ordered. "Now!"

The dog stopped at the foot of the stairs, growling.

Patricia leered at the dachshund. "You're only brave when company's here."

All eyes followed Duncan as he climbed. He stopped halfway up stairs and began inspecting a round stained-glass window. After a moment of scrutiny, he stepped back and leaned against the banister.

"Well?" Rachel hollered.

Appearing especially worried, Joan said, "Is the window broken?"

Duncan stepped up to the window again. "I think...I think it's a mouth. And an ear. Definitely an ear. There's part of a nose, too."

Chris was off the floor now, staring up at Duncan. No one spoke.

Pillsbury, after a thorough sniffing of the bottom stair, decided that

Duncan could handle the situation without her, and rejoined the others in the dining room, growling at Chris as she passed.

"Well," Rachel said to Chris, "you don't have to have a 'universal translator' to know what she just said."

Finally, Duncan looked down at the group. "Chris, you missing two earrings?"

Chris felt his right ear, then stared up at Duncan, incredulous.

Duncan returned his eyes to the window, nodding. Then, after an exchange of mumbled words, he descended the stairs.

Sauntering up to Chris, he said, "Looks like the joke's on you, Hollywood." He threw a thumb over his shoulder. "Somebody up there wants to talk to you."

"Well," Joan said, rising from the table, "I don't know about the rest of you, but I could sure use an ice cream about now." She moseyed into the kitchen, the dog in close second, both obviously more interested in Sidewalk Sundaes than talking, earring-snatching windows.

Chris couldn't move, was petrified of what awaited him up the stairs. Not counting his refrigerator, this was the kind of thing he expected when he went journeying through the human mind, or what he'd come to call Wonderland. But this wasn't Wonderland. This was Massachusetts, USA, where windows were supposed to mind their own fucking business.

With a hard and totally unexpected push from Patricia, the spell was broken, and he made his way up the stairs, albeit slothfully.

Duncan told everyone else to stay back, that this was between Chris and the window.

The stained glass window was a round multifoil, two-and-a-half-feet across its center, with an unpretentious sunburst design radiating outward in fat, orange squares, then gradually ending in narrowing rectangles of fire-yellow. The digressing pieces from there were choppily grouped, ranging from cobalt blue to blue-gray, and a ruby fringe worked nicely to capture the colors.

It appeared to Chris as if someone's face had struck the glass from the outside, at an angle, left-center, leaving the raised, multicolored impressions of a forehead, an eye, cheek, an ear with two of his own steel hoop earrings, and half of a nose and mouth.

The lips moved.

"Holy shit!" Chris shrieked. "What—who the fuck are you?"

"Sonny Bono," said the lips in a strangely familiar voice. "Now come closer."

"Come closer my ass."

The lips sighed. "Are you man, or mouse?"

"Don't mess with me, dude!"

"Just get your brave self over here."

Chris inched along the carpeted stair. The eye followed his progress with lustful anticipation, as if he were a busty blonde just two pasties and a G-string away from a table dance finale.

"Closer, closer."

"Alright, okay," Chris said, now up close. He leaned as far back as he could, as if the mouth had garlic breath. "What gives?"

"First off, kindly remove your jewelry from my ear."

Chris complied. "Okay, so what's the deal?"

"It's Juanita's fault. Like you, she has a gift. Unfortunately, she doesn't know how to use it yet."

"You mean it's, like, dormant?"

"If you'd only concentrate, you'd know, just as I do, that she just acquired it."

"Cool," Chris said. "What's her specialty?"

"You're staring at it."

"What? Like, she can warp glass into caricatures and shit?"

"Hey, stop playing stupid. It's you you're talking to here. Literally, you know as much as I do about Juanita's gift."

Chris concentrated. "Okay, it's some kind of...wait...some kind of telekinetic energy."

The eye just stared at him.

"Okay, wait, it's...she can transfer...oh shit, she can transport the essence of character, in whole or in part." He held up a victory fist. "She can move minds. Dude! She can relocate souls!"

"Ssshhh, keep your voice down," said the lips. "That'd be my guess. Except she can't hit the broad side of a barn from two feet out, as you can plainly see. She needs your help."

"What do you want me to do?"

"Before we get into that, I have something to say. You think that was pretty cute what you just did over there, feigning an epileptic attack, squirming around on the carpet like that, scaring those people? Well, I got news for ya—knock it off, asshole! That shit's getting old! Fortunately, by releasing me it worked in your favor this time. Ever hear about the boy who cried wolf? Yeah? Well, that's you, wolf-boy. Your dreaded Tourettes is gonna flare up again, but no one's gonna believe you when you're telling them in your own peculiar way that the sky is falling."

"Now you're talking Chicken Little, dude. And Sonny Bono slammed into a tree, not a window."

"That's another thing—your smartass mouth. Put a sock in it."

"Yeah, okay, whatever," Chris groused. "So, you want me to realign, calibrate, and adjust?"

The eye rolled. "No, Mr. GoodWrench, what I want you to do is play Santa Claus and put a present under her tree. Tonight."

"Dude, do you know how risky that is?"

"Of course I do. I'm you, remember?"

"Ah man, anyone but her!"

"Listen to me, wolf-boy. I'm not asking you—I'm telling you. Get Juanita plugged in before she hurts somebody. And it wouldn't kill you to straighten up and start showing a little more respect. In case you forgot, everybody's here because they're supposed to be. Hey, after tonight, we're gonna need all the friends we can get, right?"

Chris nodded. "Okay, I'll take care of Juanita."

"Gnarly," it said. "Oh, and another thing."

"Yeah?"

"Don't tell her or anyone else about our little conversation here. It could come back to haunt you in Wonderland."

"Yeah, I know," Chris said.

"I know you know."

Backing away, Chris said, "Will you be, uh...are you going to have to stay there, like, indefinitely?"

"After you get Juanita squared away, I'll be able to split. *And we'll be one again.*"

"Great, okay, well...Can I, like, get you anything?'

"Could you turn on the TV?"

"Yeah, sure. What channel?"

"The evening news," said the lips. "And hey, could you maybe turn it this way a bit? Take out just enough angle so that Katie Couric doesn't look like Karen Carpenter?"

Feeling like he'd just left the dentist's chair, Chris started back down the stairs. He opened his hand and stared at his earrings. "Dear diary..." he mumbled. He was not looking at all forward to entering Juanita's psyche. Oh, he liked the challenge of building dreamscapes, but Juanita already had it out for him, no love lost there. And if her subconscious were to somehow see behind his disguise...He shuddered. The chances of ending up a corpse in someone's mind just went from pretty good to damned likely, now that it was Juanita Santiago's.

7.

They'd gathered around the dining room table, quietly discussing their bizarre new tenant.

"Let me get this straight," Duncan said to Chris. "When Juanita hit you with her rosary, she knocked a piece of your psyche out hard enough to smash it, *mold* it into that window?"

"Close enough for government work," he said. "Can I have my Walkman back now?"

"No," Duncan said. "So, what makes Juanita so special?"

"Like, even you could have done it," he said. "Just the right mixture of anger, a religious token and a lot of faith, and bingo—Tiffany does parody."

"You're so full of crap," Patricia said.

"Ditto," said Rachel.

"Come clean—" Duncan stopped, glanced at the attentive face in the window, then turned back to Chris, his voice lower but no less menacing. "Come clean or I swear I'll beat the holy snot out of you!"

"Hey, cut me a break," he said to everyone. "I'm just as mystified about it as you guys. Well, almost."

As if just reminded by dense smoke that there was a pie in the oven, Kathy jumped up and said to Patricia, "Would you like to see a trick?"

"I thought I already did."

"Not this one you haven't," she promised.

"Kathy," Rachel cautioned, "if it's what I think it is, I don't think your mom and grammy are quite ready for that yet."

"It's all right," Duncan said. "I think they can handle it." He was sure Walt Disney himself could levitate from this very table and piss Dumbo's profile on the ceiling without so much as raising an eyebrow. He looked at Patricia. "You can handle it, right?"

She nodded, smiling. "Yeah, I guess I'm feeling pretty numb."

"Follow me," Kathy insisted, "before it's too late."

Everyone gathered in the adjacent living room.

Kathy tugged on a curtain cord, but nothing happened.

"Help her with the drapes, Duncan," Rachel said.

Without a hitch, Duncan parted the green and gold curtains to reveal a large (and, not surprisingly, clean) ordinary window. He pointed to the glass. "Hey, Juanita. *This* is how they're supposed to look."

Eyes glaring, Juanita twirled her rosary around her forefinger. It might have been some kind of obscene gesture she'd picked up from a roguish nun. It was hard to say.

Patricia stood there, arms folded. "Let me guess," she said to Kathy. "You're going to make a rabbit appear on my dead lawn."

Kathy rolled her eyes. "Just watch, silly."

After she told her grammy to have a seat on the sofa, she placed her hands on the glass.

An image instantly appeared. For Duncan, having watched it happen on a passenger window of a 747 and now on a twelve-by-fifteen feet piece of glass was a stunning lesson in contrast.

This scene was identical to the first, as if Kathy had plugged both times into the same stationary surveillance camera, one staring down upon a simple, tidy living room.

Staring at the image, Patricia swooned, though so slightly it was nearly imperceptible.

"Steady," Duncan said, almost grabbing her around the waist. But just before his hands moved, it occurred to him that Rachel might not find the gesture all that valiant.

Joan was off the couch now, walking stiltedly toward the group, her wide eyes fixed to the window. Duncan concluded that her awkward efforts were more from shock than arthritis. Concerned nonetheless, he said to Patricia, "Does she have a walker?"

"She's all right," Patricia said stoically.

Then something moved. A person entered the field of view. A white man, middle-aged, with a crop of black hair graying at the temples.

There had not been a man in Kathy's airplane show. Or anyone, for that matter. *Well*, Duncan thought, *that's what we get for flying coach.*

The man was wearing a black shirt, black pants, and a white Roman collar. He was a priest. Or, just liked to dress like one.

"Dude," Chris observed.

The priest sat down in a recliner, then reached down behind the hidden side of the chair and brought out what appeared to be a wing. It was completely white and about the length of his own arm. He sat the object on his lap, reached down once more, and this time pulled up a clear plastic box filled with buttons, spools of thread, needles, scissors...A sewing kit.

As the man removed the top tray of the box, a pile of white feathers became visible beneath.

He was sitting catty-corner to them, allowing the right side of his face to be discernible. In no time at all, he had threaded a needle and was sewing feathers onto the tip of the nearly completed wing.

As the priest sewed, he displayed an alacrity, a deftness that convinced Duncan that he was not watching a neophyte. On the wall to the man's left hung a contemporary clock with big white Roman numerals. It was pendulum-driven, and had begun chiming the hour. Duncan guessed that: A) the clock was exactly three hours slow; B) the program Kathy was airing was prerecorded; or C) the clock was tolling in Pacific time.

Duncan stared at the clock. *Yet, the ear, it fully knows...By the twanging and the clanging...How the danger ebbs and flows...* At that moment, he felt more appreciation for Poe than he did his own mother, may she rest in peace.

"The paramedic!" Rachel gasped.

Everyone stared at her as if she'd just passed wind.

"Inside the ambulance," she explained. "The paramedic said he saw a man holding wings. The wings of a swan!"

"Maybe this dude's a taxidermist," Chris offered. "When he's not dolling out communion, I mean."

Giving him the evil eye, Juanita said, "Ssshhhh!"

Taxidermy. Duncan thought that was a good guess. But the very power that was manifesting itself before them would not, he believed, be wasting its energy showing a priest who stuffed dead animals on the side.

"He's not a taxi-whatever you called it," Kathy said, her hand almost translucent now, flat and steady against the glass.

Patricia said to her, "You know who that person is?"

"Uh-huh. That's the man who killed me."

For a long moment the only sounds in the room were the tags on Pillsbury's collar clinking together as she scratched herself. The dog was obviously unaware that hushed interims always followed such bombshells, and that strict silence was to be observed until finally broken by a gasp or vulgar utterance. That, or she'd simply decided to hell with it, that etiquette was for poodles.

Kathy's revelation stunned Patricia far worse than had the window display. Mouth open, she fought for words.

"This is the man who abducted you from the boardwalk?" Patricia said. "A *priest?*"

"No, something else got me from there," Kathy said. "*He's* the one who dropped me off the cliff."

Confused, Patricia said, "Then...then...then who in the hell kidnapped you from the—did you just say this man dropped you off a cliff?"

"Yes, ma'am. He wanted me to fly."

Urgently, Rachel stepped in. "Do you know where this man lives? City, state?"

"No. But I know what he's doing."

"With the wing, you mean?" Duncan said.

She nodded. "It's just like the kind he sewed into my back."

Patricia shifted from stunned to horrified. *"He sewed wings into your back?"*

"Yes, ma'am."

"Then who's he making this one for?" Duncan said. "Any idea?"

Shrugging, she said, "Probably another little girl. He already killed one before me, because I was his second."

"Did he tell you anything else?" Duncan said. "Who he is? Where he lives?"

"I already told you, I don't know any of that. All I know is that there was supposed to be more."

Joan finally spoke. "More murders, dear?"

"Uh-huh. More angels."

Patricia walked over to Kathy, then—hesitantly—reached down and lifted her shirt.

On her tip-toes, staring over Patricia's shoulder, Joan gasped at Kathy's exposed back. "Oh, no, my poor darling, oh, no, no."

Duncan knelt beside her, then delicately drew his finger down one of her scars. "Jesus, Amy, what happened to you?" he whispered.

Kathy turned her head. Smiling, she said, "You cracked out of turn."

Duncan didn't know what she was talking about. Then it hit him. "Sorry, Kathy. And where did you pick up a phrase like that?"

"I was a con man in a previous life."

"Oh," he said, not sure if she was pulling his leg. Not sure at all.

Now leaning over Duncan, Rachel cried, "When did you get those? You never had those scars before!"

"I've always had them," she explained. "You just couldn't see them because Amy was in the way."

"Get away from there!" Juanita shouted suddenly.

During the excitement, Chris had walked over to the edge of the window opposite Kathy and breached the image with his right forefinger. He stirred the corner of the glass like a cup of coffee.

"Señor Duncan!" Juanita cried. "I tell you, he is crazy!"

"Fucking Loony Tunes," Patricia seconded, still staring at Kathy's back.

Oblivious to everyone, Chris continued with his finger, then pushed his hand all the way through. Startled, he paused for a moment, then slowly proceeded toward the priest's left shoulder. He touched it, and the man jumped.

Chris yanked his hand out before the man had a chance to see it. "Totally awesome!"

"Chris, you dumbass" Duncan growled. "Keep your hands in your pockets."

The priest looked in the direction of his invisible molester. With a devilish grin, he said, "I guess that means I'm it."

"Shit!" Rachel cried. She retreated to her husband's side, as if expecting the man to jump through and put his sewing kit to more diabolical use.

"Chris!" Patricia yelled in a soft voice. "Grow the fuck up!"

"Geez, don't panic," Chris grumbled. "We can see him, but he can't see or hear us."

"But he can *feel* us," Juanita reminded him.

"Only if somebody crosses over," Kathy said.

Very curious now, Patricia said to Kathy, "You mean, if someone wanted to, they could fully enter that house? Just by going through the window?"

"Yep," she said. "But I wouldn't advise it."

Chris, looking ready to dive right through, said, "Screw it! I say we all go through and kick his backsliding ass!"

"Just stay put, Chris," Duncan ordered.

"But he's a serial killer, dude! And God knows what else!"

"Are you absolutely positive that this is the man?" Patricia said. "I mean, he's a priest, for God's sake!"

"Trust me," Kathy said, "you don't forget someone like him."

Then Duncan saw in Patricia's eyes something that almost made him yank Kathy's hand from the glass.

Still kneeling, Patricia turned and stared at the man, his image now just inches away from her own face. He was still grinning over his shoulder in their direction, his eyes jeering them on, just begging someone to touch him again.

Finally, she said to Kathy, "From here, could a person shoot a bullet into that man's head?"

"I guess so."

Patricia stood, just long enough to seal the thought, then headed for the stairs.

"Oh, shit," Duncan moaned.

Rachel went after her. "Patricia, let's think about this."

"My daddy left a gun case just full of rifles and shotguns and pistols," Patricia declared as she bounded the stairs, three at a time. "I'm gonna find the biggest one and blow his goddamn head off!"

As she passed the face in the stained glass window, it said, "Patricia, you don't know what you're doing."

She stopped, turned. Pointing at the face, she said. "And you're next."

"So," Chris said to Joan, "do you think she'll do it from the book depository or the grassy knoll?"

Just then, the priest got up from his chair and disappeared from the living room, leaving the opposite way he'd entered.

"Señor Duncan!" Juanita cried moments later, pointing.

In the scene, located at the far end of the hallway, was a boudoir mirror. Upon exiting the living room, the priest had entered the kitchen area, leaving the door ajar. This allowed the mirror to reflect part of the kitchen counter, cabinets, half a table and two chairs, and the window above the sink, beyond which stood a telling landmark. It was a good distance away, and a thick haze was rendering it nearly invisible. Still, there was no mistaking what it was.

"The Space Needle," Duncan whispered. "Seattle."

Chris stepped in, peered closer. "You a Mariners fan?"

"No," Duncan said distantly, staring at the structure. "But then, neither is anybody else."

Kathy looked up at Duncan. "I can't hold it anymore."

"That's okay, sweetheart," he said. "You did great."

She pulled her hand from the glass, and instantly the Bently's front yard—not half as stark and fallow as it had earlier seemed to Duncan—materialized before them.

Patricia was descending the stairs with a rifle in one hand, a shotgun in the other, and two semi-automatic pistols stuffed into her jeans. Duncan recalled the old west picture of her and Kathy, and thought she looked more like an outlaw there than she did here. Now, she just looked like a frightened, desperate mother who, for all she knew about firearms and getting even, would have been better off hurrying down the stairs with her monogrammed bowling ball.

Rachel was right behind Patricia, still trying to reason with her. Burdened now with boxes of ammunition, she was having a hard time gesturing with her hands.

"Think about the possible repercussions," the face in the stained glass window pleaded with Patricia as she hurried by.

"Fuck off," she said. Then, as she neared the front window, she blurted frantically, "What happened? Where'd he go?"

"I couldn't hold it anymore," Kathy said, as if she'd just wet her pants. "Sorry."

"Well, young lady, you just march right back over there—"

"She can't," Duncan said, stepping in front of Kathy, "so leave her be."

As Patricia stared at Duncan, she let both weapons fall from her hands. They struck the wood floor like fetters on a gallows.

Her eyes were venomous. "Don't you ever tell me to leave my daughter—" She stopped, frozen in mid-sentence. Finally, she said, almost inaudibly, "You people tricked me. She's not my daughter, not my daughter at all..."

With an understanding smile, her mother held out her hand. "C'mon, dear, I've got some pills that'll take the edge right off."

As they started for the kitchen, Duncan pointed to the guns in her jeans. "Why don't you just leave those with me."

Avoiding his eyes, staring into a place only she could see, she handed both guns to Duncan.

"Don't you worry, Patty," Chris promised. "We'll catch the bastard. And when we do, he's all yours."

"Easy, Romeo," Duncan said, his words sliding down a sidelong glance. "Don't start writing checks your balls can't cash."

8.

The tranquilizers her mother prescribed had calmed Patricia considerably; however, there wasn't likely a pill in existence that could have relieved the affliction in her eyes. With the exception of Katherine, who was close by in the living room, playing fetch-the-toy with the dachshund (who she'd complained of being considerably less feisty than she remembered), everyone was sitting at the dining room table, poring over the photo albums Patricia had brought down earlier, absorbed in Kathy's maturation from infancy to a pretty, bright-eyed girl of ten.

Her evolution from there, of course, was pure speculation. Well, perhaps not entirely, Duncan thought, given what they'd just recently learned from a plate-glass window.

When someone asked about a particular photo, Patricia would answer with a short, precise history, delivered in the same stolid yet unerring manner of a bored tour guide, one shuttling her ticket-holders through her own conchology exhibit, explaining the symmetry and color and geographical distribution of every seashell. And sometimes, in spite of herself, she still couldn't help but point at a particular one and smile at its beauty.

Duncan thought she probably had the creased and grainy features of every photograph entrusted to memory. Not just duplicates of the still images before her, but titanium rolls of film, expertly counterfeited and strung along the reels of her memory should thief, flood, or fire ever take the originals.

The only person not thoroughly engrossed was Chris, who looked like he'd rather be on the carpet with the dog, chasing rubber balls.

"I have a question," Chris said lazily. "Why did you name the dog Pillsbury? I mean, it doesn't look anything like the Dough Boy."

"We didn't name her that because we thought there was a resemblance," Patty explained. "Classic case. See, one day while coming home from work, I saw her lying on the side of the road. Just a puppy then. I thought she was dead, but pulled over anyway, just to make sure. Well, she wasn't of course, but almost. Thought she'd been hit by a car, so I rushed her to the veterinarian. Found out she hadn't been run over, but probably would have been better off if she had, according to the vet. Turned out she was nearly dead with parvo, a bad doggy virus. The vet strongly suggested that I let him put her to sleep, put her out of her misery, but I said no. So, I brought her home, and the three of us—me, Mom, and Katherine—did everything in our power to get her to eat. She'd take water, but no food. We tried everything from fresh veal to Snickers bars, but she refused. Then, just when we were ready to call it quits and dig a hole in the backyard, Mom accidentally bumped the table as she was setting dinner and dropped this steaming bowl of chicken stew. It went crashing to the floor, bowl breaking, stew everywhere. Gawd, what a mess that was. Anyway, smelling this, that dog literally crawled over to the closest splatter and began eating! But she was only picking out one ingredient—the *biscuits* mom put in the stew." Patricia took a sip of coffee. "*That's* why we named her Pillsbury."

Chris looked troubled. "But then, wouldn't Dumpling have been a more appropriate name?"

Patricia laughed. "Shut up, Chris."

"These pictures, they give me the goose bumps," Juanita said. "They are one in the same, Kathy and Amy."

Patricia said to Duncan, "After having met you, I was never again able to look at Katherine and not see your face in hers."

Rachel looked up, as if she wanted to comment on that. Then her eyes rolled diffidently down to the pictures again; reserved, for now.

"The resemblance is striking," Joan agreed. "To Mr. McNeil, I mean."

"Where is her real father?" Juanita said.

"Long gone." Pouring from a carafe, Patricia warmed her coffee. "I met him at church, of all places. Well, I shouldn't say it that way. I was actually going to church at that time just to meet men. Pretty pathetic, huh?"

"Of course not," Duncan said. "Episcopalians have been doing it for years." He flipped to the next page in the photo album. "Besides, I can't think of a better reason to go."

Juanita's huge bosom rose ever so slightly in indignation, then caught there. Duncan could see she wanted so badly to remind them both that, yes, just as in the church, so could a copy of the Holy Bible be found in a motel room—but similitude stopped there, white linens included.

Contritely, Patricia smiled at Juanita, her left dimple far more prominent than her right. And Duncan was reminded that it had been just those very features with which he'd fallen in love so many years ago.

"So, what was her father's name?" Rachel prodded.

"Jack Fortune," Patricia said, her smile yielding to the words.

"Really?" Rachel said. "Sounds like some sly character from *The Young and the Restless*."

Patricia nodded. "Being tall, dark, and mysterious, he could have played a good one, too."

Chris piped in. "You forgot handsome."

With a puzzled expression, Patricia said, "That's the funny thing. I don't remember what he looked like. I couldn't even tell you for sure if he was black, Asian, Hispanic—although he obviously wasn't any of those. It's just...hard to explain. It's as if...well, as if his features have been stricken from my memory, and—and I know this sounds crazy—my mind won't even let me make up a face to put in the void."

"Sounds like you retired his jersey," Duncan said, "and now no one else can wear that number."

"Yeah, exactly," she said. "I didn't know if I was making any sense."

Recalling his own bout of bowdlerized memories, Duncan said, "No, you're making perfect sense. I'm beginning to think there's a...glitch in the program."

"Anti-virus program, dude," Chris sagely offered, then excused himself to the kitchen.

Duncan wasn't sure if Chris was offering a solution or defining the problem.

Still perusing the photo album, Rachel pointed to a picture of a man standing beside a large, if not stately, playhouse. Kathy, maybe six years old then, was at his side, gaping at the structure, the surprise on her face immeasurable. "This is her late step-father, Charles?"

"Yes," Patricia said. "He built that for her."

"Impressive," Rachel said. "But no pictures of Jack Fortune?"

Patricia shook her head.

"You mentioned his 'mysterious' side," Duncan said. "Mysterious how?"

"He was...eclectic," Patricia explained. "You know, one of those well-dressed, anal-retentive types who strut around pretending to be the cock of the walk."

Rachel laughed. "That's not mysterious—it's compulsory."

Wearing that baffled look again, Patricia said, "Well, he did have a...an ambiance about him that was convincing. An air of nobility that I never second-guessed." She glanced back down at the pictures, appearing both charmed and ashamed. "He made me laugh."

Rachel leaned forward. "He was rich, in other words."

"That too," she said. "Yeah, he was loaded. I mean, that was the impression I got. He never worked but always seemed to have an unlimited supply of cash. All he would ever tell me was that he was 'the epitome of rags-to-riches.'"

"So," Rachel said, "as long as he kept getting the check, you minded your own business."

Patricia squirmed in her chair. "No. Maybe." She laughed. "Hell, I guess I did."

Rachel pressed on. "How long did you date him?"

She sighed. "About two months."

Back from the kitchen with Twinkie in hand, Chris looked shocked, and just as he was about to comment, Juanita kicked him under the table. "Keep your remarks pleasant and to the point."

Speechless under these new conditions, Chris just gaped.

"Just two months?" Rachel said, almost haughtily. "Well, that would at least explain the lack of pictures."

Duncan, however, silently translated his wife's words into their true meaning: *"Well, well, you wasted no time in attempting to corner him into marriage, or a sizable alimony check—you slut."*

In self-defense, Patricia said, "When I told him I was pregnant, he vanished. I mean, it's like he disappeared off the face of the earth. I've never seen or heard from him since."

"Prick," Rachel said.

Duncan said, "Did you ever file a claim with the child support division?"

"No. All I had was his name, and that was probably bogus."

"Jack Fortune," Duncan guessed, "charming and debonair as he may have seemed, is probably *the* model for bogus wear." He gave the face in

184 | Jon Michael Kelley

the window an impugning glance, then looked down at Kathy playing on the floor. He whispered, "Hell, I'll even wager that Jack Fortune isn't human at all."

Patricia, staring also at Kathy, said, "Jesus, I don't want to consider that."

An hour later, still at the dining room table, Duncan and Patricia found themselves alone.

Taking what was surely going to be a short-lived opportunity, Patricia said, "You know, after Katherine disappeared from the boardwalk, I was told to make a list of all the people who'd ever been involved with her, to whatever degree. A list of potential suspects. And you were right there at the top."

It was no mystery to Duncan why she'd named him her prime suspect, at least initially, and for two very good reasons. One, just months before Kathy's disappearance, he'd been an influential—if not patriarchal—figure in her life. Having Patricia create such a list was just standard police work, and whether she'd included him or not, his name would have eventually made its way there in the course of the investigation. Two, she would have naturally assumed—again, at least initially, frantically—that he'd kidnapped Kathy for ransom. For his share of the money. Or maybe all of it. This she wouldn't have divulged (and obviously hadn't) to the authorities, as she would have implicated herself in any number of felonies, some carrying a penalty as severe as kidnapping itself. He wondered how close she'd come to telling, though, in those first twenty-four hours.

"The FBI quickly cleared you, of course," Patricia said, "seeing how you were on the other end of the continent when Katherine disappeared."

He shook his head. "Still, it would have been procedure for the FBI to contact me, to—"

"I told them not to," she said.

Duncan leaned back, surprised. "Wow. Just like that?"

"Just like that."

"Gotti should have been as convincing."

She smiled. "Gotti didn't have my dimples."

Duncan leaned in, peering into her eyes. "Still, there is a resemblance. In a *dapper* sort of way."

"Wiseacre."

Then he asked, "So, how much of the money did you burn through?"

"There's still about eighty grand left," she said. "I used only what I needed to get us out of the debt Charles left us in after his murder. And, of course, some of it came in handy when Katherine turned up missing.

Printing her fliers, quitting my job to search for her full time, and so on. I paid off this house. Some of Mom's medical bills. That's it, really."

"And the guilt?"

"Probably not as deep as yours. Your lieutenant was very persuasive when he handed me the suitcase that night. Told me how much hell you went through getting it for me. That it was our little secret, and that it would stay that way, scout's honor."

"Lieutenant Mo White's a righteous man. I owe him more than my life."

Patricia stared down into her coffee. "You lost your partner that night. I'm very sorry about that."

Duncan nodded. "It was a foolish, foolish thing I did. But what's done is done."

She reached across the table and took his hand. "Does it still bother you that you never caught the person who killed my husband?"

"Of course it does."

"Don't let it. It doesn't bother me anymore."

"I tried making it up to you, the money—"

"I know, I know."

"If I could just do it over again, I—"

"But you can't."

He sighed. "No, I can't."

<h2 style="text-align:center">9.</h2>

Silent tears streamed down Samuel Flannery's cheeks.

Despite the mugginess outside, the doors of St. Patrick's had been opened to their fullest, allaying a strong though unrecognizable stench that had earlier emerged on the heels of Father Kagan's angry exodus from the church.

For a little over two hours now, the deacon had been staring at the domed ceiling, watching all of the angels' expressions go from annoyed to utterly incensed, as his sore neck would attest.

This would be his last day at St. Patrick's. Father Kagan had flat flipped out of his fucking mind, and Samuel refused to work alongside anyone who catered their delusions of grandeur like a Kennedy wedding.

Not that it really mattered now...

But then, what if Father Kagan was anything but delusional? Could he be in cohorts with the Devil? The idea that Lucifer would chose to beguile a man of the cloth to do his bidding was such a belabored one that, nowadays, someone like himself might be inclined to look outside the clergy simply to avoid cliché—no matter how much hard evidence pointed to the contrary.

Like the nine mightily pissed-off angels above him.

He wondered if such omens were manifesting in other churches, synagogues, holy places of worship. Then he decided that it really didn't matter. He didn't have to go any further than his own backyard to know that if man's soul was ever in danger, it was now.

What could he do? He was only one man. He couldn't run. This wasn't a fifth-grade bully looking for a fight after school.

Of course, there was always prayer. But if his growing suspicions were right, that man had finally met his Waterloo, then any appeals weren't likely going to be heard through the bedlam that was most assuredly ringing the Almighty's ears.

Had he lost his conviction? Wasn't fear borne of a lack of faith?

Earlier, the Jesus statue above the front doors had winked at him. Twice. He was sure of it. It had mocked him; had reminded him that there was nothing his little mortal self could do but stand aside and let the cortege pass.

Let go and let God, Samuel reminded himself. The wisest bumper sticker ever created.

A fireman walked into the church. A rather tall figure, he was decked to the nines in firefighting garb.

He's either just come from a three-alarm fiasco, Samuel thought, *or is on his way to one.*

Then it occurred to him: Obviously, someone had mistaken the odor in or around St. Patrick's as a gas leak (though it smelled like nothing of the sort) and dutifully reported it to the fire department.

The fireman began talking to a young lady who was kneeling in prayer. After a moment, the lady rose and hurried out the doors, appearing...unsettled.

The fireman repeated this with the remaining three people, all leaving in the same pressed manner.

Samuel continued to weep silently as he stared up at the angels. The fireman's behavior did not interest him; only the soaring figures above. Their faces, their displeasure. Surely, their disappointment.

Moments later, the fireman tapped his shoulder. "Sorry to bother you, padre."

Samuel turned. "Is there a fire?" he said lightheartedly, wiping the tears from his face.

"Not yet," said the fireman. The name *Gamble* was stenciled just above the brim of his yellow hat. He handed Samuel a hymnal, one of many located behind every pew. "I was wondering," he said, "could you please read me psalm 212? You see, I've misplaced my glasses."

Samuel glanced warily at the fireman, then took the book and opened to the requested song. Dismayed, he said, "This is some kind of, of joke. This appears to be a limerick—"

"Could you please read it aloud?"

Samuel slowly began reading. "'There once was a man named—'" His eyes went wide.

"Once again, from the top," Gamble said.

Samuel just gaped at the words.

"*Read it!*" demanded the fireman.

"'Th-There once was a man named Flannery, the victim of much chicanery. He poked and prodded around, until it was hell that he found, without even a map and itinerary.'"

"Very nicely done," Gamble congratulated, clapping. "You have a lovely voice. You're a tenor, aren't you? You were a bit shaky, but that's perfectly understandable. After all, it *is* a bit unsettling when one reads one's own obituary."

The huge front doors of the church slammed shut.

The inner sanctum was still vibrating as Samuel began backing away. "I've...I've been expecting something like this," he stammered. "I knew you were coming."

Gamble laughed. "Did you, now? Why then, my learned friend, you must think I'm the Devil."

"Who else could you be?"

"Whatever I am, it ain't ol' Beelzebub, bub."

"This is it, isn't it? The end?"

Gamble's face scrunched with concern. "For whom?"

"All of mankind."

"Let's just say that you'll never know. Not from this angle, anyway."

Samuel stopped; just stood there, shaking badly. Staring.

Gamble slapped a knee. "Ha! You don't know whether to shit or go blind, do you, padre?"

"I, I'm not a priest."

"That's commendable," Gamble said, leaning forward. "But it won't be enough to get your pious ass out of this pickle."

Voice trembling, Samuel closed his eyes and began praying. "'Our Father, Who art in heaven—'"

Gamble clucked. "You fleshsacks are curious animals, with your redundant doxologies, biased almsgiving, extraneous iconolatry." He sighed. "From now on, let's leave the psalming to me, hmmm? That's *my* forte. For you, might I suggest a more philistine approach? Something, say, along the lines of, 'Hey, God! Please yank my sorry ass outta this church before this crazy fucker here makes mincemeat of my balls!'"

Samuel felt a wintry breath sting the back of his neck. A presence behind him. He turned, then screamed. It was the Christ statue from above the doors, dragging its cross. Up close, Samuel could see that its expression was more weary than plaintive; its eyelids hanging drowsily upon those dark mahogany irises. No, not despondent. Just so damn tired.

As the statue crouched to finally relieve itself of that burdensome cruciform, ambient light rolled across its slick, amber back, emphasizing as it went the skin's advanced state of crackleware motif; a patina Christ himself might have approved of, as Samuel thought it not only epitomized the weathering of time and its implications to faith, but also exquisite suffering.

Laying the cross on the floor, its gaunt, wooden physique creaked and splintered. Its hands were colorfully veined, and there were holes in both wrists. Its toes were curled slightly inward, and both feet were caked with red, flaking paint. The statue's wooden lips pulled apart with a splintery sound. Inside its mouth a vast, starry universe twinkled invitingly. It spoke in a dry, edgy voice. "Pontius Pilate. Know where I can find him?"

"He, he killed himself," was all Samuel could think to say, his voice merely a wheeze, scored by dry, trembling lips.

Grievous, the statue hung its head. "Ah, shit."

Eyes wide, fingers pressed to his cheeks, Gamble began tittering like a soused old crone winning big on bridge night. "I'm so ashamed," he said. "*Tee-hee-hee-hee*. So mortified! Oh, but this is all so blasphemous, so heretical!"

Samuel started to run, but Gamble grabbed the back of his hair.

Sounding very concerned now, Gamble said, "Tell me, Samuel, will I go to hell for murdering you?"

Samuel twisted around. "You *are* hell."

He let go of the deacon and actually began dancing in the aisle. "Ding! Ding! Ding! The closest correct answer yet! What do we have for him, Johnny?"

"An all-expense paid trip to the inferno," replied the statue.

Samuel tried to run again, but his legs seemed apprehensive, as if his astral limbs had switched places with his physical ones.

The statue reached out with both hands and grabbed Samuel around the waist; pulled him close.

"*Hay-zeus* kinda looks different now that he's off that bulky tree," Gamble said, still dancing. "Don't you think? Now, I was gonna follow the chain of command and use a Mary, but you Catholics here ain't got any obelisks of the old broad taller than Napoleon."

The statue tightened its grip and lifted Samuel over its head.

Samuel heard what he thought was a gunshot, then another—then instantly and painfully discovered that a few of his ribs had just snapped.

"Shit, I heard those suckers crack all the way over here!" Gamble laughed gleefully, standing a mere three feet away. "That must have hurt like the dickens!"

The very instant air returned to his lungs, Samuel cried, "Dear God, where are you now?"

Gamble reached up and patted Samuel on the shoulder. "Don't worry, Sam ol' boy, He's probably just caught in traffic."

Samuel's heart thundered.

"*Hay-zeus*," Gamble ordered in a Spanish accent, "let's crucify this gringo. Then you and me, we're going to party, huh? Have a few Margaritas, maybe get laid. Hey, chicks are gonna dig you, man! You're gonna be a regular pussy magnet! But first you have to take off that ratty-ass crown. Trust me, you don't want any thorns in *those* bushes!"

Samuel kicked and screamed.

Gamble snapped his fingers. "I've got it! We can go to the Temple Shalom over on 36th and Garrett and get you hired on as the new *mohel*," he said to the statue. "We'll brew up our own batch of Sweet wine, glue some alligator teeth to those Mogen clamps, and turn the next *Bris* into a scream fest! By God, we'll put the fun back in circumcisions!"

Then he and the statue wrestled Samuel to the cross.

Holding Samuel's left arm down with one hand, raising the hammer in the other, the statue cried out in an ancient, despairing voice: *"Eli, Eli, lama sabachthani?"*

Chuckling, Gamble said, "God hasn't forsaken *you,* padre. Like I said, He'll show eventually. But not to worry—me and Pinocchio here are willing to hear your confession." He positioned the spike in the center of Samuel's left wrist, then the statue drove it through.

The pain was tremendous. Samuel tried to scream, but there was no longer any air in his lungs. He quickly slipped into a breezy, almost enchanted awareness, where gradually before him emerged skeins of plaited streamers, twisting and twirling in parade fashion, donning every known and inconceivable color. And the skin of this macrocosm was resplendent in its complexity of textiles, shimmering sequins and adamantine tracers. The patterns were so intricately woven, the gossamer threads so fragile, that they could have only been treadled from an ethereal loom.

Or woven by the nimble fingers of God Himself.

Then he understood: Graveclothes. He was being fitted for death.

In a valley distant, a lonesome dinosaur cried for its mate.

No! Not a dinosaur. A train!

A pinpoint of words pierced the braided cerement. "Don't you go south on me just yet!" said an angry voice. "Wake the fuck up!"

Gamble was slapping the deacon's cheeks. Eyes fluttering, Samuel foundered back into semi consciousness. His ability to breathe had returned, but was short-circuiting.

With just enough available air, he screamed as another spike was driven through his right wrist.

"Deep breaths, deep breaths," Gamble kept chanting.

Finally, Gamble squatted on Samuel's chest as the statue prepared to deliver the last spike.

Gamble threw a thumb over his shoulder. "Kind of paradoxical, ain't it? I mean, what with the Son of God nailing your Catholic ass to a cross and all."

With journeyman force, the statue swung down hard, driving the spike through Samuel's feet.

Samuel jerked violently, nearly bucking Gamble from his chest. He did not scream; only a deep gurgling sound rose from his throat, and once again the kaleidoscope of fabric designs burgeoned in the corners of his vision, then engulfed him.

The shroud fit comfortably; was tailor-made.

He'd nearly bitten his tongue clean through, and it was all he could do to swallow the blood fast enough to keep from choking.

The train was coming. It was close.

Sweet Jesus!

"It stinks in here," the statue said.

"Hey, the man just shit his pants," Gamble replied. "Show some respect."

"Oh, so he did. Can we hang the pontiff next?"

"Whoa, you're getting way ahead of yourself, big guy," Gamble said. "We still have Mormon country to get through first." He shook his head. "Do you know how many Joseph Smiths there are in the Salt Lake City white pages? It's gonna take us forever to find the right one."

"Fuck it," said the statue. "Then let's just do 'em all."

Gamble smiled. "I think this could be the start of a bee-u-tee-ful friendship."

He lifted himself from Samuel's chest, then lit a cigarette.

Samuel heard the sloshing of gasoline before he felt its wetness on his legs, before he was overwhelmed by its vinegar-like fumes. Grimacing, he moved his head from side to side, for the vapors were, among other things, stinging his eyes and making it even harder to breathe. He caught the watery glimpses of a red plastic container, and the wooden hands that were waving it over him.

The statue then emptied the remaining fuel on Samuel's face and chest.

Gamble smiled proudly. "He's a peach, ain't he?" Then he removed his yellow hat and placed it next to Samuel's head. Folding a hand over his heart, he said, "The last fireman of station number 7734, signing off."

"They're coming for you," Samuel managed feebly.

Gamble stared repugnantly at the cigarette caught between his fingers, then coughed for dramatic effect. Seeming to ignore Samuel's comment, he said, "You know what, padre? These things'll kill ya."

For the last time, Samuel whispered, "I'm not a priest."

"No," Gamble agreed. "And you weren't a very good deacon, either."

Then he flicked the cigarette to the ground.

Samuel's head lolled to one side, and the last thing he saw beyond the flames brought a triumphant smile to his face. There upon the ceiling of St. Patrick's Church was a sign. A glorious portent.

Only eight angels remained.

The multi-winged seraph and its mighty sword were gone.

Fire roared around him, but he felt no pain. Then, on his very last breath, a rocket train coasted into the station.

"All aboard!" shouted a black man holding a pocket watch.

Samuel turned. Sitting on a steel bench was an old woman layered in tattered clothing. Her face was withered and drawn, and the few remaining teeth she had were probably not viable. She was shoeless and smelled like hot pitch and urine.

The bag lady held out both of her trembling hands. "Got any spare faith on ya, mister?"

Samuel reached into his pockets and—much to his astonishment—pulled out gobs of the stuff.

He handed her all he had. "Is this enough?"

She cackled. "Surprise! Ya don't need faith to ride these rails, deacon. Never did. But it's ok, all the same."

Samuel turned to the black porter. "Where does this train go?"

"Where would you like it to go, sir?"

"Home," he said, tears rimming his eyes.

The porter nodded. "It goes there."

Samuel turned around to wave goodbye to the bag lady, but the woman was gone. Instead, in her place on the bench sat a beautiful little girl, smiling back at him.

In her lap rested a gleaming sword, much longer than herself.

"What's your name, honey?" he said.

"Amy."

"Goodbye, Amy," he said, then boarded the train.

10.

Having to cook dinner for more mouths than she was accustomed, and at an hour that was normally her bedtime, Joan nonetheless prepared a bountiful spread. And in impressive time. Of course, she had help from Patricia, Juanita, and Rachel. And even Kathy, who'd turned out to be quite helpful.

Chris, showing some rather uncharacteristic behavior of late, had even offered his services. He was quickly shooed away, but thanked all the same.

Duncan and Rachel had insisted that they be able to show their gratitude, so they'd raided the local grocery and brought back far more food than what the present meal offered, despite Chris's rumblings that the only perishables left after tomorrow morning worth worrying about would be the human race.

So far, no one from Duncan's entourage had complained of jet lag. Far from it. The three hours they'd lost might just as well have been three seconds. Everyone seemed to be hooked up to their own IV drip of adrenaline; not so much as to be kept skittish, but enough to remain keenly alert.

Duncan did, however, remind everyone that they would crash, probably hard, and that it was vitally important that they all get at least six hours of sleep.

As Joan said grace, the face in the window stared down at them with a suffering expression. When the prayer was done, it said "Amen" with the rest of them.

Chris, having slightly bowed his head strictly out of courtesy, looked up at the window and said, "We're agnostics, you idiot."

"Yes, but two days ago we were atheists," said the face. "What's next? John the Baptist dunking our heads under the Ipswich River?"

Ignoring the loquacious window, Chris sucked a dollop of sour cream from his errant thumb. "This is one kick-ass dinner, Grandma."

"She's not your grandma," Patricia pleasantly reminded.

Chris shrugged. "Epic food, though."

Crumpling real bleu cheese on her salad, Juanita said, "How far is Seattle?"

"Too far," Duncan grumbled, not looking forward to another airplane ride. Drawing a napkin across his mouth, he said to Joan, "I may have to bum some of those pills of yours for the flight. That, or martini myself into a stupor."

"Well, why don't you go with the second option, hon," Rachel said. "Stick with something you're completely familiar with."

Duncan shot her a dirty look, but said nothing.

Reproachfully, Juanita said, "No, no, I mean the miles on the road, how far?"

"Don't know the miles," Patricia said, "but it ain't just a hop and a skip, I can tell ya."

"Might as well be Bumfucked Egypt," Chris mumbled to his chicken leg.

Joan dropped her fork. "Do you kiss your mother with that mouth?"

"My old lady's dead," Chris said. He took an enormous bite. "Died fourteen years ago, when I was sixteen. Decided to take a bubble bath with the toaster." He pulled a piece of gristle from his mouth, and grinned. "Proctor Silex, take me away."

Patricia threw her napkin on the table. "Well, that settles it. What little appetite I had is history."

Not quite leering, Duncan said to Chris, "You don't seem too broken up about it."

"My old lady hated me," he said. "But she feared me even more. Thought I was possessed. So, from the time I was, like, six until the day she died, she took me to church every Sunday." He shook his head, scowling. "She drilled religion into me, pushed it down my throat for so long and so hard that I started believing that there was something wrong with me, too." He helped himself to a biscuit. "As I got older, I started realizing that the only thing wrong with me was her. And guilt-based religion. Thing was, she was just like me—only a hundred times better."

"You mean, she had ESP too?" Joan said.

Chris rolled his eyes at the term. "Yeah, but she could see *far* into the future," he said. "I can only see a few days ahead, a week maybe. Just glimpses, really. But she could see forever—backwards, forwards, and sideways."

Patricia smiled. "I bet she cleaned up real nice at the office football pool."

Chris shook his head. "She saw our talents as a curse and was wildly afraid of them. See, when we started going to church, it wasn't just for me. She wanted deliverance for herself. Not only was she gifted psychically, but she was an addict, hooked on sex the way some people are heroin. Only difference was, she changed her needles frequently. Then, after years of bible sermons, she got really bad, really down on herself, believed she was a witch, or possessed by the devil, or both, until, eventually, she was blowing fuses from Mission Beach all the way to Sea World."

During the silence that followed, Chris asked Kathy if her chicken leg was for sale. Finding that it wasn't, he eyed both platters again, but alas...

"We haven't heard your father mentioned," Joan said. "Where is he?"

"Not a clue," he said. "Wouldn't know him from Adam. Mom never told me his name, but she talked about him sometimes. Guess he slapped her around a lot. Real tough guy. He's better off staying lost, though. I mean, if I ever find him, I'll do things to his mind..." He didn't finish, just shook his head. "He just better stay missing is all I gotta say."

"There are worse ways to die," Kathy said, rather spiritedly.

Immediately the clinking of silverware and china stopped.

"Honey," Rachel said, finally breaking the silence, "why would you say a thing like that?"

"The bad man in Seattle," she said. "He knows."

Duncan said, "You mean, because of what he did to you?"

"And the others. He knows all about pain. And death."

Chris shook his head. "Little lady, he's just a peon. But I think he might be riding the coattails of a far greater adversary: The Collective Unconscious."

Juanita grumbled something, crossed herself, then speared a baked potato with her fork.

"Ah-oh," Rachel warned, "I think Doctor Freud just walked in."

"Not Freud," Chris rectified, helping himself to another biscuit, "but Doctor Carl Gustav Jung. Dude was brilliant. Way ahead of his time. See, Jung and Freud were buds for awhile, helped bring psychology into the twentieth century. But Jung didn't agree with Freud's psychosexual view of the unconscious, among other things, and went his own way. Contrary to Freud's views, Jung believed that an 'inner' event, like a dream or vision, is as much *real* as the waking world—it's just that we don't assign those states the same objective reality that we give 'outer' events. You know, like we're doing now, eating chicken and spuds and pretending that Judeo-Christianity is the only religious truth, that physical reality is the only reality, shit like that. Our minds have become prejudiced. Since around Newton's time, everything outside Western thought and culture has had to ride in the back of the bus: alchemy, astrology—"

"So, what's your point?" Patricia said.

"I haven't made it yet," Chris said, "so sit tight. Now, Jung said that we have what are called 'inherent predispositions.' 'Deposits of the constantly repeated experiences of humanity,' he called them. Our psychic inheritance."

"Archetypes," Duncan said.

Chris grinned, realizing he had a confidant. "Exactly, dude. Jung also called them Imagos. Dominants. The primordial image. You know, demon, angel, etcetera. Jung saw man's desire for spirituality—his need to experience 'the eternal,' or God—as being an innate archetypal behavior."

"Innate?" Patricia said, spitefully pinching the tablecloth. "Our belief in God is instinctive, not learned?"

"Sort of. Like, the eternal is *pre-existent* to consciousness, and is therefore *not* an invention of consciousness."

"You seem awfully knowledgeable about these things, Mr. Kaddison," Joan said, peering concernedly at the young man. "Is psychology a hobby of yours?"

Chris took a drink of milk, then said, "Let's just say a healthy understanding of the psyche helps me in my travels."

"It's all nonsense," Juanita charged.

"All great truths begin as heresy," Chris reminded.

"Will you just cut to the chase," Patricia said. "What does all this pyschobabble have to do with our situation?"

"I'm getting there. Now, Jung called one of his archetypes the 'Shadow.' It represents the dark side of the ego, and comes from our pre-human past, when our concerns were limited to survival and reproduction. When we weren't so self-conscious, shit like that. Tokens of the Shadow include the snake—most notably your Garden of Eden variety, and elves, demons, dragons...Cool thing is, you'll find all throughout mythology that these shadow symbols often guard the entrances to mounds, caves, pools of water...The collective unconscious. So, basically, when you dream that you're fighting with the devil, it's only yourself that you're fighting with. See, we—"

"The chase!" Patricia demanded.

Chris stiffened in his chair. "Alright, fine. Look, all the archetypes, all the shadow symbols, have merged. They've solidified. Like, the collective unconscious isn't unconscious anymore. It's become an awesome tulpa."

"A what?" Joan said.

"A tulpa." Chris said.

As Chris took a long gulp of milk, Duncan arbitrated. "A tulpa. A materialization of someone's thoughts. They can take any form: spider, tree, rock, the Bee Gees. It's rumored they can act independently from their creators, and in some cases survive them." He guided a toothpick between two molars. "They're practically domesticated in Tibet."

"Why, Duncan," Rachel said, "I'm impressed."

He shrugged. "I get around."

Rachel met his smile, then glanced at Patricia. "Yes, I know."

"Mr. Kaddison," Joan heroically interjected, "are you suggesting that hell was created in man's own image?"

"Interesting way of putting it, Grandma. See, there's this thing I call the Ball of Clay, and I believe it was here long before we humans became sentient. It wasn't until we started looking into the night sky to ponder our beginnings that we began shaping our gods and their backyards. We slapped it—"

Patricia interrupted, "What do you think this 'Ball of Clay' was before man got hold of it?"

Head tipped pensively, he said, "I like to think it's something left over from creation, maybe. Something...unspent. And I don't mean creation in the orthodox sense. Anyway, we slapped—"

"Like some kind of live munitions left over from the Big Bang?" Duncan said.

"Well, something like that," Chris sighed. "Like I was saying, we slapped it—"

"And it has fallen into the hands of a child," Rachel said, finishing the allegory with barely a hint of mischievousness.

"Hey," Chris charged, "I don't make fun when you're talking." Offended, he glanced reprovingly around the table. Satisfied that he'd put an end to the antics, he continued. "So, we slapped it on a potter's wheel and sculpted the characters. For centuries they've worn a costume for every nametag. I mean, like, those gods and devils have been indulging us for almost as long as we've been indulging them. But now they've evolved into something far more radical."

Patricia looked amused. "Now why would they go and do a thing like that?"

"Because our own concepts don't define them anymore," he said. "Now they want to dress themselves, to primp in front of their own mirrors."

"We left the Petri dish open, in other words," said Duncan.

Chris nodded. "And now we can't get the lid back on."

"I'm still confused," Rachel said.

"Look," Chris said, "think of it this way. A long time ago, the mind of man created a simple board game. But now, with the advent of technology, we've programmed that game into a free-thinking computer, and are about to play our first round."

"A board game?" Rachel said. "Like Monopoly?"

"Yeah, like Monopoly," bandied Chris. "But this is the revised edition, babe, and it's got the Reading Railroad now going to Auschwitz, Dachau, Ravensbruck...See, the pieces have turned. They're no longer content to let our imaginations move them. They've become sentient, willful, corporeal. The Madonna statue isn't confined anymore to just weep and ooze blood. Now she can wear eyeshadow and rouge without the guilt. Like, those archetypes have been gazing up into their night skies for a long time, too, but they've got the advantage now because they know who *their* creators are."

"Kind of like gods realizing *their* gods," Joan said, keeping right along.

"Right," Chris said. "But do they revere us? Not on your life. All the time they've been looking up, it hasn't been to find redemption—it's been to find a way out. As we speak, a war is raging, the factions of Good and Evil. And they're fighting over us, just as we've always believed. Just like we've always *imagined*. You might not recognize the scripts anymore, the characters, the battlefields, but it's happening." Chris used his napkin for the first time, then said, "Just as surely as our minds made little green apples."

"Oh, please," Patricia wheezed.

Duncan said, "So, you're saying that there really is a God in all His glory, only *we* created *Him* and not the other way around?"

Chris's smile grew wider. "Exactly."

Rachel said, "What you're suggesting would have to also say that there were a lot of older gods running the place before Abraham's God rode into town."

Chris laughed. "If God's as jealous as we say He is, *think* He is, then I doubt that any of the incumbents from, like, Mt. Olympus or anywhere else survived the election."

"And," Rachel continued, "He would be an old man with a long white beard, and heaven really would have pearly gates and angels sitting on white, puffy clouds. And hell and its lakes of fire really would be ruled by some pitchfork-wielding demon."

"In their pre-sentient days, yes," Chris agreed, "But—"

"Tell me," Patricia said, "does God eat with chopsticks when Buddha has Him over for dinner?"

Rachel added, "If the Hindu were, say, on the fence about the whole matter, would God still be an old, bearded man, just with eight arms instead of two? And would He have one of those red ruby thingamajigs in his forehead?" She leaned into the table and whispered, "And, most importantly, do you think He'd be throwing the old bone to Shiva?"

Chris was mad. "Look," he said, "these gods aren't our puppets anymore. They have their own hierarchies now, political agendas, favorite snack foods. We can't keep a curfew on them anymore. They've grown up, but we haven't even reached species puberty yet. Things were fine when it was only cherubs and St. Peter and the burning pits of hell. But now things are changing. *They're* changing. Old time religion's still okay with us, but it's become ancient history for them. And that's because they're naturally evolving. Mankind stopped a long time ago." His fist struck the table. "I mean, like, we still burn incense and candles, confess our sins to purge our souls! We're still reading from the same dumbass scripts, performing the same rituals that our ancestors performed in the same costumes with the same convictions that the gods will look down at the sacrificial altar and be appeased and spare our lives until the next full moon. Sure, the Pope's garb is more lustrous now because it's sheared from genetically enhanced sheep and stitched in high-tech robotic factories—*but it's still a vestment.*" He glanced accusingly at Juanita. "By any other name, a rosary is still a rosary is still a rosary."

He took a badly needed breath, then, "Hey, we should all be way beyond that now. But we're not."

Juanita threw down her napkin and rose from her chair. "I think God has a special place for you—a big toilet so you can relieve yourself of all that nonsense you have packed inside!"

She tipped her nose to the ceiling and huffed into the kitchen.

Chris's shoulders bounced with quiet chuckles. "You Catholics crack me up."

"You go, girlfriend!" hollered the face in the window.

Without looking back, Chris pointed over his shoulder at the face. "The really sad part is, he's me," he said to Kathy, who was snickering into her glass of milk.

"So, who do we pray to now?" Joan said, looking perturbed that the Almighty would have the nerve to just up and bail out on them like that.

"Ourselves," Chris said decidedly. "We're our own gods. Always have been."

"That'll look good on my résumé," Patricia said. "Can type, operate DOS or MAC, answer phones, and forgive anyone their sins."

"There's just one thing, babe," Chris warned. "You won't have to worry about employment if they're able to, like, reverse the process."

"Reverse what process?" Kathy said, as if Chris had finally hit upon something unfamiliar to her.

"I think he means the tables are going to turn," said Duncan. "Our gods are going to do the opposite to us of what we did to them. We thought them into reality, now they're going to think us back into Chris's 'Ball of Clay.'" He looked at Chris. "Right?"

"Very perceptive, dude," Chris said, squinting. "That's quite a leap you just took. But, yeah, I think that would be the natural order of things. More or less."

"Whoa, back up," Patricia said. "Our own thoughts are going to 'think' us away?"

"No way they'll get rid of us entirely," Chris said. "Our souls will become the cattle of *their* collective unconscious, penned there and experimented upon. See, they've already become fruitful. Now it's time to *multiply*."

"Are you making this crap up as you go?" Rachel said.

"I'm serious," he continued. "The collective unconscious still has its limits. I mean, given that the human mind cannot grasp the full ramifications of eternity, just to mention one, then the scopes of a man-made heaven and hell—including their populations—aren't likely to reach very far."

Patricia yawned. "So."

"Sooo, if you were the devil and, after having just evolved into a free-thinking supreme being aching to pick a fight, discover that your minions are far too low in number to gain, like, a military advantage over your enemy, then wouldn't you want to get on the stick and figure out a way to multiply your troops, and fast?"

"If this being, this 'Shadow,' is as powerful as you say," said Patricia, "then why couldn't he just whip up all the legions he needs?"

"He could," Chris said, "and probably already has. But remember, these supreme beings are *mankind's* personifications of Good and Evil. And sharing that heritage has ensured that both have evolved at the same pace. Two superpowers in a cold war, each confined to the same limitation, man's inability to grasp the bigger picture." He thought for a moment, then said, "It would be M.A.D.: Mutual Assured Destruction."

Duncan said, "But if you're the bad, bloodthirsty devil, then a stalemate's the last thing you'll want."

"Is there an echo in here?" Chris said. "That's what I just said."

"So then," Duncan said, "it's safe to assume that, given the family tree, these super-'tulpas' are governed by a similar evolutionary process to our own, right?"

"In some ways, yes," said Chris, a descrying smile beginning to form.

"Then it goes to reason that one will eventually create—before the other—a weapon of mass destruction."

"Just a matter of time," Chris agreed.

Reflexively, Duncan glanced at Kathy, then looked down at his plate. "Natural order of things."

"Bombs away!" Chris said, grinning like a hyena. "So let it be written, so let it be done."

"You *do* make this crap up as you go," Rachel moaned.

"It's all made up," he said, spreading out his arms. "This reality is just another product of our imaginations."

"You really believe you're an expert on minds, don't you?" Patricia said.

"When it comes to the human psyche, I'm the best," he said. "I've probably entered Wonderland more times than any man alive."

"Give me an example," Patricia said, her coddling eyes slowly widening. "Just one little instance of what it's like inside Ms. February's head. Or did you make it that far north?"

Ignoring the jab, Chris thought for a moment, then offered, "Patty, have you ever, like, tried explaining to someone what watermelon tastes like?"

She just stared at him.

"Without comparing it to itself, it's nearly impossible. Well, that's what it's like trying to explain to someone what the psyche is like. The only people who can truly appreciate that flavor are those who've actually taken a bite. Like me." He looked at Kathy. "And you."

Kathy nodded proudly. "And me."

Rachel glared at the girl. "Oh? And whose mind have you been eating?"

"Amy's," she said, rolling her eyes. "Duh!"

"Where *do* you get your info, Chris?" Patricia said. "The Psychic Hotline?"

Chris leaned forward. "Babe, I *am* the Psychic Hotline," he reminded. "Or, have you already forgotten our visit this afternoon?"

Patricia looked away; an uncomfortable smile.

"Personally," Rachel said, "I think someone's ridin' the psilocybin." She made a gun with her hand and pushed her finger point-blank against Chris's temple. "Alright! Hand over all the 'shrooms!"

Chris shook his head, disgusted. "Look at yourselves," he said. "After everything you've seen so far, you still have the nerve to laugh. See how conditioned you all are? Even when it's right in front of your noses you can't accept it because it ain't the status quo. I mean, how many little girls do you know who can go IMAX on a picture window?" He pointed to the face in the glass: "And do you really think that every household in America has one of those? Just the sight of that alone should have all of you rethinking everything you've been taught. You're all brainwashed! Have been since day one."

Red-faced and ready to explode with laughter, Patricia said, "Speaking of brainwashing, when was the last time yours had a bath?"

"Very funny," Chris said with a smile.

Patricia broke out laughing. Just as she did, Rachel joined her.

"Okay, laugh it up," Chris said. "But I'm telling you, the mind is an incredible place, solely or collectively. It's not just one universe but untold billions, each as boundless as the one we're spinning through." He looked at Patricia. "And babe, they're all interlinked."

Patricia brought her harsh laughter down to a sort of percolator chuckle, then drew her own weapon, aiming it at Chris. "Say 'babe' one more time, surfer dude, and I'll put a subway through *your* universe."

Rachel looked at Patricia, and they both cracked up again.

"Christ, it's Cagney and Lacy." Chris threw his napkin on his plate. "I mean, what is with you chicks? 'Babe' is a—"

"Bang!"

"Bang!"

Kathy, who'd been packing her own heat, aimed and fired. "Pow!"

"—term of endearment." He stared at Kathy, hurt. "Whose side are you on, anyway?"

"You're psychic, you figure it out," she said, then blew smoke from her finger.

Patricia said, "Chris, I think your Yin has been cheating on your Yang and has caught a bad case of the clap."

Chris rose from the table. "Look, I know how weird it all sounds, but if any one of you can prove to me that God exists independently from us, then I'll stand corrected. Until then, all theories are open for debate, just as they always have been."

"What about you?" said Rachel to Chris. "Do you have any proof? Just a smidgen?"

Nearing the kitchen doors, Chris said, "If you're all really thinking about hopping a plane to Seattle, then you'd better get to the airport now. Like I said, come sunrise, nobody's going anywhere except to hell, and I'll be saying I told you so all the way down." Then he turned to Rachel. "And all that proof you're looking for will be right out front, aerating the lawn, along with all the neighbors."

As Chris disappeared into the kitchen, the saloon doors swinging wildly behind him, he shouted out lastly, "We're not the dreamer anymore, but the dream."

11.

Eli snatched the phone halfway through the fourth ring.

"Yes?" he answered, winded.

"Forgive the intrusion, Father," said Mr. Gamble, "but are you, perchance, viewing the media's live coverage of the events at St. Patrick's Church?"

Eli's heart jumped. "I'm afraid I'm busy with other things at the moment."

He was perplexed as to why Gamble was using the phone to initiate contact. Highly unusual. In fact, it had never been done before.

"Well," Gamble sighed, "it appears that someone has torched the old place. I'm afraid, my dear fellow, that your dreams of eventually turning it into a bed and breakfast are all but quashed."

"It's—*it's on fire?*"

"Lustfully."

"You cocksucker!" Eli shouted. "Why did you burn my church?"

"Watch your mouth," Gamble growled. "I've done you a favor. Your so-called masterpiece was becoming a distraction for you and everyone else. Besides, you're in possession of the seventh angel now. You don't need to carry this facade any further. Once you dispose of her—and let's not forget about Katherine Bently!—then you'll be free of all this nonsense."

Eli panted into the phone. He stood and glanced out the dining room window, in the direction of the church, four miles distant. And there it was—a faint, gray smudge on the horizon. His heart was beating so loudly in his ears that he actually withdrew the receiver a few inches from his head, fearing Gamble might hear and think him a sissy.

"You should come on down, Eli," Gamble shouted as the siren of an emergency vehicle heralded its arrival. "That busty redheaded thing from Channel Four, Sheila Livingston I think is her name, is waving that microphone in front of her mouth like it's a hard dick. Wow! I don't know what's hotter right now—her or the St. Christopher medal pooling on Deacon Flannery's neck!"

"Samuel's inside the church?" Eli said.

"Oh, you should have been here, Father. It was some of my best material yet. I'm telling you, I'm seriously thinking about trying my luck at show biz."

Eli wanted—needed—to hang up. "I've work to do—"

"Work, work, work," Gamble lamented. "Listen, why don't you whittle down a couple of olive branches, grab a bag of those great big marshmallows, and we'll sing some songs, tell some ghost stories. What'da'ya say?"

"I don't think so."

"Momma's boy," Gamble taunted. There was a short burst of static, then he said, "Sorry about the connection, Father. It's this damned cellular phone. It's geared more for long distance calling, if you know what I mean. *Looong* distance. The phone was free, but the monthly charges are killing me. Ten cents a minute my ass!"

Gritting his teeth, Eli said, "Now that the confessional is no longer an option, where will we meet?"

"Once your chores are finished, you'll finally get to meet me face-to-face. Are you excited?"

Eli hesitated, then said, "Yes, I'm...I'm looking forward to it."

"Just remember one thing," Gamble cautioned. "If and when you walk through that window, you'll still be mine. You'll never shed enough cocoons to outshine my wings. Understand?"

"Of course."

"With all of your restraints gone," he continued, "it will be tempting to imagine yourself more powerful than you really are. And with your tongue's brazen demonstration just moments ago, I might be inclined to think that process has already begun."

"I-I-I—"

"Many before you have felt the heel of my shoe, and you'll crunch beneath it just as the others who let it go to their heads."

"Yes, I...understand," Eli said amidst a thunderous noise.

"Spectacular!" Gamble trumpeted. "The roof just fell in!"

Eli winced. He didn't have to look out the window to see the surging convoy of embers. The roof was mainly stone, and he believed it would have taken more than a fire to topple it—like a little shove from Gamble, the lousy prick.

A magnificent structure razed. His wondrous masterpiece gone.

Fuck.

"Well," Eli sighed, "good night, then."

12.

Patricia smoked at the dining room table as the girl lay on her stomach in front of the television, watching *The Brady Bunch*. One of the first episodes. The girl's hands propped up her chin, and she slowly bent her right leg back and forth, as if inviting Patricia to come lay beside her but too shy to turn around and summon her more candidly. Then her leg stopped as she began giggling at Alice, who'd stepped between a bickering Greg and Marcia.

Patricia scowled. If this genie were truly her daughter, she would have sent her to bed hours ago.

But at dinner you were beginning to think—

No. This child was not hers. Her daughter and this girl shared the same likeness, that was all, that was the extent of it. And, the truth be known, she didn't think the girl in front of the TV looked *that* much like her Katherine. *Her* daughter, at the age of ten, had been leaner, her face more angular, her eyes less droopy, her hair a richer and thicker brown.

—*was almost convinced that she was*—

No. *Her* daughter had been...prettier. Yes, much prettier; her features definitely more innocent, undefiled.

"Mom?" the girl called rather urgently from the floor.

"Yes?" she answered absently.

Glancing back at Patricia, she said, "Gotcha."

"Clever," she said with a smirk, her neck and ears growing warm. "But, please, I'm not your mother."

"For a second there, you were."

"A weak moment," Patricia confessed.

Before turning back to the TV, the girl said, "We can't have too many more of those, can we?"

No, Patricia thought, *I suppose we can't.*

She recommenced staring out the dining room window. With flashlight in hand, Chris continued to pace a tight grid on her front yard. She supposed he was looking to link telepathically with some wayward wraith, or perhaps he'd discovered that her property was over some Indian burial ground and was, like, dude, eager to direct the Great Indian Chief, Me Smokem Plenty, and his empty pipe to the nearest hemp field.

Just then, Chris stopped, bent over, and pointed an ear to the ground. After fifteen seconds or so, he walked a few steps, then directed downward his fleshy radar once more.

Fascinated, she watched him repeat this act half a dozen times.

Whatever he was doing, she decided, it was definitely better entertainment than what cable was presently offering.

"He's a weird duck, that one," Patricia said.

"We're all weird," said the girl, not bothering to look away from her show. "Every last one of us. It's just a matter of degree."

Taken aback, Patricia was awed at this child's insight. It wasn't what she said, but the way she said it, with a chilling tone of wisdom.

"I guess that means you think I'm weird, then?" Patricia said.

"Especially you!" Then, barely audible, "At least Grammy never lost hope."

Patricia was shocked. "Oh, really?"

Finally disconnecting altogether from the TV, she said, "All these years you've prayed and prayed to have me back, and now that I'm back, you don't want to have anything to do with me. Now *that's* weird."

"No," Patricia started, angrier than she intended, "what's weird is that you're still ten years old, young lady. You should've been married by now, and maybe pregnant with my grandchild. But no, you show up on my doorstep with the same snotty nose and wearing the same size shoes you were in the day you disappeared!"

"My nose was not snotty!"

"Everything all right," Juanita gingerly asked, snooping through the kitchen doors. Behind her, Patricia's mother was bobbing like a cork, straining to peek around Juanita.

"Just peachy," Patricia said, exasperated. It occurred to her then that maybe everyone had left her and the girl alone like an affianced couple on their first date, hoping that they might warm to one another.

Everyone else was sold on the idea that this little girl was her daughter. Even Rachel, who had given birth to her. So why wasn't she convinced?

As Juanita let the kitchen doors swivel back into place, Patricia said, "I just can't. Not right now." Her eyes misted over, and an old ache flared in her heart. Suddenly, it was hard to breathe. "I...I'm just scared. I...I don't think I could survive losing you again."

"I understand," said the girl, standing now. "And I'm sorry I was disrespectful."

At that moment, Patricia wanted so badly to open her arms wide and hug the girl, who, upon review, *did* look just like her own daughter, *was* just as beautiful as she remembered her. *Was* just as pretty as her pictures.

But she couldn't. Not yet. "Honey, it's been a crazy day for all of us. No need to apologize—"

A loud knock on the window.

Patricia turned and saw Chris's horror-stricken face pressed against the glass. His mouth was open wide, his nose askew and mashed bloodless, and his tongue groped wetly like the foot of some desperate mollusk seeking purchase along an aquarium wall.

It was quite a hilarious sight. But she didn't know whether to laugh or be terrified. This was Chris, after all.

The girl had now joined Patricia and was giggling at Chris's antics.

"You're streaking my window, surfer dude," Patricia hollered.

"Just ignore him," the face called down from the other window. "He's an ignoramus."

Chris was now holding the flashlight beneath his chin, an obvious attempt to appear more sinister. His mouth chewed at the glass, his words unintelligible.

"What?" Patricia said, a hand to her ear.

Chris answered with another flatulent round of words.

"What?"

Perturbed, Chris backed away from the window and yelled, "They're almost here!"

"Hey, knock it off, wolf-boy," yelled the face. "You're scaring the ladies."

Patricia looked down at the girl. "Who's almost here?"

Although her eyes appeared quite concerned, she shrugged indifferently. "Monsters, probably."

13.

Earlier that morning, Eli had developed the rolls of film he'd so far taken of his seventh angel. Now that they were dry, he began artfully cutting and pasting them to the Wall of Faces. After applying the last one, he stepped back and regarded the montage with pride, if not downright pomposity.

Melanie Sands was just as beautiful in black-and-white as she was in color.

Now *his* wings were almost complete. The next—and last—series of photographs would be taken of Melanie in the throes of agony, just before her short trip into the wide blue yonder. He'd tried every time to capture each girl's terrified expression as they plummeted toward the surf and rocks, but had yet to pluck even one pose worthy of the Wall. Hell, he'd been lucky just to catch blurry glimpses of their little faces. He would click off a few of Melanie as she was falling, of course, but he wasn't going to hold his breath. Still, he couldn't help but feel that just one of those images—a portrait of consummate, mouth-wrenching, eye-bulging terror—would be worth more than all the other pictures combined.

He turned and stared at the second window. He'd finally gone ahead and dispatched another courier to assist in finding the Bently girl. And if he had to, he'd dispatch a whole gaggle.

He felt like a child on Christmas Eve night, one unable to keep his eyes from the fireplace, expecting at any moment to see the trickle of chimney ash.

His hands trembled, mostly the residual jitters from his earlier hours of meticulous sewing. But some of it was adrenaline. And before the day was over, he was confident that his circulatory system would be clogged with the stuff.

Who was this Bently girl? What had she become? And how did she manage to win a brawl with one of the couriers? Not even good old Arnold could best a courier. No mortal man could. Gamble had assured him of that. So, did that mean she wasn't mortal? Well, his mentor had so far elected not to divulge Katherine Bently's more intimate secrets. So, he would just let the questions be...for now.

Finally tearing his eyes from the window, he stepped inside the room where Melanie Sands lay prostrate, naked and bleeding. She was still unconscious, had passed out from the pain. Her mouth was taped shut.

He studied her trunk for signs of breathing. Nothing. He peered closer, squinting. Still nothing. Instantly horrified, he knelt down and crimped her nostrils shut. Within seconds, her eyes flew open as her body jerked in response. He released her nose, recaptured his own stolen breath, then stood, his knees burning and a little wobbly.

"Christ," he muttered.

A few hours earlier, with the help of his mother, Eli had finished sewing the wings into Melanie's back. She had fought hard before succumbing to the torture, so much so that Eli had to employ Jacob to help hold her.

He stared down at her body and was struck with queer wonderment. Now, he thought, just what kind of sick pervert would sexually molest a child? He'd never so much as entertained the idea, and it turned his stomach to even imagine someone taking those kinds of prurient liberties.

Help the dwindling frog population, he thought, and instead put a pedophile in every biology class for dissection. Yes, that would do very nicely.

He reached down, grabbed a handful of hair, pulled her head up, and with one swift yank removed the tape from her mouth. "I have some wonderful news," he said, releasing her. "In just a few hours, you'll be crab bait."

Wide-eyed and panting, she tried to roll onto her back. The pressure exerted on the wings tore at her sutures, and she squealed in pain.

"Hey, easy on those," he said, thumping her ear with a knuckle.

She winced, but did not cry out.

"It takes us a long time to make these wings just right," he lectured, "and I don't need you thrashing about like some harpooned seal."

Quietly crying now, she said, "Sir, where's my mommy?"

"I know where she isn't." He winked.

"Am I going to die?"

He nodded. "Yes. Horribly so."

"But why?" she beseeched. *"Why?"*

Eli turned to the window once again. "So that I won't."

14.

Behind the priest's seven windows, Amy stood naked in her adult, angel form. She was on the outside looking in upon a cold, gray basement that was much more inviting than the unremitting crypt she'd just entered. The one *this* side of those equally macabre panes.

Halloween country.

Graffiti was literally strewn across a pumpkin sky, carved out by the willful hand of a demigod. Everything from toilet habits to incestuous affinities were remarked upon, as well as some things even she had difficulty translating. An army of scarecrows hung crucified along the hilly landscape, their black-button eyes fixed repentantly toward heaven.

The ground here was crawling with thick, twisted vines, from which sprouted millions of large gourds, their rinds a pearly translucence. And within each of those knobby hulls the shadow of something rat-sized and spider-like skittered like a lightning ball.

Gamble's answer to a coyote trap.

That was okay. She could chew off her leg and instantly grow a million in its place. But she wasn't going to let it come to that. She didn't have to let it come to that, as illustrated by the two-winged creatures beside her, Tweedle-dee and Tweedle-dum, skewered upon her sword, both frozen in mid-leap, teeth bared, talons protracted, eyes blazing a hateful vermillion.

Katherine's would-be kidnappers weren't dead, just arrested in place.

An unsavory shish-kabob.

But it would make a great swizzle stick, she thought. *Another Christmas gift idea.*

Then she smiled at herself. She really did have Duncan's warped sense of humor. And, with all due respect, some of his spirit. His gall.

Unlike a few of her predecessors, Amy could, to a much greater extent, fight back.

She regarded the window with droll concern. To convince Eli that she was Katherine Bently would be easy enough, and it might keep Gamble from becoming alerted to her presence just long enough to cleanse Melanie. But that meant she would have to allow Tweedle-dee and Tweedle-dum to resume their questing duties and take her to the fallen priest.

Yuck!

She sighed, the sound knelling across the gourds like wind through fluted cymbals. Then she changed her form back into that of her ten-year-old self.

"Okay," she ordered, repossessing her sword then hurling it to a safe, distant place. "Sic me."

15.

Eli had taken his mother's phone off the hook, as it had been chirping incessantly since the six o'clock news. Most of the callers had been her fellow fussbudgets wanting to get the scoop on the fire. He'd also instructed his mother not to answer the door for anyone, that going double for the media.

Just as he was ready to break ground with the trowel, his mother hollered from the window. "Package just arrived for you, your highness. I think it's that one you sent away for with all them Count Chocula box-tops."

Eli looked up at the kitchen window, his mother's withered face ghostly behind the screen. "What the hell are you talking about?"

"Just get your ass in here and sign for it?" she yelled. "Christ, do I have to do everything?"

Cursing under his breath, he threw down the shovel and headed for the house.

As he opened the sliding back door, his mother said, "It's down in the basement, choir boy."

It took him a moment to realize what his mother was saying. Then, a jubilant smile sprang across his face.

As Eli descended the stairs, he could faintly hear their voices; impetuous whispers, actually.

He sneaked to the edge of the doorway and listened. The words were still too hushed to understand, but the voices were definitely planning something.

It was time to take a peek.

Standing now in the dimly lit doorway, he saw both couriers, seemingly free of injuries, squatting just inside and to his right, grooming one another. Beyond them, sitting beside Melanie Sands, was his second angel.

Both girls looked up, shocked.

"Well, well, well," Eli said, his voice euphoric. "If it isn't Katherine Bently."

Then Eli discovered the most criminal, most unconscionable thing he could imagine. Melanie's wings had been removed from her back and tossed into the corner like a pair of old shoes.

"What have you done?" he roared at Katherine. He looked over at the couriers, horrified. *"How could you let this happen?"*

Disconcerted, the couriers stared up at him.

"Melanie won't be flying today," Katherine said.

Currents of rage began to steadily build until they were rippling through his body. Teeth gnashing, fists clenched, he started for Katherine. "You little bitch! I'll gut you like a—" Then he stopped, suddenly struck with a wonderful idea. A smile returned to his lips; more sinister than the one he'd worn just moments ago, but stretching just as wide.

The more he thought about it, the more relaxed he became. It would save him the two hours of traveling time and another hour of preparation. And that meant he could be into his own wings a hell of a lot sooner.

He clasped his hands together. "Are either of you familiar with the expression, 'To kill two birds with one stone?'"

Neither girl answered.

"No? Hmmm. Then tell me this—do either of you have an aversion to slimy things?"

16.

Eli resumed his digging with renewed purpose.

He tossed a shovelful of dirt over his shoulder, then went for another. He didn't plan on striking any fortune cookies this evening; was just going deep enough to favor two small bodies, and a box of very hungry worms.

"Evening, Father," Jack Singletary warbled over the fence—a flimsy, truncated old thing not nearly high enough. The fence, not Jack.

Eli moaned. Living alongside the Singletarys was like getting free cable television. One of Eli's inconsistent parishioners of some years, Jack looked remarkably like Roy Thinnes, the actor from the old TV series, *The Invaders*. As the quintessential guy next door, it was unclear whether Jack was being harassed by bug-eyed extraterrestrials, but one thing was certain: if he wasn't, it was no doubt the fault of his unbearably sweet wife Janet, whose enduring impersonation of Donna Reed could keep even the most determined Martians, favorite or not, at arm's length.

But Eli knew better.

According to Janet Singletary's most recent visit to the confessional, she was continuing to bang her husband's best friend with whom she shared an expensive cocaine habit. She was also suspecting that her husband Jack was dancing the infidelity hustle himself, most likely with someone at his work, but she couldn't be sure. And at last check didn't really care.

Then there was Jack. Jack, who had indeed been tripping the light fantastic with a female coworker, among others, had once bragged during confession that he'd notched the proverbial bedpost more times than Wilt Chamberlain. Which still wouldn't come close, numbers wise, to matching the thousands upon thousands he'd embezzled from his employer of fifteen years. But Eli did not think less of Jack. He hated everyone equally. He learned long ago that abstention did not exist; everyone was a criminal, a drug addict, a fornicator.

For Eli, the confessional offered about as much surprise as finding the Indigo Girls in a new age coffee shop. Of course, that all went to the wind when he shared it with Gamble.

"Jack," Eli replied stiffly. He took a moment to retrieve the handkerchief from his back pocket and dabbed his forehead. Jack had obviously not heard about the firestorm once known as St. Patrick's Church or that topic would have already been broached with delirious remorse. "And how's Mrs. Singletary?"

"Ah, Janet's busy in the kitchen whipping up some kind of soufflé or casserole," he said, wrinkling his nose. "What'cha digging?"

"A grave," Eli confessed.

Jack folded his arms atop the fence, then laughed. "Did you finally go and snuff ol' Deacon Flannery, Father?"

It came as no surprise that Jack knew of Eli's contempt for Samuel Flannery, as did most of the congregation, he suspected. After all, he'd never tried keeping it a secret.

"No," Eli said, "Samuel's demise was accomplished by someone else." Taking a breather, he leaned against his shovel. "As I understand it, Samuel died a horrible death this afternoon and was cremated immediately."

Jack was now tittering like an infatuated schoolgirl. It had been Eli's vocational experience that people like Jack were impelled to giddy states while in the self-conscious presence of a priest, as if their sins stuck out like mortified thumbs in the pious glow of the cloth. They made small talk while keeping a safe distance, and avoided religious topics at all costs.

Then there were those who nuzzled up to the holy man like a warm fire and blathered on endlessly about the church, the state of religion, and themselves, their sad and only motive to sponge absolution, as if that were possible.

Atonement by proximity. But then, wasn't that the intention of the church? It was all so obsolete. Amnesty, Eli was sure, did not exist in this or any other world. And that was the cold hard truth of it all.

From the raised cedar deck came two loud knocks. "Here's that batch of tea you ordered, your highness," yelled Josephine, pitcher in one hand, cane in the other. "We're all out of those decorative mint leaves and fancy lemon slices, so if that insults your sense of etiquette then you and Ms. Manners can both kiss my ass."

"Cantankerous old bitch," Eli mumbled, slicing through the soil with renewed vigor.

Josephine sat the pitcher on the table, leaned herself against the railing, then began fanning her face with a round pink Tupperware lid she'd pulled from her smock pocket. "Hotter'n hellfire."

"Step Two would be a glass with lots of ice," Eli prodded her.

Without looking his way, she nonchalantly flipped him the bird.

With only his eyes and upper head visible above the fence, Jack lifted a hand and waved to Josephine. "Howdy-doody, neighbor."

Josephine glanced in Jack's direction, her middle finger extended once again.

Jack straightened himself and, with a more serious approach, said to Eli, "I think we're in for an earthquake, Father. Real soon. And I mean a big one."

"And what's drawn you to that conclusion, pray tell?"

Jack shook his head. "Sasha, you know, our dog, has been acting very strange lately. She won't eat and refuses to come out from under our bed. She just shakes and whimpers." He tossed a thumb over his shoulder. "And the Petersons' two Shih Tzus went at it last night like you wouldn't believe. Tore each other up so bad that they had to have them both put to sleep at that twenty-four hour vet clinic over on Lakeview."

"And this means buildings are going to topple?"

"Well, they say animals start behaving funny right before an earthquake. I understand some people at the San Diego Zoo are experts at knowing just what to look for."

"If I see any Mountain Gorillas or hippopotami acting suspiciously, I'll let them know."

"Good one, Father." Jack laughed, then rubbed his chin pensively. "Anyhow, something's going to hit the fan. I kinda have that, you know, weird feeling myself that something terrible is about to happen."

"It is," Eli said, finally exhausted with Jack Singletary. He turned to Josephine. "Excuse me, Mother, but would you please bring Jacob out here. I would like you to introduce him to our paranoid neighbor, Jack. Oh, and Mother," he added, "don't bother with the leash."

Enthralled, a smile pushed back the creased satchels of her face. "Why, I'd be delighted to!" she declared, then disappeared into the house.

Jack chuckled slyly. "Did your mother finally break down and buy herself a pooch? I mean, that's great, Father. I understand a pet can extend the life of its elderly owner."

Eli returned the chuckle. "Shit, Jack, if I had known that, I would have killed her parakeet years ago."

Jack smiled, nodded. "Seriously, though, what's the hole for?" he said, plucking splinters from his right forearm, courtesy of the frayed lumber.

"Nefarious as it may sound, I'm going to bury two little girls alive, along with some very nasty night crawlers."

A quizzical expression scrunched Jack's smile. "What was that, Father?"

Just then, Josephine and Jacob appeared on the cedar deck. "Jack, meet Jacob; Jacob, Jack." She reached down and patted Jacob's head. "Now go crap in his tulips!"

Jack was mesmerized. "Good God Almighty! What kind of animal is that?"

Eli laughed. "The kind, I imagine, whose scent is turning the neighborhood dogs crazy."

The creature took to the air, then careened downward, using its barbed tail to slice through Jack's throat.

"Atta boy!" cheered Josephine.

Jack's screams, only wet hisses, bubbled below his chin. He stumbled backward, then collapsed behind the fence.

Now gaping from the Singletarys' kitchen window was Janet. Her face suggested that she was watching a particularly violent clip from *America's Funniest Home Videos*. She appeared seconds later on the tiny outcrop of cement porch, just below the back door. Hands busily wringing the doily apron tied around her thin waist, she laughed. "Jack, what's going on?"

Jacob circled low over the Singletary's roof, then plunged like an osprey into their backyard, from where rending, tearing sounds immediately followed.

"Rip him up!" Eli commanded. "And when you're through with Jack, give his wife a big howdy-doody, the adulterous cunt!"

Janet Singletary was still smiling, still fussing with her apron as urine began to stream down both legs, splotching her white polyester slacks, then puddling at the soles of her blue Donna Reed slip-ons.

Josephine cupped her hands to the sides of her mouth. "And while you're over there," she bellowed, "fetch back that gravy ladle they borrowed from me last Thanksgiving."

17.

The light from the hallway bathroom eked into the otherwise dark living and dining rooms, making them negotiable.

Despite the use of some old cop techniques for stealthy prowling, Duncan's footfalls still managed to provoke chirps and creaks from the occasionally loose flooring. When one was six-foot-three and two-hundred-and-forty pounds, sneaking was a lousy option. However, once he reached the stairs, his covert intentions would be muffled by thick carpeting.

Finally there, he tightened his grip on the hammer as he climbed.

Stopping in front of the window, he stared at the sleeping face. He felt like Dorothy confronting the Wizard. "Just follow the Yellow Brick Road," Amy had told him yesterday, as if she'd known then that he would soon entertain such a comparison. At any other time Duncan would have considered it a fluke. But now it bore deific relevance, as if she'd spoken those words to him not from the environs of a hospital, but from a burning bush atop Mount Sinai.

The dim, orange glow from a neighbor's porch light was leaving rich whorls as it stirred the stained glass, tincturing the reds and blues and yellow-oranges into darker, smoldering versions of themselves. These effects also gave the resident face more amplitude, more character, than had the afternoon or even the setting sun.

Standing there, he watched its nostril move with each wheezy snore.

Its eye wondered behind the lid, the face apparently dreaming. Its lips were parted just slightly, and as he held his hand just a few inches away, he could feel warm puffs of breath against his skin.

Gooseflesh stippled across his forearms; not a manifestation of fear, but of absolute incredulity.

He tapped the hammer against his leg, watching.

"Wake up," he finally whispered.

The eye fluttered. The lips parted even wider.

He bumped the handle lightly against the glass. "Rise and shine," he whispered again, louder.

The eye flew open. It stared at him for a moment, cloudy with sleep. "What...Duncan? What's going on?"

"Keep your voice down," he ordered. "Now listen up. I want some goddamn answers."

Blinking out the cobwebs, it said, "What kind of answers?" It was now staring distrustfully at the hammer.

"What part of Chris are you?"

"The slumbering part."

Duncan raised the hammer.

"Okay, okay," said the face. "You could say I'm his psychic conscience."

"What, like you make sure he doesn't peek clairvoyantly into women's locker rooms, stuff like that?"

"Even I wouldn't discourage that," it said. "No, I'm referring to a much higher level, like keeping him from going into people's minds, and elsewhere, and doing harmful things."

"Well, you sound like a moral kind of guy, then," Duncan said with feigned delight. "How about telling me where my daughter is."

"She's just down the hall—"

"Not Kathy, smart ass," he said, raising the hammer again. "Amy."

"Look, I swear I don't know Amy's whereabouts."

"Really? Then how is it that you and the rest of Chris found out all those things about Patricia?"

The lone eye looked away. "Well, um, you see...I...we...Look, it's very complicated—"

"Tell me where Amy is!" Duncan snarled, leaning in. "Tell me *who* she is!"

"I'm not sure I should tell a brute like you. I'm bound by a conscience of my own."

Duncan brandished the hammer. "Yeah? And I'm bound by Craftsman Tools."

Just then, down in the dining room, the kitchen doors squealed open. A voice whispered, "Who's up there?"

"It's just me, Mrs. Pendleton," Duncan said.

"Are you talking to that window?"

"Well, yes, I suppose I am," he admitted.

"Alright, but you boys don't stay up too late, or you'll be the dickens to get up."

"Yes ma'am," said Duncan.

As Joan let the doors swing shut, Duncan cocked the tool over his shoulder. "Unless you want to become a draft, start talking."

"Alright!" it said. "Look, all I know is that Katherine and Amy are your daughters."

"They have different fathers, Einstein."

"Really? Looks to me like they just have the one."

"Hey, just in case you're insinuating what I think you are, I didn't even know Patricia Bently when Kathy was conceived," he stated. "And even if I were Kathy's father, what would be the odds of her and Amy sharing identical likenesses at their respective ages of ten from two different mothers—with over eleven years between their births?"

"The odds?" said the face. "Astro-fucking-nomical."

"Oh, I'm thinking even beyond that."

"Agreed," said the face. "Now, I want you to pay very close attention. Where was Amy when Katherine was killed?"

Duncan sighed as he bent over and propped the hammer against the wall. "She was either still a twinkle in my eye," he said, "or had just been recently conceived."

"I'd stick with recently conceived. So, what does that tell you?"

"Christ, I don't know. That maybe...that maybe when Kathy was murdered, her soul reincarnated through Amy?" He shook his head. "I know where you're heading, but it doesn't work. It might—*might*—explain to someone else why Amy looks like Kathy, but it wouldn't explain why Kathy carried my resemblance before Amy was ever born."

"Sure it would," said the face, "if you knew which came first, the chicken or the egg."

Duncan tipped his head as if he hadn't quite caught the remark.

Grinning, the face said, "I was making an analogy—"

"I know that!" Duncan snapped. "But while you're waxing metaphoric, I'm getting a nosebleed standing here on Mount Coincidence!"

"Alright, alright. It's like this—Amy doesn't look like Katherine. Katherine looks like Amy."

Duncan reached down for the hammer.

The eye widened. "Look, I'm not trying to screw with your brain. I just want to get you on the right path of thinking. You were there just a second ago, when you mentioned reincarnation."

"But that just doesn't work," Duncan adamantly declared. "Assuming that the literature on reincarnation is true, since when do progressing souls take on the physical appearance of their progenitors? Besides, what's the common denominator here? That reincarnation advances *onwardly.* For Kathy to look like Amy, Amy would have had to—" He stared at the face.

The eye widened. "Yes?"

"Amy's soul went back? In *time?*"

"Hmmmm."

"Oh, give me a break! Kathy is some kind of...of relapsed copy of my daughter?"

"Wild, huh?" said the face. "Gives your mind a wedgie just thinking about it."

"Okay, if Amy went back in time," Duncan said, "and occupied Kathy's embryo—" He stared at his toes, stymied. "Wait a minute, back up. In theory, Amy would have had to die at some point for her soul to be released for this bass-ackwards reincarnation to work at all. Right?"

"Right—if that's the only way you're going to approach it."

"You're starting to piss me off again."

"No, really. Consider this—what if Amy's not entirely human?"

"Well that's rather evident, isn't it?"

"Radically so," agreed the face. "But what's her *non*-human part?"

"Maybe something like...an angel?" Duncan offered pendulously.

"Something even grander than that, perhaps?" requited the face.

Leering now, Duncan said, "What do you know about seraphs?"

"Only that they once existed in greater numbers than they do now."

"You know," Duncan said, "I was muddling through just fine until you threw time travel in the mix. Are you aware of the dilemmas involved with that?"

The face smiled. "I saw this bumper sticker once. It read, 'Do it with a seraph. They take their time without creating any paradoxes.'"

Duncan sighed. "Cute. But if this is all true, then why Kathy?"

"You're assuming that Katherine was already in existence when Amy went back?"

"Then how the hell could Amy hope to influence any changes if Kathy hadn't even been conceived yet?" Then his eyes narrowed. "Oh, unless..."

As if Duncan were a baby attempting his first steps, the face said, "You can do it, come on, you can do it, I know you can..."

"Alright," Duncan insisted, "try this on for size. Amy goes back in time. Her soul enters Patricia's womb just before one of Jack Fortune's little guys scores a hit and somehow manages to plant her own essence in the egg."

"Now you're talking," said the face. "Go on."

Scrunching his face, he said, "Look, hold on, I've got to walk this through. Now, at the moment Kathy dies, her soul enters Rachel's womb. But if Amy had already gone back in time to inseminate Patricia's egg with her divine essence, or whatever..."

"Yes?"

"Then it wasn't Katherine who died at all, but Amy. It was Amy who returned back to Rachel, her original mother, her original womb. Katherine Bently is nothing but the embodiment of Amy McNeil. He looked down in the direction of Kathy's room. "By any other name..."

"A rosary is still a rosary is still a rosary," the face agreed

"But...shit...No, I just don't buy it. I mean, do you realize that we're talking immaculate conception here?"

"What else would you call it when a half-breed seraph goes back in time to fertilize a human egg? A Thursday night quickie? I hate to burst your bubble, but I can guarantee that whatever kind of hanky-panky was responsible for at least half of Katherine's conception will not be found in the Kama Sutra."

"Hold on, Duncan said. "What do you mean 'half of?'"

"I'm afraid Jack Fortune scored a bull's eye, after all."

Duncan rolled his eyes. "So, now what you're telling me Katherine has two fathers—Jack Fortune and a half-breed seraph?"

"No," said the face. "Jack Fortune's daughter is living inside Katherine as a separate entity."

Duncan ran a hand down his face. "I'm confused, again."

"Look at it this way—one of Jack's little swimmers fertilized Patricia's egg, this is true. But his little swimmer isn't anything like the item you learned about in Biology 101. It has a lot more in common with the same kind of essence that Amy used to fertilize the egg. Jack Fortune's daughter is occupying a different space inside Katherine. And he's going to do everything he can to get custody. If he does, it may have fatal ramifications for Katherine. She may not survive the separation."

"So, in all likelihood, we're going to meet up with this guy, this Jack Fortune?"

"You can count on it."

"Alright, if Jack Fortune is some kind of incubus knocking up women, then what does it make me when my daughter's part seraph?"

"Well—"

"I mean, if Amy really is some kind of angel, then what the hell am I? Her own father?"

"Maybe you're—"

"And what about Rachel? Is she an unsuspecting partner in this? Or is she the one who's passing along the angel gene? And let's just say for the moment that I am some kind of angel. Don't you think I would have at least suspected something by now? Like experiencing a twinge of regret every time I bite into an apple? Or ponder for hours over the fleshy nubs growing out of my back? A passionate urge to play a harp every time I see a funeral procession?"

"You're babbling."

"Look, I don't care what you say, I am not an angel, a seraph, a sentinel, a cherub." He felt on the verge of tears. "I'm just plain old Duncan McNeil."

"Alright. But regardless of who's humping who, doesn't it seem a bit odd to you that the seraph is breeding on some level with human beings?"

"Of course it doesn't," Duncan said. "Like the rest of what you've told me, that concept's shining through with crystal fucking clarity."

"No, seriously," it said. "Why would a seraph want to start reproducing through man?"

"Wait," Duncan said, "Amy said something about a place where angels are born. And that I'd have to deliver one. Any idea what she meant by that?"

"Not really," it said. "Perhaps she was speaking metaphorically."

"Gee," Duncan said, "that wouldn't surprise me, seeing how straight answers are like charity lately—a guy has to beg to get any."

"Look, I'm not being stingy, just purposely obscure," it said. "I want to get you thinking on a different level."

Duncan nodded. "Fair enough. So, why is a seraph breeding with humans?"

"Just think about it. Man has something it needs."

"What could it possibly need from peons like us?"

"Something that didn't come in the original box."

"Halo polish?"

"Moxie."

"Moxie?" Duncan said. "What do you call destroying cities and killing first borns? A gut check?"

"Myth."

Duncan folded his arms. "So what you're saying is, it's nothing like we've been told."

"That's exactly what I'm saying."

Duncan grabbed the hammer. He said, "You know, Chris was right about us. Man, I mean. I brought an instrument of destruction to talk with a miracle in a stained glass window, meaning to bust it if it didn't tell me what I wanted to hear." He shook his head. "Even when God wraps us in shrouds of wonder, the first thing we ungrateful bastards do is piss and moan about the quality of the weave."

"And to see what applications any of it might have militarily," the face reminded. "Now *that's* the kind of moxie I'm talking about. Besides, I had the impression that you didn't believe in God."

"There are no atheists in foxholes," Duncan said. He placed his hand gently on the window. "Thanks for humoring me and not compromising your conscience."

"Do me a favor," it said. "Don't tell Chris what we talked about. I want to be the one to tell him. You might say he has a learning disability when it comes to things divine."

"Poor bastard," Duncan said, shaking his head pitiably. "Well, there's one in every crowd."

"Trust me," said the face. "It's even worse than yours."

Duncan pointed to his own head. "But...won't he find out from me anyway?"

"Not likely," it said. "Chris's already tried entering your mind. I won't go into any details, but something in there scared him awfully bad."

"Scared him?"

"Well, as we've just discussed, he doesn't think you're entirely human."

"So, neither does my wife."

"I think you know what I mean."

"Yeah, I do," he said. "And you're full of shit. I'm no angel. Rachel, on the other hand, just might be your man. And Amy, of course."

It smiled. "Before you go, remember...you might not be able or willing to change the past, but the past might be willing and able to change you."

That fateful night isn't through with you, Daddy.

Staring at the face, Duncan said, "You're not really a part of Chris, are you?"

"Try not to think so hard." It smiled. "Just go with the flow."

"If Chris's right about tomorrow, then we're screwed, aren't we?"

"Hey, what did I just tell you?"

"I heard you," he said. "But since we're sailing down the River Styx, 'going with the flow' could mean white water rapids, and that doesn't exactly inspire confidence. Really, pal, you need to work on your pep-talks."

A half-grin fluted the indigo glass. "Just be nice to the gondolier."

Amy had advised him similarly, except that such niceties were to be lavished upon a "dead man." Interesting. But he was too tired to ask any more questions. "Goodnight, then."

"Don't let the bedbugs bite."

18.

Eli stared down into the grave, its two boarders staring back, horror-stricken. Well, that wasn't exactly true. One girl seemed considerably less horrified than the other. Katherine Bently.

Not for long, though, he thought. The worms would soon wipe away that smug look. Clean off her face.

He'd not bound their arms and legs; just taped their mouths shut. He wanted the pleasure of seeing them thrash. Seeing them flail like crickets in a toaster.

*****

Death was a damp, loamy smell.

The light cast from the nearby porch cleaved to the peaty walls like the soggy skin of a ghost.

Melanie turned to her friend, who'd told her earlier in confidence that her name was really Amy and not Katherine, and that she was an angel. Figured. Melanie had come to the grim and unnerving conclusion that she was already dead.

Amy's chest rose and fell. She looked incredibly calm. Relieved but still light years from all right, Melanie turned her eyes to the lanky man standing at the edge of the grave. He leaned on his shovel, staring down into the pit. The errant light from the porch was enough for her to see that he was enjoying himself.

Something's wrong, she told herself. *I should have woken up by now.*

The ground was cold; so much so that she almost wished the man would hurry up and throw in some dirt—just enough to make her teeth stop chattering.

A really, really bad dream

Now, that's just plain fiction, she heard her grandmother say in her immanent German accent.

It's time to recognize the facts, Melanie. Now go along.

Upon the reality of those words, her situation struck her with no less force than if the man himself had cracked her skull with a batter's swing of his shovel. Up until this very moment, dying had only been a likely prospect.

Now it was here, a raw and inconceivable certainty.

Death. How...alien. And utterly horrifying.

Panic was now pulling violently at the scruff of Melanie's neck, wanting to muscle her up and out of this dank grave. Her chances would surely be better against Eli, she insanely reasoned, than they would against a mountain of dirt.

As if sensing her intentions, Amy grabbed Melanie's arm. Her eyes wide, she shook her head.

No.

No?

Melanie shut her eyes and clenched both fists. Cheeks bulging, she was now screaming behind the tape. But the noises rose no farther than the laces of the man's soiled shoes.

Then she heard the shovel slice the mound.

Oh my God...Mommy...Dear sweet Jesus

With the deftness of a heavyweight's gloved fist, the first trowel of dirt landed squarely on Melanie's stomach. Groaning, she turned her head sideways and stared wide-eyed at the sepulchral wall of earth. Then—when it was absolutely no longer possible to keep it down—she threw up. A weak blend of water and bile spewed from her nostrils, etching the membranous passages like acid. Despite her fear that it might come back up, she swallowed the acerbic backwash, not wanting to leave it in her mouth.

Her eyes stung. Through the diaphanous lens of tears things appeared bejeweled. Tiny bits of quartz along the walls twinkled like diamonds, and the white, spidery roots dangling around her looked like crystal coral brooches.

She heaved again.

The man grunted as he slung another lump of death, this one striking both her and Amy's knees.

Muddy trails now sashayed down Melanie's hot cheeks, merging into even dirtier globs of emesis adhering to the gray duct tape.

Panting vigorously, and still choking down bile, she dug her fingers at her nostrils. Grit and snot and vomit were all conspiring to choke off her air supply.

When the man turned to refill his shovel, she loosened a corner of the tape. Sweet air trickled in. It might have been the most cherished event of her short life.

Amy grabbed Melanie's hand and squeezed it with senseless assurance.

Feebly, Melanie squeezed back.

Don't let go of my hand, she heard Amy say in her mind. *No matter what happens, don't let go.*

Maybe she *was* an angel.

A sensation flared in Melanie's palm. The feeling seeped up her arm into her shoulder, up her neck, then into her eyes, where it formed into a white-hot sun. In a wondrous explosion, the sphere's remnants were then hurled like stars into the cosmos of her being.

Then she was somewhere else.

Was someone else.

A little black boy, about ten or twelve and wearing tattered overalls, was fishing from the weedy banks of a pond. He was crying, blubbering to himself that incomprehensible language of trauma, of shock. Abiding a routine that, in these terrible moments, felt so shameful, so dishonorable—yet so alarmingly necessary, for the familiar was now the only thing between him and the utter collapse of his heart, his soul. Two perch were pulled through a string tied around his waist. A few hundred feet behind him sat a dilapidated shack, as gray as the smoke curling from its chimney. On its rickety porch a black woman was shuffling in circles, wringing her hands, sobbing. An old bloodhound lay some feet away from her, concerned but careful to remain a tolerant distance.

In a giant oak tree adjacent to the road, just twenty yards from the boy, a big black man was hanging from a rope.

Melanie knew herself to be—or rather had at one time been—this man.

He was speaking to the boy.

Crying even harder now, the boy threw down his cane pole, slapped his hands to his ears, and waded into the cattails. His murdered father was talking to him, and that just couldn't be.

"You're not alive, you're not alive!" cried the boy.

"Isaiah," the man said in a choked voice, "For the last time, son, go get yer mama and help her get me down from this branch. Those bad men are long gone now." He coughed tenuously, and as he strained to swallow, the mahogany irises of his eyes rolled back into marshmallow-white orbs, then wobbled slowly back down, as if he'd been momentarily tilted, then righted again.

The boy lowered his hands to his sides. Sniffling, he turned and slowly headed for shore. As his resolve grew, his pace quickened. Soon he was sprinting toward the house, his legs flinging water like a pair of wet dogs, the afternoon sun igniting a rainbow aura around him.

"Mama, mama!" he cried. "I think Papa's still alive!"

Melanie inhaled sharply as the cold, peaty grave embraced her once again.

Amy was still there, their hands still interlocked.

She understood the meaning of the vision, that she had been someone else in another life; had, perhaps, lived many lives. But if this divination was supposed to mollify her, then it miserably failed.

Another chunk of dirt. Seconds later, a large beetle broke through her dirt pelisse. A dot of light rolled across its black liquid shell as it lumbered away, aimlessly drunk.

In the rectangle of sky above her, stars sparkled between the willow branches like they never had, each one an enduring legacy to a sun. And now, after eons of traveling through frigid space, they'd finally found a place they could warm again. Melanie thought that hugely unfair, as those stars had searched so long and so hard for her, and now all she could offer them in return was just another cold, dark place in which to shine.

God, there was so much that she was going to miss; so much she would never see.

Another clod landed between her and Amy. But this time it wasn't dirt.

It was a gob of worms.

Earthworms. No, something similar to earthworms, but with mouthparts very much like those of the hideous bugs she sometimes found at night, crawling around the kitchen floor. Bugs that her mother called sun scorpions.

Quickly the worms began dividing, and within minutes the grave was teeming with writhing, shimmering, disgusting life.

The worms did not seem interested in Melanie, but instead began clustering upon her friend. Then, in a kind of synchronized demonstration, the worms started stitching themselves through Amy's flesh.

Each red mass grew larger as the worms continued to divide. The feeding sounds reminded Melanie of the wind pushing dry leaves across asphalt.

Amy began to convulse. Her eyes were open now, wide as saucers. Her breaths were jerking in and out of her nose, short pants that quickly turned to watery wheezes as her nostrils filled with blood. Awful choking sounds rose from her throat. Then her face began to contort. Soon, her entire body was a paroxysm. Her arms flailed savagely, legs twitching and kicking. There seemed to be an enormous pressure building behind her eyes, as they were now bulging from their sockets. Behind her taped lips, agony sung like an approaching siren.

Ligaments and tendons snapped and popped like fat on a rotisserie. Blood, black and oily, spurted now from any number of places. As she thrashed, twines of hair leaped from her head, some drifting blithely down toward the mayhem with profound indifference, while others, knotted with blood and mud and sweat, plummeted like foul to a hunter's waiting dog.

Then, from the knee down, her lower right leg dropped like a log in a crackling hearth.

Melanie turned away, praying she wouldn't vomit again.

Eli was leaning over the hole, observing with sick intensity. With all she had left, Melanie stared challengingly into his eyes, as if she could kill him with mere concentration, maybe set his brain afire with the ancient heat of all those stars that now burned defiantly in her eyes, in her heart.

He stared back at her with a longing so sick, so deviant and perverted that it doused her puny flickers of death and made her very being shudder with revulsion.

She pulled her eyes away and forced herself to look at Amy one last time. But very little remained of her friend. Only a piece of gray tape now lay where her head had just been moments before. She looked down and found the only thing left of Amy was her rib cage. Between the few remaining curved bones of her chest squirmed a greasy knot of worms, feeding on her heart.

Soon, all that was left of Amy was her left hand, still gripping

Melanie's own. Somehow overcoming a fierce compulsion to fling it out of the hole, she held on to it. Tightly.

Eli dropped two large objects at Melanie's feet.

Her tattered wings.

"It's a shame I couldn't see you fly," he lamented. "But then, this is almost as good."

He raised the camera to his face as the worms turned on her.

She couldn't tell the camera's flashes from those created by her own astonishing pain.

Amid the devouring of her flesh, the nightmare began to finally lift. She awoke not in her warm bed in Iowa, but on the edge of a pond...

Something was toying with her bobber.

"I'm gettin' a nibble," said the black man.

Isaiah rolled his eyes. "Papa, you've been gettin' cleaned out all afternoon, and I'm gettin' tired a' hookin' them worms for ya." He shook his head. "Big man like yourself outta not be afraid of a little slimy bug. It's embarrassin'."

The black man reached under his hat and scratched his head. "I reckon that's so. Just never took a shine to 'em, boy. Just somethin'...evil about 'em," he said, his massive shoulders quaking with revulsion.

"Does mama know?"

"What? That I'm a'scared a worms? Heck no. And she ain't gonna know."

Grinning, the boy pulled his bobber slowly along. "Guess that's gonna kinda depend."

"On what?"

"On if'n you buy me an orange soda down at Fender's."

"How 'bout I just drown you in this pond, tell 'em a granddaddy bluegill pulled ya in."

"And one a them licorice candies," Isaiah added, laughing.

"Alright," the big man smiled. "Bring in your pole. I wanna get back 'fore dark."

As they walked down the dirt road, Isaiah said, "I don't understand. They're just worms, Papa."

"Yeah, I know what they are." He sighed. "Just somethin' deep inside a'me can't fancy a likin' to 'em. Been that way, I reckon, since I was born."

The boy looked up and smiled. "I don't think any less of ya, Papa."

"That's just 'cause I'm buyin' you a soda."

"And a candy."

"And when that's gone, you'll be reachin' for yer mama's apron, pinchin' me for more."

"Won't either."

"Will so."

"Won't."

He grabbed the boy's neck, pulled him close. "I love ya, son."

"I love you too, Papa."

Part Four
Wonderland

1.

Now that Juanita was finally asleep, he was going in.

From a spiral space station orbiting the moon, Chris eased the ship from its mooring. This ship, this illusion, had logged the most miles, and that's exactly why he'd selected it. The more habituated the ruse, the less energy he would have to spend keeping it structurally intact. And this one remained as tangible as his first kiss.

The ship looked remarkably like the Proteus from the movie *Fantastic Voyage,* and not by any coincidence. That flick still ranked as one of Chris's favorite. Like Donald Pleasance, Chris preferred to navigate from the glass bubble on top because it afforded a 360 degree field of view. And he would love nothing more than to imagine Raquel Welch on board, to reprise her original role where all she did was squirm deliciously in her wetsuit whenever things got a little hairy.

Just moments earlier, he'd placed a beacon in Juanita's psyche, one that the ship would continue to follow in case Chris's own mind became distracted for a moment or two. And it would. He'd also psychically downloaded a special program that would not only allow Juanita to read his extrasensory software, but to interact with it, as well. This facet was imperative for the intrusion to succeed on a covert level. It would permit Juanita to play along and not be suspicious of its origins. In essence, she would believe the dream was of her own design. Chris could then get wherever he needed to go and complete the job. He was the architect. He would know the layout. Even if the dreamers participated enough to alter the landscape, he could still find his way around, unless they were excessively creative or deranged. Both cases were rare. The downside was, if the implanted dream glitched for any variety of reasons, Juanita could erase it and fill in the void with whatever she desired, something perhaps not as safe and neutral as Chris's creation.

She could even change him.

Once, a dreamer had transformed him into a skinny black lady who was throwing a baby shower for a pregnant Ed Asner. Another time he was mutated into an underwater camera fastened to the hull of the Calypso, filming a school of Yoko Onos chasing a yellow submarine. He'd always go along with his new role for awhile, behaving like the parasite that he was.

Because the last thing Chris ever wanted to do was arouse suspicion in the dreamer. Like a safari where tourists discover that the Jeep's canvass top and their screaming guide are no match for a pride of starving lions, the dawning awareness of a dreamer was terrifying. The psyche had its own lymphatic system, but rather than dispatch phagocytes or white blood cells, it eradicated prowlers and burglars with something a bit more unique: it turned their own fears against them. Chris had named this potentiality "Door Number Three."

Chris had already decided that, once he reached Juanita's subconscious mind, he would conjure the interior of a church. Since she was always lugging around that rosary, he figured some pews, an altar, and a baptismal would be great fodder. He would go in dressed as an acolyte, a liturgical task he'd shared with other teens while going through the Lutheran equivalent of catechism. And he would most certainly have to alter his face, as he was quite sure that Juanita would reap about as much pleasure in seeing him hanged by his testicles as she would getting a conjugal visit from the Pope. However, mask or no mask, given enough time she would eventually intuit that it was him.

The ship, now free of the space station, drifted lazily toward the moon. Chris started the main thrusters. On the console before him, an array of soft, blue lights pulsed with the ship's engines. A red flashing bulb to his lower left indicated that the beacon was functioning. He grabbed the joy stick with his right hand, pressed a button marked EGO, then one marked ID. The star field wavered, then was lanced simultaneously by a million dazzling trails of white light.

"Han Solo, eat your heart out."

To hook up someone could take as little as a minute, or as long as twenty. Chris had never been gone more than thirty minutes, and was estimating no more than five for this job. But that was time registered by his digital AM/FM clock radio on the nightstand by his bed. The sort of time that passed in Wonderland was almost sedentary compared to the hasty brand Timex doled out in the waking world. Chris returned every time suffering from astral jetlag, finding that he'd only been gone eight or ten minutes, when it seemed more like hours or sometimes even days.

Regardless of its gender, time was still of the utmost importance. Sometimes he got lucky and the host kept the mirage going because he or she was such a willing participant, contributing their own fun rides to Chris's traveling carnival. When that happened, the pressure was lifted, and Chris could work at his leisure. But that was rare. He had to always keep in mind the IA Factor (Inevitable Annihilation). This was when the dream started to really break down, leaving the intruder with three options. One: get out; Two: stay and let the host cast him into the next production; or Three: hastily create another dreamscape and pray it passed inspection by the host's psyche. Chris avoided option Three at all costs. He had no desire to have his tenuous carcass buried in someone's mind's eye to fester there like the proverbial splinter.

The mind was a formidable foe. Whenever the host's psyche was in defense mode, death became a real plausibility in Wonderland, ethereally and otherwise.

If there was another way to die psychically, Chris didn't know it. When younger, before he'd become more atheistic than not, he believed that if he were to ever perish in someone's mind, he would never get to heaven because his soul—the interloper—would already be dead. But he'd since learned that it hadn't been his eternal soul traipsing all these years through Wonderland, but rather its sibling; a kind of temporal step-sister that died with the physical body. Every man, woman, and child had one, but only a very select few were ever given permission to use it. When someone needed to be hooked up, the "intangibles" would call upon Chris and his talents. This communication could come in any form, be it voices routing themselves through his refrigerator, a stinky old bag lady, or a talking stained glass window.

He liked to think of himself as a younger, if not leaner, version of Maytag's lonely repairman, calmly devoted to fixing the telepathically challenged. However, he was more partial to mastiffs than he was pouting basset hounds.

Strangely, his least worry was the dreamer being suddenly awakened from deep sleep for whatever reason. That would only catapult him back into his spaceship, or whatever contrivance he was using at the time, with nothing more than a migraine. Happened all the time.

Sure, he could just barge straight in—what he called a "No-Knock," in honor of the kind of warrants SWAT teams used when making house calls. No costumes or guises or psychic software of any kind; just him and the dreamer squaring off. In his younger days, No-Knocks had been challenging. He didn't know then about hooking people up, was just there for the pure thrill of it. Now, to go in for nothing but kicks was just plain reckless.

Descending the access ladder, he jumped the last two rungs to a grated walkway below. He had to manually shut off the engines, and they were located in the rear of the ship. As he turned, he saw that the space to his right—a place where the hull should have been—was nothing but a gaping hole of interstellar matter. As he started walking, the vacancy filled itself in with stark white paneling, flashing control panels, something that might have been a fire extinguisher...And as he continued down the corridor, other omissions quickly infused with twenty-fourth century decor. To mentally picture lush, rolling hills, dense forests, a star-filled cosmic night—those were easy to maintain. But to keep a three-dimensional image fully intact of something as complex as a space ship—something entirely fictional—that was hard. To do so for any good length of time was impossible.

To patch Juanita into her special gift, he'd opted for the organ. This was part of the software he'd downloaded earlier. Once he played "Mary Had A Little Lamb," Juanita would be soldered to the ethereal plane, and could then—without the use of her rosary—eject people's psyches and souls from their bodies and slam them into stained glass windows with much more confidence and better aim.

He disengaged the engines from the hyperdrive coil, allowing the ship to coast toward a deep red nebula. The doorway into Juanita Santiago's mind.

"Where no man has gone before," Chris intoned, and thought that was probably an accurate guess, given her ugly mug and holier-than-thou disposition. He kicked on the thrusters, shaking his head. "Bible thumpers."

As the ship entered the nebula, passing through its web-like dross, Chris closed his eyes and recalled the church he'd attended while growing up in San Diego. It was Lutheran, not Catholic, but he figured it would be close enough for government work. Any conflicting aesthetics would be negligible to the point where Juanita would either overlook them or simply change them without becoming suspicious. And there was certainly not going to be a sermon, because Chris wasn't going to summon a pastor. He'd had plenty of evangelizing for one lifetime, thank you very much, not to mention enough wine and unleavened bread to choke a platoon of disciples. But if Juanita did decide to whip up a priest, a congregation, and an inspirational oration, then God could ransom her guilt, and she could fill the collection plates to her heart's content. Not a problem.

Just as long as she didn't retain an organist.

Exhaling slowly, he pictured himself standing by the organ.

The image was crystal clear.

2.

Chris opened his eyes.

Bricks of differing size, drooling mortar from their seams, composed the high, narrow passageway before him. From their iron cradles, torches licked soot upon the crude masonry, and shadows pranced to the susurrant sounds like gypsies around a campfire.

Directly behind him was a structure rising so high that the top was not visible from his perspective. If he didn't know any better, he would swear that it was the main tower of a castle. He'd played enough *Dungeons and Dragons* to know a donjon when he saw one.

To his immediate right stood a huge door, the wood planks running vertically and strengthened by long, thick ores of iron. The three clasps and hinges were massive and looked like ostracized coats of arms, painted black to expunge those clans from memory. The sand was dry and loose but bore no tracks.

Chris paused. Yes, he was now quite certain that this was not the Emmanuel Lutheran Church of his childhood, where he learned about Adam and Eve and Noah's Ark and God smiting the heathens.

Staring down at his white Adidas, he bent at his knees, swung his arms, and jumped. As his feet landed, dirt clouds rolled away from his soles, surging like waves against the walls on either side. He watched with growing concern as the settlings evanesced in the dimness.

"Dude," he said, slightly alarmed. The gravity here wasn't right because it was *too* right. Although dreams were normally born with the standard laws of physics already preset, it was only a matter of moments before they began to deteriorate. That didn't make them any less real, just more unstable. Chris knew that once the cataleptic curtain lifted for the director and his play, Sir Isaac Newton would be yanked from stage and his lead role usurped by a cute little thing from Detroit who didn't know jack about physics, and even less about acting. Eventually and indubitably, the psyche would start taking liberties with the script, not to mention the cute little thing from Detroit, and pretty soon apples were falling up instead of down, statues crapping on birds instead of the other way around.

But Chris could find no corruption of Newtonian physics here; no atrophy, no decay. By the looks of things, Sir Isaac was not only still in character but bowing before a standing ovation. If this was Juanita's dream, then she had one hell of a knack for keeping things fixed and focused.

He turned in a circle, searching for clues in the construction, in the ambience, looking for tell-tale signs that could confirm that the theater in which he now found himself was, in fact, mind-woven; rhapsodized.

No. Finally, no. The setting lacked that capricious, mercurial atmosphere so endemic of dreams. Parody, usually in abundant supply, was absent. Nothing faltered. Nothing changed.

"Where the fuck am I?" he said to the gloom.

Chris stepped to the door, grabbed the big metal ring, and pulled. As he had fully expected, the massive hinges heralded his entrance like a trio of lovesick banshees. Gusts of mildew-laden air swept past his neck and face like Chiffon ascots. He stepped through and found that he was, after all, inside a church, just one that predated good table manners. In fact, he wouldn't be surprised to find King Arthur's name scribbled in the guest book.

The interior was huge, and although he'd only seen a fraction of the structure, Chris was already left with the impression that he was, indeed, in the midst of a fortress. A medieval castle.

Groin vaulting had apparently been the rage when the place was built, lending it an eerie, antediluvian resplendence. Torches clung to the groins, gibbering in tongues like reticent monks. Shadows became black, gossamer monkeys swinging from column to column. Candles were in ample supply, as was dust, thickly suspended in the sanctum's cavernous light.

Chris stopped and listened to his own breathing. Had someone stirred the dust?

Very curious now, he strolled down the center aisle, looking for clues, anything that might help him understand what was happening. And then it occurred to him. Either he wasn't in Juanita's mind, or he was...but he wasn't her only visitor. Maybe someone else was playing him at his own game; someone who had the ability to keep his or her psychic universe so intact as to make it analogous to waking reality. After all, these were not the blueprints he'd drafted.

Or, just maybe, this was a by-product of Juanita's recent endowment. Yeah, that was probably part of the answer.

The marble altar was massive. He dragged a couple of fingers across the surface, leaving deep tracks in the dust and soot. The smell of smoldering wax was heavier here, although no candles were burning despite their abundance. To his left, at the far end of the altar beside some kind of round, clay vessel, a rat stared at him with golden eye shine.

Michael Jackson's "Ben" started playing in his mind. He immediately canceled that selection and chose Elton John's "Funeral for a Friend." *Fuck 'em,* He thought. *If they want atmosphere, I'll give 'em atmosphere!*

Most disappointing, however, was the absence of an organ. And given the apparent century, it wasn't likely he would find one hidden elsewhere in the castle. That presented a problem. He'd already programmed Juanita to receive the connection via his (albeit one-fingered) rendition of "Mary Had A Little Lamb." It didn't really matter if he played the tune from inside this ancient church or the top of Pike's Peak, just as long as he had an organ to play it on. And soon.

"I ordered *Sister Act,*" he groused, "and they fucking sent me *Excalibur.*"

Picturing a walnut organ with massive pipes directly in front of the altar, Chris strained to make the image as detailed as he could. If he was successful, it would answer the question of whether this was a waking place or a dream state. If only a dream, then he could probably conjure just about anything. If it was waking reality, then the only organ he'd be playing would be the one behind his fly.

He opened his eyes. The organ was there. But it was a ghost image, fading fast. Someone was interfering, trying to shut it down. He could feel it.

It was now obvious, however, he was in Wonderland. One of its unexplored continents, perhaps, but definitely Wonderland.

Had he finally entered a sandbox where someone else—someone just like himself—had already started working with pail and shovel? Highly unlikely.

He closed his eyes again, his face crinkling with concentration.

Afraid he might tear loose an embolism in his physical body, he finally relaxed. And there sat an organ. He rushed over and inspected it, top to bottom. It was so real he could smell the lemon wax.

"Perfect!" he said.

"Child's play," assured a suave voice.

Chris jumped. Behind him, sitting in the front pew, was a handsome gent in a gray tailored suit, burgundy shirt, and white silk tie. Slick as a greased doorknob. Beside him sat five naked little girls.

"Shit," Chris whispered. He began scanning their minds...then stopped. A stench burgeoned in his being; a stink so unbelievably fetid, so utterly vile, that if he were in his physical body and had to endure that foulness for even a fraction of a second, he would have literally been driven to eviscerate his nose from his face with the dullest spoon available.

"You're a disgrace to your uniform," the man observed, referring to Chris's surplice.

"I'm getting my 'Deuteronomy' badge next week," Chris said.

"How wonderful for you. Your mother would be very proud." He winked. "Personally, though, if I'd been your old lady, I would have gone with the Black and Decker portable space heater in the hallway. But I'm sure that's just the handyman in me talking."

The admission startled Chris. "Reading the obits is a sign of a sick mind, dude."

The man chortled. "How would you know the health of my mind, friend? You just tried making its acquaintance, but couldn't even get your feet wet. Afraid of the water?"

Chris just stared.

"Like your grandad?" the stranger continued. "I've got to tell ya, kid, for a guy who didn't have rabies he sure was one hydrophobic son of a bitch." He smiled. "But his fear of H2O is all better now. Why, I hear him screaming for it every day."

Chris laughed. "Nice try, numbnuts, but I don't scare very easy when I'm being threatened with bible stories." But Chris *was* scared now; very scared. How did this asshole know about his grandfather? Chris hadn't even thought about his grandfather in years.

"Yes, bible stories," assured the tailored gent. "Because where you're heading, son, 'slake' and 'thirst' are as likely to find wedlock as 'Baskin' and 'Robbins.'"

Chris just laughed, albeit unpersuasively.

The man stood. "I haven't formally introduced myself," he said. "My name is Gamble." He swept a hand toward the girls. "And these are my daughters."

"That's a relief," Chris said. "I was thinking you were some kind of wacked-out pedophile pimp."

"Yes, I'm afraid they can provoke the most libelous suspicions," Gamble said. Then he stretched out his arms the way a realtor does when showing a spacious living room. "I hope you don't mind, but I've taken some privileges with your church. It was lacking character, shall we say."

Chris scowled. "It's not like you put up new drapes, dude," he said. "I mean, you went from *Better Homes and Gardens* to Knights of the Round Table."

Gamble returned to the pew and sat. "Yes, well..." He crossed his legs and appeared to search the material for lint. "I'm going to make a deal with you, Mr. Kaddison. If you walk straight out that front door now, I'll see that you and your little ship make it home before the rooster wakes. But if you so much as play one fucking note on that organ, I'll rip a hole so wide in your ego that your id will need a colostomy bag."

Chris brightened. "*You're* the one who tried yanking the organ."

"Nothing gets by you."

"And you failed, dude," Chris gloated, patting the shiny veneer top. "She's right here, pretty as you please." He poked his chest. "You're looking at the best carpenter in Wonderland."

"Really? Hmmm. I seem to recall another carpenter who thought himself pretty handy. You know, I'm beginning to fear that it might be something indigenous to your profession."

Chris shook his head. "You're wasting your time, dude. Like I said, I don't subscribe to that magazine."

"Regardless, I can still bill you as the main attraction for a stormy crucifixion. But if that's not your cup of tea, then we can discuss other options. I'm privy, you see, to an illimitable number of ways to agonize the flesh. And the soul. But rather than go into them now, I'll just leave you with my brochure. As for your undefeated title, Melchizedek, you're forgetting that I've made you a prisoner of these ancient walls, strongholds which I'm sure you've noticed do not fade or bend or roll with uncertainty. I have forgotten more about your 'Wonderland' than you will ever know, so kindly remove that feather from your hat. As for Juanita, I refuse to permit the successful installation of her...whatever it is." He waved a hand. "She's not worthy."

As Gamble spoke, Chris concentrated on removing a distant section of wall. He hoped that if the man wasn't giving his full attention to the subterfuge (a rookie mistake, though Chris really didn't believe this guy was a rookie), then he might be successful.

Nothing happened. Okay, so he couldn't bring down the walls, but he could create within them. That was something.

"I'm staying," Chris said, then flipped on the organ's power switch.

Gamble stood. "You'll be making a grave mistake. I'm almost sure of it."

As soon as Chris sat down on the organ bench, a thought struck him: the girls! They're bolstering the dreamscape, jacking it up like a car so Gamble can lube it. The slick fuck. Okay, he needed a distraction. What could he pull out of his now-featherless hat that could capture and maintain the attention spans of five little girls, ages between nine and eleven? Snakes? Bugs? Wait...

Snails! Snails and puppy dog tails! Damned if he could remember how the rest of that went.

Instantly, five boys, all dressed in matching prep school uniforms, stood before the girls and began provoking them with sophomoric taunts and spit balls.

Gamble remained seated, indulging the scene with a carefree pose.

As the girls stood and confronted their attackers, Chris once again tried to make a portion of the farthest wall disappear. This time it worked, confirming his suspicions about the girls. But that wasn't good, because that meant he wasn't up against just one Cheshire Cat. He was up against a whole litter.

Who in the fuck are these people? he desperately wondered.

Just as the segment of wall vanished, all five boys began screaming.

"Not such a tough guy now, are you?" the closest girl said to her knavish suitor, who had hiked up his sweater and was now groping violently at his own abdomen. His tearing, panicked eyes pleaded for her to stop. Within moments, his short blond hair was imbued with sweat. Unable to control his hands, he gaped down in utter horror as his self-mutilation advanced to abominable levels. Pointing his nose at the ceiling, he shrieked like some forlorn crane on a moonlit marsh, then began to thrash his head. Orbs of sweat and spittle, amber in the torchlight, left his head like fireflies from a rattled bush. And the first trickle of what would quickly become a torrent of blood left his nose and stained his cracked lips. The excruciating pain began to bounce him like a Pogo stick as he dug deeper and deeper, screaming and jumping and gurgling, sounding like Pavarotti in a rumble seat down a washboard road. Then, as he ripped through the fatty tissue, he reached in with both hands and pulled back the skin, splitting himself and the immense room open with a wet, sucking sound. Each cough, each bray, each explosive scream was another interspersing of blood across the white, taut skin of the girl before him, who continued to watch with unbridled fascination. A length of intestine now hung from his avulsion like a giant watch chain, and a big, purple bulge said more was coming. All around him now, the dirt floor was sopping up the blood and fluids that were splashing from the open cavity. His face twisting in unbelievable pain, he then plucked out his own bladder and forcefully fed it to the boy on his right, who was already mashing his own shredded genitals into the next boy's mouth, who himself had a pair of eyeballs for the one next to him, and down the line it went.

The screams were unlike any Chris had ever heard in Wonderland, or anywhere else for that matter; wails filled with so much horror and insufferable pain that he had to finally cover his ears.

"Am I beaming?" Gamble said, smiling from ear to ear. "I swear, I haven't been this proud since the whole lot of them brought down that family of moose outside Vancouver."

Chris was still staring at the boys. Their screams were all but echoes now, their limbs twitching with the last, fading amperes of life. *Get a grip,* he thought. *They're just pretend, you dumbass* weenie. Then he turned away, gagging. The feculence, like everything else, was too substantive to be ignored.

Dead, and no longer desired in their upright positions, all five boys crumpled simultaneously to the ground. Then the girls began scavenging their bodies for leftovers, one occasionally nipping or clawing the other if she got too close.

A pack of hyenas couldn't have been portrayed any better, Chris thought.

He tried to make the bodies evaporate. And failed.

"The Shreveport School for Wayward Boys frowns on fraternization...and curfew violations," Gamble explained, as if he were the Dean of said institution, speaking with the parents of prospective delinquents. "In fact, both are grounds for harsh, punitive action. But I think you'll agree that these little recidivists have just been sufficiently punished."

Shocked, Chris gaped at the man. "I...I created them, dude," he finally said, more to himself. "There's no way those kids could be real. They're just like this church, this organ—they're just projections of thought."

Gamble removed an emery board from the inside pocket of his jacket, then began filing the nail of his right forefinger. "Be careful how you say that, Mr. Kaddison. I, too, was once a projection of thought."

"No shit?" Chris said, a little more than intrigued. "Then, you must feel right at home."

"This place *home?* I hardly think so. I'm only subletting this space until my new universe is fumigated."

Chris kept returning to the boys.

"I saw you peek into their minds as they were thrashing," Gamble said. "Tell me, Mr. Kaddison, do illusions so convincingly scream out for mummies and daddies? For God? For sweet death to take them...quickly?"

Chris didn't want to believe him, but had to. "You're one sick cookie, dude! You can't be from topside! You live here, don't you? In the psyche, in the mind, in the heart?"

"Chris, you're a fucking poet."

A succession of vibratory groans rippled through the church, the rings having emanated in either a distant part of the castle, or beyond the dream itself. It was the sound of imagination on a fault line; the land of make-believe shifting on its foundation.

The wrecking ball was coming, Chris knew. As were his deepest fears, no doubt.

"You know what that is, asshole?" Chris said. "That's Juanita. Because of what your little harem just did, her psyche's rejecting this dream like a bad kidney. It knows something's wrong, and it'll tear this dream apart to find us. Even your glue won't hold this place together."

"Shall we stay put then?" said Gamble. "Turn ourselves over to the authorities and take our punishment like the true gentlemen we are?"

"Fuck that," Chris said, then reached for the organ's keys.

But his hands weren't there.

"Play it again, Sam," Gamble instructed. "With your *tongue*."

Chris's tongue lolled out, all three feet of it now, and latched onto the sheet music holder. It grabbled the scrollwork like a blind worm looking for its hole. He thought of the missing segment of wall, and tried to conjure something.

Gamble softly clapped. "Play that Croche piece, 'Tongue in a Bottle'—no, no—'Tongue and Again'—wait—'Tongue is on Our Side'—I've got it!—'Song Tongue Blue' by Neil baby!"

Then Chris saw it, the embodiment of his effort, moving like oil through the opening in the wall. Its head, as large as a Volkswagen, glided in on the end of a long neck fringed with a spiny sail. Even longer than his own, its flicking tongue was mottled red and black, and classically forked. Across its buffed scales, torchlight heaved and roiled and surged like the lamentations of a dying assassin. Its nocturnal eyes were sharp and searching, each girded by a row of bony spurs.

The ground shuddered again, followed by a succession of low, booming throbs, like the cadence of a giant soldier marching in place. As Chris listened, more noises joined in: the sounds of metal turning against primal metal; the grating squeals of prison doors being opened for the first time in centuries. Then the jingling of chains wafted through; irons falling to the floor as the foolhardy guards unclasped the ancient demons from their cold dungeon shackles. And set them about their quarry.

Chris, cursing the muse, hoped it was just Juanita's demolition equipment. But one thing was certain: time was running out.

Imagining his own hands back in their cuffs, Chris hovered over the keys. They appeared, but just as he dropped his finger to play, both hands turned into shear ladies' gloves. His finger bent backwards the moment it struck the key.

The dragon raised its head. Smoke curled from its nostrils. It was maybe fifty feet from Gamble and closing quickly, stealthily.

As his new prosthetic tongue was parting his hair, Chris added another item to the beast: a thermostat. Then he cranked it up all the way.

The girls remained on the floor, snorting, sniffing, grunting. One was using her prey's femur to gain access into its skull. She was in after three more blows, pulling out her prize by the handfuls.

For a moment, Chris wondered if he might not be better off finding someone else to play the song, like that dead guy Liberace. Then he was off his stool and on the dirt. He looked up.

And there in front of the organ sat Liberace, wearing Liz Taylor's jewelry and an outfit that made Elton John look like Rush Limbaugh.

The entertainer turned and smiled his famous smile at the man in the pew, wiggled his fingers at the girls, who were now staring up at him with wary surprise, then proceeded to play "Mary Had a Little Lamb" with more than just one digit.

All five girls were now on their feet, screeching and hissing at the man on the organ.

"*Noooo!*" Gamble cried. Furious, he too was on his feet now, but keeping a watchful distance. "Your kind are dead! I personally supervised the obliteration of the last one! I was there and wove its suffering cries into chain mail! I distilled its blood and made oil for the creaking cogs of time!"

Liberace kept smiling, never missing a note.

The humor wasn't lost on Chris. Here was this guy, veins popping up all over his head, delivering some bad if not dramatic verse, and all the orchestra could play to impassion the moment was a candied rendition of "Mary Had A Little Lamb." Quite frankly, Chris felt it was doing for Gamble what 'potatoe' once did for a certain Vice-President.

Gamble boldly stepped closer, his voice supernaturally charged. "I felt the universe ascend when I pushed it off the edge! Eternity sighed when the burden of its last suckling bastard child was taken from its teat! How dare you, you extinct motherfucker! I. Watched. It. Finally. *Die!*"

Although his saliva was flying in that direction, Chris now had the strong impression that Gamble wasn't addressing Liberace, or even cross-dressing piano players in general. And that begged the question: Who was he talking to?

For that matter, he thought, *just who in the fuck is Gamble?*

The girls were jumping up and down, pointing and screaming, trying to warn their father.

The dragon hovered above Gamble, inhaled, then doused him in flame.

Just as the fire enveloped the man, it froze, encasing him in a yellow-blue tent. Behind him, as if it were a giant, meticulously assembled art form that's just been bumped by a clumsy child, the dragon began collapsing into small nuggets.

Well, so much for that idea, Chris thought.

With a tap of a manicured fingernail, Gamble sent the tent of fire, shattering around him. As the pieces fell, they reignited, burning now on his head, on his shoulders, around his feet. He began walking toward Chris, a stunt man too macho to wear asbestos.

Liberace jubilantly sang, "It made the children laugh and play."

Gamble, surprisingly, restored Chris's hands and tongue.

Smoldering, Gamble grabbed Chris's surplice at the collar. "Do you know what today is?"

"My lucky day?" he said, turning his head to the side. The man's breath was rancid.

"It's the day when I get to finally see you, and billions just like you, litter the commons with your torn and broken bodies. Then I'm going to take your souls and, one by one, pull them through my teeth, removing any evidence that might link them to a prior owner. And I'm going to make sure that you, Mr. Kaddison, become one of the first to whet what's promising to be an insatiable appetite." He smiled. "Oh, but that's right. You can't see beyond sunrise today, can you? For once in your life, you can't see the bits and pieces of tomorrow. And do you know why? Because the last chapter of the old book ends here, and the rights to the sequel have yet to be negotiated."

"All finished!" Liberace announced, the pipes still resonating from the last chord.

"Righteous," Chris said, now free to move if he chose. "Is there a green light flashing on the console?"

Liberace threw back his cape. "There sure is," he said. "Want to hear Camp Town Races?"

"Thanks anyway," said Chris. "But now that Juanita's wired for sound, I'm scooting the hell out of here."

"You're a fine man, Chris," said Liberace. He pointed to Gamble and his daughters. "And don't let those bullies shove you around. Don't cut yourself short. You've got more going for you than you might think."

Gamble returned Liberace's wonderfully warm smile. "I'll see you on the battlefields. I've killed your kind before, and I can do it again. And when it's all said and done, you ancient fuck, you'll wish you were rotting on the prairie with the rest of your herd."

"How simply charming you are," said Liberace. "But I'd leave the lights on if I were you." Then he turned to Chris. "Well, I've had a wonderful time, really, but I'm expected at a séance in Reno. My brother George wants to chat." With a bright and mocking smile, he waved his bejeweled hand and disappeared.

Gamble stared at Chris, his eyes afire. "Friends in high places?"

"That's nothing, dude," Chris said glibly. "You should be around when I have Presley and Joplin over to clean my oven."

Gamble looked truly surprised. "You pathetic moron. You really don't know what just came to your rescue, do you?"

"Yeah," he said. "A figment of my imagination. I told you I was the best in Wonderland." Chris didn't really believe he was behind Liberace's resurrection, at least not all of it. He had help, but from who or what he had no idea. Nevertheless, he was grateful.

Smiling a victor's smile, Chris said, "My imagination knows no bounds."

"You couldn't imagine *that*, Mr. Kaddison, even if you could imagine that."

Chris sucked on the riddle, perplexed.

Disgusted, Gamble leaned in and tendered a gaze that would have made Dr. Anton Mesmer cluck like a chicken. "'Do not neglect to show hospitality to strangers, for thereby some have entertained angels unawares.'"

"Hebrews," Chris said. "So you went to Sunday school, too. What's your point?"

Before he could answer, one of the girls came forward. "I'm sick of his mouth. Why don't you just finish him, Daddy?"

Another girl stepped up. "Let me do it, Daddy. Please? I'll bring him in with us."

Gamble turned and lunged at his daughters, uttering a shrill noise that sprinkled tingle-dust down Chris's back. It was a high-pitched scream, akin to a large tree monkey. It faded to a warbling mewl, followed by a series of guttural clicks and hiccup-like barks. Had his eyes been closed, Chris could have easily imagined himself deep in the Amazon, listening to the nocturnal rhetoric of a strange, undiscovered primate living high in the jungle canopy.

When Gamble was finished, he turned back to Chris. Appearing rather humored with himself, he said, "Pardon the interruption, but it was imperative that I explain to them that when one wanders the carnivals of perdition, the most sought after ride is anticipation."

Chris was certain that the man was paraphrasing. "See, there you go, that's your problem, dude," he said. "You're spending way too much time on the rides and ignoring the gaffed entertainment. I mean, win your girlfriend a Teddy bear, shoot some ducks, throw some hoops, toss some pennies..."

"I might be impressed by your gumption, but I'm afraid it's vainglory rather than brass balls that drives your mouth." Gamble nodded toward the empty organ. "Your friend won't always be here to protect you. And while your skills are laudable for an amoeba, they couldn't begin to get your worthless, protozoan ass past the welcome mat on my front doorstep."

Chris, who'd been standing against the organ, suddenly fell to the floor. The instrument had vanished.

Gamble chuckled. "Dreams are so desultory, don't you agree?"

"I might," Chris said, "if I knew what 'desultory' meant." He got up, brushed himself off. Then he saw the organ. It was upside-down on the ceiling, directly above the altar, the green light on its console still blinking.

Gamble smiled one last time. "I'll leave you to Juanita's whims. Oh, and to your own, as well, I imagine. I believe you refer to that partnership as 'Door Number Three?'" Leaning in close now, he said, "Maybe you'll get lucky again, maybe not." He straightened his tie. "Either way, you're soul food eventually. Now, if you'll excuse me, I have to muster the troops."

Then, in a blink, Gamble and his girls were gone.

3.

Appearing like a despairing usher, Chris started down the aisle, listening, carefully avoiding the dragon's crunchy remains. The sounds of demolition had ceased altogether, and now an eerie calm sequestered the church from eviction. Or so it seemed. But the lull was only temporary, just the legendary calm. He knew a storm was coming, the storm of Inevitable Annihilation. And once it made landfall, he could rest assured that it would lift and scatter the remnants of this dream to the farthest crags of Juanita Santiago's mind.

"Dude, this place is gonna fold like a bad hand," he mumbled.

Chris had tried leaving the dream without success. That meant that either Gamble and crew were still keeping him hostage or Juanita's psyche was. If it was Juanita, his chances were good at figuring a way out. If not, he was most likely going to become "soul food."

He could hear it now, distant and hungry: an encroaching tsunami that began in the deepest depths of the psyche, now threatening to crest over a vacuum where worlds were built and destroyed on white noise and nocturnal discharges.

"Surf's up," he reported to the dreary chapel.

Chris had surfed more beaches than he cared to count. He was the master of ARS, had ridden some monster bone crushers, and ate kooks and grems for lunch. And, man, there was nothing like watching his reflection in the glass house. He could line up all the betties on the beach and they couldn't come close to inspiring the kind of woody he got when it was just him and his board. He was a surfer, a dude. But nothing— absolutely nothing—could compare to beach break in the human mind.

In these last incredible moments, there was no predictable way to guess how things would eventuate; methods of annihilating dreamscapes were as individual as the minds that created them, and Juanita's psyche would do everything in its awesome power to make sure he didn't make it out alive.

A woman's voice hollered from behind the main door. "J.R.? It's time to come back now. You can talk to your imaginary friends after supper."

Frozen, Chris gaped at the door. Shit. Juanita had found him.

And so, it seemed, had his dead mother.

Door Number Three

Fuck.

"Mommy Dearest," he whispered.

"I'm coming in," she said. "Are you decent?"

"Not since I started reading Penthouse Forum," he yelled. Hell, what was she going to do? Ground him? He could only hope.

"You've got five minutes, mister, then I'm coming in after you."

He looked around, nodding. Perhaps his mother wasn't permitted to come in. This was a church. An ancient one, but a church all the same. And Juanita—now that Gamble and crew were gone—wasn't going to allow an unholy act to occur in a place of worship, even against a heathen like himself.

That was just speculation, of course...

As he turned in a tight circle, hugging himself, wondering what dear old Mom was going to do next, he saw the wall behind the altar phase into a limpid, wavy screen of bubbles, very much like a moiré effect. There were thousands of bubbles, each one no larger than a dime, and perforated like a tea ball.

Yet again, the storm fell silent.

Newton was still accepting roses from the audience, it seemed, as everything was just as it had been the moment he stepped foot inside these walls.

He was sure of it now: Gamble and his five pit bulls were still here. Somewhere.

Hands on his hips, he shouted, "What kind of Mary Poppins crap is this, Mom? Shit or get off the pot!" He was enraged. "Bring it on, bitch! Bring it on!"

Then, beyond the clear screen of tea balls, emerged the red, cloudy branches of the nebula he'd entered to reach Juanita's mind.

The ship was a mere white speck against the crimson stratus.

His self-made illusion was still here, as it always had been. It had just remained hidden behind Gamble's own chimera, which he feared was about to be eclipsed by Juanita's reckoning.

He felt like one of those Russian nesting dolls: a figure within a figure within a figure...

As hard as he tried to get back on board the ship, however, it seemed he was going to remain stuck. He made a mental note to install a transporter room and a bagpipe-playing engineer when he got back. *If* he got back.

"J.R., listen to me," said his mother. "You were two months premature. The first eight weeks of your life were spent bonding with an incubator. Did you hear me? You were never on the tit. You ate formula out of a bottle. You were robbed, J.R., and I think that's why you're always talking to yourself, are always lost in your own little worlds."

"I don't talk to myself," Chris mumbled.

"So, we're gonna get those eight weeks back. Get 'em up and running again. Aren't you just excited?"

No, he wasn't. He'd passed the bustling town of Excited many miles back and was fast approaching that frigid metropolis of Horrified, trying to figure out how dear old Mom planned on getting him back into her womb. Just as he was about to ask, the bubbles left their stationary orbits and began spreading themselves throughout the church, like the entire faculty of Texas A&M rushing out at Superbowl halftime to spell out some corny catchphrase.

"And I know I never told you who your father was," said Mom, "and that was unfair of me. No, it was cruel. So, I'm going to finally tell you."

Chris straightened, attentive to the voice behind the door. Neither he nor Juanita knew who his real father was, so the results of this paternity test promised to be entertaining.

"I'm waiting," Chris said.

"Alright, it was...was...Liberace. *Whew!* There, I said it. Satisfied?"

Chris shook his head. He was either the heir to a legacy, or Juanita was spending way too much time backstage fraternizing with the guests.

"You're not his type!" he shouted.

"Just eight weeks, J.R.," she advised. "God wants you back for just forty-nine days. Praise His holy name!"

"Forty-nine days is only seven weeks, you moron!" he yelled, goosing her.

"Maybe you're going to be the next Baby Jesus!" she cried. "Praise all that is good!"

He needed to stir the pot, get a change of scenery going. "Like, I think you failed the prerequisite for bearing saviors. In fact, I don't think you were *ever* a virgin. I think you were born getting laid."

"I need you, J.R.," she said. "I need you to make up those eight weeks."

Her voice was growing more urgent now. Privation was licking away the sugar coating. She was a starving dog on the other side of Juanita's meat locker, pacing, salivating, and just moments away from believing that, with a little determination, the crack beneath the door might just be negotiable after all.

"Why don't you take a bath and soak on it," he said. "Just lie back with a good book and the waffle iron."

"You always were a smartass, I'll say that. But you're not well, J.R., and I'm not well for putting up with it. Praise Jesus, I got bad things going through my head sometimes. But we're going to make things right, aren't we? No more of this paranormal crap, right? It's blasphemy! Just eight weeks. Eight little old weeks. Just one week more than seven. Going to get you right. Think of it as church camp. Right as a rainy day in the park, you miserable little fuck." Then she began to sing. *"Eight weeks, eight weeks, who's gonna change those dirty sheets? Eight weeks, eight weeks, who's gonna slap those little cheeks?"*

"Oh no," Chris groaned.

"Eight weeks, eight weeks, Mama's home and ain't she sweet!"

Chris did not like where this was going. At all. The scene was stagnating. Juanita's psyche wanted him, was pulling madly at its leash, but someone had tied it to the porch. And he had a fair idea who that someone was.

As a little experiment, he imagined Jack the Ripper sneaking up on his mother. Two seconds later, the muffled, twisted screams of a man fluttered through the church.

He tried the ship again with no luck. He could still conjure, but couldn't escape.

His mother rapped urgently on the door. "It's official, J.R. We're moving out of this neighborhood. It's full of English villains."

"Think, think, think," he said as he tapped his forehead.

Silently, the bubbles detonated, each one becoming a mini showerhead, spraying the church with liquid imagination. Every drop was a clever brush, adding its own prearranged piece while erasing the one before it. As the ancient venue melted surrealistically away, another was burgeoning in its place, like some chic Phoenix bubbling out of last year's duds.

This is what it would have been like, Chris thought, to watch the sprinkler system in Salvador Dali's mind try and douse a fevered inspiration.

The molten spray was not metabolizing his being; it just rolled down and off his body like mercury.

He looked for a spot to jump, a place where *what was* and *what is* didn't exist. He found one, right above the melting altar, but as he jumped, the mutating remnants of the organ fell from the ceiling, crashing upon the surface and blocking the entrance. Within seconds, the altar and surrounding area were the incomplete pieces of a long, bleak corridor of what looked like an infirmary.

His window of opportunity was gone.

Chris watched helplessly as the last fragments of the church succumbed to what was the gloomy interior of a neonate ward.

4.

Everything was aslant. Cold, stainless-steel beds lined the wall to his left, each one partially cocooned within thin, filmy curtains that dropped from oval metal tracks anchored to the ceiling. Accompanying the caveat atmosphere were sharply refracted shadows striping the slanted walls and black-and-white checked floors, as if a bright moon were piercing through the barred windows of an asylum.

Chris imagined into being an intercom system, and a woman's seductive voice filled the room. "Paging Dr. Hitchcock, paging Dr. Alfred Hitchcock, please report to pediatrics."

Chuckling, he imagined a small, unassuming cross on the wall above him. His talisman. *Not that I'm finding religion*, he assured himself. The cross appeared, and he watched it for a moment, making sure it would stay.

From what he could gather, he was in some kind of glass enclosure. Within this cage were three crude gauges located in the upper right corner, all in the process of measuring the levels of "Oxigen," "Tempreture," and "Hummidety."

Juanita's poor spelling skills brought a smile to Chris's face. Then again, he realized, he had to give her some credit. He couldn't spell worth shit in Spanish.

The enclosure resembled a standard terrarium more than it did a neonate incubator. In fact, it seemed better suited for a gerbil than a premature human infant. Sawdust and cedar chips covered the floor, not a mattress, and there was a hose at one end, one he assumed was feeding him 'oxigen.' Above him, a wire-mesh lid rested snugly over the brink. There were no holes for gloved, attending hands to fit through, confirming his suspicions that tender, loving caresses were not authorized by his HMO, and had thus not been prescribed to facilitate treatment.

He was still in adult form. Sort of. He still had on his surplice, his jeans, his Adidas...But in proportion to the rest of his surroundings, he was only eight or so inches tall.

If there had been an exercise wheel and little green pellets to munch on, he would have been a happy rodent. Juanita obviously thought him a rat, and it was showing through.

In the bed directly before him, something began to move. From within the curtains, a spectral rheostat gradually illuminated a small yet distinct form on the mattress. This mass then began to quiver like the jostled filament of a light bulb and became even more enlivened as it grew into the silhouette of a human female.

When the figure stopped vibrating, it coughed.

His heartbeat quickening, he watched the outline of her arm grab the curtain and slowly draw it aside. This maneuver, Chris realized, would have required at least a ten-foot reach from her reclined position on the bed. But this was Wonderland, where elasticity was a staple of every dreamer's diet.

This candid manifestation of dream mechanics, though, was a welcome relief from the level of waking reality that had so far dominated this trip.

Haggard, the woman's eyelids were partially drawn, and the half-circles that were visible appeared to be the lightest blue, just a shade or two this side of dead, with no noticeable pupils. Her blonde, oily hair spiked down her forehead like an EKG printout.

She was naked and in stirrups, leering waggishly.

It was dear old Mom. He wanted to turn away but didn't dare. He'd learned to never turn away from anything in Wonderland.

"J.R., you nasty little cocksucker," she said, sounding delighted to see him. "I always knew this is what you wanted to see! Eight weekie-weeks!"

"You have me confused with someone else," he said, swallowing hard.

She raised herself on both elbows and smiled, flashing him two rows of brown, rotten teeth, each one whittled to a fine point. Then she sang, *"Eight weeks, eight weeks, don't you think my pussy's sweet?"*

And his mother was growing, maybe two stories high now. Gaping through the slightly scratched window, he watched from a gynecological perspective as her clitoris elongated into a finger, and then proceed to point down at her opening the way a big neon arrow does a roadside diner. While Chris and his pseudo-incubator seemed to remain their original sizes, she continued to get bigger and bigger, as did everything around her.

When her height reached that of a grain silo, Chris could no longer stand it. "Holy shit!" He was so petrified he could barely think. If Juanita's psyche could be called brilliant for discovering that one of his (like every other male's) deeply latent fears was having incestuous relations with his mother, then it leaped to pure genius when it decided to shoot this snuff film from the Land of Lilliput.

Juanita's mind was pushing Mother closer to him. With every ten feet his mother grew, she encroached one foot upon his glass prison.

Her vagina began to open, the labia spreading like wings. But instead of the rosy luster such parts normally portrayed, these appeared the color of spoiled turkey meat.

After a quick study of the rest of her body, her face, Chris concluded that, yes, his mother was being offered as a live cadaver.

"Gamble, you sick fuck!" he screamed, pounding on the glass. Not only was this intended to be an incestuous act of unparalleled dimensions, but it was looking like he'd nuzzled up to the bar just in time to make Two-For-One Happy Hour! *Hi, I'll have an incest straight up— no, make that an incestuous necrophilia with a twist of lemon, please.*

Chris tried frantically to teleport himself out of this half-ass rat cage, to move and make objects disappear, to turn himself into a variety of religious items and symbols, anything. Nothing was working.

He inspected his surroundings again. The cross he'd put on the wall just moments earlier was now a clock the size of a child's swimming pool, but it was Jesus, not Mickey, who was pointing out the hour. And Chris thought the Savior's hands were indicating that now might be a good time for him to say his prayers. He tried turning it back into a cross, but it wouldn't budge.

"*Fuuuck!*" he screamed.

The oxygen coming from the black hose stirred his hair. He brushed the bangs from his eyes, then pointed at the tube. "Son of a bitch!"

It wasn't oxygen blowing his hair around, he was sure of it. It was something lethal, piped in from Gamble's own magic bottle.

"Just concentrate, dude," he told himself. "Don't start getting paranoid. You've been here before. Don't panic."

His mother and the room continued to expand, now at such a rate that Chris didn't know if it was she who was quickly growing, or if it was he who was shrinking.

Oh no.

5.

Georgia O'Keeffe was definitely not dreaming this picture.

Hands and face against the glass, Chris was gripped with a new level of terror that would make an attack of rabid bats seem like a stroll through a butterfly farm.

His mother's vagina had now reached such dimensions that to hear a train whistle wouldn't come as any surprise. Either the bed and stirrups beneath her had disappeared altogether, or they were now lodged in places he didn't particularly care to imagine.

"J.R.? I don't think you're taking me seriously. Hop on in, Slim! Eight weeks, boom badda bing, do ya wanna hear me sing?"

His cage vibrated with the resonance of her thunderous voice. Behind him, just below her knees, her legs vanished into obscurity. Looking up, he could see just above her breasts. From there, storm cumuli obscured the rest; her head literally in the clouds.

Chris didn't need a dream analyst to explain that one. He'd always known his mother was scatterbrained. What he did need help deciphering was the meaning for the rest of this vignette that found him no taller than a celery stick and standing before his dead mother's giant twat.

Paging Dr. Freud, paging Dr. Sigmund Freud, please report to pediatrics.

She stopped growing.

"Just eight weekie-weekies, you possessed little bastard! Come down here and see your momma! Praise his holy britches!"

Then his glass confines faded away, and he was on the floor, confronting a monster; two, if he counted the rest of his mother.

The only items remaining from the ward were the tile floors and the fluorescent ice cube trays that shone directly overhead, stopping as they neared his mother's crotch, just below timberline.

As dread and nausea rolled heavily through his stomach, he reminded himself that laughter *was* the best medicine. And he had none other than Readers' Digest to back him up.

His mother again: "Eight little old weeks can seem like forever. Oops! There goes another rubber tree..."

Then, as the last vibrations of his mother's voice waned, he heard something else. He held his breath. There it was again, faint and watery and hard to track down. It reminded him of the echoing *drip-drip-drip* of a faucet.

Whatever it was, it wasn't the cadence of his heart, which was running on all horses now and way out in front of his sphincter, which had cramped up just moments out of the gate.

As the sounds got closer, he determined their source. They were coming from inside his mother.

Someone, or something, was in the cave. He forced himself to step closer. Yes, they were footsteps. Squishy, sucking footsteps, like someone walking across a muddy field. It sounded like only one person.

Closer now, just inside the shadows. And whoever it was, they were humming. A tune, Chris thought, that sounded a lot like "Bringing in the Sheaths."

Just then, his dead mother drew her legs in at the knees, tightening the arena.

Chris was hyperventilating now, his heart pounding his knees into tapioca.

"Golden showers bring May flowers," his mother sang, who then deluged him with just a squirt, sending him tumbling backward.

On his back, Chris stared up at his mother in wild disbelief. "You fucking bitch!"

As Chris slipped clumsily to his feet, a figure spoke from the cave's entrance. "Why, Mr. Kaddison," said Gamble, his voice echoing back into the chamber, "you smell like piss." He reached around the fleshy pleats with his right hand and latched onto a single strand of coiled hair, then stepped out from the slippery entrance on agile feet.

Chris's heart felt like a castanet in a Latin musical. Drenched to the bone, he was growing dizzy, and his teeth were already chattering. His mother's urine was freezing cold.

"What?" Gamble said. "You were expecting Larry Flynt?" He was still in his gray suit, but was now wearing a white baseball cap, donning the witticism, *Help! I'm Fallen And I Can't Get Up!*, embroidered in red brush script. It was passé, but he wore it well.

Nearly breathless, Chris said, "Are you stalking me, dude?" Dripping, arms out from his sides, he was unsuccessful at conjuring even a towel.

"I can't help it," Gamble admitted. "It's just that you leave such a tempting trail of breadcrumbs."

"I like it nice and slow, J.R.," said his mother, sounding now like the raunchy end of a 1-900 number. "Is that a tractor-trailer in your pants, or are you just happy—"

"Hey, shut the fuck up, you dead, miserable cunt!" Gamble yelled. Then, smiling at himself, he turned back to Chris. "You were going to say...?"

"Why would you want to follow an 'amoeba' like me?"

Gamble looked shocked. "Why, Chris, if I had known you were so sensitive, I would have chosen a *multi*-celled invertebrate to make your comparison. But in answer to your question, it's because I like you."

"Pardon me if I get misty."

"You have every reason to be angry with me. I'm afraid I might have been a little too harsh on you back in that dreary synagogue. My temper sometimes gets the better of me. It's my Achilles' heel, you might say."

"Something's starting to stink," Chris decided, "and it ain't Mom's box."

Gamble's eyebrows shot upward. "Wait 'til you get inside." Then he offered his hand. "Come, let's take a sentimental journey."

Chris stepped back. "Let's not and just say we did."

"Why, these are your old stomping grounds," said Gamble. "The farmstead. Home sweet home. C'mon, where's your sense of nostalgia?"

"It eloped with my appetite," Chris confessed, taking another step backward.

Gamble deliberated a moment, then said, "I'll bet that if I turned you into a crotch louse, and equipped your eyes with *parasites,* you'd find your way in easily enough. Or you'd *slide* right on in as a speculum." He inspected a thumbnail. "I *could* turn you into a dickhead, but that would be rather redundant."

"Okay, okay," he barely conceded. "But, like, can I have a towel first?"

"Not even if she'd shit on you, which I can arrange *if you don't get moving!*"

Chris started walking. Every step was an ordeal, as if both legs had turned into sacks of wet sand. And the pitch of the floor wasn't helping things. Ten feet out, he stopped. "I can't go any further, dude." He was shivering. Fear had pulled his breaths into taut, wheezy strings.

Gamble walked up, tapped him on his shoulder. "Look behind you."

Chris slowly turned his head and, nearly fainting, fell to his knees. Immediately, he was crawling on all fours toward the vagina, skidding and floundering on the tilting, piss-covered tile. "Make it go away!" he pleaded in the pinched, stifled cries of a night terror. "I swear I'm going, I'll do anything, just make it go away!"

Almost upon the opening now, Chris forced himself to look just far enough to the side so that only his peripheral vision would be assaulted should it still be there. It was gone.

A nearly inaudible whine was escaping through his clenched teeth. His nostrils were flaring with each hot, eruptive exhalation. He got to his feet and, like a doddering old man, started for the opening.

"Careful," Gamble said, "that first step's a doozie."

Chris pulled himself up and in. He sank into the knobby, velvety tissue, then released a cannonade of sobs.

Standing just outside the entrance, Gamble gloated. "Bet you've never seen anything quite like that on the Friday Night Frights. Hmmm?"

A thread of saliva was pulling down from his bottom lip. Still sobbing, he wiped it away with a shaky hand. "No."

"I'll give you credit," he said, "not many people could have survived that, which only confirms what I've come to suspect about you."

"That I'm already dead?"

"Hardly." As he stepped up and in, Gamble pointed out a landmark. "Now *that* is one big clit," he observed. "Your old lady's got quite the buzz button."

"I'll make sure it's included in her biography," Chris said, recovering his poise. The urine-soaked surplice no longer a threat, he wiped his nose on the sleeve. "What do you think you know about me?"

"Let's walk and talk," Gamble said. "After you."

Chris pushed himself away from the wall, carefully balancing each wet, spongy step as he entered the dankness.

"Let's begin with your rudimentary theories of the cosmos," Gamble began. "We'll dissect a few bellies and yank out the necrotic organs, okay?"

"Figuratively speaking, this time, right?"

Gamble sighed. "If you wish. Now, you're of the belief that the heaven and hell of the dominant denomination only exist in man's collective unconscious, or some stratum thereof."

"Basically, yeah, but—"

"Mr. Kaddison, you don't have to explain the whys and therefores to me. When I started on this place it was nothing but a few pillared mansions, a marble birdbath, and acres and acres of fucking daffodils and daisies. Oh, and a pretty hefty furnace in the basement. And now look at it. Where else can you take a walk of innocent discovery through a bearded clam the size of Mt. Rushmore? I doubt that either of the other places have attractions like this," he boasted.

Chris stopped. "Whoa, *other places?* Like, are you saying that not only heaven and hell exist in Wonderland, but there's also a *real* heaven and hell...out there?"

"I assure you that, as modestly as your mind can comprehend such things, an original heaven and hell do indeed exist, but nothing like man has imagined. Granted, theologians have led you down a farcical path of ignorance, distortion and misrepresentation, but man hasn't been acclimatized to the greater truth for one very simple reason—and I'll be asking you for that answer after this review, so take notes. The same goes for my horn-bearing counterpart, whose *real* face has likewise been just as surreptitiously withheld from your puny little intellects. Now, take me for a good example. Man would view even the potentiality of my existence—his own creation, for the most part—as implausibly absurd, even if I flame-kissed Manhattan and afterward invited everyone down for ribs. He'd blame it on old Beelzebub—a myth, for the most part—before he'd ever consider hearing the truth. Now, the real 'heaven and hell' exist on a plane so vastly inexplicable that even *my* cable provider can't guarantee clear reception most of the time. Yet, that's where man will put every ounce of his faith. Why?"

"Because he's afraid of the truth, so the more out of reach it is, the more faith he'll invest."

"Well, without putting too fine a point on it," Gamble grudgingly agreed. "But yes, ignorance is the safest place to hide. Understand, man is not so much afraid of truth as he is change."

"So what you said back in the church, that you were once a figment of man's imagination—then that would mean that you're the, um...the..." As if he might have stirred a hornet's nest, he started walking again.

"The Ultimate Fraud? In a manner of speaking." Then he sighed. "But, it's a living."

"So are there, you know, like lakes of fire, brimstone, molten waterfalls?"

"Yet more props created by man." He sighed again. "No, I did away with all that, along with chariot races, those obnoxious halos, and St. Peter's guest book."

Chris was actually smiling. "I was right, then. You have evolved...are evolving."

"Like you wouldn't believe," he crowed. "You see, what I can do in Wonderland is survive independently from my negation, my flip-side. With true states, however, like the proverbial Good and Evil, there are no compromises, just polarity, existing apart but behaving conjointly when defining one another. It's really not that difficult a concept. For instance, how would you know right if wrong didn't exist? How would a woman know to blush if she hadn't been taught that having her ass tweaked on the subway was an unchaste act? You can't, in popular theory, have one without the other. But unlike the original Good and Evil twins, we don't rely on disparities here in Wonderland to justify our existence. Like yourself, I can show moments of compassion, but I am by nature an evil motherfucker. The original Evil can't do that. It only knows evil. It wouldn't know a warm fuzzy from a Valentine. And true Good could no more drown a cobra than it could a kitten. They can imitate, but they can never fully appreciate." He held up a finger. "Remember, I'm referring to the literal, genuine articles, not the counterfeits."

"That's you," Chris confirmed, "the counterfeit."

"That's me. I don't need Good to perpetuate my existence because I already have its very essence flowing through my veins." He grabbed Chris by the shoulder, turned him around and, impersonating Bob Barker, said, "Now, Mr. Kaddison, for six-thousand-dollars and the Admiral side-by-side, can you guess—no help from the audience please—who gave me that transfusion?"

Chris rolled his eyes. "Man did."

Like Mr. Bo Jangles, Gamble jumped up and clicked his heels. "That's right, baby! I'm a certifiable chip off the old block!" He put his face up to Chris's. "I'm madness personified, and *that* would have to be the scariest fucking thing I could ever imagine happening, if I were man." Suddenly, the lighting dimmed, and Gamble was standing in a spotlight wearing a white tux and top hat, spinning a mother-of-pearl cane. Then, sounding just like Frank Sinatra to the tune of "I Did It My Way," he sang, *"And now, the horns are gone, they're gone for good, of this I'm certain, my friends, the red suit, too, it's really true, they're finally curtains, my tail is but ruse, I've even tossed the cape and shoes, but more, much more than this, I did it myyyy waaaay."*

Was he trying to top Liberace's flair for the dramatic?

Not even close.

Gamble was suddenly back in his gray suit and white ball cap, the spotlight gone. "Get my drift?"

"Yeah," Chris said. "But is it the suit that makes the man, or the man who makes the suit?"

"It's the man, baby! Give me Tweed, Seersucker, Gabardine, Worsted, it doesn't matter—I'm bad! The pretense is itself corrupted by the wearer. For instance, in the guise of a hitchhiker, true evil can run out in front of a Mack truck and heroically push a deaf and blind child out of harm's way. But if you did a thorough investigation, you might find that the hitchhiker's true intentions were to make sure the driver and his truck weren't diverted from killing a family of six in a minivan ten miles down the road.

"Now, can virtue pose as evil? Can it commit atrocities? Perhaps, but I believe it will bend unto itself before it ever draws a sword, as long as the fight is for ultimate good. And you know what paves the road to hell, don't you?"

"Good intentions?"

"It's all just part of justifying their existence."

"So, where are the good guys now?" Chris said. "The counterfeit heaven?"

"The boys in white? I'll tell you, I've never seen such an ensemble of milksops in all my years." He laughed. "Why, they folded like origami under cross-examination." He slapped a knee. "Anyway, it seems I've been a naughty boy. As I've already said, the original Good will go to unimaginable lengths to avoid conflict. Man's interpretations of goodness, however, are a bit...amiss. When he created his own little heaven, he gave it a blindfold and cigarette and little else. I whipped them like the dogs they were; whipped and beat them to near death, I tell you, and they still licked my hand all the way up to the moment I crushed each and every one of their weakling skulls. But man did a bang up job on old hell, didn't he? If you humans have anything down pat, it's evil. Backwards, forwards, and sideways. And may I just say thank you—it's a wonderful fit."

Chris just shook his head. "I know if that was me, I'd have bent unto thyself far enough to kick your sorry ass."

Gamble laughed at the humor.

"And besides, I don't believe you," Chris said. "Man would have imagined 'God' as powerful—if not more so—than you. I don't think you could have taken Him out."

"How perceptive, Mr. Kaddison," Gamble said, sounding truly impressed. "You are correct. I've so far been unable to destroy the clone god, as man created us as equal opposites." Then he grinned. "But I can still bully the old buzzard."

"Isn't that an oxymoron? Equal opposites?"

"Now you're catching on."

Chris slipped, caught his balance. "Bully him how?"

A grin spread across Gamble's face. "He's drifting through a universe

I opened just for him, a universe of mirrors. Now, like Narcissus, the supercilious prick can admire his reflection all he wants. But I wouldn't count on him being transformed into any flowers, as I also have him in the continuous act of self-predation." He giggled. "Talk about being full of yourself."

Gamble folded his arms. "You could say that he has yet to bend unto himself. I'm still looking for *his* Achilles' Heel. But I'll find it, eventually."

"He'll eat you for breakfast, dude," Chris bluffed.

"I think not," Gamble said. "You see, little man—just as it is with the *real* God—it's not in his nature."

They continued walking; Chris taking small, cautious steps, with Gamble following his lead. "So, what's in store for us? In the morning, I mean?"

"Funny you should ask."

Instantly, Chris was hovering over a vast, green field of saw grass. As far as his eyes could see, armies of winged creatures were gathering; some already marching, others flying, their lines disappearing into the distance in every direction. From this height, the events below looked like the spokes of a wagon wheel. Chris could see much farther here than if he were standing on the Empire State Building. Here, there were no atmospheric distortions to hamper the view, no smog, no curvature of the Earth. If the ancient mariners had sailed their ships in Wonderland, their nautical maps would have been correct in portraying their world as flat.

And here there be monsters

Their numbers were staggering; their war cries deafening.

Then he was back inside his dead mother. "Holy shit!"

"Yes—and I imagine there will be tons of it when I'm through."

Chris shook his head. "No way God's gonna let that happen! Either of 'em. No way!"

"A believer now, are you? You fleshsacks are funny that way. Put an atheist on the stake and he'll cry for sweet Jesus! How pathetic."

Having just returned from the brightly lit scene, Chris couldn't see. His right hand landed on a portion of vaginal wall that might have been scar tissue, dry and coarse.

"I'm blind as a bat, Gamble."

"Presto!" Gamble said, and a dim, milky glow emerged, seeming to radiate from the skin itself.

"Thanks," Chris mumbled, the way a ticketed motorist might tell a traffic cop. As he lifted his right hand from the wall, he found no scar tissue. Instead, stitched into the flesh was a veronica of Christ, with *Calvary 4074 km, Ovaries 2 km* painted sloppily below in what appeared to be menstrual blood.

"Jesus," Chris whispered.

"Indeed," Gamble said, then began laughing. "Up ahead, maybe dear old Mom will roll away the boulder for you, as well."

Chris coughed. There was now a ferocious stink coming out of the walls. "Careful, dude, you're making it sound like I have a chance of getting out of here alive."

"Perhaps," Gamble admitted. "Let's just see where the road takes us, shall we?"

"If I remember my high school physiology, it takes us to a uterus." Given his mother's present size and position, Chris felt it odd that there was no slope, and the canal had already turned out to be far longer than it should have been. A flat, slippery trek, so far. He didn't know if Gamble had simply adjusted the angle for comfort, or if was part of the dream experience because Juanita (like himself) just didn't have a whole lot of experience with the damned things.

Chris said, "You're after something, dude. Something only the real heaven can offer."

"Your insight continues to astound me, Mr. Kaddison. Absolutely correct. This is about a large piece of real estate known as the Shallows. It offers an unlimited supply of souls, among other things, and the key to eternity."

"You're not eternal?"

"No," he said. "You see, I have a beginning; therefore, I have an end."

"Any chance in the next five minutes?"

Gamble slapped him hard on the shoulder and laughed. "Even without the Shallows, I will forge on for millennia. And within that time, I will have likely found a cure for my terminal illness."

Chris guffawed. "You think?"

"Even if I have to exhume Jonas Salk and turn him into a beaker-toting zombie."

"Kinda like how we created your zombie ass?"

"Yes, up until the point when I began recreating myself," Gamble said. "Now *I* have the brush, and infinity will be my canvas."

"Yeah? And what if the real God decides to become an art critic?"

Now, like a ring announcer: "Then He'd better stay His ass out of the Louvre and start gearing up for some compelling surrealism, baby, 'cuz I'm ready to *rum-bulllll!*"

"What, you and the real hell are going to, like, gang up on heaven?"

"No, I'm afraid both parties find me and my minions unsavory. They'll be joining forces to try and outwit me. I'm sure of it. Quite honestly, though, between the two of them, I don't think they could muster enough guile to trip up a one-legged giraffe."

"Heaven and hell on the same team?" Chris laughed nervously. "There's a concept."

Chuckling himself, Gamble said, "Yes, well, I doubt they'll be toasting one another at the victory party."

"So, now it's just you and your fake subordinates in Wonderland?"

"Not for long," he promised. "We're about to leave a vacancy."

"And you—a man-made, soulless, thinking hologram—think you can defeat the real thing?"

"The 'real' thing? Don't insult me, Mr. Kaddison. I'm more real now than you are." He held out his palms. "Do you see these lines? They're magnificent, aren't they? When Lincoln was President, they were just beginning to emerge." He stepped closer. Pointing with his right index finger, he said, "Do you see that one there? The one you call the Life Line? It's not broken anywhere." Then he offered his right hand. "This one's the same way. Now, I don't know about you, but it looks like I'm going to be around a long, long time. And look at my fingers! Man, I've got arches, loops, and whorls, oh my!" He held his wrists out to Chris. "Book me, Danno!"

After a short burst of merriment that consisted of odd dancing, whooping, and more of those strange animal sounds he'd made earlier in the church, Gamble said, "Now, take a look at *your* palms, Christopher-san."

Bringing his palms to his face, Chris said, "What am I supposed to find?" But he already knew.

"Degradation, dear boy. Oh, you've still got a little time left before any significant changes begin to occur. Besides, you've had more lotion on your hands than Andie McDowell. Jerkin' with the Jergens. Jesus. My point is, you're not all here. I'm more real than you are now. You and every other ignorant asshole topside, along with your reality, have begun the process of vanishing. You see, just as man wished me into being, I've started wishing him away. Just your physical selves, mind you. Naturally, I have some disturbing plans for your eternal souls. You see, *my hand prints were the last to show, so for you they'll be the first to go.*" He giggled at the rhyme. "Oh, and may I be the first to congratulate you on realizing that wonderful fact, even though it's unwarranted, since you came about it not by brilliant deduction, but through an act similar to osmosis. Each time you visit Wonderland, you absorb its essence like spilled coffee. You're a paper towel, my boy, not a scholar."

"What is it that you want from me?" Chris asked.

"I want to know everything there is to know about your friend Duncan," he said. "I've had my eye on him for quite some time now."

Chris started moving again. "Like, why don't you just leaf through my mind, tear out the pages on Duncan yourself? Being all-knowing and all, I'm surprised you even have to ask."

He laughed. "Oh, I'm not omniscient, either, Mr. Kaddison. Where would be the fun in that? No, I'm not even comfortably close."

"Still, this is Wonderland, dude. In here, you don't have to be a deity to read minds. This *is* the mind."

"Right again. And since I've already gleaned from you the knowledge that you have no idea who this Duncan McNeil is, I'll skip right to the point which you just made. Get the fucker in here!"

"Bring Duncan into Wonderland? Go blow yourself."

Gamble grabbed one of Chris's earrings, pulled him down to his knees. "I have to know, and you're the only one who can float him in."

On all fours now, inebriated with dolor, Chris looked like a teenager ready to heave up the six-pack he had for supper. He chuckled. "You couldn't get into his head either, huh? Well, join the crowd! I've tried. It's...impenetrable—"

"Again, that's why I need him in here! And since I'm being forced to redundantly make that point, I'm going to share with you a secret. As incentive for you, I'll hold off from turning Patricia Bently into my own personal sex kitten, and you into a fly on the wall." He leaned in. "Oh yes, lover boy, you've got the hots for that sweet piece. You've even taken quite a shine to her daughter. A guy doesn't have to invade your mind to see those affections." He let go of Chris's earring.

Slipping, trying to get to his feet, Chris cried, "You motherfucker! You touch them and I'll kill you!"

"Of course you will." Gamble reached down and clamped Chris's head between his hands, then pulled him up. "I'll do things to Patricia that will make your very pores bleed with envy. And pity. And I'll triple the debaucheries I intend to perform upon Katherine Bently, once I've gathered my second daughter from that fleshsack. And not only will I make you watch, J.R.—I'll make you participate, and turn that weenie of yours into a painfully long and gluttonous gash grinder. So don't fuck with me, *dude*. Just bring Duncan in!"

"Your *second* daughter?"

Gambles fingers pressed upon Chris's head, and the vagina expanded, now assuming the enormousness and personality of Carlsbad Caverns. Glistening, mucous-formed stalactites were pulling down from the shadowy upper reaches, where black, throbbing ulcers spread like bat swarms, restless as the twilight of another reality began peeking through the rifts and crevices.

Then, Wonderland imploded, forcing Chris to the forefront of consciousness.

6.

He bolted upright, his own palms pressed vice-like against the sides of his head.

Satisfied that Gamble's fingers were no longer there, he turned to the Swiss clock ticking on the south wall.

Only seven minutes had passed.

He swallowed dryly, wondering if time would stop altogether once morning found them.

Eyes wide and dazed, he began to focus on one thought: Gamble's second daughter *is inside Kathy?*

"Bullshit," he finally mumbled. "It's a lie. Has to be."

7.

Eli stood naked before the montage of wings. Although the seventh window was there, he held himself back from walking through. Oh no, he wanted to *fly* into those new and promising environs...

With his own wings.

To feel the exhilaration he had for so long awaited.

To glide and soar with his own feathered appendages.

To whip up crashing tides of air and desquamate the paper walls of what had been for so long a fragile existence.

The moment was one where time stood still. He might have been a father staring into the bright liquid eyes of his brand new baby girl.

Finally, Eli backed himself to the Wall of Faces, against the delineated space reserved for his own body.

He closed his eyes and waited.

Tense moments passed. Then...

A snap and flash of pain—what could only be described as two steel bear traps springing into his shoulder blades.

He roared in agony.

In wide-eyed, pain-generated, air-steeling dementia, he could only mouth idiocies at the windows staring back at him from the opposite wall.

Laughing at him.

He staggered forward and fell.

"Gabriel blew, and a clean thin sound of perfect pitch and crystalline delicacy filled all the universe to the farthest star...as thin as the line separating past from future..."

—Isaac Asimov, *The Last Trump*

Part Five
Transgressions

1.

Dawn was grooming the Atlantic's mane; its gusts of breath shearing off the hoary tufts, its inhalations then combing them back down into youthful blackness.

Farther inland, a shuttle bus pulled to the sidewalk in front of Joan Pendleton's house. Pillsbury was the first to notice the vehicle. She was howling incessantly at the front door with more than a hint of doggy emphysema. Every fifteen seconds or so she would stop and gag, then resume her baying with earnest.

The aroma of freshly brewed coffee wafted from the kitchen.

Joan was the second. "What on earth," she complained, cinching the sash of her threadbare housecoat as she ambled frumpishly across the dining room's wood floor. Her bedroom was on the main level, on the other side of the kitchen; an arrangement that was intended to keep her off the stairs as much as possible.

She stopped three feet from the dog. Hands on her hips, she asked, "My lord, Pillsy, what has gotten into you?"

The third was Chris. Already showered and dressed, he stepped out of the second-level bathroom, leaned his scrawny frame over the banister and began imitating the howling dachshund. He maintained a praiseworthy rhythm and even went so far as to emulate the strangling noises, all the while appearing very confused, if not frightened.

"Young man," Joan chided, "is that really necessary?"

Chris shook his head that it wasn't, but continued to howl

nonetheless as spasms rippled through his body.

Duncan peeked out from his bedroom doorway with a weary, yielding aspect, as if nothing this early could be worth fighting for. Moments later, Rachel appeared beside him, pulling a brush through her hair, her expression firm, determined. Still damp from their showers, both were dressed in Levis pants and sweatshirts. After all, only the most beguiled wore evening gowns and Armani suits to the Apocalypse.

"Knock it off, the both of you," Patricia demanded, coming down the stairs. "For crying out loud! Enough is enough!" Also in rough-and-tumble attire, she shook her finger angrily. "Bad dog!"

Not sharing her opinion one bit, the dog continued to bay. As did Chris.

Kathy and Juanita were the last. Kathy stepped out of her old room (also on the main level and adjacent to grandma's), with Juanita following, still in the same smock, now considerably wrinkled, that she'd been wearing the day before.

Walking over to the dog, Kathy silenced her with just one gentle touch. Then she opened the front door and stepped out onto the porch, returning almost immediately with the morning paper in hand. "Our ride is here," she said cheerily.

"What ride?" Duncan said, descending the stairs in Patricia's fragrant wake.

"The one to get us out of here," Kathy replied.

Now down the stairs himself, looking out the window and still jittery from his doggy fixation, Chris cried, "Dead Man! Dead Man! Dead Man! Dead Man!"

Patricia, fists clenched, turned to Chris. "Would you please shut the hell up?!"

Surprisingly, he did.

Kathy smiled at everyone. "Don't worry, Dead Man's okay. He's just the driver."

Duncan reached the door, Chris now beside him, both watching the driver make his way toward the porch. Every other step the cloaked figure would stop and lean his head toward the lawn. It was obvious to Duncan that the driver was being enticed by the very same *something* that had yesterday lured Chris to do likewise.

"Everybody stay back," Duncan ordered. He opened the front door, just a crack.

Duncan decided that whoever was hidden within the long black robe was, at best, emaciated. He could not see the person's face as the hood was pulled tightly, leaving nothing but a thin slit up the middle.

The driver reached the steps of the porch, his prowess on the unsteady planks a tribute to felines everywhere.

Duncan winced as the smell of chemicals and decay leached through the crack.

Whimpering now, Pillsbury scurried out of sight.

With a mummified hand, the corpse reached inside the door and grabbed Duncan's wrist. "Get everyone out of the house immediately."

Duncan jerked his hand away. "Jesus Christ! Who the hell are you?"

"Your driver," said the corpse "Now listen very carefully. It has begun. Everyone in this house needs to get on my shuttle, and fast."

"It's gone!" Juanita shouted suddenly, staring at the stained glass window above the stairs. "The face—it's gone!"

It was indeed.

Then, somewhere in the recesses of the house, a window shattered; a dog screamed.

"Pillsbury!" Kathy cried, then started running down the hallway, toward the commotion.

Juanita reached out and grabbed Kathy as she ran by. "No you don't!"

As if handed the torch, Joan took up where Kathy had stumbled, and started for her shrieking dog.

"Mother, stay here!" Patricia cried, going after her. "Goddammit, Mother!"

Rachel rushed over and grabbed Joan's arm, and was nearly yanked off her feet, the woman continuing to drive forward like a yoked ox. "You don't want to go down there!" she insisted.

"Pillsy's in trouble!" Joan cried. "I have to save her!" Hands waving above her head, she broke Rachel's grip and started down the hallway, informing her squalling dog that she was on her way.

"Dude's right," Chris said, now pointing at something beyond the window. "We've got company."

"Get everyone on the bus *now*," ordered the driver. "If you don't—" he pulled the hood from his decaying face "—then this reality's going on a long vacation."

It was already packing its bags, Duncan thought to say, as he now saw what Chris was pointing at. They were coming out of the ground; the same kind of creature he and Amy had encountered back at the hospital. He counted two, the duo squeezing themselves up from the dry lawn, near the big elm tree.

"Harpies," the driver offered. "Nasty little bastards."

Just then, Joan wobbled out of the far bedroom with Pillsbury's remains in her outstretched hands. One of the creatures had hitched a ride on her back, and was pulling out tufts of silver-white hair from her scalp. She appeared more grievous over the dog than she did for herself.

Blood poured down her face, into her eyes.

"Here, take this," Dead Man said, shoving Duncan a Colt .45 semiautomatic pistol. "It's special, so don't lose it."

Patricia momentarily broke free of Rachel's clutch, lunging toward her mother. Rachel caught her, this time with both hands.

"We can't help her!" Rachel insisted. "And if we don't get out of here, then we're as dead as she is!"

Patricia wheeled on Rachel, staring, shocked that she could be so cold-hearted.

Duncan turned, bringing the sights of the .45 to eye level.

"Warfare!" Chris said. "Epic, dude!"

"I want everyone on the bus now!" Duncan roared.

Joan continued blindly down the hallway, toward Rachel and Kathy, knocking down various pictures of her granddaughter and other relatives once presumed dead, ramming against the walls, trying desperately to dislodge the creature from her back. Her head and whole upper body was now drenched in blood, and her screams had all but turned into feeble cooing.

With a lonely howl, she dropped Pillsbury's remains, then stumbled over them.

Her legs finally gave out as she entered the living room. As her knees struck the floor, the creature clamped her head between its jaws. Her eyes rolled, and a blood bubble formed between her parted lips.

Duncan aimed the gun, but didn't have a clear shot.

With a lightning quick turn and pull of its jaws, the creature snapped Joan's neck.

Behind Duncan, Patricia fell to the floor in a faint.

Rachel knelt by her side and began shaking her. "No, no!" she cried. "You can't do this now!"

Chris rushed over to Rachel and, with each taking an arm, they pulled Patricia to the front door.

The risk of accidentally hitting Patricia's mother no longer a concern, Duncan fired one shot into the harpy. The .45 caliber slug struck the creature in the head, hurling it from the woman's back. As if controlled by a deranged puppeteer, the harpy began to dance upon frenzied strings. Its wings fluttered in paroxysms as its head wound ejaculated blood.

Duncan let go another round.

Its strings finally cut, the creature collapsed into a silent, motionless heap.

Juanita and Kathy were themselves already at the front door, and Juanita shielded the girl's eyes with one hand while stroking her blonde hair with the other. "It is not good to see."

From the doorway, awake though zombie-like, Patricia stared silently at her dead mother.

As Rachel and Chris steadied Patricia, another harpy waddled like a goose down the blood-splashed hallway, hissing at them.

Duncan pulled the trigger and sent the beast tumbling backward.

Another creature now, squawking as it gashed its way through the kitchen window screen.

"I'm not going to say it again!" Duncan demanded. "Everybody *out!*"

At the kitchen sink, the creature had turned on the faucet and was lapping noisily from the stream of water.

As he raised the gun, bolts of pain shot through his right lower leg. He looked down. "Shit!" A harpy was clamped upon his calf. Point-blank, he fired. The creature spun away, leaving a very nasty bite.

Duncan fell to his knees. Growling, the harpy in the kitchen was threatening to leap from the Formica counter top. Duncan wiped the sweat from his eyes. Aimed. Fired.

Missed.

Wings outstretched, the harpy pounced.

He fired again, sending the creature crashing into the cupboard doors.

Duncan looked around. No one was left in the house except him. And poor Mrs. Pendleton, upon whose twitching body now perched another creature, tugging on a cord of intestine.

Without aiming, he blasted the harpy.

He raised himself unsteadily to his feet, prayed to whoever might be listening for a miracle, then headed for the front door.

2.

Eli awoke to an unbelievable, unthinkable perversion.

Wet and pleated, his new wings glistened pink like the newborn skin of a rat.

He pushed himself up from the cold cement. Maladroit on his feet, he was unskilled with the new, encumbering appendages on his back. The combined weight of both wings easily exceeded his own, and he was certain they would each surpass twelve feet in length when dry.

They were massive.

They were hideous.

They were not what he'd ordered.

Gamble had betrayed him.

He directed his voice to the ceiling, hoping his mentor was in earshot. "GAMBLE, YOU MOTHERFUCKER!"

Then, taken aback, he wondered if Gamble might take that as a compliment. There was so much he still didn't know.

His head hung low, he began to weep, clenching and unclenching his fists.

So unfair.

His back, his sides, his entire body, it seemed, ached with his new burden.

Exhausted, he hunkered below the nearest window well, one of the basement's two, both fortified on the outside with metal mesh welded across their openings. In a few hours, the morning sun would be dropping through and, since the central heater wasn't presently an option (at least not a wise one, as any forced artificial heat might cause shrinkage, he thought), maybe he could get his wings to dry in a quicker and more natural way.

3.

Like frantic prairie dogs from their flooded homes, the harpies exited the ground.

Dead Man hurried everyone into the vehicle.

Patricia stopped. "Mr. and Mrs. Kensington!" she hollered to her neighbors, who were clutching the chain link fence on the south side of her lawn. Fascination had transfixed their eyes just as firmly as fear had gripped their legs.

"Please, get back in your house—no, wait!" Considering what just happened in her home, she turned desperately to Dead Man and said, "Can they come with us?"

"I'm afraid not," he said. "This is a chartered vehicle."

Duncan raised the gun toward the lawn and shot one harpy as it lifted from its hole. Squealing, its wings whipped up plumes of parched earth. Then it fell silent, jaws gnawing the brittle blades of dead grass.

Everyone was inside the shuttle now except Patricia and Duncan. They were both at the gate. Dead Man held the shuttle's doors open and shouted, "Goddammit, hurry!"

"What about my neighbors?" Patricia cried.

Duncan grabbed her arm. "You heard the driver. No other fares."

"But that's bullshit!"

From inside, two harpies crashed though Patricia's front bay window. They righted themselves almost immediately and began to advance upon Duncan and Patricia in macabre, synchronized steps.

Mrs. Kensington screamed at the sight, alerting the creatures to her and her husband's presence.

One harpy broke from the other and took to the air. It swooped once at Patricia's neighbors, circled, and dived again. It gouged out both Mr. Kensington's eyes with its talons and its barbed tail lacerated his wife's forehead. She stammered a few feet, then fell to the ground, a blubbering wreck.

"Three more coming from the lawn!" Kathy warned from her window.

"Fuck it, let's go!" Duncan shouted. He pulled at Patricia's arm, lugging her to the vehicle.

"But they need our help!" she screamed, pointing to her neighbors.

"*We* need our help!" Duncan said, glancing back at the two harpies now squatting like vultures upon the butchered couple. "Nothing we can do!"

Duncan pushed Patricia onto the steps of the shuttle, then pushed himself against her. "No going back!"

Both in, Dead Man closed the doors. Just as he released the clutch, two more harpies slammed like linebackers into the rear of the shuttle.

Looking around, Duncan saw that half the block was now stirring, people standing on their front lawns and doorways, still in their pajamas; some with their morning cups of coffee listing in their hands, morning papers fluttering to the ground, jaws sagging in disbelief.

Down the street, three shots in rapid procession dotted the morning.

Then a shotgun blast from the next block over. Someone screamed. A man.

Dead Man had the shuttle up and rolling to maybe five miles an hour when he had to stop to avoid hitting a black man who'd run out into the street, wearing only his silk jockeys and gold watch. A black woman chased after him, maybe his wife, screaming for him to come back.

The man waved his hands for Dead Man to stop, then began beating on the hood. Anxiously looking back at the approaching woman, he began to yell, "Take me! Take me! Goddamn you, take me!"

Pressing down the clutch, Dead Man revved the engine, trying to scare the man away, but the bluff was wasted.

The woman gained on him now and began crazily slapping him about the face and chest. "Cheatin' motherfucker!" she screamed. "Filthy, rotten, cheatin' motherfucker! I'll kill you!"

Ignoring the woman's cudgeling, the man made his way to the side of the shuttle and attempted to open the doors, his nose bleeding from both nostrils.

"Sorry," Dead Man said sincerely. He hit the gas, leaving the man to his own harpy's discretion.

To Duncan's left, one middle-age woman, arms flailing, went shrieking back inside her house, leaving her ogling mate alone on their crescent driveway, where two creatures ambushed him from behind, eviscerating him in front of his own screaming neighbors.

Up ahead, a little boy, eight or nine, silently crawled along the sidewalk, blood gushing from a severe head wound.

"Oh my God!" Rachel cried. "Stop! We have to get him!"

"No can do," reminded Dead Man.

Bolting from a hedge of azalea bushes, two harpies finished the child in seconds.

Two males, an older man and a boy in his late teens, immediately burst from a brick rancher, in front of which lay the dead boy's remains.

Firing fully automatic rifles, they advanced upon the creatures, whooping and hollering like a couple of drunken cowboys. They were nearly upon the harpies when they discovered their bullets were having no affect. They never made it back inside the house.

Juanita, blubbering now, fists clutched against the sides of her head, appeared ready to start yanking out hair. Duncan realized, however, that she was only shielding her ears from the high-pitched screams.

Duncan stared down at his Colt.

It's special, so don't lose it.

The rubber grips offered an insignia of some kind. Duncan thought the symbol looked familiar. He'd definitely seen it before, but couldn't place it. He extracted the clip and found that it had its full complement of bullets.

How can that be?

The streets were congesting quickly with fleeing people and motorists trying to escape.

Dead Man cursed.

It was stop and go, stop and go. The highway, Dead Man said, was less than a quarter-mile away, but there was doubt in his voice that they'd reach it.

An old woman passed them on the sidewalk, wearing an aluminum colander over her head. She was speaking poignantly into a spoon, gesturing with her free hand as she stumbled along. She might have been giving her listeners a harrowing play-by-play of the war, much like Orson Wells had done with his infamous broadcast of 1936.

A stray bullet struck the windshield, but left only a feathery blemish of smoke.

Shouts and orders, wails and screams, caterwauls of all kinds, distant and up-close, were filling the morning.

Patricia, her face simply blank, said, "Well, Chris, I guess I owe you an apology."

"You don't owe me a thing," he said. "And I'm really truly sorry about your mom."

She didn't respond; just continued staring out the window with the same vapid look on her face.

Just ahead, to the right, an obese woman in curlers lurched into the middle of the street to snatch her tabby. The cat didn't know where to run any more than did the screaming neighbors. From the electrical lines above, four harpies dropped upon her. The cat got away only long enough to be crushed beneath the wheels of Dead Man's bus.

"One down," Dead Man declared. "Ten billion more to go."

Kathy leaned forward and placed both her hands on Duncan's head. "Now your leg won't hurt anymore," she said.

Chris slid open his window. "What's the matter with you people?" he hollered, scared half out of his own wits. "Haven't you ever seen the end of the world before?"

4.

Fashioned to comfortably accommodate fifteen passengers, the shuttle was a banged up, rusted old thing reminiscent of the kind often seen at airports; originally white on the outside, grungy green upholstery inside, with a rather sweet musty smell that was causing Duncan to wonder if it was from years of dank storage or just the mummified driver's BO.

Duncan speculated to himself that the chassis was probably a Ford E350 RV. Then again, he thought, it was most likely nothing of the sort, but rather an older model that had once rolled crystal clean off the assembly line of a factory located nowhere near Dearborn, let alone this planet, despite its apparent earthly manufacture.

Just like Dead Man's gun.

When they'd reached the interstate, traffic had been chaotic, but negotiable; surprising, given the circumstances. Their chauffeur had skillfully woven them through infrequent snarls and smoldering pile-ups, the occasional roll-over, around corpses...

Too many corpses.

They weren't long on the highway, though, as Dead Man had chosen an exit taking them eastward, quickly out of Rock Bay proper and onto its bucolic back roads.

Thousands of harpies soared high overhead, grouped not like geese, but ranked like marching ants. For now, they seemed content to leave the shuttle and its passengers alone.

Duncan inspected his leg wound, which was nearly healed now. He turned to Kathy, amazed. For the third time, he thanked her.

"No problem," she said. *Think nothing of it.*

Patricia leaned forward. "We're going straight to Seattle, right?"

Dead Man said, "Not before we make a few pit stops."

"Pit stops *where?*" Patricia demanded.

Dead Man chuckled. "Places that Rand McNally's never heard of."

Patricia sighed, turned toward the window. "I can't cope with this."

"Did it ever occur to any of you," Chris said, "that we were selected because we can cope with it better than most?"

"We're old souls," Kathy added. "We can handle a lot more than we think we can."

"All of us were groomed for just this very occasion," Chris continued. "Not just in this lifetime, but in a long string of previous ones."

"Right-O," Kathy vouched. "Groomed."

"What do you say about all this, Dead Man?" Duncan said. "Is all of this preordained?"

Before Dead Man could answer, Patricia walked to the front and pointing past the windshield. "Why are there seven toll booths on a two-lane frontage road?"

Dead Man nodded. "We'll be running into a few like those."

Duncan, on his feet now, asked, "Who in the hell built them?"

"Angels," Dead Man said. "Funded by the seraph."

One hundred feet from the toll booths, Dead Man stopped the shuttle.

"I don't think I like this," Rachel confessed.

"Ditto," murmured Patricia.

Dead Man pointed through the windshield. "Chris, which one do we go through?"

Chris looked puzzled. "What are you asking me for? I don't know—"

"Yes you do, just concentrate."

The shuttle idled doubtfully as Chris focused. A slow tick began to pulse beneath his left cheek. Finally, he shouted, "Three! Three! Three!"

Dead Man revved the engine. "Three it is."

Dead Man eased the shuttle into the third booth and, before he could stop, the hooded figure within raised the gate and waved him through.

Chris returned to his seat, grinning proudly. "Three!"

As they passed through the gate, a different world emerged. An urban world.

A world that Duncan recognized immediately.

5.

The morning sun shone through the grille of the window well, casting a latticework of shadows across Eli's body and wings.

With her cane, Josephine nudged Eli's foot.

He bolted up wide-eyed, as if chased awake by a nightmare pack of wolves rather than the blunt end of a stick.

There was now a blanket over him, one of red and black Indian weave, obviously thrown down by his mother. And it wasted no time in making him itch.

Josephine thumped her cane twice. "Where's Robin?" she said.

Eli stared up at her. "Who?"

"Your sidekick, cape crusader!" she cackled. "I just figured since you got the role of Batman that they woulda given you a good-looking partner." She cackled some more, then pointed to his wings. "Does a cave and souped-up Cadillac come with those?"

Ignoring his crazy mother, Eli stood, cinched the blanket around his waist, then unsteadily walked to the center of the room. He flexed his wings. They were almost completely dry now, and exceeded his original estimate in length. Each one had to be at least fifteen feet long. Their color had also changed; a rich opulent brown with black mottling having replaced the neonate, rodent pink.

None of which had any redeeming value whatsoever.

With all seriousness, Josephine said, "Shall I get the bat-phone when it rings, or will Alfred be taking over those duties?"

Undaunted by his mother's jeers, Eli practiced operating his wings. Fully extended, they reminded him of a caudal fin of some monstrous fish. They neatly folded behind his back. It was as if he'd never been without them.

"How does my back look?" he said.

"Like the Joker's best prank yet."

"The wings, Mother. Do they look real?"

"I don't see any glue dribbling down your back, if that's what you mean."

He sighed. "Do they look *natural?*"

She stepped closer. "You mean homegrown? Part of the original package?" She inspected the wings, pulled and shook them. She snorted. "I imagine they'll do. But it sure is gonna be hot in that leather outfit."

For a demented old woman, Eli had to admit, she could still maintain a train of thought.

"I'm getting the wings I deserve," he told her. "Not these ugly things. We had a deal."

"Who? You and that Gamble fellow?"

"That's right."

"Ha! That asshole's been pulling you around by the tallywhacker for so long that you've got stretch marks on your balls."

"Very attractive, Mother. And just what is that supposed to mean?"

"Means you're a sucker, Eli! Wake up and smell the bullshit!"

Eli flexed his wings bombastically. "I think I'll just fan the fumes," he said.

"Not even angels were meant to have wings," she declared. "You can thank those renaissance hippies for creating that screwy notion."

"Michelangelo was hardly a hippie, Mother."

"Ha!" Josephine started up the stairs. "I know one thing—I have a bowl of rice pudding and some toast waiting for me in the kitchen." She turned, grinning mischievously. "Would you like me to make you some, batboy, or will you be switching your diet over to moths and mosquitoes?"

6.

They'd gone from day to night in a wink.

From country to city.

Boston.

Dead Man had left the interstate just moments earlier and was now cruising through the suburbs. Traffic was light, to say the least, as theirs was the only vehicle moving.

This was yesterday, Dead Man stated, the wee hours of the morning. A reprieve from the apocalypse. From here their journey would begin.

"Yesterday?" Rachel exclaimed. "We're back to yesterday? And just how did we manage that?"

"With a little help from my friends," Dead Man explained.

Finally, he eased the shuttle to the curb, killed the engine. Without turning around, he spoke to Duncan through the mirror above the driver's seat. "Remember this neighborhood?"

"Vaguely," Duncan said thickly. His face felt numb, as if suddenly impaired by a bilateral blitz of Bell's Palsy. "But you're too late. I've changed my mind. I don't want to go back."

"I'm afraid you don't have a choice," said Dead Man. "Besides, who said this has anything to do with what *you* want?"

Duncan stared at the driver's sunken eyes. "This is some kind of punishment?"

"Nonsense," Dead Man assured. "Just has to be done is all."

"Where are we, Duncan?" Rachel said, alarm etching her voice.

"Hell." He kissed her cheek, then left his seat and approached Dead Man. "What are they going to do if I refuse?"

"That night hooked into you twelve years ago," said Dead Man, "and has been reeling you in ever since, playing you to exhaustion. You might think you can still snap the line, but the hard truth is you're already in the boat, weighed and measured."

Duncan didn't like where that analogy was heading. "Next thing you'll be telling me is, I'm about to be gutted, mounted, and hung over someone's fireplace."

"Jesus, you're such a malcontent," charged Dead Man. "If this wasn't necessary, we wouldn't be here."

"Damn it, Duncan McNeil, talk to me!" Rachel insisted, standing now. "What's going on?"

"Remember those ghosts I told you about?"

She nodded.

"Well," he said, "this is their cemetery."

"And being the gravedigger that you are," Rachel said, "you're naturally going to have to rattle some old bones, right?"

"Not if I don't have to," he said. Then he turned and stared into the darkness. Something out there was strangely compelling, though. Taunting him.

Rachel aimed a finger at Dead Man. "Start this bus," she ordered, "and just slowly drive away, or I swear I'll tie you to the luggage rack like a piece of Samsonite."

"Please, Mrs. McNeil," Dead Man appealed, "understand that Duncan has to see this through."

"I don't get it," she said. "My husband has to make a pit stop and revisit something that—no matter how heinous it might have been to *pre*-Armageddon society—couldn't possibly compare to the carnage happening around us, or...above us, behind us—oh, hell, wherever the fuck it is, or we are, or—*oh, Jesus Christ!*" She was so agitated, so flustered, it appeared she might literally unhinge from herself, both halves going in different directions.

"Trust me on this," said Dead Man. "It's so very important."

"Oh, piss off," Rachel said, then motioned to their seat. "Duncan, you just sit right back down. There's no way you're going to leave us here alone with, with the Grim Reaper."

Duncan was still staring out the windshield, entranced.

So, this is what it felt like, he mused, *when sea nymphs sang the ancient sailors to the rocks.* Outside might be the early hours of yesterday morning, he thought, but that night of twelve years ago was waiting behind the subterfuge, secreted like a thief.

He met Rachel's frightened eyes and sighed. "Dead Man's right. I have to go."

Rachel turned to Patricia. "You were a part of this, weren't you?"

Patricia's eyes diverted to the floor. "In a way."

"Then get your ass up and help him, sweetheart!" Rachel demanded.

Patricia stared regretfully into Rachel's eyes. "I'm so sorry," she said. "I would take Duncan's place if I could. Jesus, I can only imagine what he's gone through for me."

Rachel's face twisted jeeringly. "Don't flatter yourself!"

Patricia countered with her own wry expression. "Listen, I know you're upset, but that's no—"

"No *what?*" Rachel snapped. "Maybe if you would have been crossing your legs instead of your T's while signing the motel register with John Cassavetes, *Rosemary*, we wouldn't be in this pickle! And I don't mean just us! I'm talking the whole fucking planet!"

Patricia bolted to her feet, fists clenched. "Why, you conceited, arrogant bitch!" she hissed. "I oughta kick your—"

"Alright!" Duncan demanded." "Enough!" He pulled the Colt .45 from his pants and handed it to Dead Man.

Dead Man said, "Stay relaxed, stay calm. Don't try to change anything. That's not what this is about." As if expecting the night to be cold, the corpse pulled his robe tight. "I wish I could tell you more."

"Nonsense," Duncan quipped. "You've been a cornucopia of information."

"Sorry," Dead Man said. The doors squealed open. "Good luck."

Duncan stared at the storm drain awaiting him at the foot of the metal steps. An oval splotch of water lay as smooth as a mirror in front of the clogged grate, capturing a yellow cleft of moon and a deep well of blackness, turning the ordinary puddle into a serpent's eye.

Omens don't get any more shameless than that, he thought.

He turned to Rachel, tipping his head toward the open door and beyond. "I was a real asshole back then."

"You still are," she said, tears running down her cheeks. Then...

Come back to me, she mouthed.

"If it's the last thing I do," he promised. He turned to Juanita. "I know I don't thank you enough—okay, at all—so, thanks for always being there for us. You're one tough, wonderful lady."

That did it; now she was bawling like a baby. She uttered something, but the words fell with her tears down into the cleavage of her huge bosom.

"Just go with the flow," Kathy said.

She was holding out on them, Duncan thought. Oh yeah, big time.

Chris, looking up at Duncan and regarding him as if he were just stepping out to get a pack of Camels and a Lotto ticket, said, "Hey, man, like Garth Brooks says, 'Do what you gotta do.'"

Duncan paused in front of the open doors. He put his hands in his pockets, as if to make certain that he had enough tokens for the colporteur and his magical gate. He lifted his head and started down the steps, his knees buzzing with adrenaline.

At last, the turnstile wrapped him in its cold, steel appendages, then delivered him into the outstretched arms of something even colder.

His past.

7.

Eli had cast aside his blanket and faced away from the seventh window when Mr. Gamble came through.

"We meet outside the confessional at last, Father."

Eli jumped, whirled around. "Gamble," he hissed.

"None other," Gamble said. "Now, I realize that this is a long-awaited moment for you, and I would love nothing more than to reward you with a gala worthy of your tremendous dedication. But I'm afraid we're pressed for time. Seems we have another problem."

Gamble's last statement immediately assumed the proportions of a boulder, one now teetering precariously above Eli's road equipment. "Oh?"

"We've been hoodwinked."

Eli leaned in. "I'm sorry?"

"Who you thought was Katherine Bently is, in actuality, an angel." He was fuming now. "A reneging, backstabbing cunt of a half-breed seraph going by the name of Amy McNeil!"

"Half-seraph?"

"And half-man, Father," Gamble said, his fury now but a flicker in the space of a breath. "I personally placed those seraph cocksuckers on the endangered species list when Greenpeace still meant Martian pussy, and followed through with their near-extinction when I killed all but one over a century ago. That one got away, and has been in hiding ever since, trying to bring its numbers back, albeit in a diluted way."

"Seraphs are real?"

"They are indeed, Father. But, as I said, Amy McNeil and the rest of her crew aren't quite AKC registered."

Despite such rumors in the Old Testament, Eli couldn't believe it. "Angels? Breeding with man?"

"You mean like, is man 'doing the deed' with the principalities, 'bumping nasties' with the cherubim, playing 'hide the sausage' with the thrones? Is that the kind of hanky-panky to which you are alluding, Father?"

"Well, yes."

"Nope. Angels don't procreate in that sense. You'd be better off knitting booties for a pair of estranged bookends. You see, God and His heavenly hosts literally don't screw each other." He raised his eyebrows. "Figuratively, however, I'm beginning to suspect otherwise."

"Then, there really is a God?"

"Holy turtle shit, Father! Do I have to put it in neon for you? Yes! There is a God!"

Eli stared at the cement floor, the cracks provoked by years of settling not so unlike the ones now extending even farther from the edges of his already tenuous belief system, reaching into its core.

"What does she want?" Eli asked.

"To put an end to me," Gamble said flatly. "And to you, of course."

"My painting," Eli said. "The seraph with the sword, it was giving us a message."

"Of course it was," he said, then began contemplatively tapping his chin with a finger. "I have to say, they've grown some rather large balls of late."

"Have they," Eli said, bewildered.

"Oh, don't worry, Father," Gamble said. "They can rattle their sabers all they want. The truth is they get squeamish when it comes to spilling blood."

Eli nodded.

Gamble slapped his hands together. "Well, ready to hop through ol' number seven?"

Eli turned and stared at his newest window. The burst of exaltation that should have followed that request rose to but a feeble murmur in his chest. "Yes," he said simply. "But...there's just one thing. I was wondering about my wings. I thought they were going to be—"

"You pitiful little shit!" Gamble said, his breath instantly rancid. "Do you think I'm some dry cleaner you can intimidate? Looky Joe, you claim ticket show you *owna awf* one cheap-cheap *Polyesta* suit, no Gucci. No Gucci *fo* you, Joe. I here when you *bwing* in bargain suit to my *chop*, cheapy-cheap. So you no try pull wool over eye." He brushed Eli's cheek with his finger, his normal inflection returning on a churlish chord. "You want the pretty stuff, then go to work for the other side. But let's face facts—your skewed sense of fashion is the reason you're working for me in the first place."

Eli stared ashamedly at his naked feet. "Perhaps I had my priorities mixed up."

"You're more interested in aesthetics than you are the big picture," Gamble said. "May I suggest that you get your shit together?"

"I'm fine...I'm...sorry."

"Apology accepted!" Gamble said ebulliently. "Now, just one little thing before we split this taco stand." He pointed to the plastic bowls beneath each of the windows. "What the fuck are those?"

"I...I keep them there just in case the couriers get hungry."

"You mean, for the last twelve-odd years you've been offering them dog food?"

"Well, yes."

"You're a devoted little fleshsack, I'll give you that. But, they don't like *Purina* any more than you do, Father. You never noticed that all this time? The hundreds of pounds of uneaten horsemeat that you must have thrown out all these years? Christ, you've been continuously insulting them for well over a decade, *and you're still alive?* I don't know of who I should be more ashamed—you or them for not tearing you apart years ago."

"Told ya," said Josephine, hobbling down the stairs. "The monkey-bats only like people food."

"Mother, not now, I—"

"Well, well, well," she said. "I finally get to meet the big shot himself."

Gamble held out his arms. "Mrs. Kagan, the pleasure's all mine. Your son has told me so much about you."

"It's all true," she said, avoiding the embrace. "So, are you the big cheese or just a sliver off the block?"

"Mother," Eli warned.

Laughing delightedly, Gamble said, "My, my, but aren't you a beauty! And in answer to your question," he said, displaying a thin gap between his forefinger and thumb, "you're this fucking close to finding out."

"Just a sliver off the block," she concluded, shaking her head. "When you get your stripes, give me a call. I want to talk to somebody who can tell me what the hell's going on with my mind. Seems I lost it."

Gamble looked shocked. "Why, Mrs. Kagan, you're right as rain, old girl."

"Don't blow sunshine up my ass. I know when I'm crazy."

"Alright, I concede. You are just a bit demented. But, hey, aren't we all?"

She thumped her cane twice on the floor. "There sure ain't anyone in this basement who isn't, that's for damn sure."

Still smiling, Gamble said, "How incredibly charming you are. I'll bet you're a real stinker on bingo night."

"I don't gamble, Gamble," she said. "I was wondering, though, can I keep Jacob?"

"Mother, go upstairs!" Eli commanded. "Mr. Gamble and I don't have time for your craziness!"

She considered Eli reproachfully. "Shouldn't you be out fighting crime?" Then she swung back to Gamble. "You think about it. I deserve something for my efforts."

As she turned to leave, Gamble said, "I agree. Not only will I let you have your precious 'monkey-bat,' but how would you like to accompany your son as he makes his way across the thrilling lands of the new and improved Hell?"

Eli's wings partially unfolded and began to quiver.

"Are there snakes?" she said.

"Josephine—may I call you Josephine?—how can there not be snakes where you'll be going? Why, hon, they're practically family."

"I see your point." She thought for a moment. "Alright, I'll go. Will I need an overnight bag?"

"Of course not. Everything will be provided for you."

Eli was beside himself. "No! She's not coming with me!"

"As your travel agent," Gamble growled, "I strongly advise that you take her along."

Eli stared hatefully at his mother.

"And you won't need that cane where you're going, Josephine," Gamble said. "Quite frankly, we don't cater to the handicapped anymore. We could never keep anyone from parking in their spaces, so we just did away with the whole concept."

"I'll bring it just the same," she said. "I might need something to shove up Eli's ass."

"She's precious!" Gamble exclaimed, wiping a tear from his cheek.

"Go get ready, Mother," Eli growled.

She started for the stairs. "Just let me run a brush through my hair. Oh, and give me a second to call Evelyn Rogers. Now, maybe I can finally outclass the old bitch and her 'successful' lawyer daughter." She turned back to Eli. "You know, the one who can't afford to run her commercials until after the eleven o'clock news? With all the rest of them ambulance chasers?"

Eli pointed to the stairs. "Just...go!"

As Josephine climbed the stairs, Eli said to Gamble, "How can you do this to me? She'll just slow me down. No! She'll bring me to a complete fucking stop!"

"Oh, come now, Father. You couldn't be pulled away if you had a comet strapped to your ass. Besides, I've got just the task for your mother."

"Task?" Eli was proud and horrified at the same time.

Gamble slapped his shoulder. "Requires just the push of a button."

8.

As Duncan stepped onto the sidewalk, the air rushed in to fill the space where the shuttle had just been, creating a minor, though nonetheless startling, boom.

Squinting at the street signs some forty feet away, he found himself at the intersection of Gansel Street and Prashe Court, the latter dead-ending in a cul-de-sac. Upon that orientation, his knowledge of this neighborhood, if not the entire Boston area, returned.

Boston. His birthplace. His hometown.

Realizing that he was on the opposite side of where he should be, he crossed the road, the asphalt blushing blond under the street lights as he made his way along the gently steepening sidewalk.

If he pointed his ear just so, he could hear the crashing surf, almost a quarter-mile away. He could smell the ocean; taste it. Like two different women, he realized, the Atlantic and the Pacific carried their own unique fragrances, not to mention temperaments. Yes, there were some frightening corollaries between women and oceans. But far more comparisons could be built upon their mutual splendor, he knew, than could ever be made upon those damning predispositions of stormy intent.

Having crossed from the even numbers to the odd, he was now able to better see the house, a large corner plot. Actually, he couldn't see the house all that well, as it was nestled within a bosk of white pine and flowering bayberry, with brakes of witch-hazel and hobblebush pushing at the fence line, an ideal hangout for the neighborhood felids and skunks.

It was different in all the ways he would normally expect after twelve years.

It wasn't his past quite yet. But he could sense that it was near, as if it were peeking at him from around the very next corner.

Two lots down, he stopped in front of an overgrown lawn where stood a lone flamingo. But this particular species was way far north of its native roost, that being any one of the priggish, geriatric-owned lawns of Dade County, Florida. The plastic body was pocked with holes, and its pink luster had been blanched the angry gray of a threatening nor'easter.

The yard bird was not what had drawn his attention, but rather a large gray dog. Upon closer examination, a wolf. There was a collar around its neck, a large silver tag hanging from it. It was an emblem of some type, but Duncan couldn't quite make it out at his distance. The animal just stood there, staring at him. There was something peculiar about its eyes...

Suddenly, the smells of timeworn flax and linseed oil took to the wing from somewhere deep inside his memory: the stink of hay and musty rooms (stalls?), the feel of warm sunlight slicing through boarded windows, the texture of frayed rope and the trill of a rusted weathervane...

These memories were not his, yet something in the wolf's eyes impassioned them.

Where were these memories coming from?

He didn't know. But he did know that they were important. Since yesterday, he'd learned not to take anything for granted, not even a trip to the john.

Up ahead, reposed against a section of chain-link fence impounding the house, was the silhouette of a man.

Duncan stopped. Stared.

With a *ching-ing-ing*, the figure came off the fence. "There once was a detective named McNeil," greeted the voice, the words steamy in the crisp night air. "I believe you know the rest."

"Well, well, you must be the poet, Mr. Gamble."

"The McDevil of the deities," he affirmed.

"And let's not forget Jack Fortune."

"Oh, let's," Gamble said, scrunching his nose. "I never really liked him."

Duncan's heart was pounding like a River Dance troop on an ant-infested stage. Gamble might have had a stamp on his forehead declaring "Man Made," but he was still very much a god, Duncan suspected, one who could shove a squeeze bulb up his ass, turn him into a perfume atomizer, and deliver to the universe his guts in little misty bursts, should the urge strike.

An image came to his mind, one of Mitch Dillard languishing in the slug's jellied throat. "You murdered the photographer."

"Yes, I'm afraid I did."

Duncan couldn't have run even if he'd wanted. His knees were locked and secured like the twin barrels of a shotgun. No, he wouldn't give the sonofabitch the satisfaction. Nor was he about to do any bootlicking.

Besides, he imagined that Gamble probably had more respect for someone who, like good old Rooster Cogburn, had true grit. Duncan knew his own grit was imitation, of course, but he wasn't going to tell.

"Fuck you," Duncan spat. "And fuck your mongrels."

"Give your sphincter a rest, Donut. That's not why I'm here."

"You have no business here," Duncan said. "This doesn't concern you."

"I'm afraid I disagree," Gamble said, closing on Duncan. "On behalf of creation, this *is* my concern. And I'm here to try and persuade you from making the biggest mistake since Red Delicious were planted in Eden."

"Persuade me from what?" he said, as if he hadn't the foggiest idea what the man was talking about. There was a frankness in his voice, though, which Duncan strongly perceived to be genuine. But then, this guy was the archetype of deception. To even think about trusting him, he reminded himself, would be a grave mistake.

Gamble stopped just inches from Duncan, the purple tassels of his muffler groping the nearly fictional breeze like the beautiful but deadly tentacles of a sea anemone. Beneath his muffler, he was wearing a blue tattered pea coat with a yellow slicker beneath, a pair of equally frazzled tan dungarees, and a shiny new pair of fishermen's galoshes.

Duncan didn't know whether to address him as Mr. Gamble or Ishmael.

Gamble shook his finger. "You're not only playing with your own existence, but existence itself. I have to tell you, going back in time is a gargantuan breach of principle."

"*You* want to play by the rules?"

"My plebeian friend," Gamble grinned. "you couldn't begin to understand the rules." He reached into the pocket of his pea coat and removed a bone, then tossed it toward the wolf.

The wolf paid no attention to the offering; just glared at Gamble.

"Listen, the fall of civilization isn't hinged on this night," Duncan assured. "This is just a personal matter. I screwed up a long time ago is all. Did some things I'm not real proud of. And, for reasons that aren't clear to me, I think I'm being treated to a replay, courtesy of my daughter." He brazenly leaned forward. "You know Amy, don't you?"

Gamble kept on smiling, remaining the true and concerned gentleman. "Yes, I know of your daughter, Mr. McNeil. I'm also aware of what happened here when you were a police officer, but we all fall from grace from time to time. In fact, I'm aware of quite a lot of things, so please don't talk down to me as if I've just fallen off the turnip truck. Just know that I'm not here to do battle with you or Amy. Not now. I've taken time out from being the rogue and am offering myself as a friend to both of you. To all mankind. Please, don't interfere here. Just hop back on your jitney and let fate take care of the rest. Really, how can we expect destiny to fulfill itself if they keep turning back the clock?" He placed a hand on Duncan's shoulder. "Don't go back in time. There's no future in it."

Duncan jerked away. "What if I don't have a choice?"

"Oh, don't let them bully you, Donut. Simply bare your buttocks and tell them to kiss it and be on your way."

"Tell who?"

"A bunch of mongrels," he said. "But the more important question is: Who are *you*?"

"Truth is, I'm not sure anymore. But I am curious, so—being the deity that you are—why don't you enlighten me."

Gamble regarded him sincerely. "Oh, I think you know, Donut."

Duncan noticed that the night had become uncannily calm; a settling lull so tangible, so lucidly crystalline that had the moon been any fuller, he was convinced that its beams would have chimed against the stillness like drizzle on fluted glass.

"Did you do that?" Duncan asked.

"It isn't in the playbill," Gamble said, inspecting the scenery himself, going one further by sniffing the air like a dog.

Duncan stared at Gamble with a mixture of fear and contempt, and with enough admiration to be nakedly ashamed. After all, Gamble was just being Gamble. Sure, he was full of pretension, but in his case it was utter verisimilitude. How many people did he know, or had ever known, who portrayed themselves so genuinely?

With a slaked expression, Gamble said to Duncan, "Tastes vaguely like something upon which I used to dine. A heavenly creature of sorts."

"An angel?" Duncan said, glancing upward.

"More or less." Like a hunter in a blind, he scanned the sky in anticipation. "A hybrid, if you will."

The ground trembled. "Step away from him, Duncan," boomed a voice; one imperially feminine.

Both he and Gamble continued searching the night, but neither could find her.

"Back away from him!" she insisted, the ground shuddering beneath their feet.

Duncan looked at Gamble, shrugged his shoulders as if it were beyond his control, and began moving away.

"I know what you're up to," Gamble said to the voice, his own just below a yell. "It's underhanded, unlawful, and, most of all, unauthorized." Then he twirled, his face beaming with delight. "Oh, baby, we were *meant* for each other!"

Duncan was convinced that Gamble knew this being intimately.

"Imp, you know nothing," assured the voice.

Gamble stared at the stars. "I know man," he said, "because I was born of him. And now that your kind have been lounging around that gene pool too, getting more than just a tan, I've been able to anticipate certain things. Like what you're planning to do with my friend here. Again."

A fusillade of heavy guns at sea. "Prattle!"

"It's intoxicating, isn't it?" Gamble said, as if he were a practiced waiter making light of a patron's rude belching of the house Bordeaux. "You keep going in with the right intentions but keep stumbling out like a slut with puke on her pumps, promising herself that she won't do that anymore. Now look at yourself—once again, you're right back on your favorite stool, showing some leg and well on your way to another idolatrous rendezvous with the porcelain god. That's what happens when you dance with man. Once you're in his arms, you soon become mesmerized to the glitter ball and begin thinking you can keep up if you just follow the pretty little lights." Appearing bewildered, he held up his arms. "But the way you keep lurching around, sweetie, how do you expect to convince me and the band that you can waltz, let alone last the marathon?"

There was a protracted silence, and it was beginning to scare Duncan even more than Gamble's own presence. He could sense the entity deliberating, and this suggested that perhaps Gamble was indeed speaking some truth. The truth about what, Duncan could only guess, since he didn't have the faintest idea what the asshole was gushing on about.

The ground was alive; the loose, shifting skin of some behemoth.

"Duncan has made his choice," the entity finally said. "Now leave."

"You can't bullshit an old bullshitter," Gamble charged. "You've been making his decisions for him. Shame on you."

Like a fossilized pustule, the asphalt ruptured, extending the width of the street, filling the air with the fetor of raw sewage. The sky quaked. Shadows see-sawed along the crater's craggy rim, as if the gates of hell had finally been opened and the first wave of tormented souls was congregating above the molten pit, pushing and shoving, their frantic intimations cast by the leaping flames below.

"Crawl back into your hole!" she ordered.

"I'll leave the same way I came, if it's all the same to you," said Gamble. "You know, the road less hackneyed?" He then grabbed the air with his fingers and tore back its skin. "Don't make the same mistake twice," he appealed to Duncan, then vanished through the rent.

More befitting an angel, her voice was soft now; a gentle wind. She said, "I will explain. The night you were shot must be relived. It is necessary for many reasons, as will be explained to you later. Do not let Gamble's visit here scare you into trying to amend the original course of events. It is not so easily done, as you will soon experience. We prefer your older self to remain a bystander. You see, your kind of time endeavors to remain on a track of linear rails."

"You mean destiny?"

"Yes, I think I do."

"Well, hey, I don't want that responsibility again. I greased the tracks twelve years ago and have no intention on throwing any switches the second time around, or third, or however many times you've brought me back here. So why don't you just put me back with the others, and we'll call it a day."

"I'm afraid you must see it through yet again."

"So you have brought me back before. How many times?"

"As many lessons as deemed necessary."

He was shouting now. "So what's your destiny? To make sure I keep the train aligned with fate or change tracks and head to Baltimore instead?"

"I only design the portages of providence," informed the entity. "I cannot make those decisions for you. But mark my warning and remain a bystander."

"Swell," Duncan said, throwing up his hands. "Then let's get on with it."

"Yes, let's do."

Without delay, the street returned to normal, and the previous lull recommenced, although the neighborhood was much louder to him now after having spent minutes in a vacuum (assuming the meter had been running at all). He could not feel the slightest breeze, yet the leaves and flowers trembled on the trees and shrubs around him, as if their roots had reached the distant interstate and, through some magical act of osmosis, tapped into the nocturnal vibrations of those heavy trucks and RVs hoping to shave some time.

There was no way for him to tell if the entity was gone, but he suspected she hadn't moseyed too far.

Moths bumped the glass domes of porch lights, electrical wires hummed, a car engine pinged and ticked as it cooled in a nearby driveway.

Turning, he saw that the wolf was still there, muzzle down, still staring at him. Staring *into* him...

Curious.

He continued to stare back, finding it almost impossible now to peel his eyes away. *Strange, the feeling...*

A glow leaked from the rims of those canine eyes.

So ...Goddamn strange...

Then another mutation of the night air. Something happening...

The neighborhood had changed; was now as it had been, twelve years distant.

Soft, advancing footfalls jarred him away from the wolf. Just as he turned, his partner, Tyler Everton, jogged not past him, but *through* him. There was no sensation whatsoever, but he flinched just the same, as animatedly as if he'd been caught in the crosswalk by a speeding car.

That would also mean that his younger self was already over the fence and coming around the side of the house.

So...it had begun.

His heart was racing again, and a fierce compulsion to merge with his other self began to build.

"Oh, shit," he muttered. Gritting his teeth, he steeled himself against the urging force, one he instantly compared to polyuria, the frequent and profound need to urinate. He'd experienced this in the hospital after demanding that someone remove his catheter, his argument being that if he was able to press the call button that continued to summon nothing but the ward's fattest, homeliest nurses to irrigate his cath, then he was able to hold and shake his own dick, thank you very much.

But nature wasn't calling from his loins. What begged release now was something way deep inside his chest; deeper. His torso was only inches thick, of course, but the force within it seemed to be emanating from the cold sable depths of a mine.

Then his surroundings began to dehydrate, the edges crinkling and curling inward like the sloughed, drying skin of a snake. Within moments, the neighborhood had become something reminiscent of a Beatles' song, a series of rice paper lawns, cellophane streets, and crackleware houses. Translucent pieces of a meal now digesting in the belly of time.

A minute crack started at his feet, then fanned outward into millions of cleaving tendrils. The corollary struck him that he was on a clear, frozen lake—and instantly he was, standing on a thin and amazingly limpid ice field, with no shoreline in sight. Beneath the fracturing sheet, the frigid waters constricted into a black vortex, giving Duncan the illusion that he was staring directly down into a whirlpool. Then the swirling blackness rose to meet his position. Like a lamprey, it attached itself to the underside of the lake's shattered veneer and began to suckle.

"Oh, shit," he whimpered. "Oh, shit, shit—NO!"

He closed his eyes and braced himself for...

Himself.

9.

Amy had been right. That fateful night was not through with him.

Everything was as it had been.

Except now there were two minds—one oil, the other water—

separated by a thin layer of years. And they were in the hands of heavenly hosts whose intentions, Duncan feared, were to shake them into solubility. For what gain, what purpose, Duncan didn't have a clue. But he was certain that this wasn't some divine civility being paid him by his daughter, as he had originally and so immodestly suspected.

No, someone or something was indulging him *and* the clock for entirely different reasons.

Maybe Gamble had been right; maybe these so-called angels had been dancing with man and were heady from the glitter ball's exhausting tempo. Then again, who was he to question divinity's aim, even if its bloodline was tainted? And how could he possibly trust Gamble?

But he was only grasping at straws. And that scared him more than anything else. Not knowing. Not understanding.

Suddenly, there was the feeling that he was being stretched. No— rounded! Like a bubble. Then there was blackness.

Nothingness.

Only the pounding of his heart.

Calm down, he reassured himself, *you're still just a bystander here.* Then...

*****

Duncan was at the front door; his partner Tyler Everton beside him.

"I hope to fuck you know what you're doing, McNeil," Tyler whispered angrily. "Like I told you at Smitty's, I'm doing this for you, not the money. I won't take a fucking dime. We're in and out like Ex-Lax, got it?"

"Like candy from a baby," Duncan assured.

Smitty's was the cop bar they frequented, and the place where Duncan had first told Tyler about his plan. Tyler agreed to help, but not without dumping a truckload of ambivalence on the table.

Duncan rang the bell.

"Who is it?" The inquiry was casual, laid-back. These were not the kind of people you could look at and conclude with any amount of certainty whether they were musicians, accountants, car salespeople, or drug dealers. They were middle-to-upper class lowlifes; not big-time but big enough, smarter than your average scum, but lacking the one vital ingredient that kept most other drug dealers out of prison long enough to put at least thirty-thousand miles on their new Mercedes'. Paranoia. Hell, according to his informant, these people didn't even have an alarm system in their house, not to mention a peephole in the door. No vicious Rottweiler.

"It's Lighthouse," Duncan said. "Tony V.'s with me." These names had been given to Duncan by his informant, who'd promised, "They'll get you in the door."

Despite the hour, a Caucasian male in Hawaiian shorts and a blue tank top blithely opened the door. He smiled, and from behind his glasses his brown eyes hesitated, as if he'd been expecting someone else. Lighthouse and Tony V. was Duncan's guess.

Duncan raised his 9mm Smith and Wesson to the man's face. "Not a peep," he said.

Tyler pushed open the door. Directly ahead, two people sat at a round glass kitchen table, a portly Hispanic man with a handlebar mustache and an attractive female, brunette, early twenties. In the center of the table lay open two Elante aluminum briefcases, one full of heroin, the other money. No paraphernalia on the table, it didn't appear to Duncan that anyone was using, at least not openly. Besides there being nearly a quarter-mil in cash crowding the napkin dispenser, and enough heroin to see Sid Vicious through his next lifetime, there were also three Heineken bottles, a cup of what might have been coffee, and a full ashtray.

Duncan frisked the doorman, then instructed him to join the others at the kitchen table.

With puckered expressions, all three stared at the two masked gunman, the reality of their situation now having fully struck them like a bad case of the runs.

"Everybody remain perfectly fucking still," Duncan ordered. "I want all hands flat on the table."

"Who else is here?" Tyler demanded.

Nobody at the table blinked.

Duncan walked into the kitchen and began patting down the Hispanic man and his female friend for weapons. "My friend asked you a question," Duncan reminded them.

"No one else is here," the Hispanic man finally said, his eyes hesitating a millisecond too long on the drugs.

He pushed the gun to the man's head, then reached over and began lifting out the bags of heroin. Beneath, he found two firearms, a Beretta 92-M9 and a Walther .P380. Each had a full clip and, upon further inspection, a chambered round.

"There's hope for you yet," Duncan congratulated. He confiscated the weapons, each one small enough to fit easily into the front pockets of his camouflaged fatigues. He then tapped the Hispanic man on the shoulder and said, "I need a pen."

The man pointed to a drawer by the stove.

Duncan found the item, then said, "Close the briefcase of money, then rearrange the sequence of numbers on the lock."

The man complied.

"Now," Duncan said, "reinstate the combination."

Removing his left glove, Duncan wrote down the sequence of numbers on his hand as the man turned each dial. "Marvelous," he said. "Now, show me it opens."

It did.

"Good. Okay, repeat step one," he instructed. "Excellent. Now, pucker up and kiss it all goodbye."

Staring down into his lap, the doorman said, almost a whisper, "Man, you are so fucking dead."

Duncan nodded. "Because I don't know who I'm dealing with, right?"

Still avoiding eye contact, the doorman said, "That's right."

Duncan put a finger under the doorman's chin, then raised the man's face to his own. "I've seen bigger shit stains on flypaper. I'm only taking the money, so just accept the fact that you and El Porko here are going to have to recoup your losses the old-fashioned way—put more cut in the product."

Tyler remained at the entrance to the kitchen, allowing himself full view of the interior. "Get it and go!"

"You guys are cops, huh?" said the Hispanic male. He spat at the floor. "Dirty fucking cops."

"You haven't been paying attention," Duncan said. "We're the robbers."

"Damn it! Hurry the fuck up!" Tyler insisted.

Duncan paused to slip on his glove, noticing as he did the young woman, shaking badly. Her long, acrylic nails might have been tapping out Morse code on the tabletop. But it was her nose that intrigued him, as it wanted to point in a particular direction, the rest of her face resisting the pull.

Body language. How wonderfully betraying.

"Just do it!" Tyler yelled, rocking on his tip-toes now, as if the walls and ceiling were spiked *a la* Indiana Jones and closing in at an extremely uncomfortable pace.

Duncan inventoried the table again: three green beer bottles, each one at least half full, a cup of coffee, an ashtray...

He grabbed the cup. It read, TO ALL YOU VIRGINS: THANKS FOR NOTHING! He held it against his cheek. Still warm; the bouquet of red lipstick still fresh.

He grabbed the girl's chin and gently pulled her face around. No lipstick there.

"Alright," Duncan said, "either you're all lying, or one of you cross-dressing faggots is chasing his Heineken down with Maxwell House." He pressed the muzzle against the doorman's ear. "Are you a Clairol man?" he growled. "Or is there something you forgot to tell me and my friend?"

Before the man could answer, somewhere in the house a baby coughed.

Tyler raised his firearm and targeted on something that was out of Duncan's line of sight. "Get your ass in here now, lady!" he commanded. "Move it!"

Duncan ordered everyone to make like statues. He grabbed the briefcase of money with his left hand, the 9mm in his other, raised and searching.

The child was squalling now, having been frightened by Tyler's outburst.

Just before he breached the kitchen's wide threshold, Duncan pointed the gun at the Hispanic male and said, "Two seconds to tell me who else is in this house or I'm gonna put a hole in that empty piñata of yours."

"It's just my wife, Sandra, and our baby," he implored. "Please, don't hurt them. Just take what you want and go."

"Gun!" Tyler cried. "She's got a gun!"

(The angel had been right. It may have been as early as yesterday when he'd decided that he wouldn't change a thing should a gust of time blow him back into this house. Earlier, he'd wanted to tell Gamble that kismet had nothing to worry about, as he had no intentions of changing so much as a light bulb this evening.

Just remain a bystander.

Damn. It was so fiercely tempting not to, knowing the shitstorm that was coming.

How many times had he been back?

As many lessons as deemed necessary...

He didn't exactly know what she'd meant by that, but he figured it was safe to assume that, throwing physics and the Dewey decimal system to the wind, the purpose of his existence might be hinged upon nothing less than the perpetual re-enactment of this night; to experience every conceivable outcome until the desired sequence of events had been achieved. And when that was finally done, then what? Would the continuity machine start back up with a hiss-bang? Would destiny's father pass out cigars?

But he was getting ahead of himself, was speculating about matters upon which he had neither rank nor aptitude. Nevertheless, the possibility that his existence might be nothing more than a phonograph needle caught in an interminable groove was as disturbing as it was antiquated.

No, he would just remain a bystander. Just...

Go with the flow.)

Duncan came out of the kitchen. "Freeze!" he ordered the lady.

She didn't freeze. Hell, she didn't even congeal, but kept right on coming with her squalling brat. Barefoot, and wearing only a white terrycloth robe that could have been pulled twice around her sallow figure, she staggered like a skid row lush as she entered the living room from the hallway. She was monstrously stoned on heroin.

Duncan saw the weapon. It was in the lady's right hand (the one supporting the infant), most of it concealed by the child's blue swaddling blanket. But enough prevailed that he could determine it was a single action .357.

Time was slowing, and the room's acoustics had become those of an empty auditorium.

"Christ, lady, drop the gun, or I swear I'll put you down!" Tyler promised, puberty revisiting his vocal chords. He was in a rigid stance, knees slightly bent, feet spread apart, both hands clutching his gun.

If his partner were to fire a shot now, Duncan thought, he would shatter from the repercussion like a cheap vase.

As if someone had flipped a switch, the baby stopped bawling, and as a bead of sweat left its salty signature on his lips, Duncan realized why. The lady had pulled back the lapel of her robe, allowing the infant to suckle her right breast.

The three people at the table remained seated; however, with each wobbly step the lady took, desperation broadened her husband's eyes.

Duncan, without looking back, said to the Hispanic man, "Easy, asshole. If you so much as blink, I'll drop her and the brat both."

Duncan was sure he could hear the man's ears begin to whistle, the rage starting to vent like steam through a kettle. But then, within the eerie silence, even a mute spider spinning a web under ten feet of water could make an obnoxious racket.

As the woman swiveled the gun beneath her baby's back, aiming for Tyler, a depraved grin formed along her mouth. The blued barrel had a sheen as liquid as her eyes, the light from the ceiling fixture gliding along its surface like the bubble of a carpenter's tool, squaring her intent.

Duncan saw something in his partner's eyes then; something imperiling. "No, Tyler!" he commanded. "Don't shoot!"

Ever so slightly, Tyler lowered his gun.

Slowing still, time began to seize. He had experienced decelerating time once before, in another life-or-death situation, and he knew that it was during these terrifying seconds when people claimed to have seen their life flash before their eyes. Duncan had been spared the replay then, and—what he hoped was a good omen—that biographical footage had yet to make the projection booth this time around.

A puff of smoke erupted beneath the infant, followed not quite instantaneously by a sluggish peal of thunder.

Within this drowsy sequence of time, Duncan thought to start running toward his partner, as if he could beat the shot and push him out of harm's way. They were both wearing Kevlar vests, but those didn't protect the head or groin, and there was no guarantee that they would save your life when struck by a bullet, the body absorbing the shock of the impact, which could kill you just as dead depending on the caliber of slug. Unlike in the movies, people wearing Kevlar weren't likely to get right back on their feet and brush themselves off after colliding with a .357 magnum round. When they did, they were the exception, not the rule.

(Desperate now, the older Duncan thought to do something, anything, to disrupt the old course of events; to throw a log in the stream and maybe misdirect the flow. But, incongruous to their quasi-lethargic succession, the events were unfolding too fast for his mind to outmaneuver them.)

The bullet spun Tyler around, his gun sailing away from his hand.

(It had nicked his aorta, the older Duncan remembered. Bullet-proof vests weren't very effective against Teflon-coated rounds either, otherwise known as armor-piercing, able to go through Kevlar and engine blocks the way wind goes through chicken wire.)

The baby screamed.

Grimacing, Tyler dropped to his knees and yelled, "Shoot the bitch! What the fuck are you waiting for? Shoot! *Shoot!*"

The lady just kept coming, staggering like some relentless, lactating mummy avenging a Pharaoh's curse.

Duncan shuffled over to where his partner now lay, and just as he raised his gun and put the lady's head between the sights, Tyler grabbed his ankle with a bloody hand. "Fuck you very much," he gurgled. "I hope she's worth it."

"Just hang on, buddy," Duncan ordered. "Just hang on."

The woman stopped. He didn't feel there was a clear, confident shot, not at their distance, not with an infant in the way. And he wasn't about to turn this mess into outright calamity by murdering a child.

He lowered his gun, backing toward the door.

Another thunderclap.

The bullet entered his chest and exited just below his left scapula.

(According to the forensics report, the older Duncan recalled, it passed through the wall, punched through the metal stanchion of a street light fifty-five yards away, and finally through the bay window of one elderly couple, Mr. and Mrs. Adam Bainbridge. It came to rest within the cranium of Sir Alec Guinness Bainbridge, "Whiskers" for short, who had been grooming himself atop the backrest of the living room sofa, 1.7 football fields distant from the point of origin.

If Tyler Everton had not suffered any fatal wounds, and had subsequently learned that a cat had perished during the ordeal, he would have died nonetheless, as his heart would have surely exploded upon such rapturous news. Duncan had never in his life met anyone who detested cats as much—

Something occurred to him just then; something Dead Man had said after running over the tabby .

One down, ten billion more to go...

No way, he thought. *Couldn't be.*)

Breathing was becoming arduous, and his vision was ebbing and flowing like a siren, which he was expecting to hear any minute. Lots of them. He had to get out of the house fast.

Two more shots sailed wide right, through the door.

Assuming the gun had its full complement of six rounds, that meant that she had two shots left.

He grabbed for the doorknob.

*****

Suddenly, the room was full of people.

His legs were folded under him now as he sat slumped against the wall, just beside the door. His breaths were coming quick and shallow, and his chest throbbed with an ache that seemed to go miles deep.

A voice whispered in his ear: "You're going to be okay, Duncan."

The voice belonged to a heavyset woman. Late forties, he guessed. Through his blurred vision, he gazed at her pretty face.

Even though there were people all around him now—fifteen, maybe twenty—the commotion was knitted with...

Stillness.

His legs were ice cold.

Then he saw Tyler's lifeless body on the floor, and the lady who had shot them both, still standing there in the living room, grinning, arms curled inward, gun in one hand. But the baby and its swaddling blanket were gone. And the more he stared, the more he realized that it was just a still frame, the scene frozen in time; a centerpiece in the midst of a bustling banquet.

"You performed wonderfully," said the heavyset woman.

"Just like the first time," said a man with a burly voice. "Almost to the letter."

Duncan tried to sit up, sliding in his own congealing blood. "Who...who in the hell are you people?"

There was a big black man standing beside him now. "I think I should answer that," he said.

That voice was familiar. Duncan craned up at the face and, as he blinked his vision clear, recognized the man as his old police lieutenant, Mo White.

"Mo?" he said. "You're not supposed to be here yet."

"This is intermission," Mo said. "And in answer to your question, we're the ones who helped bring you and the seraph back to this night."

The taste of gunpowder was still thick in Duncan's throat. "I'm sorry, the *seraph?*"

"That's right. It's living inside you. On the force, this is what we call field training."

"Translate."

Mo placed a hand on Duncan's head, and immediately the throbbing pain decreased, his breathing returned to normal. "See, McNeil, the events of this very night are what entrusted you to the seraph, why it chose you to be what has been a long line of tutors. And in your case, a breeder, too. Being a veteran police officer, and later a homicide detective, you're a veritable encyclopedia on the perversions of mankind. But a very special set of circumstances pervade this evening. The seraph's especially interested in learning from your conduct, what led you to become so reviling, so merciless against your solemn pledge to perform the contrary. And, likewise, it's fascinated by the emotions that are conversely interwoven with your actions; you know, the shame, remorse, guilt, dishonor."

"You mean, it learns from irony."

"Oh, it loves irony. And that you did it out of something that you thought was love, well..."

"My connection with Patricia and Kathy seems a bit coincidental, don't you think?"

"It knew the role you would play in their lives years before you were ever on the scene. A gifted psychic tipped us off when she passed over. I shouldn't say gifted—she was blessed. She saw this night, among others, and its connection to Patricia and Katherine Bently."

"I was snitched out?" Duncan said. "By a ghost?"

"Amy will explain it to you in due time."

"Well, I doubt the seraph commends my chivalry."

"It ain't here to judge you, m'man. It's here to learn. It's here to save its ass, and by consequence save everyone else's. When Gamble first came along, he slaughtered all of its kind. They didn't know how to fight back, didn't have a clue. They were too pure of God. But somehow this one managed to escape and hide in the mind of man. Not in the collective mind, like Gamble, but in the individual mind. From there it started breeding, creating a population of half-breeds. Us. Given our heritage, though, we'll never be strong enough to take on Gamble, even as a group. Only the seraph has the potential to destroy the clone devil."

"Then why did it find it necessary to breed?"

"The seraph figured out, because of our genetic link to man, that we'd be able to travel through time. See, it has no perception of time—not the faulty ways in which man does. We have a kind of symbiotic relationship with the seraph, as far as an understanding of time goes. It learned this the very first day of kindergarten. But I don't expect you to understand.

You don't have the dimensional capacity. So, it set about sowing its seed. We also keep a vigilant watch, making sure that Gamble never catches wind of it whereabouts."

"So, it was stuck in idle until the first of your kind matured."

"Yeah, it stayed hidden. First and foremost, it learned what it was to be secretive. As far as our maturity goes, we grow up very fast. Take your daughter. She may only be ten in human years, but in angel years she has an adult form, when she wishes to assume it."

"What about Gamble? I mean, can't he just travel through time and make things miserable for you guys?"

"No. Gamble can't time travel. That's where we have the edge."

"Okay, if you're all so clever, then why not just travel back far enough and prevent Gamble's own creation?"

"We only have a vague idea when, and haven't the foggiest idea where, to look. The collective mind is as vast as the universe. And we're not as clever as you might think. We make mistakes. And the seraph's very strict when it comes to the use of time travel. You see, the more we do it, the more degraded our ability becomes."

"When I met Gamble, just before I was brought back, he was insistent that I not make the same mistake twice. Care to tell me why?"

"Gamble knows about our travels in time. And by now he might very well know why, but there's not a damned thing he can do about it."

"What about you guys? Are you able to fight back, or did you inherit the seraph's impotence for aggression?"

"Each succeeding offspring shows a marked improvement, parallel to the seraph's level at the time of its conception."

"So the more recent ones are meaner than the older ones?"

"That's right."

Duncan managed a smile. "Then that must mean my daughter has quite the temper."

"Being the baby of the bunch, that's why she's in charge. She's one spiteful lady."

"Where *is* Amy?"

"I'm afraid she's indisposed right now. But listen, this night just isn't about the seraph reliving one of its favorite lessons again. It's about you learning something, too. It's time you straighten up and take inventory, m'man. The seraph wants you to take something back with you tonight."

"What, that I'm an asshole?"

"I can't tell you what," Mo said. "That's against the rules. The seraph still can't help but play the divinity game sometimes. You have to figure it out for yourself."

"And if I can't?"

"Then I have a feeling we'll be having this conversation once again, same time, same place."

Duncan watched a tall, thin woman remove the ski mask from Tyler's face.

The heavyset woman was back, this time with a baby in her arms. "Step aside," she said. "It's time to brand the boy."

With a great big smile, Mo said, "This is one of the other victuals that the seraph loves about this night."

The heavyset woman placed the infant on Duncan's vest and, gently rolling its head, swiped its mouth across the pooling blood.

It began to cry. The heavyset woman lifted the baby away, and she whispered, "Thank you."

"The seraph's signature is in your blood," Mo said. "Now it's in the baby."

"I don't understand."

"It's so the seraph can track it down later," Mo said.

"No, I mean, what's so important about the baby?"

"I was getting to that. Now, this boy, just given—and what will continue to be once we resume here—its extreme proximity to the discharges of its mother's handgun, will be rendered, for all intents and purposes, deaf as a stone. Interestingly, what the seraph will discover twelve years from now is that this boy, at the age of thirteen, will be the leader of one of the nastiest juvenile gangs in Chicago."

"And..."

"This boy will find a way to overcome his disability in such a way that not only will he heroically succeed in gaining the respect of his peers, but his very nature as a hardened and riotous delinquent will prove to be quintessential in the seraph's final stages of learning. You see, the seraph has a disability too—*a learning disability*. It has spent generation upon generation studying the nuances and subtleties and incongruities of wars and violence of all kind, of every conceivable atrocity committed by man against man, all the while overlooking one vital ingredient. It won't be until it begins living vicariously within the boy, throughout the pivotal moments of his life, that it finally learns something integral, something that it was lacking, something that it can finally put behind all the aggression, put behind the fight, and that something is *confidence*. Without the will, the resolve, defeat is a cruel mistress."

"The boy will teach it to have faith in itself."

"Exactly."

Duncan was listing to one side now, his right shoulder nearly touching the floor. "Are we through here, Mo? I'd like to get this night over with."

"Okay, buddy," Mo said, "tell you what I'm gonna do. As in the other times, we haven't let you remember this part of the evening, but as a gift to you, I'm gonna let you keep this memory—only because I feel confident that you're later gonna blossom with self-discovery. It's vitally important to the seraph that you do. It owes you one. So don't disappoint me. Ya dig?"

"I dig."

There was an immediate burst of light, then...

*****

He was standing again, reaching for the door, taking up where he'd left off.

In the living room directly before him stood the woman with the baby in her arms, grinning at him as she increased the pressure on the trigger of her gun. The baby was wailing to beat the band.

Everyone else was still at the table, the portly Hispanic male standing now. "Shoot that motherfucker!" he ordered the woman.

(*Get out!* Duncan warned his younger self. *She's going to shoot you in the back!*)

Duncan opened the door—and there stood Lieutenant Mo White. Instantly, he jumped in front of the lieutenant. Mo stumbled backward just as a bullet punched though Duncan's vest and lower right back. He wet his pants as he fell to the lawn and began praying for God's forgiveness, something he hadn't done since he was a teenager, when he still believed absolution was something obtainable.

Another bullet, her last, splintered the door jam.

As he rolled onto his back, he couldn't decide which burned deeper: the bullet holes, or his hypocrisy.

Mo turned him on his side.

Long blades of grass were poking at his lips. He stuck his tongue out and licked at the dew, moaning at the sweetness.

Without manhandling him too much, Mo removed Duncan's vest, ripped his blue wool sweater up the middle, turned him over, then plugged the entrance and exit wounds with his fingers.

Duncan reached up to touch the Saint Christopher medal dangling from Mo's neck.

The silver was captivating.

"Easy, buddy, easy."

(No, it wasn't St. Christopher at all, he now realized. It looked...it looked like...

It was a silver dog tag, and the insignia was evident to him. It was the same symbol that was on the grips of Dead Man's gun. And, he realized, it may very well have been the design on Dr. Strickland's necklace. It was unarguably iconoclast, as a sword was centered between seven dragons' heads, all embossed over a lambs head touting seven horns and seven eyes. When Duncan had first seen the emblems on the grips, it struck him as being fanatically Semitic, but he hadn't given it any more thought until now.

He recalled the table discussion they'd had the night before. Mrs. Pendleton had told them that the number seven was significant to many religious tomes, the *Holy Bible* included. She'd mentioned the Seven Seals, Seven Angels, Seven Candles, Seven deadly Sins, Seven Falls of Man...)

"So *you* were the wolf," Duncan said.

"Naw, that was someone else. We all got the same jeweler."

Duncan pointed to the open door. "Tyler."

"Tyler's dead," Mo said. "I'm sorry."

Just then, two men in plain clothes appeared at the doorway, guns drawn. Duncan recognized them as undercover narcotics officers.

"Freeze!" they ordered as they entered the house, one behind the other.

"Those are my guys," Mo said. "We got this all worked out. Did you see the load of heroin we bagged? We're heroes! Hell, I'll even see that you get a medal for saving my life."

Duncan reached for the suitcase that had slipped from his hand when he fell to the lawn.

Mo grabbed it before he could. "Don't worry, McNeil. I'll make sure Patricia Bently gets the money. Never figured you for such a romantic, though."

"Makes us even," Duncan said, his world beginning to spin. "I never figured you for some half-assed angel."

"Listen up now," Mo said, removing Duncan's ski mask. "This is what we're gonna do. Gonna get your older self back on the bus with the others, so I need you to look up into my eyes."

Duncan did, and found in their place two black marbles expanding in size, each containing an infinite universe. Within moments they enfolded him, wrapped him like a cocoon, then he turned into a bubble.

10.

Duncan opened his eyes, drew in a large breath of air, and realized he was standing before the doors of the shuttle.

The doors opened and he stepped inside.

All eyes turned to him. Then they left him and fixed upon the driver. Suddenly in Dead Man's place was sitting a handsome man in his early thirties, wearing a police officer's dress blues. A five-point hat was resting on his lap.

The very uniform, Duncan now guessed, in which his partner had been buried.

"Nice to see you again, McNeil," said the driver in a fuller, more replete voice than Dead Man's.

"I suspected as much," Duncan said, extending a hand. "Good to have you back, Ty. All the way, I mean."

"Tyler?" Patricia said, standing now. "*Tyler Everton?*"

"Don't look so spooked," Tyler said, then turned to Rachel. "It's better than my Grim Reaper outfit, isn't it?"

"But...I went to your funeral," Patricia said.

Rachel nodded, indicating that she'd attended the memorial service, as well.

"And I appreciate that," he said. "Really."

"Then why show up as a corpse?" Rachel said, pissed. "Damn it, why all the games?"

"To help acclimate you, for one," he said.

Chris and Juanita just stared at the driver, sharing the same bewildered expression.

Duncan said, "This was my—I'm sorry, *is* my partner, Tyler Everton."

Chris nodded a greeting. "Dude."

To his partner reborn, Duncan said, "I'm so sorry about what happened back there, Ty. Jesus, if I—"

"Don't sweat it," Tyler said.

Juanita turned to Kathy. She appraised the girl with more certainty than not, then asked, "You knew all along that Dead Man was this Tyler Everton?"

"Sure," Kathy said. Then she stood, walked over to Duncan, and put her arms around his waist, hugging him. "Thank you, Donut. You did great."

"Don't go thanking me just yet," he cautioned.

She gazed clemently into his eyes, focusing on something beyond the wetness, the glimmer. "It left in you remarkable wonders," she said. "More than I'd imagined." She stepped away from him and smiled. "Indulge them."

"You've been holding out, little miss," Patricia said. "What else haven't you told us?"

"Gobs," she said, then turned to Tyler. "Now, let's go get the boy."

"What boy?" Chris asked.

"You oughta know," Kathy said, "you plugged him in."

Truly baffled, Chris just stared at her. "Oh yeah, wait, of course, the kid in Chicago. Went in pretending I was Santa Claus." After chewing a moment on this disclosure, he chuckled. "*That* kid? No shit?"

Kathy smiled. "No shit."

"What did you 'plug' this boy into?" Patricia said.

"I don't know," Chris said. "They never tell me."

Duncan was still appraising the conversation he'd had with Gamble. Why had Gamble been so concerned with him going back in time? Was there something else about the boy Mo hadn't told him? Was the seraph living inside the boy now? He looked at Kathy. "Why are we going after the boy?"

"We're supposed to protect him."

"Fair enough," he said. "Let's go, Tyler."

Rachel glared at Duncan; not so unlike the way she had, he thought, when learning of his infidelity.

"You had better translate for me, Mr. McNeil," she growled. "What boy are we talking about?"

"Emilio Chavez," Duncan offered. "The one I just saved."

And then it occurred to him that—in this and whatever other times around—his intentions had been no less valorous than if he'd rescued the child from a burning building, as it no longer mattered that he'd set the fire himself. Yes, the circumstances were crooked, but his heart had not been, at least not in those telling moments. If his soul had ever been incorruptible, it was then. Yes, he had truly sacrificed his own life for the child's.

It was time that he forgave himself. That was *his* lesson.

And now it appeared—and by no means fortuitously—that he was going to have to save the boy one more time.

But...was it going to be the first time, he wondered, the last, or somewhere in between?

Part Six
Seraphim

1.

Aside from the fact that theirs was the only moving automobile, Boston looked very much real. Still, now that it was done with him, Duncan knew it was only a stage abandoned by time-hopping thespians.

As Tyler crested the on-ramp, seven toll booths loomed ahead on the interstate.

Tyler peeked into his overhead mirror. "Which one, Chris?"

After a few routine ticks and jerks, Chris barked, "One!"

"I hope you know where you're going," Patricia said to Chris.

As the shuttle entered the first lane, approaching the booth, a red gate descended before them.

The attendant slid aside the glass window.

"Know where the nearest Stuckey's is from here?" Tyler asked the hooded employee.

Although its face was concealed within the shadows of the burnoose, there was no doubt the attendant was humored, but not just with Tyler. It was megrim with all of them.

With a voice full of good cheer, it said, "There once was a band of do-gooders, who chartered a bus for loftier tours, but the fare at the toll, was more than they could dole, so now it's a trip to the sewers."

Duncan was already on his feet. "Back it up, Tyler," he ordered. "Back this fucking thing up now."

Tyler slammed into reverse.

"NO!" Patricia cried. "Behind us!"

There, in the gray dimness that was just moments before the carapace of Boston, stood armies of cloaked figures, not so unlike the booth's attendant, each grasping its own sickle and grinning a skeleton's grin. The Reaper, cloned to the nth power, bellicose in intent.

Overhead, thousands of harpies swooped and circled angrily; starving vultures ireful and confused over the reanimated, meatless dead below.

A crevice, as deep and black as frigid space, separated them from the ghoulish legions.

"We've already passed the threshold," Kathy said.

The attendant pushed a lever, lifting the red gate, beyond which lay a paved, narrow road sided by an ever-morphing landscape, as if an indecisive, psychotic god had been caught in the act of creation.

"Enjoy your visit," said the attendant. "And please, try to not feed the animals."

Tyler shifted into first gear. "Fuck you very much."

Clutching her rosary to her chest, Juanita turned to Chris. "You stupid little shit—you picked the wrong gate!"

Chris did not meet her gaze, just stared out at the roistering worlds ahead of them.

Duncan was already on his way down the aisle, toward Chris.

"Don't hurt him, Duncan," Rachel warned.

Yanking Chris out of his seat, he said, "Where the fuck are we?"

"I don't..." Chris started, then relented. "I had to, dude! He promised to hurt Patricia and Kathy if I didn't. Hurt them bad."

"If you didn't what?"

"Bring...bring you in."

"Bring me into *where?*" Duncan growled.

Chris's eyes were pleading now. "Into his mind, into Gamble's Wonderland."

"Oh, Jesus," Tyler moaned. "Oh sweet Jesus."

Duncan stared deeply into Chris's eyes, as if searching for the kinds of torture he would lavish upon this Judas.

"A sign!" Patricia said. "Up ahead, there's a sign!"

Chris collapsed back into his seat as Duncan released him, heading up the aisle now, toward the windshield.

As a stationary piece upon a permutating puzzle, there was nothing prototypically wrong with the sign, the kind of large green placard one so often encounters on the highways of America. It was the message, however, that would have had any literate motorist heavily pondering its meaning way into the next town. That was, if they hadn't already pulled to the curb to puke on their dashboards.

WELCOME TO THE BEAUTIFUL STATE OF KISS MY ASS

PLEASE DON'T LITTER

2.

Following Mr. Gamble, Eli managed to enter the window with little effort. His Milquetoast mother, on the other hand, along with her vituperative mouth, had to be pulled up and in; into a place even more twisted and snarled than her rants and ravings. Into a twilight world of sinking, deep-violet skies, toward which the dour delineations of massive baobab trees reached with morbid intentions. Herds of animals clustered in the far distance, their species unclear. It was dusk encroaching upon an African savannah—only this one being reminisced, Eli thought, in the Ebola-ravished mind of a Botswana tribesman.

Gamble was nowhere to be seen.

"This place stinks," his mother growled, peering around, as if searching for any signs of the pictures that had been touted in the brochure. Beside Josephine, leashed to her hand like a dog, Jacob gave his coat the once-over.

But Eli was already trotting away from them, flapping his wings, looking for all the world like some depraved lunatic determined to finally get Leonardo Da Vinci and his ornithopter out of *The 15th Century's Biggest Duds* and into the more respectable pages of *Popular Mechanics*.

"Ha!" Josephine yelled after him. "Save your strength, choir boy!"

After fifty yards, however, Eli was no longer running.

He was flying.

3.

Just minutes past the placard, the road forked yet again into seven different directions: three stretching out to their left, three to their right, or they could continue straight ahead.

Still stinging from his gallant though no less foolish decision to trick them straight to Hell, no one solicited Chris's psychic opinion on the matter, nor had he volunteered one. Rather, it had been Juanita pointing the way this time.

It really wasn't *her* way, she'd explained, but the Blessed Mother's.

"'Know now that if you pass on my right'," she'd quoted Mary, "'the fields are thin and bane, pass on my left and the river runs but a fiery wind. Continue onward and you will be blessed with the Father's own mighty hand.'"

Kathy sealed the deal when she agreed with Juanita. That was all the convincing anyone needed.

Duncan stared out at the alternating vistas; the insalubrious thought processes of a demigod wracked with fever.

Then, suddenly, the worlds united into one; the windows of a slot machine finally showing up "jackpot."

Now upon them, the prospect of nightfall bruised a sky in lethargic descent, while below ridges of razor-sharp mountains and, closer still, the gnarled and defoliated branches of immense trees aimed to shred that contused skin should it weaken and fall. Molten rivers, distant and orange amid the scabrous periphery, oozed leisurely away into the rifts and fissures, feeling no obligation whatsoever to warm the cold, settling night. Nearby, shadows groped worm-careful from their sponsors, cast by the spectral light of a meandering, non-existent moon.

Africa, Duncan thought, *in a Dali-esque sort of way.*

If the good Virgin's insinuation had been that they would enter God's mind should her itinerary be followed, then they'd arrived far too late, Duncan thought, if their goal was to save the Old Boy from a nervous breakdown.

"Company," Tyler said.

A figure up ahead, alongside the road. A man, his arm out, thumb extended.

4.

Eli hovered attentively over his mother, his wings swathing the air, though far too slowly to actually keep him aloft. But here, those old rules didn't apply. Physics was now but a dream, and the dream now reality.

Dazzled in wavering shards of heat, a gargantuan structure loomed in the distance.

The moment he'd stepped foot into the window a heightened consciousness burgeoned in his being. It was as if he were back inside a recurrent lucid dream, but with no fear of waking, this time having finally sneaked passed the veil of retrogress. Yes, he *knew* these odd environs, how to navigate them, sensed the direction he should now take, as if a long-dormant chromosome had suddenly awakened, triggering in him the sapience necessary to comprehend and, ultimately, have elite governance over this new kingdom.

Trepidation, however, was still a friend to be heeded. He would test these waters carefully, alluring as they were, and try not to drown in them.

Stick to the plan, Stan.

His covenant with Gamble had finally and so graciously been secured. And it was beyond all his expectations, his euphoria reaching critical mass, threatening to irradiate the duskiness that had for now, it seemed, postponed its slide into the inkier depths of night.

Below him, however, Josephine hampered aimlessly on; just as she had, Eli mused, throughout her preceding and much more confining reality, no wiser for the wear.

Each time Jacob would pause to inspect a smell, or to do a bit of grooming, she would grouse and yank his leash.

"He's not a basset hound, Mother. Keep it up and he'll likely have you for dinner."

"Ha!" She was shaking her cane at him now. "Get your ass down here, Eli! I mean it!"

"I've places to go," he said

"Well, don't wait for me, batboy! You can fly your sorry butt into the side of a cliff for all I care. Just stop gloating over me like some goddamn vulture!"

"If you would just let me carry you, we could be off—"

"No!" she insisted. "It ain't natural. I'll stay planted firmly on the ground, if it's all the same to you."

It wasn't. He fluttered down, reaching for her shoulders.

"Fuck off!" she cried, batting him away with her cane.

"Alright, have it your way. Just don't dally. Once you reach the aviary, stay there and wait for Mr. Gamble's instructions."

She squinted at the structure in the distance. "That what that is? Some kind of bird sanctuary?"

"I mean it mother," he warned. "No fiddle-farting around, or there'll be hell to pay."

"That supposed to scare me, batboy?"

"Yes," he said, "it is."

5.

Twilight had ripened but stopped short of falling off the vine.

Mantled in shadow, the shuttle's interior now donned the dreary attributes of a tomb.

With everyone on their feet, Tyler switched on the headlights, illuminating the hitchhiker.

"Oh my God!" Patricia cried. "That's him!"

"Him who?" Rachel said, squinting through the windshield.

"Jack Fortune," Duncan said, answering for her.

As if Duncan couldn't speak the truth if he had sodium pentothal for blood, Rachel turned to Patricia. "*He's* Jack Fortune?"

"AKA Mr. Gamble," Chris offered, breaking his shame-induced silence. "Satan plagiarized."

Juanita gasped. "The one who was shaped from a ball of clay? That is him?"

"Close enough for Government work," Chris said, moving up the aisle.

Another figure now, approaching from their left. Low in the sky, it soared majestically toward them.

"Well, looks like we won't need to go to Seattle, after all," Rachel said, staring at the winged entity. "It's come to us."

"It's the priest," Kathy confirmed.

Alighting upon the road, his appendages folding crisply behind him, the priest made his short way to Gamble's side. A winged emissary, steadfast and true; shirtless, wearing only khakis and white sneakers. And a smile that said he was now curator of this shop; eyes that relayed a confidence just a breath below the certitude spangling in Gamble's own.

The prodigal son, Duncan thought.

As Gamble approached, Tyler rolled down his window.

"Mr. Kaddison," Gamble began, peering in, "I ask for a grape, and you bring me the vineyard." He winked at Juanita. "Migrant workers included! Now, in light of your generosity, I'm almost inclined to become a man of my word. But then, that would make me one of the good guys, wouldn't it?"

Thrusting a finger at Gamble, Chris said, "We had a deal, you asshole!"

Gamble clucked. "If I had a day for every time some poor schmuck said that to me, I'd be ten years past Tuesday."

"Alright," Duncan said. "You want me, you got me. Just let everyone else go."

Feigning surprise, Gamble placed a hand over his heart. "Why, Donut! And to think I was recently informed that chivalry was dead." He waved a finger. "But first things first," he said, rolling his eyes to Kathy. "You have something of mine, you little winch. And since I'm under the incontrovertible impression that you're not going to hand yourself over, I suppose I'm going to have to get creative, eh? Smoke you out, as they say?"

Kathy remained seated. Accosted again by a voice not her own, she said simply, "You can't have her."

"We'll see," Gamble said, then turned to the priest. "Fetch me the package, will you, Father?"

As if suffused by a sudden gust of wind, the priest's leather sails billowed outward. "Right away," he said, then took to the air.

6.

The first worm wriggled from the soil and stretched its glistening, vermicular body across the mound. In quick peristaltic movements, it disgorged a viscous substance. With serrated mandibles it began shaping the matter the way a bee fashions wax. Another worm wriggled beside the first and affixed its own pulpy retch to the tiny segment.

Then a third arrived.

A fourth.

Within minutes, a multitude of worms squirmed upon the surface, each one focusing on a particular area, adding vomitus to a puzzle as yet unrecognizable.

Upon the leafless branches above, marsupial-like creatures skittered in uncertainty, squeaking their displeasure, their whiskered noses bobbing frantically in the air.

Faster and faster, the worms worked; snaking and slithering and undulating, up and around, over and under, spewing and ejecting, shaping and constructing.

Still not yet discernible, the project was nonetheless taking greater form. The freshly forged parts shone like polished silver, turning a rich vermillion as they cooled.

Then, finally, into bone and muscle, flesh and hair. *Eyes.*

The squealing creatures above were now delirious, tripping and hopping and loping over one another to get to higher branches.

Completely reformed, Amy took in a huge breath of air. She turned her head, but found that Melanie Sands was no longer with her. Not only had she failed to cleanse Melanie of Gamble's daughter, she'd failed to save Melanie, period. Her magic proved successful against the worms, but somehow the link had been broken between her and Melanie by Gamble's own sorcery. Just one more sign that she was still too weak.

Now Gamble had six daughters, making him even more powerful.

She sat up, assuming her adult form.

This was not the first time she'd tried saving Melanie, but that didn't make her failure any less painful.   .

7.

Eli soared, his thoughts gliding cleanly and evenly through his mind; as unimpaired as his wings upon the windless twilight.

It was magic. And it was magic*al*. No longer would he need to shake the glass ball to incite glittering confetti upon miniature landmarks once visited, to excite flurries of snow upon cheesy winter vistas—or perturb any such unimaginative keepsake for nostalgia's sake; those mementoes, those old frames of reference purchased from the roadside displays and curio shelves of vacationlands utterly aseptic in comparison.

No longer was he on the outside looking in.

In *this* world, he would terminate any illusion of reality as he'd once known it, would eradicate with extreme prejudice those sentiments that are likely to skulk away amid the unbridled novelty and seek haven in the deepest ravines of an erstwhile imagination. Then, upon those quivering, obsolete notions, he would, with a single stroke of thought, commence creating lands and peoples—and set upon them astonishing wickedness should they forget to kneel and give thanks.

Yet, something continued to mar his exultation; something disturbing him. Blotches had begun appearing on his wings; initially only a dappling affect created by shadow, he was sure, and from there enhanced by his own imagination into more valid, more permanent shapes. But now, the closer he got to the boy, he was aware—and annoyingly so—that his eyes weren't playing tricks.

Something *was* showing through. But what, he didn't have the faintest idea.

Far below, he could now make out the boy, his bleak form alone within a circle of bushes. No, not bushes, he now realized, but animals of some kind; hyena-like. Gamble, it appeared, had taken precautions that the boy stay put, or suffer a mauling he was not likely to crawl away from.

The boy's eyes, as pursuing as his ears were reined, now fixed skyward upon him.

As Eli descended, he was reminded of a verse from Psalms. "'Be still,'" he cried, arms outstretched for the boy, "'and know that I am God!'"

8.

The sky bowed inward with each inhalation, then reset as Gamble breathed the slow, cadenced breaths of a transcendental practitioner reciting a mantra.

"...ohmmmm, ohmmmm," he chanted before them, now cross-legged upon the roadway, hands on knees, thumbs and middle fingers fused in harmony. "...ohmmmmm, ohmmmmm..."

Patricia was staring at Chris, wearing the evocative expression of a customer irksome over the proprietor's inability to speak the English language. "Excuse me?" she said.

Chris sighed. "Okay, look, I'll explain it this way: without his daughters, Gamble wouldn't be able to maintain the charade as well. Like, they free him up so he can concentrate on more important things, like being a dickhead."

Rachel said to Kathy, "And you said he needs seven offspring to succeed, and that one of them is inside *you?*"

Kathy just nodded.

"Why seven?" Duncan said to Chris. "And why girls?"

"That's just his way, dude. I believe it's a spoof on biblical innuendo. The number seven. Like, if he'd elected to go with forty masturbating chimpanzees in hoop skirts, it wouldn't matter. You're trying to figure him out from a rational perspective. Gamble is the antithesis of rational. He made his own rules, set the criteria, and for reasons none of us can fathom, he feels obligated to follow them."

"If he's some kind of god," Patricia said, "then why doesn't he just come inside here and get Katherine himself?"

"First of all," Tyler said, "this bus is special. It would take Gamble a long time to bust inside here."

"Like your gun is special?" Duncan said.

"That's right."

"So, what's so special about them?"

"They're products of the seraph's imagination."

"Then why doesn't the seraph just imagine Gamble away?" Rachel said.

Tyler shrugged. "Because it just doesn't work that way."

"Then how do we defeat Gamble?" Patricia said.

"Just be patient," Tyler said.

"Patient my ass!" Rachel said. "I want some goddamn answers! Just how the hell do we get out of here?"

"We're in Gamble's mind, his universe," Tyler said. "The only way out is to kill Gamble, or at least bring him to his knees."

Patricia threw her hands in the air. "Oh, great," she said. "We're screwed."

"Speak for yourself!" Rachel said.

"There *are* certain rules to this game," Tyler offered. "Our hope of dethroning Gamble won't be in understanding them, but exploiting our own. Gamble's playing with multiple decks of cards, but that doesn't mean we can't trump him with our own lousy hand."

Duncan eyed Tyler suspiciously. "Translate."

Chris piped in. "We have an ace in the hole. Juanita. And, if I'm guessing right, she'll know just when to pull it from her sleeve." He smiled proudly. "After all, I'm the one who went in and got it going."

Aghast that Chris had been inside her without her explicit permission, Juanita said, "Where have you been in me?"

"While you were sleeping," Kathy explained, "Chris went inside your mind and left a present."

Juanita stared mistrustfully at Chris. Almost a whisper, she said, "What kind of present?"

"I kind of calibrated something that was already inside you," he admitted. "Someone else gave you the present."

"The Mother Mary!" Juanita said, suddenly understanding. "At the hospital. She gave it to me!"

"What is this present?" Duncan persisted.

"Remember when she knocked a part of me into that window?" Chris said. "Well, that's what it is."

"What? She's going to knock something out of somebody?" Rachel said.

"That's what I'm thinking," Chris said.

Patricia rolled her eyes. "Oh, that's just ridiculous."

Smirking, Chris said, "We'll see."

9.

Eli returned with the boy.

Inside the shuttle, everyone crowded around the windshield.

"Oh, no" Kathy said. "He's got Emilio."

"The boy we were going after?" Rachel said. "But how did he know?"

Duncan put his hands on Rachel's shoulders. "He's a god, remember?"

"Is this the boy you're all so concerned over?" Gamble hollered. "Mischievous little shit. Found him in a juvenile detention facility in Chicago. Oh, he wasn't that hard to find. Fact is, I simply sang out the name Emilio Chavez, and all those tympanums that fluctuated dismally on my pitch, I sought out. You see, this here brat's deaf as a stone." He smiled at Duncan. "Ain't that right, Donut?"

Duncan nodded, the gunshots that inflicted the malady still fresh in his own ears.

"So, tell you what," Gamble continued. "Being the sport that I am, I'm gonna let the delinquent here go, and give whoever wants to play a generous head start. If you can catch him, you can have him." Then, to the boy, he signed adeptly with his hands.

Wide-eyed now, Emilio burst from Gamble's side, leaving the road for the interior of the trees; a macabre network of cindered capillaries.

"No!" Kathy shouted. "We can't let him get away!"

Tyler opened the shuttle's doors. "She's right. Duncan, Chris, move it!"

There was no time to argue. Duncan and Chris dashed through the open doors and into the night.

"Go after them, Father," Gamble instructed. "Let's see what you're made of."

10.

Josephine stopped, gaping at the enclosure. It was colossal. As were its occupants; flocks of them, a series of creatures not so unlike one another, the smallest standing no less than twenty feet high, she guessed, the largest easily exceeding that times two. She didn't know how many there were but guessed that if they'd all cooperate by lining up, it'd take her a good week to count them.

They reminded her a little of moas, those large flightless birds of New Zealand; now extinct, thanks to man and his dog. There were no feathers here, though, elephantine or otherwise. Just grotesqueries aplenty. And derivations of beauty, as well, she had to admit; the way the pinks and purples of twilight glazed along their knobbed and bony fringes, made even ruddier along the onyx keratin of their mandibles, more insect-like than bird.

The cage itself was surrealistic in fashion, its bars comprising a menagerie all their own, of coiling and sleuthing and flying serpents, scaled, beaked and taloned, as if Sir Arthur Conan Doyle had—during an onerous bout of schizophrenia—prodigiously emulated in bronze sculpture the inhabitants of his own Lost World.

The closer she got, the more Jacob protested until, finally, he convinced her to let him go. The instant she pulled the collar from around his neck, he was off like a shot in the opposite direction, half-flying, half-hopping, his tail literally tucked between his legs.

"Ya big sissy!" she yelled after him. "Christ on high!"

Upon reaching what was obviously the gate, she read the note attached, a white spec of paper snared upon a colossal bramble of metal.

*BE A DOLL AND PRESS THE LITTLE RED BUTTON WHEN I
GIVE THE WORD
P.S. YOUR SHOE'S UNTIED*

Josephine peered down at her shoestring-less loafers, then back at the note, which had changed.

HA! THANKS FOR PLAYING!

"Smartass," she grumbled.

Off to her left rose one of those dispensers often found beside the Giraffe pens of a local zoo, the ones that with a quarter and a turn of the knob you can purchase a granola-looking treat for the animals. Despite its proportionate immensity—and that the knob and coin receptacle were at arm's reach and designed for *her* physical dimensions—there was no guessing its function.

Yessir, she thought, *there has to be some mighty big biscuits in there.*

But it wasn't Gamble's brand of humor that was pissing her off so much. She, unfortunately, was without any change.

11.

Eli heard voices. Murmurings, undecipherable, as if becalmed in the vacuum of this alien atmosphere. But voices nonetheless.

Now in a kind of slow, eerie animation, the blotches were becoming more focused. With rising determination those blurry images continued to struggle within their rarefied encapsulations; hatchlings straining against the embryonic membranes that were his wings.

They were blistering.

The voices getting louder now; clearer. They were coming from his wings.

Diving, lest he should suddenly be without ballast, Eli aimed for an outcropping of rock.

He was going to have to leave the chase. But just for a moment.

Fluttering down, he reached a level spot. Then, with something fast approaching revulsion, he began scrutinizing the voices.

"...finished, Eli, finished, you're finished..." said the voices. Pustules were taking the shapes of faces, the faces of demons, declaring, "...you're finished, Eli, finished..."

"Be gone!" Eli commanded, but the images remained, squirming in delight, as did their decrees, rising in his ears.

"Be gone!" he cried again. "Be gone, all of you!"

Stymied, Eli considered the possibility that the demons inside his wings were artifacts of this new world he was in, were demonstrations of the kind of skullduggery he should no less expect in a carnival world where Gamble was ringmaster. Perhaps, he thought, if he were to change the venue back to a more earthly flavor he could banish the intruders. He imagined the first place that came to his mind—

Instantly, surrealistically, the goblin world gave way to that of the Pacific Northwest, the very landscape that saw his evolution from pawn to king.

The surf below him washed loudly against the rocky shore, but still did not drown out the jeers issuing from his wings.

"...finished, Eli, finished, you're finished..."

Eli clamped his hands over his ears, tightly closed his eyes, then fancied the only thing left he could think of.

He envisioned the wings gone from his back.

12.

The change had come like a breakneck wind, an astounding storm of transformation sweeping across horizon to horizon, so swiftly that the eye could barely keep up. The sanguine purple of twilight had given way to the warm yellow light of a mid-afternoon sun. The air, now redolent of moss and rain and dirt, still crackled as if statically charged.

Up ahead, Emilio Chavez had stopped; was signaling with both hands for them to hurry.

Duncan nearly tripped and fell, the ground suddenly thick with fern and vine. They were in a forest of Douglas fir and hemlock, and Duncan's instinct was telling him that, for whatever reason, the priest—not Gamble—had changed their surroundings into his old stomping grounds, the coastal regions of Washington State.

And damned if it wasn't to the T, he thought, right down to pesky mosquitoes. The world before seemed almost cardboard in comparison; had lacked a particular depth, the atmosphere almost antiseptic. The scenery before them now was so real that Duncan wondered if the priest had not just imagined their surroundings into being, but had literally brought the real thing to them somehow.

There were running footsteps behind them. Duncan looked back, expecting Gamble to be in fast pursuit. But it wasn't Gamble. It was Kathy and Juanita.

Jesus Christ, that was all he needed.

"Just what the hell are you two doing?" he said.

"You'll get lost without me," Kathy said.

"In case you haven't been paying attention, we were already lost the moment we entered this damned place."

Winded, gasping for breath, Juanita said, "I go where Kathy goes."

As Kathy approached Duncan, she said, "There's a stable not too far ahead. We need to get there."

Finally catching up with Kathy, Juanita bent over and placed her hands on her knees, gasping.

Up ahead some thirty yards, Chris had caught up with Emilio.

Duncan nodded toward the boy. "The seraph's inside Emilio, right?"

Kathy shrugged. "Could be."

"But Gamble thinks it's in Emilio, too."

"No," she said. "He believes it's in you."

After Juanita had caught her breath, they started walking. "What do you believe?" Duncan said.

"Only that it's close," she said. "Very close."

Juanita said, "Thee seraph's our only hope, isn't it?"

"Yes."

They stopped in front of Emilio. The boy appeared frightened out of his mind, and was signing briskly.

"Slow down, dude," Chris said.

To Kathy, Duncan said, "What's he saying?"

Kathy watched him for a moment, then said, "He wants to wake up."

"Don't we all," Duncan said. "How does Gamble plan to get his daughter from you?"

Kathy explained that Gamble would try using the priest first, and that would buy them some time. But that once the priest failed, and she was most assured he would as there was already a contingency plan in affect for him, Gamble would most likely come after her himself, or that his daughters would, and that either scenario was not a comforting one.

"Where's this stable you were talking about?" Duncan said.

She pointed. "Just over the hill."

"What's so special there? Horses?"

"No," she said. "It's long abandoned. But there's a tunnel there we can hide in."

"I don't think a tunnel is going to hide us very well from Gamble," he said.

She took Emilio's hand and started walking. "It'll do, for now."

"Hold up a second," Duncan said. "I'm confused. How did you know about the stable in the first place? I mean, how did you know the world was going to change from Dali's Africa to the Pacific Northwest, let alone know the neighborhood?"

"Amy told me."

"Okay, then how did she know?"

"She's an angel."

Duncan rolled his eyes. "Oh, of course. How silly of me."

13.

Naked, Amy stared at the thousands of dead worms cloaking her, plaintive over Melanie's loss.

She crinkled her nose, the putrid smell overpowering.

"For a sneaky little bitch," Gamble said, suddenly perched on a low, thick branch above her, "you sure can play the organ. Forgive my surprise, but it's just that I thought a harp would have been your instrument of choice."

"Sticks and stones," Amy replied, not bothering to look up. "Besides, you put on some show yourself. *'I distilled its blood and made oil for the creaking cogs of time'...'I was there and wove its suffering cries into chain mail.'* Give me a break." She finally turned, loathing him. "But what you did to those five boys was inexcusable."

He laughed. "All for Chris's benefit. And Juanita's, to be sure. Oh, how I do love a melodrama. And judging by that spiffy cape you were wearing, and its incriminating intentions, one might suspect that you have a penchant for theatrics, as well—all because we wouldn't want to raise anyone's suspicions that there might be something going on between us, right, Liberace? Don't forget, my stage mask may be tragedy—but not nearly as tragic as the truth that I did, in fact, slaughter all but one of your ancestors."

She stared up at him now, grinning. "And you almost screwed it for yourself, didn't you? Found out almost too late that the only way you were ever going to get the Key to the Shallows was through one of the seraphs. After rifling through God's pockets—and don't think for a second that it never crossed my mind that you would, *despite* your promise to the contrary—you found that even *He* doesn't own a set. So now I'm your only hope of ever seeing eternal rein. At least in your manmade part of the kingdom."

"Only temporary housing," he assured, then jumped from the tree. "Need I remind you what a real sport I've been throughout this whole affair? I've refrained from making things difficult. And don't *you* think for a second that it never crossed *my* industrious mind to do so. I've obliged you in every way, half-breed. I've left your proxy family virtually untouched, along with your globular maid, who believes she's on some holy crusade for the Virgin Mary. And not only have I refrained from turning Chris and his surfboard into chum, I've left Patricia Bently alone with her grief." He stepped closer, his lips stretching across his face. "But now, you show up in Wonderland and allow Chris to hook your housekeeper up to something that, I strongly suspect, might be integral to finding the seraph's whereabouts. Now, why you would entrust such a power to a flabby fleshsack such as Juanita?"

"You play your little games," she said. "We play ours."

"Yes, but the simple fact is, I'm tiring of the games," he said, angrier now.

She finally stood and wheeled on him. "I said you could have your apocalypse in exchange for your promise to leave God alone."

"It's not the Almighty I'm after," he said, "as you so very well know. Furthermore, in light of your own deceitful ways, I believe it's time you confirm for me the whereabouts of the last seraph. That, or personally give me the Key, or give me back my remaining daughter. If you don't comply to any of these requests, then I'll have no other choice but to end this miserable stalemate by finally destroying you and your mongrel cousins, and your merry band of misfits."

She laughed. "And forever lose the Shallows? I hardly think so. Besides, if you really think you can take us on, then you'd better pack a lunch. You just might discover that we're not the pushovers of old."

"I might be testing that theory sooner than you think." He grinned. "The seraph, the Key, or my daughter. If you really want to score some points, all of the above."

"Even with seven, you have nothing," she lied.

"Oh, I heartily disagree," he said. "Seven's such a magical number."

"Look, I've stuck to my end of the deal by letting you have your Armageddon. Do to the world what you may. But if you break your end of the deal again by harassing God, and that goes for the clone god, too, or try and remove your daughter from Katherine, then my 'mongrel cousins' will remodel your world so completely that even your memory won't reflect on the newly waxed floors."

"Oh, please. And if *memory* serves me correctly, you've yet to answer the question I posed in the beginning. Why would God appoint a bunch of conscientious objectors to guard the Shallows and its eternal waters?"

Amy didn't answer.

"I'll tell you why," Gamble said. "Because He never perceived my kind of threat. And let me remind you, sweet little Amy, that your tinkering of so-called time has yet to yield the desired results. I am still here, yes? And we both know that the more you indulge that fallacy-laden concept, the more degraded it will become until, finally, you will no longer be able to navigate within its stream effectively." He brushed his right fingers against the material of his jacket, taking a moment to admire his nails' restored luster. "As for God and your pacifistic subordinates, well...they don't even register on my shit meter."

Amy sighed. "Are you finished?"

"Not yet," he said. "You see, I've begun realizing that the reasons for your ventures in 'time' aren't all what I initially thought them to be. For instance, that each trip has been an exercise in deception, to hide the seraph in a new place, and always in a different time, simply to keep me guessing. But what you've really been doing is trying to teach an old dog new tricks. Like letting it live inside a juvenile delinquent of some caliber. Oh yes, I know all about the boy, among many others. Of course, since I don't share this miscreant ability of yours, I'll be left to my own suspicions. As for the last seraph, I believe that it remains in your father. Oh, I imagine that it ventures out from time to time, as I've just proposed, but it roosts there. You see, I've searched every other mind in existence, and Daddy Duncan's is the only one I can't get in. I've run into minds like his before, down through the years. I know the game."

Amy said nothing.

"Gotta hand it to him, though," he continued, "that's one hell of a wall he's built. Just like the boy had at one time. But now I really do believe there's a fortress behind those battlements, and not just subterfuge. And do you know what? I think I may have finally found a way to scale those walls and rescue the maiden from the tower."

"Not without my help, you can't."

"Ooooh, Mommy, I'm scared," he said, shivering. "We used to call the seraphs the poltroons of creation, the whales of eternity. But you and I and that one remaining seraph all have something in common. Although the womb within which you were conceived was a biological one, mine idealistic, and the last seraph's, I suspect, now a combination of both, we all share the same mother, more or less." He folded his arms proudly. "The stork dropped us all on the doorstep of Man."

"The point is, you can't be sure. And when you finally do realize just what did happen with the last seraph, you'll be begging it to pull its foot out of your ass."

"I sincerely doubt it," he said. "Just like you, it hasn't the nerve, despite your efforts to teach it aggression. Its heart is simply not in the game." He adjusted the knot in his tie. "Now, as you can see, I've gained my sixth daughter. All I have left to do is get my remaining daughter from that fleshsack Katherine." He shook his finger. "Fool me once, shame on you, fool me twice...

"Now, if you ever want to see your friends and family again in one piece, adhere to my requests."

She glowered at him. "If you so much as look at them wrong—"

"My dear angel, your threats have become as wearisome as your attempts at hiding the seraph. I now have Duncan where I want him, as well as Katherine Bently."

She bowed her head. "I'm tired, Gamble. I just want an end to the whole damn thing."

"I thought hell would have come to your rescue by now," he said. "Seems I gave those boys more credit than they deserve."

"You just haven't backed me far enough into a corner yet," she said. "But I don't want things to go that far. That's an IOU I can live without."

"I imagine it is," he said. "Come, let's make a deal. You give me Katherine and unimpeded access to the Shallows, and I'll let you and the rest of your half-breed family have God and all the acres of heaven. You have my word, as a gentleman."

"Your word as a gentleman, to leave God alone? Both of them?"

He placed a hand over his heart. "My word."

"Alright," she said. "You can have Katherine. As you know, the Key to the Shallows can only be gotten from the seraph. Juanita is the only one who can release it. We'll meet you at priest's old launching pad."

"You do know that I'll have to kill it to get the Key?"

She met his gaze. "Yes, I'm aware of that."

"Just so long as you are." He smiled winningly. "Very well, then. At the cliffs. Bring everyone. It'll be a party." He began walking away. "Oh, and one more thing—put on some clothes. You wouldn't want to embarrass Mummy and Daddy, would you?"

14.

Josephine Kagan was more than pleased with the change of scenery. That weird old African stuff was for the birds. She was still in front of the sanctuary, steadfast and true. She was a trooper.

She missed Jacob and called out for him again.

Something fluttered then, something behind her, on the gate. She turned and found another piece of paper speared upon a vertex of metal.

TIME TO PUSH THE LITTLE RED BUTTON, DEAR

YOURS FOREVER, GAMBLE

She wadded up the paper and tossed it over her shoulder. She then walked over and pressed the little red button.

That wasn't so hard.

The massive gate began to open outward. Slowly at first, the creatures began to muster near the entrance, then trickle out one by one.

Josephine banged the gate with her cane. "Come on, come on, what are ya waitin' for!"

The herd began to move faster. Soon there was a stampede of creatures great and not so great charging through the massive opening, their cries deafening over the thunder of their feet.

Josephine clamped her hands to her ears, stumbled backward. It was an astonishing sight to behold.

It felt like she'd watched the commotion for a good fifteen minutes before the last one came out, stopped, regarded her with a quizzical expression, then loped over to her and, with startling swiftness, devoured her in one single bite.

15.

Whimpering, on his knees, Eli scratched at the grass, listening to the surf below. It had a calming effect. And the mild breeze washed over his sweaty torso and brow, cooling him.

His mighty wings were gone, and so was the vocalizing that had sprung from them. But now he was without power. He had tried repeatedly to conjure a new pair. But without success. It seemed that Gamble was the only one who could fit him with new ones.

He was useless without his wings.

The boy and the others had a major head start on him now. How was he going to chase them down? He could run after them, but where was the supremacy in that?

Gamble was going to be hugely pissed at him. But what could he do? For all he knew, this was just another test, another trial by fire set by Gamble's own incendiary hand. Another riddle, another conundrum, another fucking infantile limerick that he was supposed to solve.

But this one made no sense whatsoever. Why let him taste the wonders of flight, then take the gift away so quickly, so cruelly?

What had he done to deserve this punishment?

He gazed into the sky and wished a moon upon the stratus. Suddenly there appeared a gray crescent, mordacious upon the blue sky. He then imagined Zeus fast about in a fiery chariot. Not two hundred feet above him roared a sleigh, arcing across the sky, pulled by a hundred flaming horses, and at the reins was a long-bearded god adorned in lambent white robes and a golden crown.

He could conjure anything. Except a pair of wings.

What were his options?

Wings. That was his only option, to have a mighty pair lift him into the heavens once more.

Did he dare summon his mentor?

Yes, he would have to risk losing face. Or more. There was just no other way.

He stood, then reached for the sky. "Gamble! Come! I need you now!"

16.

Tyler saw her coming before she had a chance to knock. Now in blue jeans and a white tank top, Amy McNeil stood in her adult form in front of the open doors of the bus. Her hair was shoulder-length, strawberry blonde, and the sunlight pranced along the fibers of red as the breeze lifted and parted the strands. The freckles on her face were now more prominent around her pug nose than on her cheeks, as they had been when she was a little girl. Her eyes had changed from aquamarine to the deepest, cobalt blue, her eyebrows thin and silver-blonde. She looked to be around twenty-five.

"Hi, Tyler," she said. "I see the seraph's been good to you."

He smiled, as if he'd been expecting her. "Got me out of the ground for awhile. Come on up."

Rachel and Patricia were already on their feet.

Squinting, Rachel stared at the woman. "Oh...my...God," she said. "Is that you, Amy?"

"It's me, Mom."

Eyes welded to her daughter's maturated image, Rachel slowly, gropingly, sat back down. "My, you've...you've grown up...fast."

Amy looked down, as if ashamed. "Not fast enough. We have to leave now; you, me, and Patricia. Tyler's staying on the bus."

The adoration in Rachel's eyes conceded to the inevitable. "Okay," she said. "Where are we going?"

"To meet Gamble," Amy said. "Not too far from here. It's in walking distance."

Still standing, Patricia said, "Where are the others?"

"They're safe. They'll meet us there. Kathy knows the way."

In a long-suffering sigh, Rachel said, "This is it, isn't it? This is where it all comes together?"

"It'll be a showdown," Amy assured.

Rachel, straightening her already taut posture, said, "I...I just can't believe how lovely you've turned out to be. Your father's going to be awfully proud, you know."

She smiled. "I know. Now, we have to go."

17.

"You rang," Gamble said. "I must say, Father, that with all of your newly acquired inclinations, one would have imagined a more exotic decor than what you've just laid out for us." He tapped his chin thoughtfully with his forefinger. "But...I have to admit, it is apropos, as it's come full circle. Yes, I think I'll let it remain." He turned to Eli. "I told you you'd have quite the magic wand once you passed through the seventh window, didn't I?"

Nodding, Eli swallowed hard, wiping away the tears that were streaming down his cheeks. "I...I lost my wings," he stammered. "I wished them away. They were...infested with...demons."

"You let a bunch of mongrels get under your skin, Father," Gamble said, a pitying tone in his voice.

"M-mongrels?" Eli stammered.

"Angels, Father. Given your profession, I'm surprised you didn't realize it, least of all expect it."

"Then...it wasn't you who...did this?"

"Why heavens no," Gamble said. "Why would you even consider such a thing?"

Immediately ashamed, Eli's tears began anew. "I tried to make new ones, but I...I can't seem to—"

"There, there, now, Father," Gamble said, his arms outstretched.

Eli slowly fell into his embrace. "Why can't I make new ones?" he cried. "I seem to be able to make everything else..."

"But nothing else seems to matter," Gamble said, "isn't that right?"

"I...I..." It had been so long since Eli had been in the embrace of another, had been the recipient instead of the giver of solace, and it felt so good, especially in the arms of his mentor, of his counsel, of the one who had brought him so far after so many years of scrupulous devotion, of dedication to a cause to which he virtually remained ignorant. In the arms of the one who was always there for him, rain or shine, through the good and bad times; the one who always kept his promises.

"You're only at your best when you can fly, right, Father?"

"Yes."

Gamble tightened his hug, lifted Eli from the ground, then began walking toward the edge of the cliff. "And that's why you're no good to me anymore, Father. You can't get your head out of the clouds."

Gamble reached under Eli's armpits, pushed him out, dangling him over the edge.

"Fly" Gamble said, then released him.

18.

As they neared the stables, Duncan counted at least a dozen gray wolves. All remained back in the trees. Watchful. Duncan was reminded of the wolf he'd encountered in his sojourn back in time and was acutely aware that they were in the presence of heavenly hosts and not indigenous wildlife.

Moving closer to the structures, he saw a weathervane on top of one of the buildings, could hear the trill it made as the wind pushed it along. As they entered the stalls, the sunlight sliced through the cracks in the boarded windows and was warm on his face. The smells of timeworn flax and linseed oil and hay were frail but ever-present. He reached up and ran his hand across a coil of rope hanging from a nail, and he was suddenly reminded that these were the memories he'd briefly experienced while walking toward the drug dealers' house, just before Gamble had come off the fence and introduced himself.

A glitch of reminiscence, he thought, out of place and time. So, he *had* been here before. How many times? he wondered.

Duncan stopped; heard a rumbling in the distance.

It was getting closer.

"Ssshhh, you hear that?" he said.

Kathy nodded. "Crap. We have to hurry."

"That does not sound good," Chris offered. "Sounds like a stampede."

They pushed hastily through more stalls.

"Over here," Kathy said. "There's a trap door leading to a long tunnel. Goes for maybe fifty yards to the main building."

What the tunnel had originally been intended for was anybody's guess.

The rumbling was close now. Very close.

Then the screeching started.

19.

They'd entered the edge of a meadow. Amy led the way, Patricia and Rachel behind her.

"Are you sure they're all right?" Patricia said.

"Kathy knows the way," Amy said. "Don't worry, they'll meet us there."

"Tell me something, Amy," Rachel said. "What was Duncan doing back there in Boston?"

Amy said, "I think Patricia should answer that."

Patricia sighed. With some diffidence, she related the story of how Duncan had stole nearly two hundred thousand dollars from some drug dealers the night he got shot, and how it had made its way to her via his lieutenant, Mo White. She explained how Duncan, because of his involvement with her husband's murder, had become aware of her financial crisis because of her husband's death, and this led him to commit the crime. She went further and said that she felt guilty for accepting the money at first, but later decided to hell with it, that she would only spend what was absolutely necessary to get out of debt. The rest, she said, would stay hidden for a rainy day. Or maybe she would someday donate it to an orphanage or children's hospital.

Rachel was stunned. *"He gave you two hundred-thousand dollars?"*

"Yes."

"Holy shit!"

"Yeah."

"The same night Tyler was shot and killed?"

"Yes."

"And Duncan's lieutenant was in on it?"

"Apparently so."

"Christ almighty."

"Uh-huh."

"Well," Amy said, "maybe I should clear the air on that. You see, Lieutenant Mo White is one of us."

Patricia stopped. "The lieutenant is...what, an angel?"

"I'm afraid so."

"But...he did such a bad thing."

"Got you out of debt, didn't it?"

"But it was against the law!"

"Trust me, Patty," Amy said. "In the grand scheme of things, it'll be overlooked."

Grudgingly, Patricia started walking again. "I thought your kind were supposed to be decent and pure."

Amy laughed. "We're half-human. What do you expect?"

"So," Rachel said, "why did Duncan have to go back and relive that night again?"

"You'll have to ask Duncan that question," Amy said.

They reached the end of the meadow and entered a dense, steep-sloping forest.

"We're almost there," Amy said. "Just over the hill."

"I can smell the ocean," Rachel said.

"Oh, my God," Patricia said. "Look at the *wolves!*"

To their left, there were at least twenty wolves standing among the trees.

"Don't be frightened," Amy said. "They're friends."

Rachel shook her head. *"Two hundred-thousand dollars?"*

"Yup."

20.

The going was pitch black.

Before climbing down into the tunnel, Chris and Duncan had just enough time to peek out a window and see what kind of animals were making those frightful screeching sounds. They were huge, flightless, featherless birds with taloned feet and horrific sets of insect-like mouth parts. They were terrifying.

Even underground, the thunder of their passing was near deafening.

Crawling on hands and knees, Duncan stopped. "Wait a minute," he said above the din. "Gamble can do better than that."

In front of him, Kathy said, "What do you mean?"

"I mean, if Gamble wanted us, he could pluck us from the ground like carrots."

"So?"

"So, those creatures really aren't interested in us, are they?"

"Not really," she said. "We just had to get out of their way. Gamble's just showing some muscle."

"Any idea where they're going?"

"To the Apocalypse."

"They're going topside?" Chris said.

"And where are we going?"

"To meet the others," Kathy said, "at the cliffs."

"To the same cliffs where the priest took you?" Duncan said. Now it was all making sense. *A place where angels are born*, Amy had told him. And she'd been speaking metaphorically, just as the face in the window had suggested. Sewing angel wings into the backs of little girls didn't get more metaphorical than that.

"And we're going to deliver an angel," he said. "The last seraph."

"That's the plan."

Duncan started moving. "And you couldn't have told me this earlier?"

"I knew you'd figure it out, sooner or later."

Emilio and Juanita were ahead of them and had apparently found the other entrance, a shaft of light now shining down some twenty yards ahead.

"Señor Duncan," Juanita called out, "the monsters, they are almost gone. Is safe to go up?"

She was right. The thunder was diminishing to a low rumble now.

"Go ahead, take a peek," Duncan said. "If they're gone, we'll move on out."

"It's less than a quarter mile away from here," Kathy said. "We'll be there in no time."

21.

Duncan and the others saw Patricia and Rachel standing just within the tree-line. There was another woman with them. And the closer they got, the more the woman resembled Amy.

The adult version of his daughter.

"My God," Duncan said. "Amy?"

Chris was equally benumbed. "Dude."

"Hi, Dad," she said, then hugged him. "How was Boston?"

"I learned my lesson," he said.

"Well, it's about time."

Juanita was stunned. "Amy! You've grown to be a woman."

"Juanita," Amy said, "you've been a wonderful guardian to me all these years. Now it's my turn to protect you." She looked at everyone. "It's time to go."

When they broke tree-line, they saw Gamble and six naked girls standing near the cliff's edge.

Juanita reached for Kathy's hand. "You hold on to me," she said. Now Kathy had Juanita in one hand, Patricia in the other.

"Let's do it," Chris said, bravado staunch in his posture but lean in his voice.

As they approached, Gamble held out his arms. "And I was beginning to think you wouldn't show."

Amy said nothing, just kept on walking. She was in front of the group, Duncan directly behind her.

Below them, hundreds of feet down, waves crashed rhythmically against the rocky shore. Except for a large bank of clouds to the west, the sky above was light blue, and a gentle wind rustled through the fir just behind them. The setting was more befit a picnic, Duncan thought, than it was a showdown of deities.

"I don't like this place," Kathy said. "I really don't."

Patricia pulled her close. "I know, baby. I know."

Amy stopped ten feet from Gamble; Duncan and Rachel now by her side. The rest stayed close behind, Kathy now in Patricia's clutches, Juanita in close orbit. Chris and Emilio took up the rear, both apprehensive but steady.

Gamble waved a hand toward the naked girls. "These are my offspring," he said. "They'll be judging your demeanor, so mind your manners. It might also please you to know that my protégé, the priest, has suffered a hopeless accident and thus will not be joining the festivities." He shook his head. "You know, it's so true what they say about finding good help."

Kathy glanced back at the tree-line and saw the wolves, all silent and still within the dusky perimeter.

Gamble had noticed the wolves, too, and said to Amy, "I see you brought your *other* family along. Unless you want them to become an endangered species again," he warned her, "then keep them at bay."

"You just stick to our bargain," Amy said, "and they'll keep their distance."

Patricia was staring, too. She said, "My God, how many are there?"

"Not nearly enough," Gamble assured, then walked over to Kathy. "Now, it's finally time I gather my remaining daughter from you."

"No!" Patricia cried, stepping in front of Kathy. "You leave her alone!"

Juanita was now alongside Patricia, shaking her head wildly. "No, señor! No, you don't!"

As Gamble stood before Katherine, the wolves began slinking from the shadowy timber, their steely eyes fixed ahead, their noses to the ground. They stopped their advance when Amy held up a hand.

Then Amy looked at Patricia and Juanita and said, "Step aside, the both of you, and let him have her."

Patricia was stunned. "W-What?"

"Amy, what are you doing?" Duncan said.

Amy was now beside Gamble. "Just do as I say and let him have her."

"Patricia, Juanita," Duncan said, surprising himself. "Do as Amy says."

Juanita, still protesting madly, had to finally be pulled away by both Rachel and Chris.

With stark resignation, Patricia slowly moved aside. "I'm so sorry, baby," she said. "Forgive me."

Gamble placed his right hand upon Kathy's head. Instantly, as if suffused in electrical current, her arms jerked outward, her body became rigid, and a white mist began spiraling from her back like a thin rope, stretching toward his six daughters. At the other end of the cord a wispy form began taking shape, gathering there, and quickly coalesced into a body, that of Katherine Bently.

It was quite the magic trick.

Behind them, a baying rose from the woods; a lamenting chorus of howls from a symphony of wolves.

The wind was picking up, and, looking west, Duncan saw that the clouds had moved considerably closer, their docile color having changed to an angry gray, their bellies bulging.

Eyes rolling back into their sockets, the Kathy beneath Gamble's right hand crumpled to the ground.

Patricia was immediately cowering over her, shaking her. "Kathy, baby! Kathy! Wake up!"

"I'm afraid she's no longer with the living," Gamble said, briskly wiping his hands, as if the chore had been a dirty one.

Juanita fell to her knees and wailed.

"Dear God, Duncan," Rachel whispered. "What have we done?"

"You asshole!" Duncan roared. Fists clenched at his sides, he was about to charge Gamble when Rachel grabbed his arm. "No! That's a fight you can't possibly win."

Something arced across his mind then, something Kathy had told him upon his return from yesteryear. "It left in you remarkable wonders," she'd said. "Indulge them" And upon that musing, he was suddenly granted insight into what she'd been referring. It was crazy, of course, but he had to try. He walked over to Kathy's lifeless body and, kneeling down, placed both hands upon her head, just as she had done with her own hands when healing his leg wound. But she had only healed the flesh. He, on the other hand, was attempting to revive the soul.

"Come back," he said.

For a moment there was nothing.

He leaned over and pressed his ear to her chest.

She stirred.

Her eyes fluttered open.

"Donut," she said softly. "I was at the Shallows."

"That's great, sweetheart," he said, smiling.

Rachel, tears in her eyes, said, "My God, Duncan."

"Why, Donut, I'm impressed," Gamble said. "But then, I suppose it only confirms what I've suspected for quite some time. You see, only God and the seraphim have the power of resurrection."

Duncan ignored Gamble as he helped Kathy back to her feet. Patricia, tears streaming from her eyes, kneeled in front of Kathy. "Oh, baby, oh, baby," she said, brushing her hands through her daughter's hair over and over. Juanita, now back on her feet, stood close by, clutching her rosary to her chest and thanking the Blessed Mother, her own wet eyes heavenward.

Gamble's insinuation that the seraph was inside him was no longer true, he felt. It had been at one time, that was certain. But why did Gamble feel that the seraph was still a part of him? After all, that was why Chris had tricked them into Gamble's Wonderland. And why was that? Because the seraph had built up some kind of barricade inside his mind, one high enough that Gamble couldn't enter. That was obvious. So, if Gamble couldn't get inside his mind, then he would bring him inside his own, where they could square off. But Gamble was able to bring the boy in without Chris's help. So, did that mean that the boy did not have the same kind of barricade? Did that mean the seraph wasn't inside the boy? Or had Gamble found someone else who, like Chris, could psychically maneuver him inside.

No, that was doubtful. Duncan had the sneaking suspicion that Chris was one of a kind.

But if the seraph wasn't inside the boy, and if it wasn't inside himself, then where was it hiding? It was close, he could feel it; a sapience, almost sacrosanct in its quality, knotted in his gut. The more freedom he gave this cognizance, the more the knot unraveled, becoming an umbilicus to a forbidden knowledge that divinity was at play here, that this was all preordained. After all, he'd been here before. They all had.

The big question: Would they get it right this time?

"Behold them," Gamble said, swinging an arm toward his seven daughters, "the devils that they are."

All of his daughters, starting with Kathy, had begun to morph into grotesque forms. Bat-like wings matured from their backs. And tails, growing long, barbed and sword-slender. Their hands and feet elongated, became scaled and taloned; a mixture of something canine, avian, and reptilian. Horns sprung from the foreheads, curling down and around. Muzzles burgeoned from their faces, sprigs of wiry hair cropping up here and there, niched deeply into the crevices that pocked the mutation, each one savagely ranked with long, pointed teeth. Menacing now, they regarded everyone with snarls and snorts, their eyes black as marbles.

"Ain't they a sight," Gamble said; then he turned to Juanita. "It's my understanding that you have the power to release the seraph. Is this true?"

Juanita looked terribly confused. "I...I did not know I could do this," she said. Then she straightened. "But if it is God's will..."

"God's will?" he said. "*God's* will? Sweetie, you've been shanghaied by a bunch of interloping mongrels who don't know squat about God's will. They've been making it up as they go along."

"I do not care," Juanita said. "I do what they tell me."

"Do you?" Gamble said, walking over to Emilio. "Then, just for grins, let's see what's hiding inside the boy here." He waved a hand. "Come along."

Juanita hesitantly made her way to Emilio. Standing in front of him, she shrugged, then reached out and, with her rosary, touched her hand to his chest.

Nothing happened.

"No, no," Amy said, "you've got to hit him, Juanita. Get pissed, goddammit! Hit him hard!"

This time Juanita hauled off and punched Emilio in the chest. Not real hard, but hard enough. A tiny, solitary moth escaped from the impact, fluttered upward, and was lost from view in seconds.

Gamble turned to Amy. "As I knew all along." Then, with a simple touch of Gamble's finger, Emilio began to swell. Within moments he was immense, off the ground and floating upward like some Thanksgiving Day Parade balloon. Now the size of dinner plates, his eyes conveyed, in stereo, the horror he was experiencing.

"Dear God!" Rachel screamed.

"I believe he just might pop!" Gamble declared .

And Emilio did just that, stridently and in hundreds of thin, rubbery pieces.

"Full of nothing but hot air," Gamble said. He turned to Duncan and said, "Let's see you bring *that one* back to life."

Duncan was reeling from the spectacle. It all happened so fast, was so dreamlike, that he could hardly fathom that it occurred at all. All he could do was stand there and stare.

"Why, Donut," Gamble said gleefully, "I believe you've gone dreadfully pale."

"You rotten bastard," Duncan finally mumbled. "No good rotten bastard."

"Motherfucker!" Chris declared.

"Easy, Christopher-san," Gamble said, "you might just pull something." Then he turned his attention back to Juanita. "Now, let's see you sock the stuffing out of old Duncan McNeil, eh?"

Juanita, now a jumble of wobbly nerves thanks to Gamble's horrific prank, staggered over to Duncan. "Please forgive, Señor Duncan," she said, then punched his chest. Again, only a tiny moth appeared, fluttering aimlessly away.

Juanita appeared mildly surprised.

Duncan didn't appear surprised at all.

Gamble whirled on Amy. "Don't toy with me, bitch! Produce for me the seraph, or I'll rip the maid apart!"

"There's still one place you haven't looked," Amy said.

Gamble stiffened, his eyes going round.

This is it, Duncan thought. *Here we go.*

Amy stepped forward. "Right under your nose."

Gamble guffawed. "Surely you don't mean...?"

A smile slowly broadened across Juanita's face, and she turned to Amy for permission.

"Go ahead," Amy said. "Punch him. Hard."

Gamble did not back away as Juanita ambled toward him; just stared virulently at Amy.

The moment Juanita's fist struck his chest, Gamble was thrown hard to the ground. A bulbous shape of opulently brilliant, pulsating light shot from his mouth and nostrils, then surged into a greater form, one struggling within those luminous confines to become something more tangible, more corporeal. As it soared higher toward the approaching storm, the clouds parted, and as the entity entered the rift a ferocious salvo of lightning swept across the ocean, each strike of fire turning the waters to the smoothest glass.

Gamble cried out for his minions, and within moments legions of winged demons had darkened the western horizon like a swarm of locusts.

Then above them, the nimbus parted again in deafening thunder, and amid the noise the seraph descended upon multiple, luminous wings. It was colossal. Through the glaring brilliance, Duncan thought the creature resembled many forms, the sleek head of a horned serpent, the scaled and sinewy body of a dragon, the deadly talons of an eagle. It looked mythical and, in a fantastical way, elegant, despite its bulk, the way it undulated, the way its many wings moved in perfect synchrony around its entire girth. It reminded him somewhat of a whale; its gracefulness flawless upon an ocean of air.

The baying from the woods grew to a crescendo.

Still upon the ground, Gamble shouted to his daughters. "Kill it!" he cried. "Kill it now!"

His daughters took to the wing, caterwauling. From the seraph's eyes erupted bursts of deep blue fire, each barrage perfectly aimed at the ascending demons. One by one, Gamble's brood was reduced to cinders, their smoking remains falling to the crystalline surface below.

Gamble, back on his feet, threw out his hands, and a truculence of flame shot from his fingertips, toward the descending giant. The sky erupted in a molten storm as the seraph countered with its own breath of fire, turning Gamble's volley to a river of ashes.

"*Nooo!*" Gamble cried. "How can this be?"

Gamble raised his hands and the sky parted, unveiling a starry universe.

"Be gone!" He cried.

But nothing vanished into the void. The storm clouds remained, and the seraph continued its descent, crashing into the mirror ocean. The ground shook forcibly as a volcanic eruption of glass went scattering into the sky. At the epicenter, a perfect circle remained, where a whirlpool began to form, counterclockwise. Slowly, Gamble's Wonderland began spiraling inward as the vortex pulled it down. Multitudes of Gamble's demons now swarmed over the fractured surface, pouring down into the pit, their cries rising to the angry, swelling clouds above. They came from all directions, from the smallest, monkey-sized bats to the behemoths, flying amalgamations pieced together from the most wretched imagination, many as large as the seraph itself. The sky was full of them.

Bright blue and orange flashes burst beneath the ocean's glassy surface; bombardments and cannonades reverberated throughout the landscape.

Gamble once again raised his hands and called forth more legions, this time a troop of giant beings made of stone, with six arms, standing fifty stories high. They came from the north. Faceless, without eyes, they proceeded across the mirror ocean toward the swirling vortex, their synchronic cadence vibratory; each granite footfall fracturing the glass surface. In three of their six hands were long, stone maces; in the other three, stone shields.

As the first of the soldiers reached the vortex, they rode the swirling waves down like a carnival ride.

Everyone stared in silence, waiting.

Suddenly a scream broke from the hole; a high, vehement wail of such magnitude that it made the skin on Duncan's back crawl.

It was the seraph, he knew. It had been injured.

Gamble raised his hands triumphantly. "Yes!"

Then a terrific explosion. From the vortex, fragmentary rock went spraying into the air, from boulder-size to the tiniest of pebbles.

The seraph rose slowly, almost decrepitly, from the fissure. It was black with demons, those creatures teeming over its body, clawing, biting, slashing at its skin. At the approaching stone titans, the seraph shot bursts of concentrated energy, reducing each one to piles of rubble. When through, it descended once more, resuming the war with Gamble's minions below.

"*Noooo!*" Gamble cried.

Amy raised a hand, and upon a tremendous peal of thunder a striate of lightning burst from the roiling clouds, delivering upon its dazzling end a long golden sword. The weapon struck Gamble mid-chest, impaling him to the ground.

Still upright, Gamble stared down at his chest, then began to laugh. "How archaic! And yet so superbly realized! My dear angel, what's stopping me from calling down my beasties and having them tear you all limb from scrawny limb?"

"Because you're more man than you are god," Amy said, "and through grace you've discovered an appreciation for life that one seldom obtains until the end game. It's over, you've lost, and are content to leave the arena humbly. Because, Gamble, thanks to the human in you, you can be a true gentleman and see the fairness in the fight."

"But are you so sure this is the end of me?"

"Look at your hands," Amy told him.

Gamble stared uncertainly at her, then, hesitantly, peered down at his palms. "My lines...they're...gone," he said.

At his feet, a mass of worms had begun congregating.

Gamble glanced down at his feet, at the worms about to devour him. "So, you succeeded in turning the humble giant into a killer, after all. I never thought it possible." Then he looked at Amy. "But to have concealed it inside of me for even a breadth of a second—that was truly cunning."

"Your grandiosity was your downfall," she said. "There were countless places within you to hide. Besides, it learned its last chapter from you."

"Checkmate," he said, grinning.

"Please, call back your armies," she said. "Don't make the seraph do battle any longer than it has to. And, for the love of God, stop your apocalypse."

"Come now, I'm not *that* much of a gentleman," he said with a wink.

"Very well," she sighed. "Go down with your ship, then."

"Do I have a soul?" he asked.

"That's not for me to decide."

"Then there's a chance for my salvation? A chance that I might taste the Shallows?"

"A chance, perhaps."

"Then, my dear angel, I shall keep my fingers crossed."

"Oh, and just in case you should decide to change your mind and try something slippery, like not letting us get out of her alive, the seraph and I have arranged a babysitter to make sure you remain a true gentleman." She tapped his shoulder. "Turn around."

Gamble turned. Standing behind him was a figure adorned in khakis and majestic, white feather wings. He smiled, his arms folded proudly across his chest. A furnace blazed behind his eyes.

"Father Kagan," Gamble groaned. "Charmed, to be sure."

"I wouldn't piss him off," Amy said. "Hell *has* come to my rescue, and he is it."

"We have to go," Kathy said, pointing to the ocean. The whirlpool had grown much larger; was now encroaching upon the cliffs.

They started for the shuttle.

Epilogue

Tyler Everton turned off the dirt road onto a paved, two-lane highway. "Beautiful country," he remarked. "Too bad it's going down the shitter."

"It's Gamble's shitter," Kathy reminded him.

Amy turned to Chris. "It's time I told you about your mother."

Chris' eyes went wide. "Tamala?"

"Yes, she was Gamble's first seduction. Gamble chose Tamala because of her unique ability to enter minds, just like your own. Not only was she going to bear his first daughter, but over the years was going to seek out the six remaining women for him and psychically prepare them to receive his offspring. 'Hook them up,' as you say. But, as you know, your mother was also gifted with the ability to see the future, and, while pregnant, she began having visions of Patricia and Katherine. And Duncan. It was from these visions that she perceived her own situation."

"Wait a minute," Chris said. "She was pregnant with Gamble's first daughter?"

"Yes, and that was one of the reasons she killed herself, knowing she was going to give birth to, in essence, a devil."

"What were the other reasons?"

"To keep the secret. She knew that if she stayed alive, Gamble might have ultimately stayed in her mind long enough to have seen her visions of, and the days leading up to, this very day."

"So, what, like my mom tipped you off? Before or after she died?"

Amy laughed. "After, Chris. And it wasn't me she tipped off, but those who came right before me."

"Right," Chris said. "Then she's a hero."

"Yes, Chris," Amy smiled. "Your mother's a hero."

"But...since her death, who did Gamble find to replace her? I mean, I bet there's maybe one or two people out there who can do what my mom could do; what I can do."

"Oh, Gamble can hook people up. He just likes to dole out the work, feel important. No, he had to finally resort to doing it himself. Because you're right, Chris—there's no one else out there like you and your mom. You're two of a very special kind."

Duncan shook his head. "So why Emilio Chavez," he said. "Why take me back to that night, then get me thinking that the boy was the key to the whole thing?"

"This time around, Emilio was placebo," Amy said, "as Gamble had guessed. But all the other times before, he wasn't. It was those times we failed, and Gamble got the better of us. You see, because the seraph cherished the deaf boy, it decided to use him as a vehicle for delivery. But each time we unleashed it from the boy, it was overpowered by Gamble and his daughters. It wasn't until we finally found a way to accelerate its final stages of learning—to hide it inside Gamble himself—that we stood a chance."

Duncan said, "So why didn't you just hide it inside Gamble from the start?"

"No, that would have been devastating. All that abhorrence at once would have destroyed it. The seraph had to learn in increments over many generations, had to build up a threshold before we could plant it inside Gamble. And please, don't think Emilio died in vain. He was crucial in the seraph's final development." She winked at him. "And so were you, you criminal."

Duncan grinned. And that was okay. After all, he'd forgiven himself. "So, how many times did we go back in time trying to defeat Gamble?"

"Just a handful, Dad. I doubt we could have made the trip too many more times. We've just about used up our ability to time travel. It's become very degraded."

"So what was it that I hooked Emilio into?" Chris said.

"A failsafe device," she said. "Say we're at the cliffs and Gamble somehow manages to kill all us angels after we've just released the seraph from the boy. Consequently, without our help, how does the seraph hope to return back in time and escape certain death? Easy. By wiring the boy into our own schematics, we made it so that if the seraph ever encountered such a situation, or felt the least bit in jeopardy, it and the boy would instantly be whisked back in time to a pre-selected point of origin before anybody got the wiser. Fact is, that's exactly how the seraph saved itself in all the previous attempts. Still, not without some scars, to be sure."

Chris nodded heavily. "Righteous. But still pretty risky. All Gamble would have had to do is kill the boy right off the bat."

"It was never without its risks," she affirmed.

"What was Gamble ultimately after," Rachel said. "God?"

"No, not God," Amy said, "but a place called the Shallows. He would have had access to an unlimited number of souls. And, most of all, immortality for himself."

"Bad news for us if he would have gotten there," Kathy said.

"Bad news," Amy agreed.

"Tollbooths up ahead," Tyler said. "Which one, Chris?"

Chris concentrated. "Two," he said. He looked at Amy, smiling. "Two."

With rosary in hand, Juanita crossed herself.

"Where's this one going to take us," Patricia said to Amy.

"Back to the apocalypse," she said. "I still have that mess to clean up."

"Can you do it without the seraph?" Chris said. "I mean, it's gonna be tied up for awhile, right?"

Amy sighed. "Yes. But with Gamble gone, my cohorts and I will find those harpies easy pickings."

"What about the other god," Rachel said. "What will you do with him?"

"That's up to God to decide," Amy said. "Who knows, He might just open up another universe just for him."

"Maybe we could use another set of ears," Patricia said. "I mean, God's got a lot on His plate as it is. Maybe He could use a fill-in."

Amy laughed. "Maybe He could, Patty. Maybe He could."

"Like, where's the real hell been throughout all of this?" Chris said.

"Accumulating shadows," Amy said.

"One thing's for certain," Duncan said. "After today, man's never going to be the same."

"Oh, I don't know," Amy said. "Man will have more faith in his demons now. And with his faith bolstered in the devil, so will his faith be bolstered in God. It'll be a more united front all around, mind you, but the same song and dance, just with the music turned up a notch."

"Do you think maybe that's been God's intention all along," Chris said, "to get man back on track, to get him polarized again? I mean, to tell the truth, this whole thing stinks of destiny."

"I have to agree with Chris," Duncan said. "Big time destiny."

Amy thought for a moment. "I'll tell you something. We broke every rule in the book to achieve what we did today. I doubt very seriously that God is breaking out the champagne right now. My relations and I have got some serious answering to do, the seraph included. If you think this was all preordained somehow, you're barking up the wrong tree. I don't think God ever saw Gamble coming."

Rachel smiled. "I know I'm just a silly human, but I don't think you're giving God enough credit. I think the old boy's still full of surprises."

Amy laughed. "Alright, Mom. Maybe He is." She stared at the tollbooths ahead, smiling. "Maybe He is."

The smile waned from Rachel's face, and she said, "Am I ever going to get my little girl back?"

Lamentably, Amy said, "No, Mom, I'm afraid you're going to have to get used to seeing me this way. I've been through too much to ever going back to being a little girl."

"Look at the bright side," Duncan said, "At least we won't have to put up with her as a teenager."

"I have a question," Patricia said. "If you were able to keep Gamble's second daughter—the one occupying Katherine's soul—away from him initially, then why weren't you able to keep the rest of his daughters away from him?"

"First off, remember that it was Chris's mother who tipped us off about Katherine. After we saved Kathy, we *did* keep an eye on the priest, and the rest of the girls that he prepared for Gamble. But, we really only needed to make sure Gamble didn't complete the seven before we confronted him with the seraph," Amy said. "Each time I tried saving the seventh girl, Melanie Sands, just for some cushion, it didn't work. Gamble had grown far too powerful."

"Just for some cushion?" Patricia said. "God, that sounds so...heartless."

"Cliché as it is, this was war, Patty. Those girls bought us the time to get where we needed to be. Sacrifices had to be made."

"The apocalypse was a huge sacrifice," Chris said in Patricia's defense. "Something tells me you let Gamble get away with it."

Amy nodded. "Yes, but it was only for a day. Imagine the casualties if it would have lasted a year. Or a decade. Or eternity."

Tyler pulled to the tollbooth. The red gate lifted, and the cloaked attendant waved them through.

Suddenly they were back where they had begun, in Rock Bay. Harpies dotted the trees like patient vultures. Carnage was everywhere; smoldering pile-ups; dead, mutilated bodies.

"Here we go," Tyler said.

"Here we go," Amy agreed.

"Look!" Kathy said, pointing excitedly out her window.

To the west was a large, gray mass covering an expanse of open field. It was moving.

"Wolves," Patricia said. "There must be thousands of them."

Then, before their eyes, a glorious resplendence erupted from the mass, as each wolf suddenly changed into a human figure, each adorned with wings, carrying long, golden swords.

Tyler stopped the shuttle, and Amy headed for the doors.

"Don't wait up for me," she said. "This is going to take awhile."

"Wait!" Juanita said. "What happens to us?"

"Tyler's going to take you to a safe house," Amy said. "You'll all be fine."

As she exited the shuttle, a sword of magnificent light bloomed in her right hand.

"Let's get it on!" she said. *"Let's get it on!"*

18076795R00193

Made in the USA
Lexington, KY
18 October 2012